Praise for *Murder Take Two*
by Charlene Weir

"...fast-paced and chilling..."

—*Redbook Magazine*

"A suspense story with plenty of excitement. Ms. Weir has a winning series on her hands."

—*Dallas Morning News*

"A highly recommended read."

—*Booklist*

"...high-pitched suspense..."

—*Kirkus Reviews*

Praise for George Baxt and
The Humphrey Bogart Murder Case

"Baxt scatters wisecracks through every scene; the celebrities are all convincingly portrayed; and the book...is great fun to read."

—*Houston Chronicle*

"An author of rare integrity."

—*Peter Lovesey*

"Baxt knows his show-business history and scatters names and lines like an anthologist in a stiff wind."

—*Los Angeles Times*

MURDER AT THE MOVIES

MURDER TAKE TWO
by Charlene Weir

THE HUMPHREY BOGART MURDER CASE
by George Baxt

SOMEWHERE SOUTH OF MELROSE
by Maxine O'Callaghan

WORLDWIDE.

TORONTO • NEW YORK • LONDON
AMSTERDAM • PARIS • SYDNEY • HAMBURG
STOCKHOLM • ATHENS • TOKYO • MILAN
MADRID • WARSAW • BUDAPEST • AUCKLAND

MURDER AT THE MOVIES

A Worldwide Mystery/April 1999

Murder Take Two and *The Humphrey Bogart Murder Case*
were first published by St. Martin's Press, Incorporated.

ISBN 0-373-26305-8

CONTENTS

MURDER TAKE TWO
by Charlene Weir

To Patty and John Westley

Heartfelt thanks to Jane Paul for reading the manuscript; to my daughter, Leslie Weir, without whose help, etc., and who went above and beyond; to Leila Laurence Dobscha for many things (in all my books—it's about time I thanked her), including the color of the carpet; to Kullikki Kay Steen, M.D., for medical advice; and to Detective David Pires of the Daly City, California, Police Department and Alexander Kump of the Kansas City, Kansas, Police Department, who answered questions about police procedure from a frantic unknown author. These busy people patiently and graciously answered all my questions. Any errors are mine, either because I didn't ask enough questions or didn't understand the answers.

ONE

YANCY WISHED they'd get to the murder. He shifted his belt—gun, ammo clips, handcuffs, radio, baton, and flashlight—aware of the sweat it left around his uniform shirt. Slapping at the buzz of flies by his face, he leaned a shoulder against the inside barn wall. Anything to break up the boredom, and him being a cop it wouldn't have to be more than mildly interesting. He stood well out of the way, by the small door at the side of the barn, a big old limestone place, the uneven stone floor littered with coils of cable—cable, cable everywhere—cameras, lights, mikes, and people constantly moving in a hurry. The huge lights on tripods were off right now, so the far corners dipped into dim shadows.

"Clem, for God's sake, what's the problem? We're ready." Hayden Fifer, big Hollywood director, stood on a raised platform with camera and cameraman. His voice thundered through the more than three-story height of stone, rattling rafters and raising dust. Livestock were long gone, but the effluvia lingered and seemed to rise up with the dust and hang in the air to be caught on the rays of sunlight rushing through the big open doorway.

Clem was Clem Jones, a skinny kid, female, with spiked pink hair and an attitude. Yancy didn't much care for Clem. They stared fish-eyed at each other. With her weird hair, far-out clothes, and air of serious intent, he found her slightly ridiculous. The feeling was probably mutual. She was Fifer's assistant, and, Yancy thought, not responsible for shepherding actors onto the set, but Fifer yelled at her anyway. He yelled at Clem a lot. She muttered into a handheld radio, and Yancy barely heard her words through the static. "She won't come out of her trailer."

"Tell them to get her in here! What do you think I pay you for?"

Clem jammed the radio in the pocket of the ankle-length, prison-striped smock she wore and scuttled over cables, around cameras and mikes, through clumps of crew, and out the big doorway into the fierce sunshine.

For two weeks Yancy'd been hanging with the movie crowd, doing nothing, just being there: handy, making sure they weren't bothered, had everything they needed, turning up whenever one of them hollered. Some assignment, right? Shit. It didn't take more than two days before he was brain-dead. Nothing ever happened. Nothing. Ever. Happened. Near as he could figure, movies were made by herds of people milling around for hours until the director called, "Action." Cameras rolled for sixty seconds, or ground away for hours to get sixty seconds of usable film.

If he'd ever had any inkling of running away to became an actor, this would cure it, one giant yawn giving him nothing but slow time that let his mind tick over. Which he didn't want. He should do something, but he didn't know what. And if he did, ten to one, it'd be wrong. What about simply running away? Now there was a thought.

From Mac, one of the teamsters he'd been idling away time with—teamsters hauled in all the trucks necessary for the making of a movie and chauffeured around the stars—Yancy had gotten the hot tip about the murder on the call sheet today. So far that was just as unreal as everything else.

He had no idea what the movie was about, except it was a thriller. *Lethal Promise*. He knew that much because every vehicle had a placard on the dash with the name printed on it. Filming wasn't done in any sequence that allowed perception of a story.

Movies weren't a cushy way to go, long hours and hard work. Today, they'd started at six a.m., which meant *he'd* started at six a.m. It was now after one, temperature ninety, humidity ninety, and the hot wind that blew in was more irritating than welcome. It was so hot he wondered they didn't all pop off of heat stroke. Being from California, maybe they could survive anything. He smacked the fly feasting on the back of his neck as his mind played through who he might get to swap duty time with. Could he get away with that? It might nettle the chief, she wasn't exactly all sunshine these days.

"Officer?"

Startled, Yancy turned. He hadn't heard her slip through the small door behind him. Laura Edwards. Big-time actress. The Star. "Uh—" Oh, yeah. One cool cop. *There she was.* Remote fantasy from the movie screen standing right beside him. In the flesh. Spectacular flesh. Up to now, he'd only seen her at a distance, on the set, or disappearing into her town car. She was beautiful. Small, maybe five two with hair of pale gold that dazzled like sunlight on new snow, and blue eyes, the soft warm blue of a Kansas sky on a spring morning, a body that only Hollywood could dream up—taut and tawny and ripe.

He clasped his hands behind his back, lest they stray of their own accord toward all that female lushness. "They're looking for you," he said.

"They can look."

Director Fifer, still on the raised platform, bellowed for the harried Clem who was nowhere to be seen. "Will you, for God's sake, tell them to get her up here?"

They'd been using the platform to shoot a bad-guy-menaces-heroine scene in the hayloft. Villain had caught the beautiful Laura and had her bent backward over the railing, whether to send her falling to her death or choke the life out of her hadn't been clear. Since she was the heroine, the murder most likely wasn't of her.

Before lunch, hours had been spent setting up lights with a photo double hanging head down over the railing. Fifer, up on the platform peering at a monitor, issued instructions that resulted in minute changes in the position of lights, or cameras, or various appendages of the hapless female upside down over the railing, and ditto the villain, primarily his hands around her throat.

After achieving whatever effect he was striving for, Fifer had called for Laura Edwards to drape her beautiful form exactly as the stand-in had been. Therein followed more minute moving of appendages. Hours later all was perfection.

"Roll cameras."

"Speed."

"Scene twenty-four, take one."

"Action."

Before anything much happened, a young female with a clipboard trotted onto the set. Fifer called, "Cut!"

An argument ensued. Fifer got irate, the female stayed implacable.

"Now what?" Yancy asked his teamster buddy.

Mac grinned. "It's been six hours."

"Only six?"

"Contract. A break after six hours or the pay goes up at thirty-minute intervals. Meal penalty. Fifer's way over budget already. He can't afford more."

Polaroid pictures were taken of Laura and the villain from every conceivable angle and then Fifer called a lunch break. The barn couldn't have emptied out faster if he'd shouted, "Fire!"

After the break they all trooped back, except Ms. Laura Edwards. She was not on the rail and Fifer was royally pissed.

Now she was standing right by Yancy. She put an index finger, featherlight, on his forearm and looked up at him long and intensely. "I'd like you to do me a favor." Her voice was low with promise, the spot beneath her finger was warm as a downy duck.

What might she want from him? She smelled like fresh air and wildflowers. In her tight black pants and scoop-necked white blouse, she looked ready for a romp in the hayloft, but not with the likes of him; we're talking light-years away. So what's with all this luminous intensity? Obviously, she wanted something from him. The question was, what? He'd been with this bunch since they'd rolled into town, and she'd ignored him so far. She hadn't gotten a speeding or parking ticket she wanted him to take care of, hadn't caused any riots or broken any laws. Unless maybe after filming shut down and he'd gone home? Naw. He'd have heard about it. The guys at the department were using all kinds of heavy-handed humor, they wouldn't let anything like that go by. So what did she want from him? "Yes, ma'am," he said.

She inched closer. "Come to **my** trailer after the shot," she whispered. "It's very important."

Is it now? You have intrigued me, lady. "Yes, ma'am." She was so compelling he found himself whispering back.

"Clem!" Fifer bellowed.

That much put-upon young woman materialized at the foot of the platform and yelled up at him. "The designer said Laura won't come out of her trailer because the blouse looks like a potato sack."

Fifer held a muttered conversation with the stunt coordinator who was agitating to block out moves. "Enough assing around," he said. "Kay!"

A shadow angled through the open doorway and paused. Kay Bender, the stunt double, backlit by bright sunshine, dressed identically and wearing a gold wig, was the image of Laura Edwards without the passion: a doppelgänger.

Laura glanced at her and shivered. "Please," she pleaded and floated away through the small door.

The apparition in the wide doorway and the appeal in Laura's single word made the hairs stand up on his neck. Don't be a goofus, he told himself. This is the land of make-believe.

The stunt double clambered up wooden rungs to the loft.

During the lull the bad guy had been up there lounging against the hay bales. Instantly, he put on a murderous expression. Kay draped herself with her back over the railing, head hanging down, hair trailing. So far as Yancy knew, haylofts didn't have railings, but what the heck, this was Hollywood. The villain grabbed Kay by the throat.

The stunt coordinator gave instructions.

Fifer gave instructions. Cameras rolled.

Then everything seemed to happen in slow motion that took up a fraction of an instant.

There was a splintering crack. The railing gave way. Kay plummeted.

"Cut!"

Kay seemed to gather herself into a ball in midair. She landed hard on her back on a layer of straw, jerked convulsively, then lay still.

"No!" Fifer yelled. "Wrong! What's the matter with you people?"

Looked pretty good to Yancy, except maybe that athletic pulling together on the way down. And she didn't scream. Surely

Hollywood would want a scream, but that maybe got put in later. He moved closer to where he could see a little better over equipment and people. Not much blood; he was surprised by the small amount, almost none. He would have figured these folks to ladle on lots of artistic blood, made with Karo syrup and sugar and red coloring so it wouldn't poison the actor who had to let it dribble from the corner of his mouth as he died.

He watched Clem scurry across snarled tangles of cable. Fingers at her throat, she knelt and peered nearsightedly at the stuntwoman, touched an arm and sprang back. She covered her mouth and made a strangled squeal.

Yancy moved without thinking, a cop's conditioned response. Standing in front of Clem, he put a hand on each shoulder and stared in her face. She was sobbing and gagging.

He pivoted her to one side just in time for her to spew all over the straw. He anchored her by the waist. When she straightened, she clung against him, gasping and shuddering. He patted her back, made soothing sounds, and looked over her head to see what set her off.

No genius was needed to figure it. Clem lived in the world of make-believe, where nothing was what it seemed. Phony horror was dished out all the time; broken and maimed bodies strewed the landscape, features distorted into death masks.

Only this one wasn't make-believe. Kay lay motionless with the tines of a pitchfork through her chest.

TWO

"PORNOGRAPHY." Mrs. Oliver, on the other end of the phone line, spat out the word as though it tasted bad. "Filth."

"Yes, ma'am." The sun glaring through the window slats left stripes on the desk that made Susan squint. She swiveled a half turn, putting her back to them. A fly circled and landed on the wall at knee level. She kicked at it; it flew to the ceiling.

"I was the one who had to scrub it off. And let me tell you, that was no easy job. It took hours. Hours, do you understand? Getting rid of that smut. I expect you to do something about this."

Mrs. Oliver hung up before Susan could utter another "Yes, ma'am." She swiveled around and replaced the receiver. The phone rang again immediately. Another art critic?

"It's the mayor," Hazel, the dispatcher, said. "You want to talk with him?"

She did not. "Put him through."

"Chief Wren," Bakover said.

"Mr. Mayor."

"What is going on with this vandalism?"

Well, let's see. Vandals will be vandals? Vandals for the sake of vandalism? Vandals unite? The fly landed on a stack of papers on the desk. From another stack, she rolled up a report and smacked the damn thing. With an irritated buzz, it took off. "We're looking into it."

"Not good enough. It's upsetting people."

Some people. Pornography being more or less in the eye of the beholder, there were those that were upset and those that were amused and those that felt honored to be chosen and those that said sometimes a garbage can was just a garbage can.

"You are perfectly aware these Hollywood people are in town. We don't want anything like this to offend them."

She trapped a laugh in her throat by coughing around it. Hollywood? Offended by nudes? Oh, boy, it was this weather. Who was it who said this was the kind of weather when wives sharpened their knives and eyed their husbands' necks?

"Put a stop to this," he said and hung up.

She replaced the receiver, rolled the report tighter, and chased the fly around the office, swinging wildly. It took shelter behind the blinds at the top of the window, buzzed angrily. Yeah, well, you think you got troubles.

She tilted the slats to get rid of the glare, then shifted folders until she got to today's *Hampstead Herald* and spread it open. Page two. Headline: Mad Painter's Latest Raid. There was a picture of a garbage can with a female nude tastefully draped in plastic grocery bags so as not to upset the delicate sensibilities of those who saw porn in the unclad human form. The mad painter—a reporter had come up with that one—hit only garbage cans, and left a nude figure—either male or female—equal opportunity salaciousness—and disappeared into the air.

Chase Reardon, San Francisco police captain and Susan's former boss, had drilled his maxim into her: *Evidence is always at the scene of the crime. If you didn't find it, you didn't search enough.* They'd better go more carefully through the garbage.

She picked up the phone and told Hazel she was going out to look at the scene of the crime.

The pickup's fuel gauge hovered around empty. Not wanting to find herself without gas while hotly pursuing the mad painter (if she learned who he was and he ran) she U-turned into Pickett's service station. Kevin Murphy came from one of the service bays, wiping his hands on a greasy rag.

"Ma'am?" He shook black hair from his face, stuffed the rag in a rear pocket, and tucked in the brown shirt with Pickett's stitched on the back. Sullen kid, high school football star, fire inside, so far no trouble.

He squeegeed her windshield, she paid for the gas and was headed for Ohio Street when the muttering radio caught her attention. She picked up the mike. "Wren."

"Osey, Chief." O. C. Pickett, her country boy detective, the youngest son of the service station owner, sounded hesitant and apologetic. "I'm at Josiah's barn. I thought you'd better know there's been an accident. A stuntwoman's dead."

"Oh, shit."

She didn't know she'd spoken aloud until he said, "Yes, ma'am."

THE SKY, vast and blue and empty, stretched forever over the low hills. The midday sun of early June blazed relentlessly on the field of high grasses and goldenrod, struck sparks on boulders, and created shimmering heat illusions in the distance. Occasional hot gusts of wind whirled dust devils on the dirt road.

She kept the pickup at a moderate speed, no lights, no siren, not that it would make a difference. News traveled with the speed of lightning in a small town, and there would already be a crowd. Movies and actors always drew them, especially when the actors were in the megabucks category, as these were. Nick Logan and Laura Edwards.

When word had come that Hollywood was coming to Hampstead, Susan was the only person in town who wasn't thrilled. Her experience was—from directors and actors on down to cameramen, lighting techs, and grips—the whole bunch and their moviemaking was a gigantic pain in the butt. They moved in, took whatever they wanted, broke it, altered it, mangled it, and dropped it when they were finished. They pulled out and left the place trashed, like picnickers who left litter and breakage in their wake.

San Francisco—oh, yes, summer fog, cool ocean breezes—she leaned forward and plucked at the white blouse sticking to her back—was the site of many a movie. They'd even managed to close down the Golden Gate Bridge on one occasion she knew about. Irate drivers trying to get into or out of the city were not thrilled to be watching a movie in the making.

They did spread money around like syrup over pancakes. Which was, of course, why they were given the red carpet treatment and why the mayor was so ecstatic. He'd informed her that as police chief she was to make sure they felt welcome and to give them everything they wanted.

She rolled past the field where they'd parked their trucks and trailers, vans and cars, and drove on another quarter mile to old Josiah's barn. Good Lord, thinking like a native, referring to a piece of property by the name of a long-dead owner.

Josiah Hampstead, an early settler before Kansas was a state, made himself wealthy in land, cattle, and oil, got a town named after him, and late in his life donated some of that land for a college. The house was long gone, but the barn remained, a large weathered stone structure. Off to one side was a power and light truck—the generator that ran all those huge lights. Cables, taped to the ground, snaked inside the barn.

An empty squad car, overheads blinking, was parked parallel to the wide-open door. An ambulance, rear doors open and waiting, was pulled up behind. A dozen or so people stood in what shade the two tall cottonwood trees provided. Susan's arrival separated the media from the spectators and they rushed at her with mikes and questions.

She edged the pickup in beside the ambulance and slid out. Heat came up to greet her as though she'd opened an oven door. When she'd dressed that morning, she'd tried to strike a compromise between dignified businesslike and what she could survive in given the heat. Tailored white blouse and beige cotton pants was the best she could do. Linen jacket, if the occasion demanded. The pants were wrinkled and sweaty where her legs had rested on the driver's seat. She left the jacket on the passenger side. Hot wind caught her full-face and lifted her dark hair, blowing it straight back.

"Can you tell us what happened?"

"What's the name of the person killed?"

"Was this an accident or do you suspect foul play?"

"Is this going to affect the movie?"

"How long will the filming be stopped?"

"What happens when a death occurs in—?"

"I just got here," she said. "I don't know anything yet."

Just inside the big sliding door, two paramedics in navy blue jumpsuits leaned against the wall, arms crossed. One glanced at her and gave a brief shake of his head. No need for urgency.

Despite the wide doorway, the interior was gloomy. The barn was cavernous, easily over three stories high: hayloft overhead in the rear, above that a steep-pitched ceiling with rough-hewn beams. On the ground, box stalls ran the length of one side, on the other were open stalls. Actors and crew were contained inside these with White and Demarco riding herd. Cameras, lights, snarls of cable, and dollies cluttered the large open area in the center. Just below the loft, on a layer of straw, the dead woman lay on her back, the tines of a pitchfork jutting through her chest.

Susan picked her way closer, careful to stay back from Osey Pickett taking photographs. Dr. Fisher waited patiently for him to finish. She studied the victim. Young, no more than twenty, she judged. Cascade of blond hair, one errant strand across her still lips, eyes slitted, but not enough to tell color. Alive, she would have the attractiveness of youth, health, and fitness. All that had been taken by death and now she was gray and flat. The heavy theatrical makeup seemed a mockery. She wore tight black pants, a white knit shirt with a scooped neck, and black ankle boots with fringe up the back.

When Osey finished snapping pictures, Dr. Fisher drew on latex gloves and knelt for a close look at the body. Susan took out her notebook and made a rough sketch even though Osey would be doing the same. Habits from her years on the San Francisco force stuck with her.

She backed carefully away and left them to it. Yancy was waiting for her at the edge of the cleared area. "Ma'am," he said quietly. His tentative tone made it clear he was wondering whether an ass chewing was coming his way.

She'd like to chew somebody's. This would come down like an avalanche on her and her department. The movie crowd might make trouble, the mayor would be furious and worried. More media would turn up. She was beginning to understand why the brass was so quick to jump on someone. Sheer frustration.

"What happened?"

"Her name is Kay Bender," Yancy said. "The stunt double for this film."

Oh, my. Film, not movie. He'd been infected with showbiz.

"She did all the risky stuff for Ms. Edwards."

If there was anything to be thankful for about this, she could be thankful Laura Edwards wasn't lying dead with a pitchfork through her chest. A stuntwoman would rate a paragraph in the back pages of the newspapers, maybe a brief mention on television news. Only *Hollywood Reporter* would care. The media would still come, anything touching Laura Edwards was news, but they might not descend like locusts as they would if she'd been the one killed.

Susan made quick notes while Yancy gave a clear, concise account of what had occurred, ending with Ms. Edwards asking him to her trailer. "When Kay fell, I had Mac call nine-one-one."

"Mac?"

"Laura Edwards's driver. I prevented anybody from going over there and secured the scene. I wouldn't let them move her. That meant they had to stop filming. Fifer, the director, got furious. I got a cold whisper that I had no idea what I was costing him." Yancy paused, giving her the opportunity to yell, if she was so inclined.

"Go on."

"I think he wanted to shove the body aside and get on with the movie. I told them all to move over into those stalls along the side there." Yancy nodded. "I figured that's the best I could do. Everybody's been in and out of them all day anyway, and at least I could keep an eye out till backup arrived. Fifer refused, said he'd be in his trailer. Short of cuffing him to a manger, there was nothing I could do."

"Was there any reason to make you think this was more than an accident?"

"No." He hesitated. "The director kept yelling it was a tragic accident and I was being an asshole." Yancy took a slow breath. "Damned if I can figure what this movie is about. Laura Edwards was supposed to be thrown backward across that railing"—he nodded up at the loft—"with the bad guy choking the life out of her. Then Kay Bender, the stuntwoman, would take over. The rail breaks and down she goes."

He shifted his weight to his other foot. "Down below they would have it set up such that when she fell she wouldn't get hurt. Except, Ms. Edwards wouldn't leave her trailer."

The star having a fit, Susan thought. Not a rare occurrence.

"The stunt coordinator then insisted he wanted to work something out and the director agreed. The railing broke. There wasn't supposed to be a pitchfork under it." He shrugged. "I didn't want to take any chances."

"Laura Edwards wanted you to come to her trailer. Why?"

"No idea."

"Cop business or because you're tall, dark, and handsome?"

Yancy smiled. "Much as I'd like to think it might have been the latter, I doubt it."

Yancy was tall all right and dark-haired; handsome didn't say it. He was soft-spoken, with soft brown eyes, and a smile as sweet and soothing as a summer night. Trim and fit in his blues, he was dynamite. She could see even Ms. Big Hollywood Star being interested.

"I assume you asked her what she wanted."

"Yes, ma'am. She said she'd tell me later."

"Where is she now?"

"In her trailer. At the base camp. I went to check."

More movie talk. Base camp was the place where all the trailers, cars, trucks, et cetera were set up. In this case, the field a quarter mile back.

"You go baby-sit. I'll be right there. I want a word with Dr. Fisher. Oh, and Yancy, have somebody move the newspeople back."

Owen Fisher, a man of solid bulk, wasn't able to tell her any more than she already knew. He brushed straw from his dark trousers and peeled latex gloves from his hands. Those hands always fascinated her; they were perfectly shaped, delicate, and long-fingered, a total mismatch with the rest of him, which was thick and bearlike.

"Well?" she said.

He peered at her from under dark heavy eyebrows, a sharp contrast with his white hair. "Yep, she's dead all right."

"Anything else?" she asked dryly.

"Just what you can see. Newly dead. Body temp not even lowered yet. Course it is hot in here. Lividity just beginning. Mucous membranes just beginning to dry." He bent over and snapped his instrument bag shut. "Something might show up when I get her on the table."

Susan clambered up the wooden rungs to the loft and found Osey on his hand and knees sifting through straw. Needle in a haystack. When she stepped off onto the loft, Osey unfolded his tall, thin body in a series of jerks. Hair the color of the straw he was fingering through, guileless blue eyes that were deceptively naive, hands and feet that seemed to get in his way, brown pants and white shirt with the sleeves rolled up, tie askew. The impression—harmless country boy, not too bright. Reality—mind like a gin trap.

"Anything of interest?"

"Naw." He whacked at his pants legs. Dust filled the air and sunlight slanting through the small window under the peaked roof sparkled on the motes. "Not yet anyway. People all over the place. Up here, down there. Now that railing there. That's maybe a mite interesting. I'm going to have to get both pieces together and see. They got a rail that's rigged to break. It's part of the action. But this one was supposed to be solid. Was solid right before they all took off for lunch. Now it looks like it was cut most of the way. Then with weight on it, it just gave." He showed her the spot where the rail gave way.

Damn, Susan thought. Murder? Accident would have been bad enough. And who was the intended victim? Stunt double Kay Bender? Actress Laura Edwards? Any hint of an attempt on Laura Edwards's life and the media would be all over it.

"Where's Parkhurst?" she asked. Ben Parkhurst was her most experienced officer. She used him to sound out data and surmise, he pointed out the difference. They made a good team. At least, they had until personal stuff started leaking over into cop stuff.

"On his way. He was up in Topeka dropping off some water samples at the lab, from the Sackly well."

"When he shows, I'm at Ms. Edwards's trailer."

PALE GREEN. Laura my beloved. The universe is pale green. The spirits are worried. I know you're in there. I know you're not hurt. I saw you go in. You're afraid. I can feel your fear. Don't be afraid. Everything's going to be wonderful. I'm here. Near.

My love, my light. The light of truth. Sweet and lovely. I'll watch. I'll wait.

He watched the tall, black-haired policewoman knock on the trailer door. He didn't see Her inside, but he sent love.

YANCY OPENED the trailer door at Susan's tap and she walked into welcome coolness. The only sound was the hum of the air-conditioning unit. The kitchen area had sink, cabinets, and a table with a green padded bench. The living-room area, carpeted in pale blue, had two blue-tweed couches at a right angle to each other with a large round coffee table in the bend, two end tables, large television set, and a VCR. Watercolors hung on the walls, flowers done with intricate detail.

The woman sitting on a couch brought a split instant of surprise before Susan's mind caught up. A stunt double would of necessity be made to look like the star. Laura Edwards wore the same form-hugging black pants, white knit scoop-necked shirt, and black ankle boots with fringe.

She sat perfectly still, legs crossed, hands palm up in her lap with the fingers loosely curled, staring blankly ahead. She took no notice of Susan.

Even frozen in shock, Laura Edwards was stunning. A thick tangle of hair the color of pale gold curled away from a smooth forehead and high cheekbones, it fell in loose swirls along her neck and shoulders. Long dark lashes over blue eyes that tilted up slightly. Perfectly shaped nose, generous mouth.

"She won't say anything," Yancy said. "Hasn't even moved. She didn't answer when I knocked. I'm not even sure she knows I'm here."

Uh-huh. This stricken beauty had aroused protective instincts in Yancy the cop. Susan could understand it, even she felt a tug to protect the vulnerable maiden. Laura Edwards was as still as a stone sculpture.

Let us not forget here, the woman is an actress.

"Ms. Edwards?"

No response, not even a focus in Susan's direction. Kneeling in front of her, Susan took one of her hands. Cold and limp. "Laura."

No reaction. Susan put the hand back in Laura's lap and rose. "We'd better get a doctor in."

There was a tap on the door. Yancy opened it and Parkhurst stepped inside. He nodded curtly to Yancy and said to Susan, "You wanted to see me?"

Laura blinked her beautiful blue eyes, shiny with unshed tears. "Ben?" Her voice, low and husky, caught on a sob.

Parkhurst's face went hard. Laura hurled herself at him, wrapped herself around him, and nestled her face against his neck.

Yancy's jaw dropped. Susan's eyebrows shot up.

THREE

LAURA'S MUFFLED SOBS and the hum of the air-conditioning blended together for a stretched-out moment. Parkhurst, arms around the actress, held himself board stiff, a muscle ticked away in the corner of his jaw the way it did when he was angry. Susan, startled by the woman's actions, was even more startled to discover tiny seeds of jealousy. What's all this?

Confusion. She'd known Parkhurst a little over two years. They'd gone from suspicious dogs snarling at each other to grudging mutual respect to just recently something else that she didn't want to admit to but had attraction thrown in and would, if not stomped, lead to trouble. So why was she getting all prickly around the edges because Ms. Movie Star was sobbing all over Parkhurst's chest, and acted like she'd done that very thing before?

Why Parkhurst? If Susan were the flinging type, given the choice between Yancy and Parkhurst, she'd choose Yancy every time; any limpet would. Yancy had a gentle look, with "pliable" and "kind" thrown in. Parkhurst looked dangerous. Everything about him was hard, from his dark eyes to his tight back, and when he lowered his voice it wasn't soft, it was menacing. So what the hell?

She eyed Yancy and gestured with a thumb. He slipped out the door without protest. His curiosity was probably as high as hers, but she was the boss. Parkhurst peeled Laura's arms from his neck and held both her hands in one of his. He put an arm around her and edged her to the couch. She dropped, not at all gracefully, and clutched his hand tight when he tried to pull it loose. Short of a clip to the jaw, his only choice was to perch at an angle beside her and allow her to keep the hand. Which she did, clasping it to her bosom.

Every male's fantasy. Parkhurst's? She never could tell what

he was thinking; he had a great ability at self-concealment. Thick
dark hair, medium height, mid-thirties, he was self-assured, self-
contained, intelligent, and a good cop. Just lately, she'd learned
that stuck back there behind the air of reined-in violence was a
sense of humor.

Laura kept her eyes fastened on him, as though he might disappear if she so much as blinked. Tears glistened and left smeary
trails through the heavy makeup. This did not detract one whit
from her beauty, if anything it made her more attractive by
throwing in vulnerability and an appeal for help. Susan poked
around in the tiny pale-rose bathroom and found a box of tissues.
She plunked it on the coffee table and backed over to the padded
bench in the kitchen area, out of Laura's line of vision but able
to watch her.

Laura snatched a tissue, then another, wadded them together,
and rubbed at her eyes. Susan reminded herself again that this
woman was an actress. Yet the crying was real, red eyes,
splotched face, and runny nose. Even Susan wanted to help; any
red-blooded male would grab his lance, leap on his horse, and
gallop to her defense. Susan caught Parkhurst's eye and gave
him a short nod. His show. She pulled out her notebook.

"It's good to see you, Ben," Laura said. "You look great."

Parkhurst knew Laura Edwards. That was a little like the sun
rising in the west. The whole Hollywood circus had been in town
almost a week and he never mentioned he'd known the famous
Laura Edwards.

Susan wished she could read him better. Whatever was going
on inside, he had it under control—face set, eyes flat—but he
had to work at it. His jaw muscles were so tight, she wondered
if he'd ever be able to speak again.

He worked his hand free. "Likewise."

They were mouthing platitudes, Susan thought, while they
fought off the emotions of the underlying situation. She noted
the pulse beat in his throat and judged his heart was banging
around inside his chest.

Laura smiled. "You haven't changed, have you?"

"No," he said, "and right now I need to ask you some questions."

"Still the cop. You have a title?"

"Lieutenant."

"Really? I expected by now you'd be chief, or commissioner, or whatever is at the top."

A tiny bit of hostility oozed through here.

Parkhurst responded with raised hackles. "Don't tell me you've forgotten my personality. It always did get in my way."

"All right, Ben, ask your questions." Tears overflowed again and Laura grabbed another handful of tissues. "I know you have to. I just didn't want to think about it."

"How well did you know the dead girl?"

"I've worked with her several times. She looks a little like me. Basically same height and weight. Not that it really matters. The camera takes great care to protect the deception. You know, dreams of shimmering illusions."

This seemed to refer to something Parkhurst knew about. "Cut the crap, Laura. It doesn't have to be me. If you'd rather talk to somebody else—"

"No." For a moment she looked panicked, then as though she wanted to challenge his getting down to business, then she dropped it and sighed. She drooped. "Oh, Ben, unbend a little. I'm nervous. Aren't you?"

It was a direct appeal and Susan could see Parkhurst try to ease up on his tight emotional hold. "I know this is awkward, Laurie, but—"

Laurie?

"Would you ask her to leave?"

He tucked up the corners of his mouth in a wry smile. "She's the boss."

Laura's eyes widened in a parody of surprise and her mouth rounded into an O as she looked around at Susan, then flattened into a tiny smile.

It was quick, but Susan caught it. I don't know what you're working here, lady, but there's a plan rolling around in your mind.

The smile vanished and was replaced by bewildered sadness as she turned back to Parkhurst.

"Tell me about Kay Bender." His voice was quiet with underlying anger.

They stared at each other, squaring off for battle. "Still hostile," she said.

"It's what I do best."

"You're an insensitive prick!"

"Good. Now. How old was the stuntwoman?"

Laura took in a breath; tears filled her eyes; she scrubbed at them with balled-up tissues. "I don't know. Twenty. Twenty-one. Around there."

"How well did you know her?"

Laura hesitated, either to collect her thoughts or to sort through and pick and choose. "Not very. When I try to think I guess I really don't know anything at all." Look of remorseful sorrow.

"What about her family?"

"She's from San Diego, I think. I guess she has a family. I don't recall her ever saying anything about them."

"Boyfriend?"

Susan studied the woman's hands, small and shapely with tapering fingers, they were in constant motion twisting and untwisting the tissues, crumpling them into a ball, smoothing them out—nervous movements that didn't seem a deliberate way of stalling or evading answers, but a try at controlling the shock, and maybe grief, that sat waiting just beyond the mind's focus.

"Boyfriend," Laura repeated. "Yes, I think so."

"Name?"

She shot him an angry look. "For God's sake, Ben, soften up a little. I'm trying to think— I don't— You're treating me like a suspect. There are always romances on a shoot, especially on location. It happens. It's like not real time, you know? Away from home, temporary, and the place doesn't seem real either. It's like it doesn't count. It's aside from life, part of the make-believe. Kay is—was a professional. She did the job. It's a risky job. No matter how careful, stunt people get hurt. Accidents—"

A horrified expression came over her face. "It was an accident," she said very carefully with more statement in her voice than question, as though by sounding positive she could make the answer come out the way she wanted it to.

Parkhurst, as far as Susan could see, didn't respond with so much as a flicker of an eyelid, but what little color there was behind the makeup on Laura's face drained away. Susan was afraid she'd drop over in a dead faint. Parkhurst apparently thought so too. Before Susan could move, he had Laura's head down around her knees.

Seconds passed, then she started making muffled mewling noises and he released her. The heavy smeared makeup was still the only color in her face. Susan retrieved a glass from the cabinet in the kitchen area, filled it from the tap, and handed it to Parkhurst.

He did a surveillance of Laura's face as he placed the glass in her hand.

"It should have been me," she whispered.

"Why do you say that?"

"I was supposed to be up there—on the railing—when—"

"Why weren't you?" Parkhurst asked, but he'd lost her; her attention was caught on something in her mind. Probably the fall. Her skin got a little green; her eyes went unfocused.

Putting his hands on her shoulders, he said quietly, "Talk to me, Laura. Concentrate. That's right. Now, where were you when you were supposed to be in the loft?"

"Somebody killed her? Why?"

"We need to find out the answer to both those questions. Who would want to kill her?"

Laura simply looked at him, then shook her head. "Accidents happen, you know. Even when everyone's being very careful. They just do. They—"

"Laura—"

"Deliberate?"

"Maybe. How long have you known Kay Bender?"

"I don't know. Two years. Maybe longer. What does it matter?"

"Did she have any conflict with anybody, anybody dislike her?"

"I don't know. I don't think so." Laura's head swiveled around to look at Susan.

Parkhurst turned her back, held his hands on both sides of her face like blinders. "Never mind her, Laura. You're bright enough to know that if Kay wasn't the target, you were. You in any trouble?"

"What kind of trouble?"

"You tell me. If someone tried to kill you, or hurt you, there must be a reason."

"No. I don't know. Something is wrong on this film."

"What do you mean wrong?"

"I don't know. It's not anything I can point to. It's a feeling. Something going on underneath the surface."

Under whose surface? Susan wondered cynically.

"Always, or just since you came here?"

Laura hesitated. "I'm not sure. But it's certainly been stronger since we got here."

"Have you made anybody angry? The director?"

"Fifer would never try to harm me. That'd mean his movie wouldn't get finished. You've no idea how much money would be lost."

But there would be insurance, Susan thought. A possibility? Director kills, or seriously injures, star to collect? She made a note to check into the financial situation of this movie.

"Your co-star?" Parkhurst asked.

"Nick? Why would he try to hurt me?"

"That's what I'm trying to find out. Maybe you eat garlic right before the love scenes and he's tired of it. Maybe a lover's spat, true love not running smooth."

"Okay, so we have our moments. We're both professionals. It doesn't affect our work."

He stared at her. She lowered her head, shiny gold hair obscured her face. Her breathing got quick and shallow. Parkhurst was getting to her, Susan thought, but damned if she knew what was going on here.

"All right, Laurie," he said. "You're smart, even observant when you want to be."

She raised her head, tried to look him in the eye, but her gaze slid away and her face flushed a soft pink.

"You're not being straight with me, Laurie. You're holding back. That's of great concern."

"Damn you, Ben. I'm not holding anything back."

Susan heard the almost imperceptible catch in her throat.

"You care about finding out what happened to this girl?"

"Of course I do. I honestly don't know anything that could help."

Parkhurst let a couple beats tick past while he pinned her with his eyes. This time she held up to it without flinching. "I don't know anything. Honestly, I don't. Don't you think I'd tell you if I did?"

"Laura, something doesn't feel right here. What are you hiding?"

"Nothing. I've told you. Nothing. Jesus, you haven't changed a bit. Get your teeth into something and you shake it to death. For God's sake, why would I hide something?"

"I don't know. That's what I'm trying to get to. Where were you when she fell?"

"What?" He'd jumped too fast and left Laura a step behind.

"You were supposed to be on the railing when it broke. Why weren't you?"

"Oh. I was on my way back here after talking with that very nice officer."

"Why were you talking with him?"

"I wanted to ask him if he would do something for me."

"I'm sure, Laurie," Parkhurst said tightly, "if you asked him and it was remotely within his power, he certainly would. Now, stop playing coy and tell me what you wanted from him. I assume it wasn't simply his hard, lean body."

"Don't be crude, Ben." Her blue eyes lost the glazed look and flashed anger. "I wanted him to ask you to come see me."

"Why?"

An impish smile played around her mouth. "You can't think of any reason? None at all?"

"Can it."

Laura's eyes teared again. "It's hard to explain. It's like smoke, when I try to catch hold of it, there's nothing there."

"What's like smoke?"

"Something brooding and ugly. It worried me."

"Threatening? Directed at you?"

Susan didn't know what to make of this under-the-surface ugliness story. There was way too much emotion here. Too damn much drama. She'd been a cop a long time; her ears were tuned to pick up false notes, and there was something false here.

"What did you want from me?" Parkhurst asked.

"I wanted to ask you to help. I knew you'd want to do all you could for your wife."

FOUR

I WANNA KNOW!"

Exactly, Susan thought, but while the words were hers, the voice wasn't. It was male, loud, and came from outside.

Parkhurst at her elbow, his eyes guarded, she opened the trailer door to see what was going on. A tall young man, red hair, both fists clenched at his sides, was demanding to see the cop in charge.

Fiery eyes shifted to her. "Who are you?"

"This is Robin McCormack." Yancy put a restraining hand on the young man's arm, a hand that looked casual but was firm enough to make McCormack wince.

"It's okay," she said to Yancy. "I'll talk to him. And would you get Ellis over here?"

Feet planted, hands loose by his side, Parkhurst stood ready for any aggressive moves from McCormack.

Cast and crew were all staying at the Sunflower Hotel. They were transported back and forth to base camp or set by vans. Superstars like Laura Edwards had their own personal town cars with drivers, muscular guys who could respond as bodyguards if needed.

Susan told Officer Ellis, another big muscular guy, a weight lifter and boxer, to stick on Ms. Edwards's tail like a burr. Anything happened to her and his ass was on the line. When the actress was tucked in and rolling away with Ellis in a squad car on the bumper, Susan asked Yancy to find Nick Logan and bring him around, then turned her attention to Robin McCormack.

He thrust out his jaw. A rangy young man in cutoff jeans and a T-shirt with the sleeves ripped out, he looked sullen and every inch belligerent, from his longish hair, closely trimmed red beard, and turquoise earring right on down to once-white Nikes now coming apart at the seams.

She invited him inside the trailer. Parkhurst stayed on his heels, avoiding her glance.

McCormack shot her a confused look and demanded of Parkhurst, "What the hell happened?" His fists were still clenched at his sides and he seemed to bounce on tight springs.

"Have a seat, please." Parkhurst aimed an index finger at the couch.

After a moment of internal struggle—which she thought he would lose and end up taking a swing at Parkhurst—McCormack did sit. Barely. Feet planted, ready to leap up, fists on his knees.

"What's your job?" she asked quietly. She'd do the questioning on this one. With this kid's attitude, Parkhurst's manner would strike sparks. The matter of a marriage they'd go into later.

"Your job?" she repeated to get his attention.

He looked at her. "Props. I want to know what happened to Kay."

"How long have you known Ms. Bender?"

"Two years, a little more." Short words, clipped.

"You were friends?"

"Yeah, friends. Now will you tell me?"

"Close friends? Lovers?"

"So what?"

"We're trying to find out what happened, Mr. McCormack. It seems to have been an accident."

"The hell it was! Kay was an athlete. Physically fit. She didn't have *accidents*. She was careful. She always checked everything. Always."

She undoubtedly did, Susan thought, but stunt people got injured, it went with the job, and Kay wasn't expecting to go through a railing, or to hit a pitchfork when she landed. "Have there been problems in making this movie, Mr. McCormack?"

Parkhurst, once he decided the kid was going to keep his fists to himself, drifted to the kitchen area and slid onto the padded bench at the table.

McCormack made a sound somewhere between a grunt and a snort. "There are always problems. Actors get moods. Weather doesn't cooperate. Directors have fits. Things break. Props get lost. Doors don't open."

"Was Kay blamed for any of these things?"

"No."

"Who didn't like her?"

Robin glared with such fury she could see Parkhurst set himself to intervene. "Nobody. Kay was a stunt double. They can't afford anybody not liking them. They don't have tantrums. No matter how bad it gets, they just do the job."

"Other boyfriends? Someone she rejected?"

"Who left a pitchfork lying around? No!"

"It wasn't lying around, it was below the railing hidden under straw."

He winced.

"Where did it come from?"

"The prop cart." That probably played over and over in his mind.

"It was yours." Accusation in her voice.

"It was a prop, yeah. Used in a scene this morning. When we broke for lunch, I left it on the cart for a scene coming up this afternoon."

"Did you notice it missing after lunch?"

"Yeah."

"Why didn't you look for it?"

"I did." He rubbed a hand, hard, over his face. "Fifer told me to stay out of the way and shut up, he was filming." He pressed thumb and forefinger against his eyes. "She wasn't supposed to fall."

"If Kay wouldn't have an accident and nobody would want to hurt her, what do you think happened here?"

He took in air to prevent an explosion. "Laura Edwards."

"What about her?"

"She was supposed to be there, wasn't she?"

"You're suggesting someone wanted to harm Laura Edwards?"

"I'm not suggesting anything. She was supposed to be there. Kay wasn't. Laura's important. Kay isn't."

"Who would want to hurt Laura?"

"How the hell should I know."

"Was she mean? Nasty? Selfish? Did she trample on somebody?"

With a thumbnail, he scratched at a cut on his forefinger. "You better ask Nick."

"What did she do to Nick Logan?"

Robin looked at Susan as though she were two beats slower than the rhythm. "Huh. They're this great Hollywood success story. Great romance. Making a great movie."

She dearly wanted to glance at Parkhurst and get his reaction to this, but she kept her eyes fixed on Robin McCormack. With Parkhurst's ability at concealment, he probably wasn't reacting anyway. "Not true?"

"No," Robin said, but his eyes looked through her.

She'd lost him again; he'd tuned back into the tape playing through his mind. The one that was edited so the ending turned out differently. "Which part isn't true?" she said. "The love story? Or the great movie?"

His clenched fists tightened until the knuckles stood out white. There was much anger in this young man. He might react in violence if told by Kay she didn't want to see him anymore. "What's wrong with the movie?"

"Nothing," he said definitely. "It's coming good. The dailies—" He glanced at her to see if she knew what dailies were. She nodded.

"They're good. Fifer gets all lit up after seeing them. We're running over budget and we're running out of time. He'd be all silent and tight like he'd set himself for the chop going in and then he'd come out with a face like there was gold in the mining pan."

"So he was pleased with Laura's performance? Was he ever angry at her?"

"Never. Not her. He only sometimes got quiet and cold. Scary. He yells at everybody else, especially Clem..."

Clem? Oh, yes, Fifer's assistant.

"...but not at Nick and never at Laura. With the dailies so great I think he didn't want to risk an upset of a good thing."

"Laura's a good actress?"

"Yeah," he said as though anyone with half a brain would know that.

"So if there is nothing wrong with the movie, then it must be the great romance that's in trouble."

"You might say that."

"Have Laura and Nick been fighting?"

Robin looked undecided, then said, "Yeah."

"Screaming at each other? Throwing things? Hitting each other? What?"

"Some of that." He shrugged. "The screaming part. Mostly just charged-up attitudes. Never being in the same place. Not seeing each other if they were."

Charged-up attitudes. Uh-huh. How much do we place on that, coming from a kid who didn't seem quick to pick up nuances? "How long has this been going on?"

"From the start."

"Why were they fighting?"

Robin propped an ankle on the opposite knee and held on to it with both hands. "Sheri, I guess. Sheri with-an-I Lloyd."

"Who is she?"

"Another actor. There was a rumor going she thought she had a shot at the role."

"The role Laura's playing."

"Yeah. Laura had something else going and wasn't available. Then all of a sudden, she was available. Sheri gets offered a nothing part. 'Supporting role,'" he stated in a passing good imitation of Fifer's clipped, staccato enthusiasm. "'Very important. Pivotal. Only you can do it justice.'"

"Mr. Fifer wanted Ms. Edwards for the starring role?"

"Damn straight. Fifer wants a hit. Better get one. His last two bombed. He's counting on Laura to pull him out of the toilet. Sheri sure couldn't do it. Your name doesn't last long if you have a couple of losers under it. Especially multimillion-dollar losers."

"How does Sheri feel about this?"

"What do you think? She's not real smart or she'd never of believed she'd had a chance in the first place."

"What does that have to do with Nick Logan?"

"Well, the great romance wasn't so great after he started snuggling with Sheri."

So what have we got here? Kay Bender dead, maybe in mistake for Laura Edwards. So far—and we've only just begun—no known reason for anyone wanting to harm Kay Bender. Laura Edwards, on the other hand, seemed to bring out motives. Another actress who'd hoped to snag the role. Nick Logan, co-star, finding love and romance, not with the star but with the starlet.

This was beginning to sound like a soap opera. Did Sheri try to kill Laura to obtain the starring role? (Would that happen if Laura were gone?) Was Nick Logan, handsome, sexy co-star, tired of Laura? Was Laura not letting go and needed to be gotten rid of? Tune in tomorrow. Maybe somebody's evil twin will show up. Susan looked at Parkhurst to see if he had a question, a comment, an expression. He looked impassively back in true Parkhurst style. She told Robin McCormack she had no further questions at this time.

He lit out, but before she could get to Parkhurst about this wife business, Yancy had Nick Logan coming in. The actor stood in the living-room area of the trailer, taking up too much space, smelling of expensive aftershave and cigarette smoke. And somehow, she didn't know quite how, he brought with him an air of California. Maybe it was the suntan, or the sun-streaked light hair. Whatever, it made her homesick. For San Francisco, that is. This man—denim shirt unbuttoned halfway, gold chain with some kind of medal hidden in chest hair, denim pants, thongs on his feet—was strictly Los Angeles and never the twain shall meet. But still, California is California.

Rugged in appearance rather than handsome. Coarse features, questing hazel eyes that examined her, moved on to Parkhurst, and stayed there taking in some inventory. Logan then quirked a famous eyebrow and waited. Despite her preset notion that he was going to be a self-centered, arrogant pain in the butt, she found she liked him.

"Please, sit down, Mr. Logan." She indicated the couch and he flip-flopped over to it, waited until she seated herself on the other couch, then settled in with an elbow crooked along the back, a hand on his thigh. There were fine lines around his eyes and down a path from nose to mouth. Early forties, she thought.

"Call me Nick." Low gravelly voice, but not grating to the ear. He twisted his head and looked at Parkhurst sitting unobtrusively in the kitchen area. "Don't I know you from someplace?"

"I doubt it," Parkhurst said.

Nick looked unconvinced.

"We're investigating the fatality that happened this afternoon," Susan said.

Nick nodded. "Making a film seems frivolous in this context, doesn't it?"

"You were in the barn this morning. Is that correct? Scenes were filmed."

"Right." He stuck thumb and forefinger into his shirt pocket and pulled out a pack of cigarettes. "May I?"

"I don't mind. Laura Edwards might. It's her trailer."

Nick stretched out a leg, stuck his hand in his pants pocket, and fished out a lighter. He flicked it and inhaled deeply, tipped back his head and blew smoke at the ceiling.

Susan took a deep lungful of secondhand smoke and wondered why she'd quit. She got up and found a saucer in the kitchen that she handed to Nick in lieu of an ashtray.

"You don't care," she said as she sat back down, "if Ms. Edwards gets upset, or are you deliberately trying to annoy her?"

Nick smiled and Susan realized the smile came from somewhere deep inside; he'd switched something on and the muscles around his eyes created a smile that gave out warmth. It had made him famous, also made him a megabucks star and she could see why; he exuded sensitivity and understanding and, being big and strong, gave the impression he could take care of any threatening dangers.

"She won't mind," he said with a touch of malice, suggesting Ms. Edwards would mind very much.

The first lie, she thought. "Where were you during the lunch break?"

"In my trailer."

"The entire time?"

"Most of the time."

"When you weren't in your trailer, where were you?"

With a thumb, he flicked the end of the cigarette to get rid of ashes. "Uh—the caterer's truck, wandering around to work the kinks out. Uh—I don't know. Around."

"How well did you know Kay Bender?"

"Not at all."

"She worked on this movie."

"Yes, but we did no—socializing."

"Did you ever talk with her?"

"Maybe."

"What did you talk about?"

He didn't have his mind on Susan or her questions, or even on his answers; he kept craning his head to flick glances at Parkhurst. Parkhurst made a lot of people nervous, especially if he was behind them just out of their range of vision, but Nick didn't seem nervous.

"You know," he said after a moment's thought. "I don't believe I ever did talk with her."

"Tell me what you know about her."

He puffed on the cigarette. "Nothing. I didn't know anything about her." There was surprise and sadness in his voice. "Who said no man is an island?"

"Who went into the barn during the lunch break?"

"Oh, hell, I don't know. People might have been in and out. They're always in and out."

"You?"

"No."

"Who wanted to hurt Kay?"

Nick again focused attention on Susan. "I thought the fall was an accident."

Lie number two. She'd questioned too many suspects to miss the slight rise of shoulder muscles. "That's what we're trying to determine. Who had problems with her?"

"Nobody that I know of. You have to understand, I really had nothing to do with the girl. She did her work, doubling for Laura, and that was it. I mean, she must have been around, but—" He shrugged. "Sorry. We have dividing lines here just like every place else."

"Were you aware a pitchfork was on the set?"

"Sure."

"When did you last see it?"

"This morning. I used it in one of those cutesy bits where city slicker male ineptly spreads around straw." Engaging self-deprecating smile.

"What happened to it then?"

"I don't know, the prop man would take it."

"And do what with it?"

"Put it in the prop truck, most likely."

This was said with such offhand sincerity that Susan didn't know whether it was lie or truth.

She glanced at Parkhurst over Nick's shoulder and gave him a nod. Let's see how Nick Logan responded to Parkhurst. Moving fluidly, like one of the big cats, Parkhurst slid from the padded bench and came around where Nick could see him, then took a step closer, forcing Nick to look up at him.

"What's the conflict between you and Laura Edwards?"

Nick stubbed out his cigarette. "Conflict?"

"Love gone sour?"

Nick paused. "What does that have to do with Kay?"

"What do you know about her death?"

"Nothing."

"You didn't find her attractive?"

Nick answered that with a look of "come on, you can do better than that."

"You only interested in actresses?"

"What does that mean?"

"Sheri Lloyd."

"I see you've been picking up the on-site gossip."

"You're sleeping with Ms. Lloyd. How does Ms. Edwards feel about that?"

Susan wondered what Parkhurst felt about this whole tangle of lovers and ex-lovers. His face gave nothing away, it was cold and hard.

"That," Nick said, "is none of your business."

"Wrong, Mr. Logan." Parkhurst backed off and slid a haunch

on an end table. "A young woman was killed. That makes it our business."

"The two aren't connected."

"Ms. Edwards was supposed to be on the railing when it went down. Figure it out, Mr. Logan."

He already had, Susan thought.

"You accusing me of trying to kill Laura?" There was something wrong about the way he said that. No explosive anger, the way an innocent man would normally respond.

"Why would you harm Ms. Edwards?"

Parkhurst's questioning differed greatly from Susan's soft-voiced, "Let's find out what happened here." He dripped disbelief and made suspects so angry they got tangled up in explanations and said things they didn't mean to.

There was none of the laid-back California slouch about Nick Logan now, he was paying close attention, but if he was angry he was keeping a lid on it.

"I wouldn't harm a hair on her head."

"Who wants her dead?"

"No one that I know of." Nick swallowed.

The third lie. A suspect often swallows when he lies.

"Guess. Give me names."

"Laura's a beautiful woman," Nick began.

Parkhurst waited, the panther in the brush patiently waiting for the right moment.

"She raises passions..."

"Names." Parkhurst waited a little less patiently, the panther flicking the tip of his tail.

"I don't have names," Nick said. "You have to understand a lot of emotions run around on location. It comes from being so close together and being focused on the film. I don't know of any anger or hatred toward Laura, but that doesn't mean there isn't any. The costumer because Laura always slumps during fittings? The script writer because she transposes two words of his dialogue? None of that means anything and it's all forgotten when the director calls a wrap."

"What part do you play?"

"What?"

"Part," Parkhurst said slowly and distinctly, "as in role. In the movie."

"The hero," Nick said dryly. "I play a cop."

"Uh-huh. That's all for now, Mr. Logan. You're free to go."

Nick remained seated, took a breath, opened his mouth to ask a question, then changed his mind and got to his feet. He nodded and strode firmly—even in thongs—out. Hero exits trailer.

"Got a little carried away, didn't you?" Susan rose, stood behind Parkhurst in the doorway, and watched Nick Logan's back.

"He was using me."

"Using you?"

"Research for his role. I thought I'd show him how a hick cop conducts an interrogation." Parkhurst smiled, the panther seeing the antelope stumble. "Before I'm done, I may show him a thing or two he's never seen before."

FIVE

WHERE THE HELL was Clem Jones? Yancy was worried about her. He hadn't seen the director's assistant since she'd upchucked on the barn floor. She didn't have sense enough to take care of herself, he'd known smarter geese. With her pink hair she wasn't easy to miss, so how come he hadn't spotted her anywhere, in his sheepdog missions to separate one individual and herd him along to the Edwards trailer? The director, Hayden Fifer, took some nipping at the heels to keep moving.

"This is wasting time," Fifer said.

He wasn't a large man, but he had a large voice. It must come from all that commanding of actors, the power went to his head. It sure didn't go to his heart, that was black like his hair. Black hair threaded with gray, gray beard and eyes the color of slate. Or flint maybe, the state of his heart. He had a good line in scowls, one of which he was using on Yancy. Yancy ignored it. You wouldn't pick him out of a crowd as the great Hollywood director. No jodhpurs, no beret, no long cigarette holder. Plain jeans—they did have somebody's fancy name on them, but jeans nevertheless—and a plain white T-shirt. Not even a smart-ass message. His forehead was sunburned and so were his arms.

Just as they reached the trailer, Nick Logan opened the door. Fifer barely waited for his male star to clear the doorway before he barreled in. Logan took a side jump off the trailer steps and raised a puff of dust and pollen from the dried grass. With a mock salute to Parkhurst, he strode off.

"How long are you going to hold me up?" Yancy heard Fifer say as the trailer door closed.

"I'm sorry to keep you waiting," Susan said. And she was, too.

Hayden Fifer was tightly wrapped, either worry about his movie or maybe just plain irritation that someone else was calling the shots. "Please sit down, Mr. Fifer. We'll try not to keep you long." No longer than necessary and she intended to pour deferential regard all over him, soothe his ego, and anything else that needed doing so he wouldn't get in her way while she did her job.

"I can't sit around wasting time."

"Just a few questions," Susan said.

Fifer slid onto one of the couches, sat with his hands on his knees, ready to get this nonsense over and get back to the important substance of life.

"Disruption and waiting are inevitable after an unexplained death, I'm afraid." Susan used her best cool voice, the one that stood her in good stead in numerous situations: with irate superiors, malcontent subordinates, drunks, belligerents, and just plain when she didn't know what the hell was going on. A voice that allowed her to skate around on potential thin ice with the best of them.

"It was an accident."

"If the pitchfork hadn't been where it was, Ms. Bender would probably be alive. We'll need to speak separately with everybody who was present, and we'll try to do that without causing undue inconvenience."

The fingers on Fifer's left hand danced against his knee. His eyes clicked left and then right, he nodded. "Sure, sure. How long?"

"We won't be certain of the cause of death until after an autopsy."

Fifer's eyes fixed on her face, the fingers became still. "She fell."

"Yes, sir. There will also be some lab investigations and that will take time. We'll try to take care of everything as quickly as possible."

The fingers resumed dancing. "It isn't that I'm not affected by the girl's death."

"I understand, sir. We will need a list of all the people employed by you, and it would be helpful if you could give us their room numbers at the hotel."

"Clem can do that," he said.

THERE WAS STILL no sign of Clem Jones as Yancy tromped around in search of Sheri Lloyd. These fields used to be pastureland. Way off in the northeast corner was a small stock pond, scrub pines grew here and there. Knee-high weeds and grasses had been mowed down in one section to accommodate the vehicles. Trailers for superstars and director. Trailers divided into cubicles called honey wagon rooms for lesser actors, photo doubles, stand-ins, and stunt people. Trailers for wardrobe, makeup, and props. Caterer's truck—Better Than Home Cookin'—from Los Angeles. Ha. Probably afraid we didn't have calamari and garlic ice cream out here on the prairie. A tent staked out for serving hot meals from behind a row of steam trays, long tables and folding chairs for eating. Semis and vans and town cars, flatbed trucks and an electrician's truck and a grip's truck. Bicycles. Did these California people know it rained here? One solid Kansas gullywasher and that's it, Joe. No movin' anything except the bicycles.

Sheri Lloyd was in her own cubicle with her name on the door, but she didn't care to come with him. After some convincing, she got up and followed along, high-heeled sandals tottering over taped cables on the uneven ground. She made her displeasure apparent when he then asked her to wait, standing right out there under the cottonwood, in the heat if not the sun. "It's too damn hot," she repeated many times. He had to admit she had a point there.

"Where's Ms. Jones?" he asked.

"I have no idea. You said they wanted to see me." Sheri twitched her shoulders, raised a hand, and flicked long bronze hair over her shoulder.

"Yes, ma'am. It'll be only a moment." He wanted her all lined up to go as soon as they were finished with the director. With Lieutenant Parkhurst looking like a storm about to happen, Yancy didn't want to give him any aggravation. You couldn't tell so much with the chief. She just always looked poised and classy, kind of haughty with her blue eyes and dark hair, but he didn't think she was any too cool either. She hadn't wanted the movie here from the start, back when everybody else thought it was more exciting than Fourth of July fireworks.

"Well—" Sheri smiled at him. She had the prettiest, whitest, straightest teeth he'd ever seen, dazzling bright in her tanned face. Everything about her dazzled. Well-toned muscles. Surfing probably. Wasn't that what they did in southern California? When they weren't in aerobics classes.

She surely did not like to be kept waiting. She pointed that out to him over and over. Not that he blamed her. It *was* hot; little beads of sweat stood out on her smooth forehead. She constantly tugged at the ends of her skimpy white top thing. No bra. He admired the flexibility of the red shorts that were just a little bit too short—exposing small half-moons of her buttocks, also tanned, he noted—and the shapely length of thigh and curve of calf.

"How come they want me? I wasn't even in there when she fell."

"I wouldn't know, ma'am."

Delicately, she patted fingertips at the hollow of her throat. "Is it always this hot here?"

"No, ma'am. Only half the time, the other half you're freezing your butt off. Being from California, I figure you must like heat."

"I don't like it here, I can tell you that. I can't wait to get out of this place."

Yancy nodded. Hollywood go home. He could go back to being a cop. But this accident that smelled like homicide sure beat all to hell whatever story they were trying to film.

"If you want to know the truth," Sheri said, "I'm not terribly terribly surprised this happened. Laura's been hyper-uptight from the beginning, you know?" She stopped for a second, then added, "Like just waiting to mess up super bad," in case he wasn't following along with his dim countrified brain.

"If you want to know the truth," she said again, "Fifer knows it too. You can be *sure* he isn't telling it like it is in there. You can be sure of that. He needs a great success artistically and financially and I'm afraid—" She shook her head sadly.

"I understood this movie was going well."

"Oh, that's what they *say*, but Laura—well, she was quite good in her day. With a certain type of part, one that didn't require—how shall I put it—a quality of vulnerability—she was okay. She has no subtleties. Just a certain hard—ah—brittle, you might say, archness. It's all just so—so—TV miniseries.''

"Isn't Ms. Edwards supposed to be a great actress?"

''*Pa-leese.*'' Sheri laid a hand on her chest, fingers fanned out over a breast. ''I have nothing but the greatest respect for her as a performer, but I'd have to admit, since you force me, that her—talents are limited. And this film—she was killing it.''

Why was she wasting all this stuff on him? In her view, he could only be a gofer, sent to fetch and carry. Rehearsal maybe? "Fifer isn't pleased with Ms. Edwards's performance?"

Sheri lifted her hair off her neck, making her nipples poke against the halter top. "You have to know the kind of man he is. In control, very circumspect, on the outside, but inside—inside he's really—screaming. And I know—only because I know him so well—I know he realizes he made a mistake with Laura. As a matter of fact...'' She leaned closer, stroked a long curl of hair, and twirled it around her finger.

He knew he was supposed to be spellbound here, lost in all her sexy shimmering. He smelled her musky perfume, got a glimpse of those incredible boobs.

"I just happened to overhear—and I wouldn't want you to think I was eavesdropping—I mean, I wouldn't *stoop*—but he was on the phone and there was this despair in his voice and he was saying''—she lowered her voice—"'I know something has to be done.' And then there was this pause, like the other person was speaking, you know? And then Fifer got this really cold—I mean actually frightening, it was so cold—look on his face and he said, 'I'll take care of her. She won't be a problem.''' Sheri widened her eyes at the enormous implications.

"You believe he was talking about—?"

"Laura." A little impatience here. She caught it right away. "Laura forced him to take her on. I personally know he didn't want her. She has some kind of''—Sheri searched her mind for a word of enough devastation—"*something* she's holding over his head." Sheri nodded sagely. "That's the only reason she's in. And she's destroying this movie."

"Who was Fifer talking with?"

"Well, one of the investors, of course." She was a wee bit

exasperated he was wasting time on the nonessentials. She moved constantly while she talked; her hands fluttered and her hair swayed and her butt jiggled and her boobs bounced. No wonder she was sweating, all that action had to be exhausting.

She was putting on quite a performance. He had to give her flawless skin, mouth-drying shapeliness, hair asking for fingers to get tangled in, and certainly gorgeous teeth, but she wasn't lighting any fires. He'd never, at work or at play, found contempt a turn-on. All right, she probably didn't have much experience with homicide. Maybe this was her way of coping, handling fear, shock, anxiety, grief even—anything's possible. Or maybe she was just a cold, emotionally stunted, selfish little bitch. Or maybe she had a hand in the fall and there was some purpose behind this titillating display.

"Oh, pay no attention—" She laid her fingers on his arm. "It's just—oh, I just—everything is too much. There's a curse on this movie. Something more, something very bad—" Tears glistened in her eyes.

Now Yancy was impressed. When the emotion got turned on, he'd have expected heaving bosom and muffled sobs.

"Yes, ma'am," he said.

Suddenly she stopped all the jiggling and bouncing and stood stock-still. A breath caught going in. He turned to see what got her attention. Ambulance out on the road. Slow and silent. The very stuff of which movies were made. Endless blue sky. Not a cloud. The tortured scream of a jet plane and then a thin white jet stream. Ambulance rolled by leaving a cloud of dust in its wake.

She paled. He took her elbow. "Ms. Lloyd?"

She swayed. He eased her around so she couldn't see the road. She shivered. The ambulance, swaying and bouncing, moved on.

"Listen," she said. "I can't wait around here all day. I can't help any anyway. So—"

The trailer door popped open and the director shot out.

"Fifer?" She put out her hand to stop him.

"Later, baby." He patted her arm. "I'm busy now."

With a little pout, she watched him stride off. Lieutenant Parkhurst got her attention and invited her inside. She turned on the smile and the jiggle and bounce and tripped up the steps, managing to slide very close to Parkhurst as she went by. Hey now, must be some kind of performance she was planning for the lieutenant.

"Yancy," Parkhurst said, "round up Clem Jones. Tell White he can turn the rest of them loose. Make sure he has names, local and permanent addresses, and phone numbers ditto."

Yancy nodded and headed for the caterer's tent where White was keeping two dozen or so people corralled. They sat in folding chairs at long tables, or stood around in clumps, yakking with each other. Soft drink cans, glasses, cups, and plates with various snacks were all over the place. Nobody was pounding a fist and demanding to be let go. These people were used to hanging around waiting. He did notice all eyes shift to him when he passed along the message to White. Clem Jones wasn't with them. He asked if anyone had seen her.

"Here somewhere."

"Around."

"Every time you move, you trip over her."

But nobody could tell him where she was now and the last time anyone remembered seeing her was in the barn after Kay Bender fell.

Had she slipped through in all the confusion? Gone back to the hotel? He was getting all tense about her. He hoped nothing had happened to the silly little twit.

Tapping at Nick Logan's trailer got him Nick, but no Clem Jones.

"You mind if I talk with you for a bit?" Nick asked.

"I'm looking to find Ms. Jones. Any ideas?"

"I'll help you." Nick stubbed out a cigarette and shoved his feet into thongs.

"You work with that guy in there?" Nick gave a hitch to his jeans and fell into step beside Yancy.

"The lieutenant? Sure."

"What's his name, Parkhurst? How is he to work for?"

No way Yancy was going to reach into that funny little can of worms. Sometimes the lieutenant was a volcano about to go off, and sometimes he wasn't. You didn't know. You paid attention. "He gets the job done," Yancy said, sidestepping the obligation to be specific.

With a mocking expression in his eyes, Nick acknowledged the diplomacy. "You been a cop long?"

"Six years."

"Like it?"

"Sometimes."

"Tell me about being a cop."

"What do you want to know?"

"Why a cop?"

Yancy shrugged. That was simple; he'd needed a job. If he had a father somewhere he'd never met the guy. His mother didn't live in the same world as everybody else. Sweet, yes, and beautiful, but loony as owl shit.

When he was a little kid he'd come home from school hoping there'd be something to eat in the house. Like as not, his mother would hug him fiercely, grab his hand, and race with him to the woods. She'd point out butterflies and wildflowers, touch a petal with a fingertip as gentle as a puff of spring breeze. She'd sing in a soft clear voice, eerie haunting songs about blood and murder and revenge and unrequited love. He'd have made a pact with the devil for one peanut butter sandwich, would even have shared it with his sister who used to fantasize about food until he yelled at her to shut up.

"It's a job," Yancy said. He'd wanted to be fireman. Saving children from burning buildings, rescuing kittens from treetops. A hero. God help him, he was his mother's son. She'd marked him with all her fairy stories without him even knowing it. The fire department wasn't hiring, but the police department was.

At the makeup trailer, a man told him Clem wasn't there, he didn't know where she was.

"What kind of man is he?" Nick asked.

"Who?" Yancy's mind was still running along the track that read what to do about his mother. By this time it was worn into a deep rut. For a moment he thought Nick was asking an oblique question about Yancy himself. And it startled him. Not only because he didn't know the answer, but also because it seemed to hold echoes of his sister's accusatory voice.

"This Parkhurst guy."

"What are you getting at?"

Nick smiled, shrugged. "Oh, hell, I don't know. I got the impression a whole lot of hostility was coming my way. Made me wonder why. Does he not like outsiders? Is that it? Or is it me in particular he doesn't like?" Nick hooked his thumbs over his belt and loosened his knees. "All right, stranger." Good John Wayne imitation. "This town isn't big enough for both of us."

Yancy smiled. For a big movie star type, Nick was an okay guy, they'd even gotten friendly over a beer or two. "The lieutenant's a good cop."

"Yeah? Good enough he won't be swayed by trying to solve this immediately? Just to get it cleaned up?"

"What are you getting at?" Nobody answered his tap at the wardrobe trailer. With Nick at his heels, he went inside. Clothing on racks filled it until there was barely room to walk the length of it. Stacked washer and dryer at one end, worktable for sewing, mending, et cetera by the door.

"Hell if I know," Nick said as Yancy closed the door behind them. "I'm just concerned. Kay was an okay kid. I didn't know her well, but she was a part of this game and if it was more than an accident—somebody has to look out for her. She can't do it herself."

"What does that mean?"

Nick hunched his shoulders and shoved his hands in his pockets. "Oh, hell, justice, I guess. If that doesn't sound too high-principled."

Yancy stopped and looked at the actor. "Are you asking me if the lieutenant has the smarts to recognize a clue if he trips over one? What are you going to do? Step in and clear the case? Real movie stuff. The cops are so stupid they don't know what they're doing. But, by God, you're going to track down the killer. See justice is done for this woman, because she can't do it for herself and she's one of your own."

"Something like that, yeah."

"You've been seeing too many movies, Nick."

The actor gave him a smile. "Yeah, I guess." After a moment he sketched a wave and started to flap off in his thongs. Not the best footwear for the terrain, his feet and ankles would likely be covered with chiggers by the time he got back to his trailer. For half a second Yancy wondered what that was all about—with these people you never could tell what was real and what was made-up—then he went back to worrying about Clem Jones. She was always around, looking at him with withering scorn, mouthing at him. She chewed bubble gum, for God's sake, and had pink hair.

"Oh, Yancy?"

He turned. "Yeah?"

"You might try the barn," Nick said. "Clem's a morbid little thing. She might be there."

Yancy headed for the barn. The yellow tape was down, that meant Osey had finished taking prints and picking through straw for evidence. The chief really was moving this along as fast as possible. He looked inside. Body gone, no Clem, no people, but everything else still there, tangles of cable, cameras, booms, mikes. Just as he turned away he heard noises, muffled sounds from the loft, then a high thin keening that stirred the hair on the back of his neck.

He clambered up the ladder, halted when he got to eye level, and cautiously peered into the huge shadowy space. It took a moment to spot her; the ankle-length prison-striped smock sort of fit in with the dimness. Pink hair didn't. She sat at the edge of the drop just where the railing had broken, knees drawn up, arms around them. She froze when she saw him.

"Ms. Jones?"

Like a wild thing, she scrabbled away, ended up against the rough wall, eyes wide with panic, mouth open for air.

"Hey now," he said softly. "Take it easy."

She was a mess; black eye makeup smeared all over her face, nose running, pink hair all every which way.

Recognition slowly seeped into her eyes. They were an odd tan color and a shaft of sunlight angling through the small window at the peak of the roof picked out gold flecks. Tears spilled.

"I killed her," she whispered.

SIX

SLOWLY, Yancy levered himself up into the loft. Go easy here, Clem didn't look too well wired together. A sudden move on his part and he'd have her exploding, then there'd be raw nerve ends dangling all over the place. He edged along to a spot where he was between her and the broken rail, then squatted, facing her.

"It's all right," he said. "Nobody's going to hurt you." He kept his voice loose and slow.

She brought an elbow up over her eyes, gulped, and sniffled on a ghost of a sob. "Yancy, you got a sweet voice, but you're full of shit."

Her flip, so quick from damp misery to attack, surprised him. Relieved him too. As long as she was mouthing off she wasn't likely to throw herself over the edge. She looked like a homeless cat, scared and spitting at everybody.

He'd better treat her like a stray, she seemed better able to handle that. This brought up thoughts about her life he didn't have time to go into at the moment. He stood up, took four strides, sat beside her with his back against the rough wall, and rested his forearms on his bent knees. "What are you doing up here?"

She pinned him with a gaze like rifle barrels. Leaning forward, he pulled a handkerchief from his back pocket and held it out to her.

She looked at it like she'd never seen such a thing before, then she scrunched it and scrubbed it over her face, mixing tears and black mascara and blue eye shadow and white makeup into one big muddy mask. She blew her nose. "Go away, Yancy. I hate men."

"You said you killed her." He waited. "What did that mean?"

"Life is all one big gigantic joke. Nothing but banana peels and pratfalls. A fart in a cathedral. It was my fault."

"What was?"

"Take your questions and your busy little mind and your dithyrambic little self and get away from me."

Dithyrambic? He better get himself a dictionary. "Why was it your fault?"

"If I'd gotten Laura up here like I was supposed to, Kay wouldn't have fallen."

"Then it might be Ms. Edwards who'd be dead."

Clem grimaced. "I'm slaying dragons."

"I've slain a dragon or two in my life. Maybe I could help."

"Are you deaf? Get lost."

"Sorry. I didn't just wander up for a straw to pick my teeth with. I was sent to get you."

"Good boy. You did what you were told."

"Yes, ma'am, I usually do."

"Your mother must be very proud."

"As is yours, I'm sure."

"I don't have a mother. Go away."

"You don't have a hope of making me go away. You will come with me, docilely and mutely, or I will cuff you and drag you."

Clem looked at him seriously for a long minute. "Can you really do that?"

"No. So I'd appreciate it if you'd just haul ass out of here and come with me."

She let a beat go by, then another, then tossed off, "Okay."

Yancy attempted to help her down the ladder and got a kick for his attentions.

"Where are you taking me?" she asked when they passed from the dimness of the barn out into bright sunlight.

"Laura Edwards's trailer to answer some questions by the higher-ups."

"That guy that looks like a grizzly about to attack? What's his name?"

"The lieutenant, that who you're talking about? Parkhurst."

"He's a cop," she said, getting everything clear.

"Yeah."

"I don't want to talk to him."

"They just want to find out what happened."

"I saw him before."

"Before what?" Yancy asked, sitting hard on exasperation.

"He was hanging around the barn during the lunch break, when nobody else was here."

Yancy delivered her at the trailer and wondered if that crack about the lieutenant had any truth in it.

SUSAN PULLED her blouse untucked as she opened the door of the pickup. The sky was taking on the hue of cobalt blue. The air was finally cooling down a little—it damn well should at almost seven-thirty—but the pickup, having baked all afternoon, was like an oven. She pushed on the air-conditioning, then pushed it off and cranked down the windows. With the truck in motion, a little air passed through and it smelled of coming dusk and recently cut grasses and lilacs. Cicadas hummed somewhere. Her mind replayed the session with Clem Jones. Susan couldn't get a clear fix on Clem. One minute she was world-weary, the next smart-ass, the next lost and bewildered. Parkhurst was surprisingly easy on her. Susan wondered why.

Parkhurst and Laura Edwards. Talk about surprise. Wife, for God's sake.

Lately, her interest in Parkhurst had just as much to do with hormones as business. She'd listed all the reasons why it wasn't a good idea, why she'd be a damn fool. And then this famous actress comes along, wraps herself around him, and Susan is as green-eyed as any teenager. Jesus. What a mess.

Focus on the dead woman and how she got that way. Get over to the Sunflower Hotel and go through Kay Bender's room. Find out next of kin and notify. Go through all the statements of cast and crew and see what doesn't fit. Find out when Owen Fisher had scheduled the autopsy and be there. Probably early tomorrow morning. Attending autopsies, while not her favorite activity, sometimes turned up important information that got to her quicker than if she'd waited for the formal report.

Okay? That enough to keep your mind in check? It still wandered back to Parkhurst and Laura Edwards.

Get a grip.

She drove along Main Street, a street paved with red bricks and lined with tall maples, and thought as she had many times before that Hampstead was actually a pretty little town. In the gathering dusk, the old-fashioned lantern-shaped streetlights glowed softly throwing out pools of gold. The buildings, many of them made of native limestone, were old and impressive with fancy cornices and parapets. At Seventh Street, she turned left past the courthouse, a Gothic-style type with a clock tower; the stone had mellowed over the years to a warm cream color. It had been built in 1906, the year of the San Francisco earthquake.

San Francisco. Maybe now was the time to go back where she belonged.

Can't. Work to do.

She pulled into the lot behind the police department, a relatively new building, red brick with white trim, and nosed in beside Parkhurst's Bronco. Sliding from the truck, she glanced up at the communications tower to make sure the owl was still standing sentry. Birds tended to roost there and interfere with transmitting and receiving, sometimes to the point of reducing everything to fuzz. The stuffed owl was to keep them away. Detective Osey Pickett's idea. He'd also been the one to scale the tower. Good kid, Osey. Chock-full of local lore.

Inside, she took the corridor covered with indoor-outdoor carpeting in an icky brown color and paused at the doorway of Osey and Parkhurst's office. Osey wasn't in. Parkhurst stood by his desk, back toward her, and turned before she could speak. The room was dim, not dark, but murky enough that she couldn't see his eyes clearly. His face was carefully blank.

"Right," he said. "I'm on my way." *To your office* was unspoken.

Well, at least they were still a team, no need for dialogue. Her office had glass halfway down across the front. She flicked the light switch—more light, more clarity, right?—and adjusted the blinds to half-mast. During her first year the natives had stared at her like she was a strange and wondrous fish. She was from

San Francisco. We know what that's like. Freaks and perverts. The fishbowl effect still made her self-conscious. The carpet here was dark blue, not much better in quality, but at least better in color. The desk was gray metal, standard government issue, also the chair, swivel with green vinyl. The visitor's chair was a wooden relic with arms. She hung her shoulder bag over the coat tree in the corner.

She'd started as acting chief, temporary. The mayor didn't like her; the townspeople didn't like her and didn't want an outsider, especially a woman, in the job. Members of the department agreed with both. There was no danger of permanence. Well, the acting recently got dropped. Now she was the real thing, and the mayor still didn't like her, the townspeople still didn't want her, and some of her officers still agreed with both.

Parkhurst came in with two soft drink cans—a delaying tactic, she assumed—and handed her one. She bent up the tab and took a sip. He looked at her, paced to the window, held down a slat, and looked out at the street where streetlights were coming on.

"Wife?" She'd meant to be a little more smooth, work up to it with some finesse, for Christ's sake, but the word just popped out. She put her feet on the desk, legs crossed at the ankles. Why had she given up smoking? This was a cigarette moment, if ever she saw one.

With a knee, Parkhurst nudged the wooden armchair closer, sat low on his spine, and stretched his legs out. "Once upon a time," he said. "Long long ago. Not now."

"You were married to Laura Edwards."

He made a sound, half laugh, half snort. "She was just plain Laura Edwards back then."

He tipped the can, took a long drink, and rested it on his chest. "It was twelve years ago. We were a couple of kids. She thought I needed my horizons expanded. I thought she needed taking care of." He gazed at the can, rubbed a thumb through the condensation, and took a quick swig. "It turned out we were both wrong."

His voice was flat: don't push it, this is as far as I intend to go. If it had been only personal, Susan would have dropped it, but a death had occurred. She couldn't simply let it hang there.

"It seems like you might have made at least a mention of the fact that you were married."

"Oh, hell, it was an awkward *fact* to just drop into conversation. Lovely weather we're having. Oh, by the way, I used to be married to Laura Edwards."

Yes, actually, any normal person would have done just that. Especially when news got around that Laura Edwards was coming to town. Susan hadn't known he'd ever been married at all, let alone to an actress of Edwards's note.

Parkhurst sat quietly, his hard gaze playing over her face. She had no idea what thoughts were behind the silence that stretched out. This case was going to be a bitch no matter which way she turned it.

"Have you kept in touch with her over the years?"

"No." He looked perfectly relaxed, except for the little knot of muscle at the corner of his jaw.

"God damn it. I know this is awkward, but we have an investigation going on. You're involved, simply by your relationship to what may be the intended victim. At this point I don't even know which side of the fence you're on. It doesn't help any when you answer emotionally loaded questions with yes or no. I can see there's all kinds of stuff here you'd rather not go into. I'd like to respect your wishes"—the hell, she would—"but that's not possible. You will talk to me or I will put you on suspension until this case is cleared." She kept her voice calm and low with no hint of challenge. Challenge would set him off like a rocket.

"You're the boss."

Yes, and she didn't like to hear that response. It meant he wasn't going to cooperate, he was going to be combative, and that made her angry.

He continued to look at her, then to her great surprise, he smiled. A quick, apologetic "you're right and life's a pie in the face" smile that disappeared fast, but nevertheless a smile. That was such a rare occurrence she immediately got nervous.

"I'm sorry," he said. "You don't know what I'd give for this film company to be shooting their damn movie somewhere else."

She could make a good guess. "You didn't leave town."

He gave her a sour look. "The thought crossed my mind. It seemed cowardly. Besides, they're probably going to be here too long. And she had no idea where I was. With a little care, there was no reason our paths should cross."

"Sometimes life is interesting that way."

"Oh, yeah." He studied the cola can as though he were memorizing it. "We were from different worlds. Me, slums and street gangs. She lived in a nice middle-class house with a nice middle-class family. Her father was an accountant. He used numbers and pencils. My father used curses and fists."

"How did you meet?" If the question wasn't strictly pertinent, it was one she wanted answered.

"It was a dark and stormy night." He took a drink. "She was on the highway with a flat, drenched to the bone. I changed the tire."

Susan waited for him to go on. He didn't, but she could imagine how it went. Laura damply grateful, intrigued by this dark man in uniform. It probably started with coffee somewhere first, moved up to a drink, and then dinner. From there everything took off.

"I courted her," Parkhurst said with mocking humor. "Flowers and chocolates. Very traditional. Very unoriginal. We were married two months later. Her father gave her away in the family church while her mother wept and her brother looked manly."

"Do you feel any bitterness?" Susan emptied her can and set it silently on the desk.

"After twelve years?" He tipped up his can, drained it, and sailed it to the wastebasket with a little more spin than he intended. He picked up Susan's—held it easy. Lots of other stuff maybe, but no bitterness. It clinked when it hit.

LAURA HAD BEEN swept away by the idea of marrying a cop, especially a hard-ass like him. She'd never known anybody like him, he smelled of danger and violence, she could pretend to dance close to the edge. He was crazy in love with her. Laura was all that was good and kind and warm and clean; everything he wanted and assumed he'd never have.

She was a drama student, going to be a star someday. And so

were all her friends. They liked classes, they liked each other, they liked to party. They didn't like him. They thought he was a dead brain and they couldn't understand why she had saddled herself with him. He was a rookie then, finding it difficult to play all night and function on the job. He kept going with it until the drugs finally tore it. Her friends, used to him, got more and more open about what they were smoking, shooting, or snorting. Finally, they got so blatant, he couldn't turn his head anymore. His job put him on the other side of the fence. One evening he lost patience and dragged her out of there. They slung words at each other that ricocheted around the enclosed car.

That night he came close to hitting her, close enough it scared the shit out of him. He had a temper, legacy from a drunk, abusive father, about the only inheritance he got. And at that exact moment he knew he was losing her. Anger and frustration grew in his belly and built a hot rage so fierce it roared through his head. His mind flashed on the old man, face red, fist raised. He lit out and walked for miles, then walked some more, solemnly promising himself it would never happen again. Never would he get that close, never would he become his father.

He and Laura had stayed together a few more months, shouting at each other, inflicting pain, but he didn't ever come near to hurting her with his hands. Feelings ran high between them. They rolled around in bed with a hot passion, then lay dripping and spent, not speaking a word. Through it all, he had the sense she was standing to one side and observing: this is the way tragic, doomed love is played.

"ANOTHER DARK and stormy night," he said to Susan, "she had enough of my mundane character, my repressed personality, my provincial thinking, and my exceptionally closed mind. She took off for California."

"You have any unfinished business?"

"No." Before today he'd have bet his life on it. He shouldn't be so careless with his life.

"Anything else you need to tell me?"

"What do you want to know?"

"Whether you have any reason, real or imagined, old or new, for trying to harm Laura Edwards."

"No." Embarrassment. He'd known when he heard she was rolling into town that someday she'd land him in a shitload of embarrassment. And she came through like the trouper she was.

"No conflicts? No, she took your collection of baseball cards and you vowed to get them back?"

"No." Laura took her dancing and dazzling and curious and exciting self and left him sad and ashamed and failed and relieved. "We didn't have anything except our clothes. She took hers and left mine."

Susan let her feet drop to the floor and leaned forward. "As I see it, we have two paths to explore. Someone tried to kill Laura Edwards and we need to prevent another attempt and find out who."

She picked up a pencil and threaded it through her fingers, tapped eraser end and sharpened end alternately. "Or Kay Bender was the intended victim. In which case the perp could be Laura Edwards. She didn't show up when she was supposed to. Who better than Laura could manage that?"

Parkhurst took a breath, let it out. "Yeah," he said, "I realize that."

"You realize that because of your relationship with Laura Edwards I have to consider you a suspect?"

SEVEN

IT WAS AFTER EIGHT, with only an hour or so of daylight left, by the time Yancy turned in the squad car and got into his own vehicle. Rolling his shoulders to work out the knots left by the fourteen-hour day, he cranked the windows down to let the hot air inside mingle with the tepid air outside and fired up the Cherokee. It idled rough. He needed to take care of that.

Shoving the gear in reverse, he backed out and took Eleventh Street for a block, then swung right on Vermont to get out of town. He was late. Beyond the city limits, he accelerated past barbed-wire fenced fields of buffalo grass and wild flowers, a few dark green cedars dotted over the hills.

What should he do about the little nugget Clem Jones had tossed him? Ask the lieutenant? Yeah, right. With all due respect, sir, what were you doing at the barn just before the stuntwoman got killed? Forget about questioning Clem. She'd tell him whatever suited her fancy at the moment, with no relationship to the truth.

Drop it on the chief's desk? Bad idea. Ratting out a superior was never a good idea. Anyway, he liked the lieutenant, would trust his life to the man. And Clem was some kind of nutcase. Okay, then what? Ask questions? See what turned up. If Parkhurst was there, somebody else might have seen him. Maybe Yancy's teamster buddy Mac would know something. A crow sat on the mailbox, and as Yancy made a left, it fixed him with a bright malicious eye, uttered a jeering "caw," and took flight.

"You're probably right," Yancy muttered as he jounced toward the house. A white wood frame, in this kind of light, it didn't need paint so bad. Small, one-story, it had a quiet pitch to the roof, wide windows all around, and a porch that extended the whole length of the front. Trees reached up behind, flowers—snapdragons, bluebonnets, poppies, hollyhocks, and God knew what else—ran unchecked front and back. Tall structures like birdhouses sprouted here and there, looking like they'd simply grown taller than the other plant life.

He backed up the drive and parked the car ass end against the garage door. As late as he was, it couldn't hurt to have a fast getaway in the making. Joke.

"Finally decided to show up?"

Startled, he turned. The hammock strung between two walnut trees sagged under the solid weight of Dallas Walsh, all spiffed up in suit and tie. A suit and tie kind of guy he wasn't.

"Hi, Dallas. Sorry I'm late."

With a polished shoe tip, Dallas shoved at the ground and swung the hammock. "Tell it to your sister, buddy. Last I saw her she was crying at the kitchen table."

"I had to work."

Dallas waved a beefy hand. "Take it to Serena."

Yancy found his sister sitting at the table in the graying daylight taking lemons, one by one, from the blue pottery bowl in the center and carefully placing them in a circle around it. He flicked on the ceiling light. She squinted at him. She wasn't crying, but she had been, eyes red and watery.

"Serena—" He sat across from her and took both her hands, they had a strong citrusy smell. "I'm sorry."

"You might have called." She jerked her hands away and went back to lemons.

"I didn't have a chance. I'm sorry."

"Sorry won't do it. I've been looking forward to this evening for weeks. Dallas and I had plans. It was all arranged. I bought a new dress, for heaven's sake." She touched the high neck of the green dress and stood to shake the folds from the flared skirt, a pretty green that matched her eyes and set to advantage her auburn hair.

"You look fantastic."

"Frankly, Peter, it wasn't you I was trying to impress." She tip-tapped across the wood floor to the stove in the center. With its copper hood, it was the only modern touch in the old-fashioned room. Open shelves packed with supplies lined two walls above the counters, and glass-fronted cabinets took up the third.

She clicked on the burner under the teakettle, then went to the window, turned to face him, and crossed her arms. "This can't go on."

"Why didn't you go to your party? You knew I'd get here as soon as I could."

"Haven't you heard anything I've said?"

"Serena—"

"She's your mother too, and right now I'm feeling like you don't fully appreciate that, because if you did you'd give some consideration to the fact that I'm still living here. I've been doing it for a long time now and I haven't voiced many complaints."

She stared at the three glass flycatchers on the counter, ran a fingertip over the middle one. "I'm trapped here, Peter. And I'd like to move out. Dallas and I—we want to move in together."

"That's great."

Serena spun around. "She set herself on fire today."

"What!"

"Sit down. She's okay. She's asleep."

"What happened?"

"I was a little late getting home and she decided she would fix supper. She was making an omelet and her sleeve caught on fire."

"You're sure she's all right?"

"Yes, Peter, she's all right. This time. Fortunately, I came home and managed to get it out before she got burned. Since the stroke, she's just not—"

A stroke didn't seem right, not at forty-six.

"She can't be left alone, Peter. When I came to fix her lunch today and make sure she was okay, she wasn't here. I was frantic."

"Where was she?"

"I have no idea. I drove around looking for her as long as I could. I had to get back. I called and called and kept calling. Finally, she answered the phone."

"Where had she been?"

"Who knows. She couldn't remember."

Scooting the chair to a slant, he stretched out his legs and rested one arm on the table. "What do you suggest we do?"

"You know perfectly well what we have to do. I can't be here every minute. I have a job. And don't tell me to quit. Maybe it's your turn to quit." She glared at him. Tears ruined it; you can't glare effectively through weepy eyes.

He went to her and folded his arms around her, rested his chin on the top of her head. He couldn't quit, even if he wanted to. While his salary wasn't diamonds and caviar, it beat hers by a country mile, and they needed the money.

"This can't go on," she said.

"I know," he murmured. "I'll think of something, I promise."

"Oh, Peter." Hands flat against his chest, she gave him a push, went to the towel holder next to the sink, and yanked off a paper towel. She ripped it in half and blew her nose. "Thinking won't do it. There's only one solution and you know it. We have to find a place for her to live."

"This is her home."

Serena started crying again. "I know."

"Okay." He smoothed her hair back. "I'll look into it. We can't do anything tonight. Why don't you and Dallas go—"

"Peter!"

"I know it's too late. Isn't there something? I don't have to be back till six in the morning. I could stay here tonight."

"It won't do. You can't make atonement by staying one lousy night. You might ease your conscience, you won't solve anything."

He kept his voice low. "I only want to do what's right."

"That's what we all want. The problem is what's right for one isn't right for all. Right depends on viewpoint. What do you think is right? She stays here and everything goes back to the way it used to be? That's not going to happen. She had a stroke, Peter. She's not ever going to be like she used to be, and all your wishing and ignoring the facts isn't going to make it so."

Eyes closed, he rubbed a hand down his jaw. Fighting with Serena made him feel small and beady-eyed. They'd always stuck together. Growing up as they did, it was the only way to survive. "What do you want to do?"

She sighed, part sadness, part irritation. "You know what we have to do."

"She's afraid of that very thing."

"Damn it, Peter, you think I want this?" Serena blew her nose on the other half of the paper towel. "You think I don't ache for her? Wish she was all right?" A high giggle popped out. Yancy smiled.

All right didn't fit with their mother. She'd always had a flexible attitude toward reality.

"That's not the only option," he said. "We could find somebody to stay with her."

"Twenty-four hours a day?"

"I could move back, be here at night."

"That's great. And what will you do when you have to work nights? And how will you pay for it?"

"I don't know. I'll work something out." He didn't suggest Dallas move in here. In her more lucid moments—as lucid as she ever was or could be—their mother liked Dallas fine. Other times she got him confused with the villains in the grimmer Celtic tales. Besides, Dallas had a larger, more livable place of his own. "And the money for some kind of home?"

"The house."

Yancy suddenly felt bone-tired; sadness—the kind that clings after grief ebbs—oozed over him like an oil slick. "What about Elmo?"

"I don't know about Elmo. I just don't know."

"Peter?" Their mother's voice came from the other room. "Is that you?"

"You mind if I see her?"

"Stop that!" Serena slapped the cabinet with the palm of one hand, the sound was like the crack of a circus whip. "I won't be the bad guy here."

"No. I'm sorry." His hands cupped her head so she couldn't look away. "I don't know what to do. That makes me mean."

"Peter—?"

Serena poked him in the chest with an index finger. "Go. You always make her happy."

The house was basically four rooms, kitchen and living room

in front, two bedrooms behind, bathroom tucked in between. Their mother's bedroom was on the right of the hallway, Serena's on the left. Until he was eight and Serena ten, they'd shared it. For his eighth birthday, he got to move into the garage. A little nippy in the winter, but all his.

On the floor in the corner, Elmo, the giant schnauzer his mother had rescued from the pound, inched himself up to a sitting position, gave Yancy a swipe with a soft tongue, and inched himself, toenails clicking, back down. Time to trim those nails again. His mother sat in the white wicker rocking chair tucked into bright yellow cushions. Outside the window, a fiery sun was slipping behind the hills, the dark blue sky was smeared with violet and pink and purple. Jasmine scented the night air.

A small fan purred on the table beside her gently lifting the ends of her dark hair. When he was a little kid, he'd thought she looked like Snow White, fairest in the land. At forty-six, Raina Yancy was still lovely, white skin, oval face, brown eyes, air of innocence and wonder. She brought to mind fireflies and moonlight and silvery wind chimes.

She sang quietly to herself in a clear voice, a song about blood and murder as she worked on a quilt square.

> *"...Then he cut off her head*
> *from her lily breast bone*
> *and he hung't up in the kitchen*
> *it made a' the ha shine."*

Before the stroke, her fingers would dart like hummingbirds over the bright colors; now they were slow and awkward.

"Peter." A smile lit up her face. She dropped the square of cloth in her lap and held out both hands.

"How are you, Mom?" Squatting beside her, he took her hands and kissed her soft cheek.

"No longer very skillful." She nodded at the square.

"It's perfect." He backed up and sat on the edge of the bed. It was covered in a quilt she'd made of white squares with stars of every color and a blue and yellow border.

"I'm so glad you're here."

He reached past her and switched on the lamp sitting on the bookcase. "This might help."

Light pooled on a white pitcher with blue flowers and a framed photo of himself in uniform brought out the cheery yellow of the striped wallpaper and paler yellow in the tied-back curtains.

"I've been watching the bats leave," she said.

Other people had birdhouses in their yards; his mother had bat houses, way back before bats were popular. Little differences like this had made his childhood difficult.

"It's just that they're ugly," she said. "They suffer from bad press. And they do so much good. Think of the thousands of mosquitoes they eat."

Elmo, supercilious expression, bushy eyebrows, and mutton-chop whiskers, stretched his forepaws out in front of him and raised his rear end in the air, then righted himself, moseyed over and butted his head up under Yancy's hand. Yancy obliged. The *Herald* daily ran a picture of a cute puppy or kitten needing a home. Why they chose Elmo, he couldn't guess, but his mother had taken one look and raced right out to save the beast. Elmo hadn't strayed from her side since. He knew lady bountiful when he saw her. After bestowing a lick of appreciation on Yancy, he swung his large head into her lap and looked up at her with eternal love and loyalty.

She stroked his pointy ears. "Tell me about your day, Peter. What happened to make you so late? Serena's upset."

"I'm sorry."

"I know, dear. I told her to go ahead. What kind of trouble could I get into sitting right here?"

"She didn't want you to get hurt."

"I'm not a child, Peter."

"No, you're not, but sometimes you get—confused."

She laughed. "I hate to be the one to tell you this, but I've been confused all my life."

"Well—" He smiled. "Maybe different." Nobody else's mother put fairy tales and Bible stories in the same bin. He grew up with a steady diet of things in the world that needed doing, missions to accomplish, wrongs to correct, causes to champion. "And what have you been up to?"

"Watching movies."

"Yeah? What did you see?"

She frowned in thought. "Somebody was trying to kill her. The weapon was hidden in the basket. It broke and fell."

"What fell?"

"I'm not sure. Remember Lucy Locket?"

"I don't think so, Mom."

"Of course, you do. She had two eyes on a platter."

"Oh."

"Obsession." She examined his face. "You look tired, love. Are you getting enough sleep?"

"Sure, Mom. It's just been a long day."

"You know, Peter, I've lived here all my life." Her voice was soft. "Elmo and I like to sit out there under the ash tree." Her voice grew softer. "Are you going to make me leave?"

"No, Mom. No, I won't."

EIGHT

SUSAN MANAGED to be at the hotel, the lobby dim and deserted, by ten o'clock. Howard Gilbert, the assistant manager, handed her the stuntwoman's room key—an actual key, not a coded plastic card.

"This is the first time since I've been here," he said, "that we've had a guest die."

He didn't look over twenty-five, round face more suited to smiling than somberness.

"Tell me about Kay Bender," she said.

"Quiet. Tell you the truth, I hardly remember what she looked like. Never any trouble. Not like some of them."

"Who caused trouble?"

"All of them," he said darkly. "They're worse than fraternity boys on a weekend drunk. They play football in the hallways, pull down chandeliers. I think they swing on them. Once they took lobby furniture and jammed it all in the elevators. And you wouldn't believe the state of the bathrooms. One maid out-and-out quit, said I couldn't pay her enough."

"That's showbiz," Susan said. "Did Kay make any calls? Receive any?"

"Not that got charged for. Maybe local or room to room."

"Are you sorry this whole bunch is here?"

He grinned. "I'm not and that's a fact. It's the only period in my time that we've turned away guests."

"Is everybody staying here connected with the movie?"

"All except for two or three. And I have to say they're really something."

"Who?"

"You know. From California. Making the movie. Laura Edwards. I mean, right here. I'm an extra," he added proudly.

She congratulated him.

On the third floor, she slipped the key in the lock, opened the door, and flicked the switch. A ceiling fixture with four tulip-shaped globes bloomed into light. She'd never been in one of the rooms. It was pretty much standard hotel room of the past type, which was, she assumed, what the decorator had in mind. Brass bed with floral spread, small tables on each side, two easy chairs with a table between, a low chest with a television set—a bow to modern times—alcove with mirror and vanity table, and a bathroom with the usual fixtures, albeit of a bygone era.

Everything was neat and tidy. The stuntwoman had left before six in the morning and never come back. The maid had been in around nine. There was no way to be sure, but the room seemed undisturbed by any unauthorized individual; certainly no one had sneaked in and tossed the place.

She checked the bathroom, making sure an ax murderer wasn't skulking behind the shower curtain—she'd actually encountered that once—then pulled on latex gloves and began a methodical search. She missed Parkhurst's help, but all things considered, it was better that he had no more connection with this case.

Osey could be doing this search, and he was a little miffed that he wasn't, holding unspoken resentment that she didn't believe him capable. It wasn't that; he was a good cop with a quick mind and thorough in his work, but this situation was a potential bag of trouble, and she was the most experienced investigator the HPD had, including Parkhurst. Though he came from a fair-sized city, with all the mess and pain and horror and inhumanity that cities have, her background was more extensive. She wanted this death cleared in record time, before anything happened to Laura Edwards, before the media got wind of a threat—if there was one—and got into a feeding frenzy.

Kay Bender had been a neat young lady; nothing was left on tabletops, not even a note or paperback book. T-shirts, shorts, and underwear lay folded in drawers; three dresses hung in the closet—two casual, one for a more fancy occasion; shoes were lined on the floor, two pairs of white Reeboks, one pair of black pumps with medium heels. The bathroom counter held a tooth-brush and toothpaste; a neat row of cosmetics, only a few, sat on the vanity table.

One of the drawers turned up a scrapbook and Susan paged through it. Pictures and newspaper articles of Kay Bender in high school. An accomplished gymnast, she'd won competitions and awards, had even been an alternate for the Olympic team. Toward the end of the book were articles and stills about the movies she'd been in, stunts she'd done, pictures of her with the actresses she'd doubled for, both smiling into the camera. She'd been very focused, this young woman, and devoted her entire life to gymnastics, and then movie stunts. Nothing frivolous or frothy. Twenty-one years of life, Susan thought as she laid the scrapbook on the bed. She hoped Kay's dedication had brought her fulfillment, satisfaction, happiness, whatever was most important to her.

The room revealed no more surprises than had Kay Bender's body. Susan hadn't expected it would, but she searched thoroughly. She checked under the bed, between mattress and springs, in the toilet tank, under the lamps, through all pockets and in the toes of shoes. She emptied all the drawers, pulled them out, and checked the bottoms. She'd never found anything taped to the bottom of a drawer, but there was always a first. No cryptic messages, hidden treasures, or meaningful items. It all added up to a picture of a young woman caught in somebody else's hatred. She hoped she wasn't dismissing Kay Bender too blithely.

Peeling off the gloves, she took one last look around before she left, making sure the door locked behind her. She headed for the elevator and poked the button.

The doors slid open, and Sheri Lloyd stepped off. A denim-clad Nick Logan gazed above head level with polite indifference. When he realized who she was, he smiled. "Working late?"

And there she was getting into the elevator with one of the rich and famous. "It's in the job description."

"Time off for dinner? You pick the place, I'll buy."

Now, there was a bang-up idea. "Another time. Murder investigation."

"Murder?"

Watch your mouth, Susan. "Or accident. We're working on it."

The doors slid silently shut leaving her in a small confined space with a man who took up too much of it. Something about him was so big and so vivid and so directed, it drew you in.

He pulled on an intent look of idiocy. "If you could tell me," he said as Inspector Clouseau, "where you wear. 'Wear?' Yes yes, wear. 'A pin-striped suit, a white shirt and gold cuff links.' No, you idiot. Not the cluths you had on. Where you wear at the time of the murder."

She smiled. Talented man, Nick Logan. How about that dinner invitation? She could file it under suspect, interrogation of.

"I thought you always worked in pairs," he said. "Where's your partner?"

A casualness in the question brought her mind back to a sharp point. "Was there anything you wanted to say to him?"

Nick shook his head. The elevator glided to a stop at the fourth floor and the doors opened. "Good hunting," he said.

With her thumb on a button to keep the elevator in place, she watched him stride along the corridor and knock at Laura Edwards's suite.

LAURA WRIGGLED OUT of her pants and stepped into the shower. She felt hot and sick and worried. Seeing Ben after all these years brought emotions and memories and regrets and desires like a tidal wave. There she was standing on the beach and this twenty-foot wave rose up and flattened her. She hadn't expected it. She was only curious to see him, and she wanted to talk to him. The thing about Ben was, she could trust him. There was nobody else she could say that about.

Turning off the water, she groped for the towel and rubbed herself dry, then slipped into a white silk robe. Was somebody actually trying to kill her? She'd worked hard to get where she was. That didn't happen in a vacuum. Had she offended somebody along the way?

Well, maybe. Okay, probably. But that was just the business. She'd never schemed and manipulated in any underhanded manner. Never deliberately tripped up anybody. Never stabbed anybody in the back. Never pushed anybody down the stairs. Never lied—well, of course, she'd *lied*, but nothing vicious. Like she

could speak Spanish when her Spanish was two words, like she
could ride horseback when she never got on anything that didn't
have wheels. Never slept with anybody either. Not for gain. Except her first agent and she'd married him. He didn't have murderous thoughts about her. Did he? Of course not. It hadn't been
very long into the marriage when she discovered he was unfaith-
ful, and they'd parted with no hurt feelings, except hers, maybe.
She'd been heartbroken. The betrayal had left her devastated.
Anyway, he was in L.A.

She'd had love affairs, two serious. They'd ended the same
way. With the guy betraying her. No man had ever been faithful,
except Ben.

There she was all set to believe Nick was the one. He'd been
married twice, so had she. She was madly in love, so was he.
They were supposed to live happily ever after. Yes, well, it just
goes to show. She pulled a tissue from the box on the counter
and blew her nose. Along came Ms. Overdeveloped Spider and
sat down beside him. Instead of being frightened away, he hustled her into bed. Laura never could stand spiders.

She didn't know how she felt about Nick now. Only once,
he'd sworn. Well, maybe. She didn't know if she believed him
or not, and even if she did, once was too many. She didn't know
what to believe anymore. She felt alone and afraid. Could he
want to kill her? Impossible. Why would he? Because he didn't
love her anymore? Well then, why wouldn't he just say so?
Afraid she would make a scene?

She slid her feet into high-heeled white slippers. Well, of
course, she'd make a scene. Was that any reason to kill her?

What about Sheri? Little Ms. Sex Object. Sheri wanted Nick
and also wanted Laura's role. Was she so dumb she thought she
could get it if anything happened? Nobody's that dumb. But she
was a vengeful spider. What about that? If Nick really did say
he wasn't interested, she might think getting rid of me would
change his mind.

And that would also get back at Hayden Fifer. What about
him? He have any reason to harm his star actress? No, he loved
her. He'd wanted her for this movie. Of all the directors she'd

ever worked with, he was the one she liked the best. He'd never harm a hair on her head.

The knock made her heart skip a beat. She edged to the door. "Who is it?"

"It's me."

Nick. Come to finish what he'd failed at earlier? Her heart kicked in so fast it threatened to choke her. Then she took herself in hand. Everything is not a movie, Laura May. And Nick does not want to slaughter you. Open this door.

When he tried to kiss her, she stepped back. "What do you want?"

"What kind of line is that, coming from my beloved?" He sprawled on the Victorian sofa and gazed up at the crystal chandelier.

"You gave up any rights to being beloved when you took up with the Lloyd person." She flipped on the chandelier; a zillion teardrops blazed into light.

Nick blinked, rubbed his eyes, and hauled himself up straight. "I just saw the police."

"What police?"

He gave her a look. "The woman police chief."

"So?"

"They're looking at the stunt double's death as a murder."

She backed up to a wing chair and sat, crossed her legs. "How do you know?"

"Who'd want to kill her? All she ever did was work out, or work on stunts. That's all she ever thought about. Nothing else was ever on her mind. How could any of that turn into a reason for murder?"

"What are you saying?"

"I'm saying, I'm worried."

"You suggesting someone wants to kill me?"

"Laura," he said, "the world is full of nuts."

She recrossed her legs. "You're not being very comforting. Why aren't you holding my hand and saying, 'There, there'?"

"I would, if I was sure you wouldn't spit in my eye."

"What's that supposed to mean?"

"Love scenes between us lately have been only on the set."

He reached for a low vase on the table behind and eased a cigarette pack from his shirt pocket, then stretched out a leg to get his lighter from his pants pocket.

"What do you expect, you bastard? And if you're going to smoke that, go to your own suite."

He smiled. "That's my girl. I'm glad to see a little fire. It means you still care."

"I care about the air I breathe and the company I keep."

"Well, let's talk about that for a minute. What company have you been keeping lately?"

"What does that mean?"

"That small town cop?"

"Don't be ridiculous. After your antics, you can't in all good conscience expect to play the jealous suitor."

"Come on, Laura. Stop playing to the camera."

It was true, everything was a scene for her. Well, she had to have some way to get through the pain. They weren't even married yet, and he couldn't keep his pants zipped.

"I told you the thing with Sheri just happened."

She jumped up; the shiny robe swished as she paced. "You couldn't help yourselves. Love like yours couldn't be denied."

"Oh, hell, no. She's a beautiful and determined lady. I had just enough to drink that it seemed like a good idea. I'm sorry."

"Sorry it happened? Or sorry that now she's got her sticky fingers clutching at you?"

"Don't be snide, Laura. You don't do snide convincingly."

She stopped in front of him and crossed her arms. "I'm a damn sight more convincing than your girlfriend. She's a lousy actress."

"She's not that bad."

"She's wood. And just barely managing to get by without cue cards."

"My darling Laura, I've told you I'm sorry. I've groveled at your feet. What more do you want?"

An ugly bust sat on the table at the end of the sofa. She considered hurling it at him. Better not. She might miss and break it. Or not miss and break his nose. Fifer would never forgive her.

Nick was watching, waiting to see what she'd do. She turned, swirling the skirt of her robe, and tossed herself in the chair.

"One thing I could always count on, Laura," he said.

He didn't go on. The bastard was going to make her ask. "What?"

"Your honesty. Behind all your emoting, you've always been straight. With yourself, with me, with everybody."

"Well, thank you very much. What has that got to do with your betrayal?"

"Betrayal, is it? My self-esteem just went up a notch. If you're betrayed, I'm important."

"Not anymore, you slime."

He stretched both arms along the back of the sofa and crossed his ankles on the coffee table. "Have you ever done anything you regretted?"

She eyed him warily. "Yes." Probably lots if she made a list. "So?"

"This is one of those things, Laura. It was a mistake. It was stupid. I regretted it from the moment it happened."

"Ooohh. All this regret doesn't keep you from letting her hang on to your arm."

"Yes, it does."

"Oh, really. I suppose it wasn't her in your trailer this morning. Who was that? Somebody selling Girl Scout cookies?"

"You're beginning to piss me off, Laura. I came to do a little more apologizing, a little more groveling, but there's a limit. I told her there was nothing between us."

"Maybe you should try words of one syllable."

He leaned forward so abruptly he scared her. Her heart started doing that thing again. "Aw, Laura, come on now. Was there ever somebody in your life like that? Who got a scenario in his mind that wasn't anywhere near reality and wouldn't give it up?"

There was, actually. A man who swore undying love. Wanted to marry her. That he was already married never fazed him. He wouldn't give it up, he even left his wife so they could be together. She eased one slipper off and let it dangle from her toes.

"All clear? Enough groveling? Can we have dinner now?"

"I'm tired, Nick. And there's something I need to take care of."

"Yeah? With a cowboy cop? What is it? Unfinished business? Sweet nostalgia? A thing for a man in uniform?"

"He doesn't wear a uniform."

"He does in that photo you have of him. I knew I'd seen him before. Maybe we should talk about that."

"Talk about an old photo?" She sighed, weary, stagy. "I can't deal with this, Nick. Just leave."

"That the best you can do? No storming fit? Flashing eyes and flaring nostrils?"

She smiled, then pointed to the door. "Out."

He got up and left without a backward glance. She was considering being outraged. At least he could have put up more protest.

THE PHONE TORE through the fog wrapped around his mind, collected a fistful of nerves, and jerked him awake. He grabbed the receiver to shut off the noise. "Yeah."

"Oh, Ben, I'm so sorry. I woke you."

He cleared his throat and tried to do the same with his mind. "Ben?"

"Yeah, Laura. What is it?"

"I need you."

"I'm no longer working the Bender case."

"Please."

"What's the problem?"

"Just come."

"Where are you?"

"My hotel room." The dial tone hummed in his ear.

He swung his legs over the edge of the bed and stared at the floor under his bare feet. My ex-wife, who is now a Hollywood sex goddess, has just invited me to her hotel room in the middle of the night. He replaced the receiver. It couldn't get any better than that.

He got into the shower with the idea of clearing his mind and stayed only long enough to sluice the sweat off his body. What Laura wanted teased at him while he brushed his teeth, zipped up his jeans, and rolled up his shirtsleeves. In ten minutes he had the Bronco headed for the Sunflower.

LAURA WRAPPED her arms around his neck and hung on as if she were drowning. She kissed him; the kiss was slightly aggressive. His arms went around her automatically, his hands felt the muscles of her back under her silky robe. Her perfume filled his mind with memories. The physical responses were still there; maybe they were always there between old lovers.

She tilted her head and smiled up at him. "Oh, God, Ben, you don't know how much I've missed you."

"You got me here in the middle of the night to tell me that?"

"It isn't the middle of the night. It's only eleven. Did you ever think about me after I left?"

"Never."

She laughed: light, pleased. "Liar."

He smiled. "I read about you now and then, after you got famous. You did good, kid." He let his arms drop, felt awkward, like he'd stumbled onto a movie set. Fancy hotel, subdued light, beautiful woman in slinky attire, and a rube who didn't know what the hell he was doing here.

She stepped back and tightened the belt on her robe, then took his hand and led him to the sofa. He sat; she perched beside him, hands together on her knees, and leaned slightly toward him. A small lamp on the end table created a halo effect around her platinum hair, picking out gold highlights.

"Regrets?" she asked softly.

"Laura, what are you doing? We made a mistake a long time ago. After all the hurt, and the scraped pride and ruffled feathers, there was sadness, and then there was relief."

"I had regrets. Lots of them. Still have sometimes."

That tugged at desire. Irritation came along. Well well, just like old times.

"Don't, Ben." She barely touched his jaw. "This muscle always jumps when you get mad. Please don't. I'm scared. I need you. I don't have anyone else I can trust."

"What are you afraid of?"

"Don't be a cop!" Her hands clenched. "Jesus, why can't you just be human?"

"I was under the impression you wanted a cop. Did I get that wrong?"

Her blue eyes glistened. "I wanted a friend."

Which made him feel like a total shit. This too was just like old times. He wondered if she was as snared in the undersurface nuances as he was. "To help, I have to ask questions. The only way I know how is as a cop. What's the problem?"

"All business. No drinking a cup of kindness for auld lang syne."

"What do you want from me, Laura?"

The tears filled her eyes and trailed down her face.

Oh, shit. He slid over, put his arms around her, and held her close. The cynic that he was pointed out that histrionics were her forte. The mind might twist situations with complications, or worry at them to find the hidden meanings, but the body cut to the chase, and his body responded to hers just as it always had.

He still didn't know what she wanted from him; he still didn't know how much he was willing to give. He didn't know what Susan would do either, about him being here since she'd told him to keep clear.

"Laurie." Putting both hands on her shoulders, he looked at her. With a thumb, he rubbed tears from her cheek. "Just talk to me. Okay?"

She stared back, blue eyes, wide and full of emotions he couldn't guess at. After a second that stretched thin, she nodded. In confusion, she looked around, then went into the bedroom and came back with a handful of tissues.

"This is hard for me too." She stood in front of him.

"Yeah."

"What would you like to drink? Wine? I don't know what kind they might have. Scotch? You still drink that?"

He got up, took her elbow, and steered her to the chairs at a small round table. "Sit," he said.

Somewhat to his surprise, she did so without comment, protest, or struggle. He sat opposite her. "Now," he said.

"Maybe somebody does want to kill me." Her voice was low but matter-of-fact, with no overtones of great drama.

"Who?"

She got up, went to the bedroom again, and returned with a burgundy briefcase that she placed on the table, snapped open, and took out two newspapers.

With a raised eyebrow, he picked up the top one. It was a copy of the *Hampstead Herald,* dated two weeks ago. Page one had a photo of her getting out of a limo in front of the hotel. With a red ballpoint pen somebody had circled her name in the caption. The second paper also had her photo on the front page, but this time the focus was on Nick Logan, sitting at a picnic table near the old barn where they were shooting. Laura's back was toward the camera. In the same red ink, a circle had been drawn on her back.

"How long have you had these?"

"The dates are on them. The first one the day after I arrived. The second one a few days later."

"You handled them?"

"Of course I handled them. I looked through to see if there was anything else in them."

"Was there?"

"No."

"Where did you get them?"

"I always get the local paper on location. I told the person at the desk when I got here. He said it would be at my door every evening. I didn't know whether I should be worried or not when I saw the first one. I mean it could be a fan. I do have fans, you know."

"Yes."

"And then the second one and it's not exactly—I mean, it's creepy."

"Who have you told about this?"

"I don't know. Nick. I guess my hairdresser. The makeup girl. Mostly it's letters, you know? This kind of thing, it's part of the game. I guess any celebrity—some are nice and some are not so nice. This feels threatening. Then—" She took a white envelope from the briefcase and slid it across the table.

He handled it carefully. Plain white, drugstore variety; Laura's name and room number. Inside a piece of cheap typing paper with a crudely sketched gun and, in block letters, BANG.

"When did you get this?"

"This evening."

"Anything else?"

"No. And now after Kay—" Laura shivered, crossed her arms, and clutched her elbows. "What can you do?"

"They aren't clearly threats." He watched her like a snake after a rabbit. She could be doing it herself, the papers, the note. Like the chief said, Laura could have arranged the accident that killed the stuntwoman. Laura should have been on the railing, Laura wasn't. Kay Bender was. This might be reinforcement. But he didn't know why she would.

"Ben, you're not going to do anything?" She grabbed at his arm. "You do believe—"

"Calm down. I'm going to take care of this." He took her hands and looked at her steadily. "I need to ask some questions. They're going to sound like cop questions because they are cop questions. Understand? Just the facts, ma'am."

She nodded.

"Have you hurt anybody?" He forestalled her protests. "I don't mean minor hurt feelings. I'm talking about serious injury. The kind that could destroy someone's life."

"Oh, God, I hope not. Hurt feelings and irritations and that kind of thing. You know, the sort of 'I hate her' thing. There must be lots of those. I've had my share of both sides."

"Not minor grievances, people who are just pissed. Normal people get over it after a while. The exception is a nutcase. Some guy you wouldn't go out with, or an actor who feels he didn't get a part because you didn't like him. This type can put in three, four years plotting out revenge."

"How could I know if it was something like that?"

"They don't usually keep it to themselves. They send hate mail, make threatening phone calls."

"Nothing but this. It feels threatening."

Yes, it did.

She started to put her hand on the papers and he stopped her. "Don't touch it."

Startled, she jerked her hand back. "It's so scary out there. You know? All those people and some of them—you never know what they are. You never know what's coming or who's going to jump out at you with acid or a knife."

Yeah. A stalker who'd fastened on her. He hoped not. The thought of a psycho who mixed fantasy and reality and fed both through a sick mind scared the shit out of him. "They usually send mail too. Or try to see you." And often the creeps believed the victim had a romantic interest in them.

"Anybody who always shows up when you're filming? Tries to get close? Tries to talk to you? Touch you? Get past barriers? Anything like that?"

"I don't know. I don't pay close attention to the crowds. I need to focus on what's coming up, otherwise my performance would be—on a level with that of Ms. Lloyd."

Laura wasn't so frightened that she could pass up an opportunity to throw a dig at the other actress. "Why didn't you mention this stuff this afternoon?"

She looked at him, then got up and stalked to the bedroom. When she came back, she smacked the box of tissues on the table. "It knocked me out, if you must know. The accident— Kay and—and then seeing you and—I just—I didn't expect it to hit me so hard and there was that other police person."

"Yancy?"

"No. The woman."

"The chief."

"Anyway, you were so hard. Like you always were when you were mad. I mean, you came in angry."

With a sour smile, he acknowledged the truth of her assessment. Old memories and old responses had come over him. He'd felt she was going to shove him into the stew pot.

"And I wanted to talk to you without all those other people. Just you." She rested her forearms on the table and clasped her hands together. She fell silent, looking at him with wonder, then tilted her head. "We were so young."

"Yes."

"Oh, Ben, I've missed you."

"Don't get carried away," he said dryly.

She laughed. The laugh roused memories; it was the same delighted, life-is-so-interesting laugh she'd had when they were married. For reasons he couldn't figure, it made him sad. Lost youth maybe, lost promises, lost chances.

It also said that underneath all the Hollywood glitz was the girl he'd married. Pretty little girl who looked up at him with curiosity and interest, made him feel like maybe he was worth something after all.

Suddenly he was aware of exactly where they were. Hotel suite. Just through that doorway was a bed.

Laura, eyes alight with impish malice, said in a velvet voice. "For old times' sake?"

NINE

SERENA, sitting at the table, busily dunked a tea bag in a cup of hot water and barely gave Yancy a glance when he came in. "Well, you certainly took care of that, didn't you?"

"What do you expect?"

"Right. You're the only one with feelings." She threw the tea bag at him. He ducked and it landed with a splat on the floor.

"You think I want to toss my crazy sick mother out of her home?"

"Serena—"

She shoved the chair back, got up for the tea bag, and dropped it in the trash, then wiped up the floor with a paper towel. "You want something serious to happen? Maybe even fatal?" She plopped herself back in the chair. "How would you feel then?"

"She doesn't want to leave here."

"You keep refusing to look at the point. She needs to be safe, Peter. Sometimes she's perfectly all right. Sometimes she isn't. I don't know about you, but it scares me silly to come home and find her on fire. What if I'd been fifteen minutes later? Or an hour?"

To get away from her demanding gaze, he went to the refrigerator and reached in for the carton of orange juice. He shook it, then poured a glass and took a sip. "I told you, I'll think of something."

"You'd better hurry because time's running out."

"Oh, hell, Serena. She doesn't want to leave here. It'd be different if she was totally out of it, didn't recognize us, didn't know what was going on. She loves this place. She loves the flowers. She loves the trees. She loves—"

"Maybe we can find a place with flowers and trees."

"And a place that will let her have Elmo?"

"That's something else we'll have to do something about."

He gave her a startled look. "You want to do away with Elmo?"

"No, you jerk. One of us will need to keep him."

Yancy's beeper went off, saving him from having to respond. This beeper was something that came with his assignment to the movie bunch. If they needed anything, wanted anything, got bored, lonely, or wanted another hand for poker, he got beeped.

"Don't answer it," Serena said.

He didn't much want to; a fourteen-hour day ought to be enough. He downed the orange juice and set the glass on the counter. "I have to." She might not like his job, but it was the only one he had and he wanted to keep it.

He'd be the one in trouble if he didn't respond, and if he got fired, they'd really be in the shit. Who'd pay for the old folk's home then? He rubbed his face. Damn it, damn it.

In the living room, he dropped into the old green easy chair by the front window. A rectangle of light spilled in from the kitchen. Night had closed in while he'd been talking with Serena. Fireflies blinked on and off in the soft black air. After a second, he picked up the receiver and punched in the number.

"Hi, buddy. How's it going?" It was Mac, his Hollywood teamster friend. "I have a mind to get something to munch on. How about you and me go out and find us some barbecued ribs? You folks know how to barbecue ribs around here?"

"Yes, sir, we do. If you'll give me"—he held up his arm to catch the light from the kitchen and squinted at his watch—"twenty minutes, I'll take you to a place with barbecue sauce hot enough to blow off the top of your head."

"That a promise?"

"No, sir, that's a threat."

Mac chuckled and hung up.

Yancy leaned back and closed his eyes. His mother often sat here in the dark. She watched the moon rise and the small animals come out with the night, the foxes and possums and skunks, the occasional coyote. Sometimes she talked to them. No big deal.

Sometimes they talked back. That was a little different. She listened.

He didn't feel like being with movie people anymore today. Aw hell, Mac wasn't really movie people. If Yancy wanted to ask about the lieutenant being near the barn around noon, now was the time to start.

Get a move on then.

Serena was still drinking tea. He rested a hand on the table and leaned down to look into her face. "I've got to go."

"You always do."

"We'll talk about this later." He kissed her forehead and left, told Dallas, still in the hammock, that maybe Serena needed him, and got in the Cherokee.

The stars lost some of their brilliance as he got into town. He drove through on Fifteenth Street, took Crescent Road past campus, and then turned west on Mississippi. In the driveway at the side of the old Victorian house, he parked under the maple tree and fished keys from his pocket. Alice Blakeley, the owner, divorced and struggling to keep afloat, lived downstairs. In addition to tutoring students in math, she gave piano lessons and rented the upper half of the house to Yancy.

Outside stairs went up to the second story. Stephanie, his landlady's daughter, sat on the bottom step. At thirteen, mother and daughter didn't always see eye to eye.

"Hey, Steph, what are you up to?"

"Writing."

"Isn't it a little dark?"

"I'm just making notes. Have you solved the murder yet?"

He sat beside her. "Not yet."

"Would you like a clue?"

"Do you have one?"

"You're just like my mother, you treat me like a child."

"I'm sorry." This was his evening for apologizing to irate females.

"No, you're not. You just say that. I'm making character studies. You're one of them," she added darkly.

That was a little daunting. "How come you never let me read what you write?"

"Maybe I will sometime."

"Tell me your clue."

"Those eyes the greenest of things blue,
The bluest of things gray."

"What does that mean?"

"Nothing, but it sounds great, doesn't it?"

"Yeah." He patted her knee and took the stairs two at a time to prove he wasn't tired. Just as he stuck the key in the lock the phone rang. He rushed in and grabbed the phone.

A breathy voice cooed in his ear. If he didn't know females didn't go in for that kind of thing, he'd have thought he had a heavy breather.

"Hello, Officer Yancy."

"Ms. Lloyd. What can I do for you?"

"You recognized my voice."

"Couldn't miss it." Nobody else he knew sounded like a seduction scene.

"So businesslike," she pouted. Even over the phone he could hear the pout. "And here I was trying to work up the courage to ask you a favor."

A favor, is it? And what might that be? "Yes, ma'am." Her usual disdain wasn't apparent, but the promise of good things to come was a shade overdone.

"If you'll come over here, I'll explain. I might even tell you a few things you don't know."

Oh, yes, lady, I'm sure you could. He bent his chin to his chest, squeezed the back of his neck, then stretched his head backward as far as it would go. He had a little dilemma here. He was due to pick up Mac in a few minutes. Within the confines of his edict—take care of these show biz folks—actors probably beat out drivers any old day.

What was clear was, he should tell Mac he couldn't make it and hie himself over to Ms. Sheri's hotel room.

He hauled in a breath on the wings of fatigue. Hotel room. Breathy coo. He wasn't important enough to warrant the usual attention that would suggest. In her opinion, he was just some clown hired to guard doorways, so what was the favor she wanted? Anything pertinent she'd lay on a higher-up. If she wanted information... Now there was a thought. She'd think he'd spill it. With the right lure. "How'd you get this number?"

"I went to a lot of trouble." Sexy and cute.

Howie, he thought. His old friend Howie Gilbert, assistant manager at the hotel. If Sheri did her song and dance for him Howie'd give out state secrets, let alone a little thing like Yancy's home number. Yancy wished he wasn't so tired, he could think better if his brains weren't mashed potatoes. He was curious about what she wanted, but too tired to trot into her room, the mouse accepting the cat's invitation.

"Well, ma'am. I sure am sorry but I'm on my way to pick up Mac."

"Who's Mac?"

"Ms. Edwards's driver. Hey, I've got an idea. Why don't you join us? We're going to get a bite to eat." Boy, would she be a hit. "You like barbecue?"

"It doesn't sound like my kind of place." Her voice was losing some of its warmth. "Call this Mac and tell him you can't come."

"Well, yeah, that's an idea all right, but he's nowhere I can reach him. How 'bout I come right over to the hotel as soon as I can."

"That'll be too late."

Too late for what? "Oh, gee, yeah, it will be getting late. Tell you what. I'll see you first thing in the morning."

There was a frosty silence, then she said in a tart, irritated, dealing-with-the-help voice, "You just made a mistake."

He probably did at that. And he probably wouldn't get another chance either. He stripped off his uniform and got in the shower. If this favor had to be granted right now, it most likely couldn't be about the investigation. Mac would have been routinely questioned, but Yancy wanted to get at questions that Mac probably hadn't been asked. Like had he seen the lieutenant near the barn.

Toweling dry as he went, he padded to the bedroom and pulled on jeans and a blue knit shirt long enough and loose enough to cover his gun. Hot as hell up here. The ficus plant his sister had given him was dropping yellow leaves in the corner.

This old Victorian was a great place to live: lots of space—

bedroom, kitchen, living room, everything sparse and barren, the way he liked it. Hardwood floors, bookshelves in the bedroom floor-to-ceiling that he'd put up himself. Gray couch and chair in the living room, round table to rest his feet on when he watched television. Built-in desk. Walls papered in gray stripes with dark gray and dark rose trim around the top. No pictures, no knickknacks.

He thought about getting up at five in the morning and wondered how late barbecued ribs with Mac would run. How did actors do it? The hours alone would kill him.

He shoved keys, change, and wallet in his pockets and headed out. Moths were flying around the light intent on suicide, and a couple of june bugs dive-bombed the door. He accidentally stepped on one and it made a loud crunch. He hated the things, big and lumbering.

Mac was pacing up and down the walkway in front of the hotel. When he saw Yancy's Cherokee, he stepped into the street. Late forties, big belly and flat butt, dark hair receding up his forehead and hanging long around his ears. He wrenched open the door and slid in.

"Hey, buddy." With a friendly fist, he punched Yancy's shoulder. In the interests of projecting male bonding and macho toughness, Yancy did not flinch.

ROSE. Laura my beloved. The universe is rose. He stood under the trees and watched the taillights, red eyes of the evil spirits, retreat down the street. He was careful not to get directly in their path. If he did, they'd see into his soul and scramble his plans. He must never allow that. They were forming, falling into place. The universe had told him the most humane way was a gun. Now it told him he had to kill that cop and take his.

THIS CLOSE TO ELEVEN, the Blind Pig wasn't overflowing with business. Red padded booths ran along two sides, tables in the middle. Western flair for decoration—ten-gallon hats, spurs, tack on the walls. Tex Ritter sang in the background.

"I should warn you," Mac said as he slid into a booth, "I take barbecue sauce very seriously."

The waitress brought menus and a basket of hush puppies. Yancy looked the place over.

"Cops always do that?" Mac asked.

"Do what?"

"Check the place out. Like you're looking for felons, or escape routes."

"Yeah." He wondered what kind of a cop he was. Now that he was here, he figured he probably made the wrong call and should have gone with Sheri Lloyd.

Mac ordered the ribs with the picture of a red-horned devil holding a pitchfork beside it. Yancy went for a milder version.

"Tell me about this movie," he said, slyly working up to his questions.

Mac took a slug of beer, leaned beefy shoulders against the seat back, and raised his eyebrows. "What, kid? You all of a sudden getting star struck?"

"I'd like to know what your thoughts are about this bunch."

"One thing you gotta understand. There are the top cats and there are the rest of us. Except for what's strictly necessary, like driving all their crap out on location and driving them around, we don't have anything to do with each other."

"Well, thanks. That's a big help."

"You gonna ask me if somebody was jealous of the big cheese, wanted her out of the way, was itchin' for the part. Hell yes."

"Who?"

Mac laughed. "That's what I'm telling you. Jealousy, fighting back and forth, spreading dirt—it goes with the territory. It's a given. Just the same as cameras and mikes and clapboards. As to specifics—" He shrugged. "There I can't help you. The fat cats don't hobnob with the rest of us."

The waitress plunked steaming platters of ribs in front of them, refilled Yancy's iced tea, and brought Mac another beer. Mac pushed up his sleeves, gave Yancy a look of this-better-be-good good, and grabbed a rib dripping sauce. He chomped down and chewed. Tears sprang to his eyes. He swallowed, grabbed his beer, and took a long drink.

"Not bad," he allowed. He pulled off another rib and worked his jaws.

Yancy did likewise with his sissified version. "Who had it in for Ms. Edwards?"

Mouth full, eyes streaming, Mac shook his head.

"Anybody feuding with anybody?"

"Well, I'm not one to be sensitive about atmosphere and pretentious crap like that, but I gotta admit these clones didn't give out like happy campers." Mac wiped his greasy fingers on the oversized napkin. "All covered up and hidden away poison was coming through somebody's pores."

"Whose?"

"Don't know. I'm just a driver. I go where I'm told. It's all these other folks with sensitive souls that'll have to tell you about that. I know Fifer had a sling-out fight with his big box office star."

"Ms. Edwards?"

"Naw. The other one. Nick Logan."

"When was this?"

"Right after we got here."

"Where?"

"Out there in that barn. Everybody else had split. The director asked his big moneymaker to hang back a minute. And then told him to get his ducks in order."

"Meaning?"

"Oh, hell, how do I know? I walked in in the middle of it. The director was saying it took more than reputation to carry a career."

"What did that mean?"

"My big guess would be Fifer wasn't real ecstatic with Nick's performance."

"What did Nick say?"

"Laughed a not funny laugh and said, 'Go careful. It wouldn't be much of a movie if you lost your star.' That's when I blundered in with my big feet and they both turned around to look at me. I got out of there."

Yancy hadn't picked up anywhere that Fifer was dissatisfied with Nick's performance. On the contrary, he was under the impression both stars were doing great and the director was dancing around hugging himself. "What were you doing there?"

"Laura sent me in to tell Nick she'd be at the hotel."

"Is she hard to work for?"

"At her level, they're all hard to work for."

"You ever have any trouble with her?"

Mac, greasy rib between thumbs and forefingers, looked at him. "What are you getting at?" Everything changed: voice, eyes, posture. He went from good ol' boy to steel-jawed driver/ bodyguard.

Yancy wouldn't care to tangle with him, he could see how Mac would be good at this job. "What did you do, make a pass at her?"

Mac snorted. "That'd get me killed. No, I was late picking her up. The car wouldn't start. A kid from a service station came out and replaced the battery. It took him a while. She threw a hissy. Wanted to fire me."

"You're still here."

"Yeah, well, she cooled off and threatened, 'Once more and you're gone.'"

"Why'd she do that?"

"It gave her an edge."

"Edge?"

"Something to hold over my head."

Artfully, Yancy changed direction. "Around noon, were you anywhere near the barn?"

"Yep. Well, part of the time. You gonna ask me next if I smuggled a saw in there and cut through that railing?"

"No smuggling was required. The saw was already there. I was going to ask if you saw anybody."

"Like who?"

Like the lieutenant. "Anybody."

"Naw. I didn't see anybody sneak into the barn, but back at base camp Nick was in and out of his trailer, Laura Edwards too. And Clem Jones, our director's assistant with the personality plus." Mac cleaned the meat off the last rib, then picked through the bones making sure he hadn't missed anything.

"Nobody else?"

"Who you getting at?"

Yancy shook his head. "Just wanting to know."

"Well, you gotta remember I wasn't exactly standing there with my eyeballs glued to the barn door."

So much for checking up on the lieutenant.

Mac finished up with apple pie and ice cream.

By the time Yancy dropped off Mac in front of the hotel and started off for home he was so tired his eyes were beginning to cross. Five a.m. wakeup. Ah, the glamorous life of moviemaking. His mouth opened with a wide jaw-creaking yawn that nearly unhinged it. Side vision caught a dark shape staggering in front of the headlights. He stood on the brakes.

There was a thud.

"Oh, shit."

TEN

YANCY HIT THE STREET. Oh, Jesus, the man wasn't moving. Crouching, Yancy shined his flashlight in the guy's face. It was Robin McCormack, the stunt girl's boyfriend. He ran the light over Robin's T-shirt and cutoff jeans.

Robin stirred, put an elbow over his eyes, and muttered, "The moon in June is goddamn soon."

"Don't move." No blood, arms and legs seemed to work all right the way he was thrashing around trying to get up.

"Stay where you are," Yancy said. Alcohol fumes rolled over him like fog.

"Can't."

"Can't what?" Yancy felt eyes staring at him from the darkness. A quick glance didn't spot anybody.

"Can't stay. Have to find the bastard pushed me."

"Somebody pushed you?"

"Didn't fall over...er...er."

"You hurt anywhere?" Yancy couldn't see any injuries, just grime from the street.

Robin made swimming motions trying to get up; Yancy held him down. "Did you hit your head?"

"Quit helpin' me, man. I can do it." His arms flailed and he tried to roll.

Christ, if he was injured, this was making it worse. "Robin?"

It took him a long time to respond, processing through a thick soup of alcohol. When he did answer, his voice was slow and sleepy.

"Yesss...sss...sss?"

"Robin? I want you to lie still. You understand?"

"Yes. Fine...ine...ine."

"Robin, don't try to get up."

"What?"

"Stay where you are."

"No," he said. "I have to go...go...go." He tried to crawl.

"Robin—"

"Stop calling me Robin!"

"It's your name." Yancy shined the flashlight in Robin's face. "Look at me!"

"Fuck off!"

He grabbed Robin's chin and held his head still. Pupils reacted sluggishly, not surprising as smoked as he was.

"Knock it off." Robin closed his eyes. "Tired."

"I can see you are. What day is this?"

"Today."

"What is the date?"

"Monday. It's the Monday of June."

"Robin, where are you?"

"Never been here. Kay. Never Kansas."

The poor bastard was just soused out of his mind, Yancy thought, but that left him in a little bit of a quandary. He had no radio on him, none in the Cherokee. He didn't think this guy was hurt, but he wasn't a doctor. Concussion. Spinal injury. Fracture. To get Robin to stay lying down, he'd have to sit on him. If he left Robin to go into the hotel and ask somebody to call an ambulance, Robin would get up and stagger around, further aggravating any possible injuries. Loading him in the Cherokee could do the same, plus Yancy might have a fight on his hands. Or if Robin passed out on the way, there was nothing Yancy could do. Or any way to stop him if he got it into his head to get out of the moving vehicle.

Lights inside the hotel shone brightly over the entrance, but not a soul was visible.

Yancy stopped trying to hold Robin down and helped him up. Draping one of Robin's arms over his shoulder, Yancy put his own arm around Robin's waist and aimed them both for the door.

"Where we goin'?"

"Inside." And we're hoping like hell there's no spinal injury.

"Over there in the anywhere and Kay in the nowhere." Robin sobbed; his whole body shook.

Yancy steered them to the entrance and was wondering how

to get them both through the door when Howie came dashing up and held it open. Yancy needed to talk to Howie, sometime friend and assistant manager, about giving out cops' phone numbers to sexy actresses.

"What happened? Is he hurt? Oh, my God." Howie held the door, stood back, and peered anxiously at Robin.

"I seriously hope not. Would you get an ambulance?"

"Sure. Yes. Right away." He loped off to the desk.

BLUE. Laura my beloved. The universe is blue. He didn't know why he'd pushed that drunk. He was just there and it seemed right. Maybe it was out of sequence. The cop got out of his car and was bending over him. If he'd obtained a knife or a hammer, he could have done it right then. Killed the cop, and taken the gun. He should have thought ahead. He could have bought a knife. Damn. Was this a test? Did he fail?

He had to have the cop's gun. That was the most humane way. Shoving and cutting through railings was wrong. The spirits had been against it.

AN AMBULANCE drove up, lights flashing, but no siren. Two guys jumped out and opened the rear doors. They got a stretcher and wheeled it up to the entrance. A minute or two later, they wheeled it back with the drunk strapped on. The cop got in his car and followed.

ONE GOOD THING, Yancy thought, this late on a Monday—he glanced at his watch—one-thirty—early on a Tuesday morning—the emergency room wasn't stacked three deep. They were all home resting up from the weekend. He trotted up the ramp to the admitting area where the ambulance attendants were unloading Robin. The glass doors slid open and they trundled him through and along to a treatment room.

Mary Mason—he'd gone to high school with her—was on duty tonight. "What have you brought us this time, Peter?"

"Just a drunk, I hope." He explained what had happened.

"Since he's one of the movie people, give him every test you've got."

"Sure. We do that anyway, you know. Go sit down. It'll be a while."

For a few minutes he sat in the waiting area, but all that unneeded adrenaline was jazzing through his bloodstream. He told Mary he'd be outside.

It was still hot, probably seventy-five degrees. They could use some rain, cool things off some. Not a cloud in the black starry sky.

He made his way to the courtyard on the side of the building. Light poles with round globes lit the area of shrubs and flower beds and wooden benches. In the center was a three-tiered fountain and water spilled endlessly down.

"What is it about moving water?"

Startled, Yancy turned and saw a woman sitting on a bench, middle-aged and plump with short gray hair. She wasn't crying but her face was slack and dull as though she was long finished and there was no emotion left.

"It's just there." Yancy sat on a bench at a right angle to her. "It's soothing."

She gave him a ragged smile. "I wish I smoked. Then I'd have an excuse."

"You need an excuse?"

"My husband is dying."

Yancy had assumed as much, a relative or someone she loved. "I'm very sorry," he said.

"I stay in the room until I can't stand it, and I have to leave. But I feel so guilty when I'm not there I have to go back. I sit and listen to him breathe. Awful strangled breath, then nothing. I pray, 'Oh, God, please let him take another breath.'"

She wasn't talking to Yancy, she wasn't talking to anybody really. Her mind was so full of darkness, she had to let some spill, like the water trickling over the fountain edges.

"And he does," she said. "Another awful strangled breath. And I pray, 'Oh, God, please let him go. Give him peace.' I feel so ashamed because I want him to die."

She rubbed the heel of her palm up and down her cheek, a

gesture of rubbing away guilt. "I'm so afraid he'll go when I'm not there. I'm terrified he'll go when I am there."

The fountain trickled water down its tiers, crickets chirred in the grass, the moon shone full, and the air smelled of jasmine.

After a long silence, she said, "Someone you love is here?"

"No. A minor accident. I don't think he's hurt."

After another long silence, she stood and dusted off the back of her skirt. "It was a pleasure meeting you," she said. "I guess it's time to get back."

Yancy silently wished her the best, whatever that might be.

Later, Mary came looking for him. "There you are," she said. "You can come get your boy. He's been poked, jabbed, X-rayed, lab tested, and, aside from some bruises, pronounced suffering from the excesses of alcohol."

Yancy let go of a long breath he'd been storing up. He had no idea what kind of trouble he was in, but he knew one thing: running over one of the movie people was not permissible. He loaded Robin into the Cherokee and drove as carefully as if he were delivering unboxed eggs.

He went with Robin into his hotel room, placed the key on a chest, and switched on the lamps on both sides of the bed. Robin slumped on the edge of the bed with his head drooping. He managed to prop it on his fists. He wasn't as way-out drunk now, but he wasn't sober either, and he looked thoroughly miserable.

"You need to get some sleep," Yancy said.

"No," Robin mumbled, tipping his head back and forth. "I need to see Sheri."

"Why?"

"She did it."

"Did what?"

"Knows—she knows—"

"Ms. Lloyd knows who hurt Kay?"

"Nobody wanted to hurt Kay. Laura."

Yancy leaned back against the door. He thought if he sat down, he might fall asleep.

"Had a fight." Robin's eyelids were at half-mast.

"Sheri and Kay?"

"Nick."

"Nick and Kay?"

"No." Robin's eyes closed. He forced them open and settled for slits. "Nick and Sheri."

"What about?"

"Not gonna throw everything over for her."

Yancy wondered if it was worth trying to follow this drunken rambling. The lieutenant would have retrieved whatever was to be had from Sheri, and Yancy was overstepping his duties. A dull headache was developing just behind his temples, the result of long hours and hanging with these California people.

"Oh, God." Robin took a deep breath, shoved himself up, and stumbled into the bathroom. Yancy heard water running. Robin came back drying his face and hair.

"We were getting married. After this shoot." He twisted the towel. "You want to hear something funny? She liked working with Laura. Ain't that a kick? Twenty-one." He glared at Yancy. "Twenty-one goddamn years old."

Robin wasn't much older, Yancy thought. Twenty-three or four.

"She lived in Van Nuys. You know? Family. Normal people. Two older brothers. Daddy a history teacher. Mother works for some business, secretary. I called them. I had to tell them—" Robin clamped his teeth and swallowed rapidly. His fingers dug into the towel until the knuckles whitened.

"She got along with Ms. Edwards?"

"Sure. Who knows what Laura thought. But stars don't suffer in silence. If she didn't like Kay, you can bet your bottom dollar she'd have said so."

"What do you want with Ms. Lloyd?"

A crafty look came over Robin's face, then it turned blankly innocent.

Oh, Christ. He's got it in his head to find out who killed Kay Bender. Be an avenger? Slay the slayer? What the hell was the matter with this Hollywood bunch? Couldn't any one of them tell reality from a movie? Yancy sighed. Actually, they couldn't.

He took a deep breath instead of yelling at Robin. He didn't go over and slap him around either. Partly because that wasn't the done thing, partly because Robin had just toppled over and started snoring. After removing Robin's shoes and shoving a pillow under his head, Yancy left him to it.

He debated with himself all the way to the elevator. Any information should go to Osey. The trouble was, he didn't have anything concrete. Drunken ramblings, facial expressions. The hallway was discreetly lit. Yancy felt hairs prickle on the back of his neck. He jabbed the button and looked around. A door seemed to be just closing. Optical illusion. Or somebody was watching him wait for the elevator. A little creepy music and he could turn this into a slasher flick.

When the elevator arrived, the room door opened quickly and a male in his thirties came out. Brown and brown, five ten, hundred eighty, brown pants, white shirt. Small brown backpack. Yancy ran down the description like he was eyeing a suspect. Careful, boy. You don't watch it, you'll be as nutsy as the movie folks.

Inside the elevator, a kid from room service, holding a tray with covered dishes, balanced the tray on one hand and wrapped the other hand around the edge of the door to prevent its closing.

Yancy got in. The hotel guest veered off toward the stairway. Two floors up, Yancy tapped softly at room three-eighteen. It wouldn't do to wake Ms. Lloyd; she most likely wouldn't take that too kindly.

The door was yanked open so fast it startled him. For a fraction of a second Sheri Lloyd smiled in welcome, then anger flushed her face. She was wearing something pale pink and flowing, semi see-through. Obviously, she had been expecting somebody. He wondered who.

"What are you doing here?" She didn't invite him in. Behind her, an ice bucket and two glasses sat on a small table.

He came in by dint of simply stepping forward and forcing her to move back. He closed the door and leaned against it.

She poured something in a glass and tossed it down. "Well, what do you want?"

"You invited me." He crossed his arms. "You said you had something for me."

"It's too late." Sharp. Sexy coo nowhere in sight. Back came the usual disdain.

"What were you going to tell me?"

"Nothing."

"Who were you expecting?"

"None of your business."

Yancy was tired, his head ached, he wanted to go home, he wanted to go to bed. He did not want to be looked at like yesterday's dinner. "Ms. Lloyd, you could find yourself under arrest for withholding information in the matter of the death of Kay Bender." He sounded like such a pompous ass, he expected her to laugh.

She topped up her glass and slugged it down.

"We don't have to talk here. I can take you in. Book you. Take your prints, and your picture. It would be in the paper, but hey, you know what they say about publicity."

"Are you trying to scare me?"

"No, ma'am. I'm just explaining what could happen in the event that you did not cooperate."

"You are a low-life shit."

"Yes, ma'am."

"You know—" Her voice got husky, breathless. She glided toward him, one hand extended in invitation. "If you'd be nice to me I could be very nice to you."

"Let me make it perfectly clear here, Ms. Lloyd. Whatever the game is you're playing, you don't have to be so nice you need to sleep with a cop. Just answer a question or two and I'll get out of here. All right?"

She dropped her hand, flounced to a chair, and threw herself down in it. "Ask."

"Who were you expecting just now?"

"Nick." Very clipped. The lady didn't want to talk with him. Fine. What he wanted to do was go home. He also wanted to know why Robin McCormack thought this woman either knew something or was guilty. He sat in an easy chair that was so comfortable, he was tempted to close his eyes. Just for a few minutes. He fixed her with a steely-eyed stare, projecting authority and low-life shittiness. "Go on."

"He's been cool toward me ever since we got here. It's because *she's* been giving him a hard time."

"She being—?"

"Laura! Nick is just too sensitive for his own good. And he doesn't want to do anything that might have repercussions on the film. He's a professional that way. She's just barely carrying it off anyway. This role is way beyond her. Nick has asked me to be patient. *Begged* me to understand."

"Patient?"

"Of course, I told him I'd be patient, I did understand. But there's a limit." She smiled, like the evil stepsister. "So I asked him to drop by."

"And he agreed?"

"Oh, yes. He said he would try. And I could hear in his voice how much he was longing to be with me."

"You think he no longer loves Ms. Edwards?"

She glared at him. "He wanted me. On a permanent basis."

"Marriage?"

"Yes."

"What time was he going to do this dropping by?"

She flashed him a look of irritation. "Nine-thirty," she snapped.

"Have I got this straight? You wanted me here at nine-thirty and Nick here at nine-thirty. Wasn't that going to be a little crowded?"

"He is a man who could be spurred by jealousy."

Yancy thought maybe he ought to be flattered here, if she felt Nick would be jealous of such as he.

"We are exactly suited for each other," she said. "I know it and he knows it. He's a brilliant, highly successful actor and I—well, I like to think I have my own brilliance even though I'm not quite as established as he is. We can help each other. We're both concerned with social issues. We both have intellectual pursuits. A little jealousy—well I must admit, it's exciting. Just the beginnings, you understand. It makes him very *attentive.*"

"You think he loves you?"

"Of course, he loves me."

"Then why isn't he here?"

Her face hardened to porcelain and her eyes took on the intent focus of a raptor spotting a rabbit. "I saw him," she said. "This morning. He stayed behind in the barn when everyone else left for lunch.''

So much for true love.

Going to the elevator, Yancy got the same prickly feeling of being watched. He stopped and looked around. Nothing. If he didn't get some sleep, he was going to be just as out of touch as these film folk. He poked the button, heard something behind him, and spun around. Guest. Same one he'd seen earlier.

The man held himself stiffly and rocked slightly forward on his toes. He fiddled with his backpack and never looked Yancy in the eye.

To Yancy's surprise, when the elevator door opened, there stood the lieutenant. Muttering something about forgetting something, the guest went off down the corridor.

''Yancy,'' Parkhurst said with a curt nod.

''Sir,'' Yancy replied. What was the lieutenant doing here? He wasn't working this case anymore. Oh, Lord, will this day never end?

ELEVEN

LAURA TWISTED THE LOCK after Ben left. She hadn't really expected him to stay; she hadn't expected to be quite so disappointed either when he said he didn't think that was a good idea. Odd, all those years since she'd seen him and there it was, the same old excitement, the same old rush of hormones.

One thing about him, he made her feel safe. He couldn't let anything happen to her. He had some kind of code that wouldn't let him. She could trust him to find who was sending weird pictures and notes. Someone trying to kill her? It didn't seem actually real, yet she knew it was a possibility. They all lived with it. Stand out there in the open and you catch attention. The world was full of crazies. If you let it get to you, you'd never go anywhere.

They lived in different worlds, she and Ben. Yet here he was in the very place she was sent out on location. Karma?

She'd been restless lately, twitchy, unlike herself, unhappy, feeling like something was missing in her life, who knows. Nick playing footsie with that no-talent nitwit hadn't helped. Maybe maybe maybe a few changes would come along. Would that be interesting?

There you go plotting again, Laura May. Remember what your mother always used to say. You're never satisfied with what you've got, you always have to be planning and plotting for something else. Well, all that planning and plotting got her where she was.

The muscles across her back, just below the shoulders, were pulled up tight. She shrugged and moved one shoulder forward and one back, then the other way, to ease them. It was all very well to tell yourself there might be some idiot out there tracking you, but that's the way it is and just carry on. The body had its own responses.

An aromatic bath was what she needed.

In the bathroom, she turned on the taps in the old-fashioned tub with claw feet and let it fill to the brim. She dug out the chart given to her by her aromatherapist. Bergamot for tension, worry, and anxiety. Agitating the water, she carefully allowed two drops to fall. Two drops of lavender to balance the emotional extremes of stress, shock, worry, impatience.

Interesting impatience was included. By all means include lavender, she was getting impatient.

Patchouli, she noted, was an aphrodisiac. Lure Ben over and push him in the tub. Except it wasn't a physical thing that stopped him. It was that personal code again. Anything to do with that woman cop?

Two drops of vetiver for anxiety and tension ought to do it.

Slipping off her robe, she stepped in, slid down until water rose to her chin, and let her skin absorb the essential oils. A little guilt was always a useful thing. Maybe something could be done along those lines.

SILVER. Laura my beloved. The universe is silver. In the world of magnificent palaces we will love each other in a new life. He stared up at the window, all he could see was light behind the curtains. He couldn't even see her move around, the curtains were too heavy. But in his mind he could see his beloved. Her beauty surpasses all others. She is the princess of the universe, the angel of all that is caring, the countess of all that is good. My soul mate. Hand in hand we will walk through a meadow of buttercups. We will spend eternity together.

THIS DAY seemed to last an eternity. Clem stepped from the shower, grabbed a towel, and wrapped it around herself. She was totally wrung out. With a hand towel, she made one swipe over the steam on the mirror and looked at her reflection. What a mess everything was, including herself. Fifer walking around like God creating the world with his very hands. Laura and Nick at each other's throats. Big surprise the film wasn't run out of Eden. A snake handing out apples right and left. Fifer should direct a new film. *The Snake That Ate His Career*. He was so uptight all the time it made everybody jittery. His butt was on the line here, and the accident—

She pulled on an oversized pajama top patterned with zebras, then tried to call room service for some ginseng tea. It was after midnight, room service was closed. She knew that. No room service after midnight. Her mind wasn't working right. She padded barefoot around the room, touching the table, the chair, the chest, the lamp. How could she go to sleep without ginseng tea? Her mother always brought it to her.

Pulling back the curtain, she peered up at the night sky. The moon was full. A cloud like a wispy piece of gauze floated across the face of it. The Patio below, with chairs and tables, lights strung through trees like fairyland, was deserted. Except someone stood on the very edge looking up. There was something creepy about him. He blended into the shadows and she couldn't tell who it was.

Creepy, quivery, bump in the night, bad will. Even before the accident, astral influences were stacked against this film.

She shivered, let the curtain fall back, and rubbed her arms. Go to bed, get some sleep. Business as usual in the morning. Oh, Laura's scenes might be postponed, the dangerous ones, but not in acknowledgment of Kay's death, only because the new stunt double wasn't due until afternoon.

The bed was tall, high off the floor, a good place to leave a body under if you had one lying around. The phone rang, sending her three inches into the air.

"Hello?" she whispered.

"Oh, did I wake you?"

"Not really."

"I'm sorry. I didn't realize how late it was. Listen, I'll let you go back to sleep. Tomorrow I need to talk with you. I think you can do something for me."

"What?"

"You shouldn't have any trouble with it."

CLIMBING UP the outside stairway, Yancy had trouble lifting his feet high enough to clear the risers. They tended to catch on the soles and pitch him forward. His landlady had turned the light off again. He'd explained to Mrs. Blakely more than once that the best way to discourage prowlers and burglars was to keep lights on after dark. She always nodded, then turned them off anyway, worried about the cost. With the full moon shining down he could see well enough, but the stairs stretched twice as high as normal. At the top, he shoved his key in the lock, then raised his head. Noise. The concrete driveway below was empty, silver in the moonlight. The Cherokee, parked by the storage shed, cast a black shadow.

The house next door was dark. At one-thirty, they would be in bed and long asleep. As he should be. The yard behind the neighbor's house was shadowy with trees and shrubs. Occasionally, a shadow moved, nudged by a warm breeze.

He rubbed his eyes and squinted. He couldn't see around to the rear of the house. Honeysuckle was soft in the air. Night sounds came on the wind, of birds nesting in the trees, frogs conversing with each other, and crickets sawing away.

As he turned the key, he heard the whisper of a shoe on damp grass. Fatigue cut so heavy through his mind, he wasn't sure he could trust his senses. A metallic clink sounded, silenced almost immediately.

Wishing he had a flashlight, he ran down the stairs and hugged the house as he inched toward the back. A footstep came from the driveway. He stopped, looked behind him. Nothing. He imagined it. Or somebody had melted into the dark below the stairs.

Three-quarters of the way to the rear of the house, he tangled with Stephanie's bicycle. It clattered onto the driveway as he sprawled across it, banging a kneecap and scraping a hand. Oh, Lord, little cat feet.

He pushed himself up and dashed to the Cherokee for a flashlight. When the dome light went on he ducked low—even though he didn't think precautions were necessary at this point, unless the prowler was deaf and blind he was long gone—and snatched the flash from the glove box.

In the backyard, all was quiet. Holding the flash at arm's length, he clicked it on. He was still a pretty good target if the prowler was so inclined.

Whoever had been here had hightailed it over the fence disturbing the lilacs and spreading their scent through the night air.

The mad painter had struck again. Somebody with an artistic soul or a keen sense of the absurd started creeping around painting nudes on garbage cans when people were away on vacation, then when they were out for an evening. Lately, he—or she—had gotten even bolder. But to come here, with a cop in residence, was downright insolent.

Yancy checked all ground-floor doors and windows, then went back and studied the artist's rendering. Mrs. Blakely now had a garbage can with a female nude on it. He wasn't sure what they'd charge the guy with, if they ever caught him. Defacing private property? The garbage cans actually looked better. Lewd and lascivious?

The bicycle belonged in the shed. Stephanie was thirteen, an age when things didn't always get where they belonged. He put it away and limped up the stairs. Sufficient unto the day.

WHAT A DAY this has been, what a rare mood I'm in, Susan thought sourly as she let herself into the house. She checked the messages on her machine. There was only one, from her father. It could wait. Upstairs, she took a quick, tepid shower to wash away the sweat, dirt, and irritation of the day. In the bedroom she dug a white T-shirt from a drawer and slipped it over her head. It hit her about midthigh. Her husband had been a tall man. He'd been dead now about a year and a half, sometimes it seemed only days, sometimes it seemed forever.

She reversed the cassette in the portable player and pushed play. Soft sounds of Boccherini floated around her. She shoved the window all the way up and invited in any breezes. They came, but they were hot. San Francisco nights—most days also, but especially nights—were cool. A soft puff of air, like a baby breathing, touched her cheek. The silver moon shone full, crickets sang, fireflies blinked. They intrigued her, those fireflies.

Perissa, the Siamese kitten, squeezed her furry little self between Susan and the window screen. Perissa gave it a chance and when she was still ignored, she jumped from the sill to the floor and bit Susan's ankle. The cat had been an unwelcome gift from Sophie, a nutty old woman with a passion for cats and snooping. Susan didn't know much about these cat creatures, but this one seemed to sense when her thoughts were far away; if she was reading the cat would spread itself across the book; if she was staring thoughtfully into space it would climb up and pat her face. Weird creatures, cats. She rubbed Perissa's chocolate brown head and thought about Kay Bender. Dead at twenty-one, almost certainly killed because she was in the wrong place. A stunt double for Laura Edwards at dangerous moments, and a double for her murder.

A shadow of cloud passed across the moon, leaving a dark blotch on the dark lawn. An owl called, then some other night bird.

She hadn't yet come up with much of a motive for anyone to ice Ms. Edwards. That she didn't need to show motive didn't matter, she wanted one. That it had been only about twelve hours since the death didn't matter either, those were crucial hours. She got impatient when nothing showed. She needed movement on a case or she got irritated. Not enough was happening here.

She had Sheri Lloyd, jealous of Laura Edwards and wanting the starring role. Ms. Lloyd was not superbright, but could she really believe she'd get the part of the star if the star was out of the way? Maybe. Some people simply couldn't see beyond their own wants.

Nick Logan. Susan liked him. That didn't mean anything, she had known charming killers before. He was easy in himself, not handsome, but had rugged good looks, and that flavor of southern California. Large, talented, charismatic, a man whose very presence commanded attention. He'd had an affair with Ms. Lloyd, was supposed to be madly in love with Ms. Edwards. Would he kill Laura to be with Sheri? This was sounding like a soap opera again. Someone in a coma ought to show up here pretty soon. It just wouldn't fly. Why not simply walk away from Laura? It was done all the time, and these two weren't even married.

She listened to the cello concerto on the tape and felt homesick. Her mother played cello for the San Francisco symphony. When Susan was a child, she could remember lying in bed at night hearing her mother practice.

Fifer, the director. His motive seemed even weaker. Get rid of Laura and collect the whopping great insurance he had on her. The movie was in financial trouble, it was true. It was way over budget. But everybody except Sheri Lloyd—and that was maybe jealousy—said Fifer was ecstatic about how it was going, fully confident that when it was released he'd have the hit he needed.

Parkhurst. No motive at all. True, spouses and ex-spouses headed the list of suspects, but she wouldn't believe it. However, as her former boss used to say, what she believed didn't cut any cake.

Laura Edwards herself. Which meant Kay Bender was the intended victim. No motive at all that showed so far. Early days, early days.

Sheri Lloyd, Nick Logan, and Hayden Fifer, all with weak motives for doing in Laura Edwards. Laura Edwards with no motive at all for doing in Kay Bender. None of them had an alibi worth looking at. Okay, making great progress here. Damn it, she missed Parkhurst. Much of a homicide investigation had to do with theories. She tossed them out. Parkhurst said, that stinks, that's asinine, or maybe you've got something here.

She looked at the clock by the bed. Almost one, nearly eleven in San Francisco. Her father would still be up. Did she want to deal with him tonight? When she was a child she felt she always had to fight or her life would be his. As an adult, she still sometimes felt that way. It was ridiculous at thirty-five to be still rebelling against a dynamic father who loved her very much, but she could only deal with him when she felt she had the necessary strength. Tired or drained, forget it. He'd swoop down and engulf her. Oh, hell, wasn't it time she grew up?

"What do you think, cat? Time to make my own decisions? Uncolored by choices made because they're the opposite of what he wants?"

Perissa stared back, unblinking.

"It's probably why we're still here, instead of back in San Francisco where I belong. Unless the power has gone to my head. Chief of police, impressive, yes?"

Perissa washed a paw.

"That impressed, I see." She stretched out on the bed and

reached for the phone. It rang before she could pick it up, startling her.

She sat up. "Hello."

"Parkhurst."

Unsaid things growing like vines filled the silence.

"Sorry to call so late. I just drove past the house and saw the light." Parkhurst also lived on Walnut Street, but way on the other end. He told her about his visit with his ex-wife.

"That likely means," he finished, "we have a stalker in our midst."

"You're off the case."

"Yes," he said. "I'll turn all this over to Osey."

"And stay away from Laura Edwards until this is cleared."

"Yes," he said.

She hung up a little harder than was necessary, a mixture of emotions bubbling around: jealousy—of a woman Parkhurst had been married to before she even knew him. Yes, but this woman was beautiful and famous.

Worry about this new information and keeping Laura Edwards safe. Irritation that he'd disobeyed her orders. What was she going to do about that? Let it ride for tonight.

Oh, hell, call your father. That'll take your mind off things. She picked up the phone again and punched in the number. "Hi, Dad."

"Hello, baby. What are you doing up so late?"

His rich resonant voice sounded tired. Her father never got tired. "Is everything all right?"

"Sure, except my only child is way off in the middle of some unreachable, forsaken jungle contracting rare swamp fevers instead of by my side where she belongs."

That was better. "I had the measles, Dad."

"You okay now?"

"Fine."

"Spots?"

"All gone."

"You got running water yet?"

"Downhill. We also got California." She told him about the movie being made.

He snorted. "That's not California."

She smiled. North and south never quite got along; periodically there was commotion about splitting into two states.

"I just read something about that," he said. "Nick Logan had to turn down fifteen million and a role he wanted because of the commitment to this one."

Oh, really? "Where'd you read that?"

"The *Chronicle*."

She asked him what the weather was like there, that led him into a soliloquy on the beauty and desirableness of coastal fog and a comparison with heat, humidity, and general awfulness. She fended questions about when she was coming to visit, then talked with her mother.

When she hung up, she propped pillows behind her head and stared at the ceiling. Nick Logan had just moved from no motive to a fifteen-million-dollar one. She spent at least sixty-five seconds in serious thought before sleep took over.

TWELVE

THE TENNIS COURT wasn't the only thing sizzling. Laura Edwards and Nick Logan dashed around zinging the ball back and forth, with the tension hot enough to strike sparks. Yancy kept his eye on the ball.

According to Mac, Ms. Edwards's driver and Yancy's buddy, this was the time of the second murder attempt. Yancy never did figure out who the first victim was, but the tennis game was supposed to be a tense moment in the movie. Some kind of explosive was inside the ball. There was a lot of close-up stuff of the ball flying to a racquet, the racquet making a big slow arc. The *thwock* and the ball flying. Yancy followed the ball like a myopic puppy. It wasn't going to explode. That's what he'd been told and he'd looked at every tennis ball around. Still, he clenched at each smack. Another accident, this time with Laura Edwards scattered in pieces all over the court... Stupid way to try to kill someone. It would have to explode when the intended victim was near. How could anyone make sure of that? He wanted this piece of filming finished.

The aging Lockett mansion had been given a face lift. It was a large rectangular place with two-story white pillars across the front. Sparkling white paint, gray-blue shutters, double doors replaced at the entrance, windows repaired and replaced, and spanking clean. Shrubbery had been planted, thick green grass rolled out, and pots of purple, yellow, pink, and red flowers set across the porch. That was the front of the place. The north side looked fantastic too, but the back and south sides were left in their faded and peeling paint, boarded-over doors and windows. The maple trees were real though, tall and green against the cloudless blue sky.

The mansion, used as the main set for *Lethal Promise*, had everything a mansion should have. It had been built for the new wife William Lockett was importing from the east. Nothing was too good for Lucy. Marble bathrooms, stone fireplaces, kitchen appliances big enough to handle restaurant crowds, tennis court, swimming pool, small lake stocked with fish, and stables.

Poor Lucy never saw it. The private plane William had sent to fetch her had gone down in a storm, killing all on board. Shortly thereafter, the oil business fell on hard times and William lost buckets. He put the house up for sale and went off to Texas. There were lots of lookers, but no buyers. Mostly people were just curious, they just wanted to see the inside of the place, but even those who might want to buy couldn't afford it.

The place sat empty, except kids breaking in for parties or homegrown vandalism, until Hollywood came along. They cleared out the rats and the spiders and the old beer cans and the used condoms, and painted and fancied up all the rooms they wanted to use in the film.

Yancy stood on a pathway under the shade of the maple trees, almost kissing the fence around the tennis court, sweat trickled down between his shoulder blades. Whenever a camera operator yelled he was in frame, he moved back a grudging inch.

A dozen or so onlookers—boring as this was, he'd expect them to get tired of it, but they were always around—were behind a roped-off area back of the trees. He kept an eye on them too. Some he was beginning to recognize, like the guy with the backpack.

The temperature once again approached the mid-nineties and the humidity topped that, too damn hot for early June, and too hot for Fifer's artistic demands. Periodically, Fifer stopped the action and a team moved in to mop up his stars. Apparently, stars weren't allowed to sweat. For all Yancy knew this was supposedly taking place in the dead of winter. That made as much sense as anything else. People with umbrellas and battery-operated fans would swarm out, makeup and hair people, people carrying bottles of water with straws. Actors couldn't just grab a bottle and chug it down, that smeared the makeup.

It must be torture out there. Yancy could barely tolerate the heat and he was standing still. These Californians were tough, you had to give them that.

In the far corner of the court, Sheri Lloyd waited, with somebody holding an umbrella over her, for the director's call. Robin McCormack, the dead woman's boyfriend, looked pale and sweaty. In shorts and sleeveless T-shirt, even the snake tattoo on one bare arm looked subdued. He wore dark glasses and moved carefully, obviously protecting a pounding head. Yancy saw him speak to Sheri. She turned away. He grabbed her arm. In her snotty way, she tossed her hair and took a step back, distancing herself.

At Fifer's word, the swarms cleared and the actors went back out in the sun and smacked the ball back and forth. Yancy pulled tight on all his muscles and clamped down on his back teeth. Nothing could happen. This ball was just an ordinary ball, the exploding one was locked in a safe under the eye of the special effects man, and wouldn't be used until Fifer called for it. Then the new stunt double would be on the court.

Fifer was beginning to look like a candidate for sun stroke, his face taking on the color of rare steak. Khaki shorts and white T-shirt left a lot of skin exposed to the sun and all of it was turning brick red. Nick seemed to know how to play tennis and moved with the sureness of an athlete. Laura could hold the ball up there and place an okay serve, even make the right moves, but she wasn't quick with it. She looked beautiful though. Periodically, a man behind a wind machine would turn it on making her gold hair flutter.

"She had lessons in preproduction."

Yancy looked around and found Clem Jones, narrow face looking pinched, coming up behind him, eyes fixed on Laura. Envy of all that beauty and perfection? Clem would be better off without the black mascara, white makeup, and pink hair. The men's black swimming trunks and huge shapeless orange shirt didn't help much either. Maybe she was also just hoping nothing would go wrong.

Fifer called, "Cut. Beautiful, children. Just beautiful." He granted everybody a twenty-minute break.

PINK. Laura my beloved. The universe is pink. He watched Laura, his lovely Laura, go into the mansion surrounded by cast

and crew. The cop went in too. Soon, my beloved. Do not get
discouraged. Soon we will be together in a land of beauty
throughout eternity. He needed the gun. Always, too many people
around. The gun was his. I'm coming my princess. It will be fast
and painless. We'll be together. He edged up to the barrel of
trash that held the water bottle and straw she'd used. He grabbed
the straw and walked off. Away from the court he put the straw
in his mouth, moved it slowly back and forth, sucking gently. It
tasted of the sweetness of her lips, the purity of her soul.

BOTH NICK AND LAURA, along with a herd of people whose job
it was to soothe and succor, trailed up to the mansion. Yancy
followed. On the way, he snagged a doughnut and bottle of foreign water from craft service. Inside, the stars climbed the big
staircase side by side, without touching, without looking at each
other. At the top, they split and Nick went into one room, Laura
into another, with Mac on her heels, Officer White on his.

Yancy plopped in a love seat in the hallway and downed the
water. Knowing Laura's minders were on her tail—and beautiful
as it was—he zeroed in on Sheri Lloyd's petulant face as she
chugged up the stairs. He let her get settled, then barged into a
room that had obviously been meant as a child's bedroom. The
switch plate was a train with a smiley face, the wallpaper had
trains, trucks, and hot air balloons. William Lockett had been
planning a male heir.

The two females patting Sheri's cheeks, forehead, and the nape
of her neck with damp cloths looked at him with astonishment.
He pointed, they stomped out, he closed the door.

The room had a bed, two chairs, a bar stool, and two carousel
horses. Why carousel horses? Sheri had, naturally, arranged herself on the bed with pillows propped around her in such a way
as to show off her body. "It's so terribly hot. I feel ill. I can't
talk with you."

He pulled a blue bottle of water from the six-pack on the table
next to the bed, twisted off the cap, and handed it to her. "Sit
up and drink it. You'll feel better."

She took it and glared. Apparently, he wasn't being sensitive.
Hard-faced, he pulled one of the chairs close to the bed and

sat on it. Ms. Sheri Lloyd would be apt to misinterpret anything else, so in the interests of intimidation and the pursuit of information, he sat rigid, eyes flinty.

Automatically she wiggled herself around on the pillows so that her tits were thrust forward in maximum position for distraction.

"What were you talking about with Robin McCormack?"

"I don't believe that's any of your business, but if you must know I was extending my sympathies."

Miss Sheri was not one to drop sympathy around where it wouldn't do her any good, and it had been Robin who'd approached her. "Ms. Lloyd, I told you before the consequences of withholding information in a murder investigation."

"When two old friends make a date to get together, it hardly constitutes *withholding evidence.*"

"You and Robin are old friends?"

"Of course."

"When are you getting together?"

She studied the veins in the back of her hand as though they were a road map. "There's nothing definite."

Yancy wondered if maybe Sheri Lloyd was one of those people who simply lied all the time.

"Now, if you don't mind, I really need to regather my strength." She flipped on her side and mashed another pillow under her head.

He left her to the ministering women and went in search of Robin. In the condition Robin was in, it wouldn't need thumb screws; a loud voice ought to do.

Six or seven crew members were schmoozing in the kitchen, Robin sat glugging down a Coke.

"Talk to you a minute?"

"What about?"

Yancy looked at the other guys. "Maybe we could step into the pantry."

Yancy could see him want to refuse, but in the end it was just too much trouble. He drained the can, crushed it, tossed it in a trash container, and grabbed another.

The pantry hadn't been spruced up, it remained in its cobwebbed seedy condition. Robin propped himself against a wall of empty shelves. "What is it?"

"How you feeling?"

"I been better."

"Remember last night?"

Robin gave him a rueful grin, and rubbed a hand along the back of his head. "Not crystal clear. Didn't you run over me?"

"You said somebody pushed you."

"Did I?"

"Who?" Yancy slouched against the door frame and crossed his arms.

Robin popped open the Coke and took a long drink, giving himself time to think, or because he was thirsty. "I don't know."

"You see anybody?"

He started to shake his head, grimaced, and thought better of it. "I wasn't exactly in top condition."

"Why would anybody push you in front of my Jeep?"

"Nice guy like me?" Robin shrugged. "I can't imagine."

Yancy was getting a little irritated. "You loved Kay Bender, right? If you had anything to help, you'd give it to me, right?" Yancy paused. "Who'd you see?"

"Could you, maybe, not talk quite so loud? I don't know." He tipped up the can and swallowed. "A kid, I think. And—oh, yeah, another guy."

"The kid, male or female?"

"Male."

"What do you mean by kid? Ten, twelve?"

"Seventeen, eighteen."

"What'd he look like?"

"I don't know."

"The other guy, it was a guy? Male?"

"Yeah."

"What'd he look like?"

Robin closed his eyes, kept them closed so long Yancy wondered if he'd gone to sleep. "Somebody who came out of the hotel."

"Describe him."

"You're asking an awful lot, man. Medium. Medium everything. Not tall, not short. Kinda stocky, maybe. That's it. You think I was studying him?''

That description would fit any number of males, including his old friend, Howie. ''Age?''

''Youngish. My age or so.''

''Who else?''

''Only you.''

''Why do you think Sheri killed Kay?''

''I don't.''

''You wanted to talk to her last night. Just a few minutes ago, you did talk to her. Why?''

''I need to get back to work,'' Robin said.

''Not until you lay it out for me.''

''It's nothing, okay? It's only a feeling. You ever heard the expression the cat who ate the cream? That's the way she looked, Sheri. Like she knew something and she was going to use it to her advantage. Okay? That anything you want?''

''You're reading an awful lot into an expression.''

''I told you.''

''What else?''

Robin hauled in half the air in the room. ''She was singing. 'Take what comes and use it your way.'''

''That's a song?''

''Yeah, man. A line from the theme song for this movie. I gotta go.''

FROM THE BEDROOM WINDOW, Sheri looked out at the tennis court and watched Laura hit the ball back to Nick. It should be her out there. She'd be much better. And she could play tennis, for God's sake. None of this holding the ball up and serving and then cutting in the stunt double. Laura was hot and sweaty and not at all sexy. Sheri hoped she'd drop over from the heat. Sheri patted at moisture on her own forehead. It was so hot. Even when they managed to get the air-conditioning going, it kept breaking down. Fifer would yell and they'd fix it again.

Maybe this might have been some house when it was new, but now it was a dump, falling down and moldy. Even if it was all remodeled it wasn't practical. She was nothing if not practical.

She knew what was important, like the right script, the right money, a limo and driver. She should have a trailer of her own. Not that little crummy cubby she was stuck with. She'd tell her agent, her own trailer from now on.

She liked things to be right. If they weren't, she would make them so. Like her name. She'd been born Martha Gutlet in Newark, New Jersey. As soon as she got to California, she knew immediately that wouldn't do. Gutlet was impossible and Martha was a plain, obedient kind of name. The whole name just didn't have a euphonious—her high school English teacher would be surprised at the use of that word—ring to it.

The way she found her name, she was taking the bus home to this shitty apartment that she shared with another girl and somebody'd left a paperback book with this handsome guy on the cover. It turned out to be this really sweet story about this girl who fell in love and the guy loved her too only she didn't know it and the girl's name was Sheri Lloyd. Then and there she knew that was her name. Her best friend from high school laughed and said it was just like her to choose such a dumb name. Well, she got the last laugh. She made it. And her best friend wasn't her best friend anymore, she was a housewife. Sheri knew the name was right. She knew a lot of things. It was just a matter of figuring out how to use them. She wasn't as dumb as people thought.

She frowned, then consciously smoothed her face. Frowning caused wrinkles.

And she was not only fulfilled as an actress, she was a right-thinking member of society, advocated the right causes. She was against pollution and offshore drilling and oil spills. And for endangered species, saving trees, and AIDS research. Women who wore fur coats deserved to have red paint thrown over them. People who picketed abortion clinics should be dragged away and shot. Except, of course, that would be capital punishment and she was against that.

And then there was religion. Religion was all right, even though it was the opiate of the masses—see, Miss Strickler, I was paying attention—and everybody had the right to worship in his or her own way, but the God squad wasn't satisfied with choosing for themselves, they wanted to ram their choice down everybody else's throats. You couldn't even talk to them, because they wouldn't hear and you might as well be talking to a brick wall, or they made you feel like the biggest sinner since Pontius Pilate. Or they wanted to pray for you. She hated it when they wanted to pray for you.

And that time on the *Tonight Show* when she said she was for abortions. Of course, she didn't mean that. She meant for choice. Picketers followed her around for days. Good Lord, you'd think she'd recommended slaughtering whole nurseries full of babies. Most people didn't have the scope to transcend their own narrow horizons.

She swung the crystal on the gold chain around her neck. Wasn't it ever anything but hot and sticky in this godforsaken place? Even at night, it was hot. Dreadful place. She watched Nick out on the tennis court smack a ball that Laura missed completely. She wasn't even graceful about it. Not that it mattered, the finished film would only show what Fifer wanted, the stretch and the hit and the bouncy flouncy. Sheri studied Nick and wondered how she was going to get him in bed again. And get him she would. It was only a matter of working it out.

Laura ought to understand. Good God, they weren't even married, and these things happened. Sheri knew Nick was much more suited to her than to Laura. Look at how they were fighting all the time. If that romance wasn't already dead, Nick wouldn't have been interested in the first place.

Out on the tennis court, Fifer called a break. Everybody rushed like commuters to the mansion. If Laura's fans could see her now they wouldn't think she was so sexy. Her face was red and she was sweating like a pig.

"People!" Fifer called after them.

Sometimes Sheri thought Fifer didn't appreciate her. She'd mentioned it once, tried to bring it right out in the open like you're supposed to do for good relationships, but somehow they'd ended up talking about team playing and the good of *Lethal Promise*.

"I want everybody in the ballroom," Fifer said. "That means everybody."

THIRTEEN

SHERI took tiny sips at her drink. The moment of silence was turning into a cocktail party. It had started out all quiet with everybody in the ballroom and kind of avoiding looking at each other, and Fifer making that sweet speech about the stuntwoman. How Kay Bender was one of us. What a tragedy it was. How sorry we all were. How good she was at her job. How much we'd all miss her. How we were a family and what happened to one affected us all. Everybody had shuffled their feet and looked at the floor, but Sheri thought it was touching. After he finished, alcohol was poured. Ice cubes tinkled and glasses clinked, hors d'oeuvres on a long table were being perused and eaten. Sheri liked cocktail parties. People tended to drink too much and say things.

The sound level rose. Eighty people in one room with alcohol and food and you had a party. Sheri was drinking rum and Coke. So what if it was sneered at? She liked it. She usually tried to limit herself to one drink unless she felt really comfortable and knew what was going on. She didn't know what was going on here but something was. There was a really bad aura, and she kept feeling somebody was watching her. She couldn't catch anybody, just people standing around wondering how soon they could leave. It was tense in here. Really tense. She was sensitive to these things.

She didn't know why Fifer picked this room. It wasn't like it was nice or anything. Just this one huge empty room, nothing in it but the folding table brought in by the caterers. There wasn't even anyplace to sit down or anything. It was scummy, cobwebs on the ceiling and patches of wallpaper missing.

That Yancy police person stood by the wall looking like he was watching everybody. Laura was holding court in the middle of the room like the Queen of Sheba. Sheri tipped a teensy bit more rum in her Coke and plopped in another ice cube. Nick was standing by the fireplace. Kind of a nice fireplace. Stone, sort of massive, all the way to the ceiling. She weaved around through people, wedged herself between Clem and a makeup girl, and slipped her arm through Nick's. He gave her a smile and tried to step sideways. She stayed with him.

Laura glared at her. Sheri smiled. Stupid bitch. When would she realize Nick and I are meant for each other?

"Excuse me, darling." Nick tugged his arm loose and set off for Laura.

"You shouldn't do that." Clem fingered the locket at her throat.

"Do what?"

"Upset Laura like that."

"Poor Laura. She just won't admit it's over between her and Nick." Sheri turned to make her way to the snack table and found Robin McCormack standing beside her.

"I'm so sorry about Kay." Sheri put her fingertips on his forearm so he'd know she really meant it. She was sorry she'd been so short with him earlier. After all, he'd suffered a Loss.

"Yeah? Then help me."

"Help?" What did that mean? Of course, she would make allowances because of his grief, but what did he want? No way would she sleep with him if that was what he was working up to. That's usually what they wanted, starting with her step-father. "What?" she asked in a voice that slipped a little from sympathy.

"What do you know about Kay's death?"

"Oh." She was relieved. "I told you earlier, I don't know anything."

"I'm not in the mood for coy." His voice was awfully cold for somebody who was grieving.

Her hand closed around her crystal. Too many bad feelings were coming from all around. This movie just had bad karma. She needed to meditate, to get herself centered. And call her astrologer. Her astrologer would tell her what to do. Sheri concentrated on putting out good thoughts. "I don't know anything."

"It's not smart to play games with me."

"Really, it's true. If I did, I'd tell that police person. He's supposed to help if we need anything. Although when I asked him for one teensy favor he said he was too busy."

"Things happen," he said menacingly.

"What's that supposed to mean?"

"It means"—he spoke very slowly like she was an idiot or something—"that you could find yourself in a situation your conniving little mind won't be able to get you out of."

"Are you threatening me?"

"Just a warning."

How dare he talk to her like that? She left the snack table and went all the way across the room. With her back toward the wall, she peered around for Nick. He was over there with Laura. Sheri elbowed through to him and stood on his other side. Her arm slid through his, just where it belonged.

"Fifer seems to be trying to get your attention," Laura said with sweet poison.

Sheri, fingering the crystal dangling between her breasts, glanced over at the director.

"I doubt that will help you any, darling," Laura said.

What was she talking about? All of a sudden it seemed everybody was talking from pink pages that she didn't get. "If you have the idea—"

"Sheri, darling, in all the time I've known you I don't believe you've had a single new idea. Or a single old one either."

"Now just listen here—"

Nick detached her arm and gave it a little pat. "See what Fifer wants, sweetheart."

"Sheri." Fifer beckoned with one finger. She couldn't believe it. Like she was some kind of underling. Oh, this had to be straightened out. Hayden Fifer didn't appreciate her at all. Dialoguing was the only way to clear this up. She had to work really hard and make sure he listened to her this time. Well, of course, she was all for team playing and the good of the film, but there was such a thing as making her own needs known.

He just walked out like she'd follow and didn't even look back to see if she was. People parted for him as if he were Moses at the Red Sea. Or whoever it was, she couldn't remember. By that big wide stairway, he studied her and said, real quietlike, "My hotel room. Eight o'clock."

Then he left, just like that. Back inside the ballroom, she searched out Clem and caught her arm. "What does Fifer want with me?"

"I'm not always in his mind, but I'd say he wants you to stop getting our star all ruffled by trying to steal her boyfriend."

"But that's just silly. Nobody steals anybody. He wouldn't be interested if he still loved her. I didn't do anything. It just happened."

"Great line."

Sheri looked at her, puzzled. "Maybe I should talk to Laura. I mean, just explain that Nick loves me and we need to be together."

"You really believe that's going to happen?" Clem asked curiously.

"Of course. It has to."

"Why does it have to?"

"Because that's what my astrologer said. I shall win out over my enemy."

"Well," Clem said, "if I were you I wouldn't mention that to Laura."

"It's always better to dialogue and get everything out in the open."

"Right." Clem snorted and made her way over to the drinks table.

Clem was a really odd person, Sheri thought. Into her self too much. Did she ever have a boyfriend? The way she looked what could she expect? That awful makeup and those awful clothes. Maybe she had one once who gave her that locket and that's why she always wore it. There were times when Sheri really didn't think Clem liked her. Sheri would show Christian charity. Clem's life was hitting too many wrong planes. Sheri had offered the name of her astrologer, but Clem had refused. What more could she do?

She slid the crystal back and forth on its chain. The bad auras were making her jumpy. Of course, Nick loved her. He was going to marry her. Hadn't her astrologer said her true love would return that love twofold? Besides, she was twenty-two. Laura was old.

SHERI LEANED OVER the bathroom cabinet and frowned at her image in the mirror. There wasn't enough light. This really wasn't a nice hotel. Compared to the Four Seasons, it was just crummy. Why was everybody so thrilled with old?

She examined her makeup. It was perfect, but her eyes were a little puffy. Nobody had dared leave the mansion until Fifer said they could, and then she'd come straight to her hotel room and taken a nap. It was so hot and awful, she'd felt just really drained, and she'd slept too long.

Now she didn't even have time to get anything to eat. Hayden Fifer didn't like it if anybody was late. She turned her head a little to one side and then a little to the other. She took a step back. She couldn't even see her whole self in the dinky mirror, only the top half. Although she had to admit that part looked pretty good. The white blouse with a wide neck looked great against her tan. The skimpy skirt, green to show up her green eyes, hugged her hips. Slipping her feet into high-heeled sandals, she grabbed her room key.

Fifer had a suite, of course. He answered her knock, motioned toward a couch, and went into the bedroom. He swung the door shut, but it didn't quite latch. She sat down, crossed her legs, smoothed the skirt, and waited.

She recrossed her legs. What was taking him so long? If she'd known he was going to make her wait, she could have picked up something to eat. The snacks at Kay Bender's moment of silence hadn't really appealed. From a carafe on the old-fashioned desk thing she poured herself a glass of red wine and took a sip. She grimaced. She never could understand what people saw in wine. The murmur of Fifer's end of the phone conversation drifted in from the bedroom. She tiptoed to the door and put her ear to the crack.

"...not any trouble...I keep telling you."

Silence a moment, then he said, "Yeah, yeah. Don't worry about it...if there's trouble, I'll take care of it."

Silence.

"Just leave it to me...I told you...little setback...can be fixed..."

Silence.

She was caught taking a giant tiptoe toward the couch. He grabbed her wrist so tight she couldn't even twist it.

"Interested in other people's phone conversations?" He released her with a little push and she landed on her butt on the edge of the couch and slid to the floor. She got up, eased onto the couch, and rubbed her wrist. What was the matter with him? He didn't usually push people around, he just yelled, or got creepy quiet. That's when he was scariest.

He went back into the bedroom and she heard him say, "I'll get back to you." When he came out again, he poured himself a glass of wine. "Refill?" His voice was dangerous.

Since she had a glass she'd only taken two sips from, she shook her head.

"Want to know what that call was about?"

She shook her head again.

He gave a little laugh that wasn't really a laugh, drank off the wine, and poured another glass. He started to pace. "The money people. They hear rumors. They get twitchy and make noises about pulling the plug. That makes me nervous. I don't like getting nervous. Understand?"

She nodded.

He stopped in front of her, leaned over too close, and stared in her face. "Who's the most disliked person on the set?"

She shrank back.

"The director." He straightened and continued pacing. "You want to know why? I'll tell you why. He makes people act. He doesn't allow them to get away with what they think is acting. He makes them be things they never thought they could. They might think the actions are stupid, or wrong for the situation, but he insists. He demands too much and ignores their carefully considered suggestions. He's never satisfied and makes them work their butts off. He has no understanding of the sensitive artist, sets impossible goals, and doesn't make allowances for weather or technical problems. He demands the impossible and yells when he doesn't get it.''

He sat on the arm of an overstuffed chair. "Why is that, Sheri?"

She stared at him.

"He has a vision. A vision of what he's working toward. The final product. He feels each section, has an overall sense as the work progresses, even if it gets changed along the way. He has to fight to create that vision. You understand? Sympathy on the set isn't possible, or tolerance for individual foibles. That would create chaos, turn out a project with no focus. A cause without a leader.''

His voice got even scarier. "I'm not a person who yells a lot. I've found it's more effective to speak softly. I believe in *Lethal Promise.* I want to see it finished. I'll fight to make that happen.''

Her heart was beating fast. She shivered. Her fingers found her crystal.

He waved toward the bedroom. "They heard about Kay's accident. They heard about the possibility it was an attack on Laura. I'm running the line that any publicity is good publicity. By the time *Lethal Promise* hits distribution, the public will be clamoring to see it. An attack on Laura will bring them charging in.''

He pinned her with his eyes. "What is not good is your upsetting Laura. I don't care about your hormones. I care about this movie. Drop all your sexy little plays for Nick. Don't give Laura even a smell of anything to complain about. Understand? Or I will be forced to take care of you.''

He stood up, took away her almost full glass of wine, set it on the table, and opened the door.

As if hypnotized, she got up and walked out. She didn't get mad until she was in the elevator going down. How dare he talk to her like that? He couldn't tell her what to do. When the doors opened at the lobby, she was momentarily confused, then realized she'd pushed the wrong button.

She stomped out, then stopped and drew in a deep breath. Calm. Ease the anger. Deep breath in. Let it out slowly. Release all the tension. Deep breath in. Out slowly. For a moment she wasn't certain what to do. But only for a moment. That pathetic man at the counter, assistant manager or whatever he was, was watching her and pretending not to. With a smile on her face, she walked to the desk.

"Hi," she said with a throaty purr. At least he appreciated her. Hadn't he been so kind as to give her that Yancy person's phone number? It wouldn't hurt to be nice to him. She might want something else, you never knew.

Howie, who had been acutely aware of her from the instant she got off the elevator, looked up from the papers he was pretending to work on. "Hey, Ms. Lloyd. Is everything all right?"

"I'm going out there." She pointed. "Could you have someone get me a drink?"

"I'll send someone right out."

"Thank you so much." She glided across the lobby, then marched down the corridor and out through glass doors to the Patio. She paused and blinked to let her eyes adjust to the dimness.

The area was glass-enclosed. Shrubs, growing in big pots and draped with strings of tiny white lights, sat on the uneven flagstone floor. Little round tables with two or three chairs placed here and there. Most were unoccupied. A ring of large trees outside screened the area from the rest of the grounds.

She waited for somebody to notice her. A hicksville kid, sitting in the corner where it was almost pitch-black, couldn't take gawping eyes off her. And a local nobody in a white dress. She'd been gazing out at the stars or something. A big black dog lay at her feet. Dogs shouldn't be allowed. She intended to complain. Laura and Nick were at a table with their heads together. They pretended like they didn't see her, but she knew better. Clem and Robin were over there with a makeup girl and somebody from wardrobe.

With her chin up, Sheri tip-tapped across the flagstones, high heels on the uneven floor making her stumble a little. "Okay if I join you?" Without waiting for an answer, she pulled a chair from a nearby table and joined Nick and Laura.

A waiter was at her elbow the moment she sat. She gave him a captivating smile and asked for a rum and Coke, then turned the smile onto her companions. Laura glared daggers. Somebody really ought to tell her how unattractive she was when she did that. It made her look haggard. Caused wrinkles too. At her age, she needed to be careful. Nick didn't seem really happy to see her either. That frightened her. She needed to get him alone so she could fix everything. It was Laura, sitting there sending out hateful auras, who made him act that way. Sheri felt very discomposed. She really did.

When the waiter came back with her rum and Coke, she took a tiny sip, tipped her head, and looked out at the moon, full or almost full, like she was enjoying its beauty. This was an awful place, she hated it here, she'd be so glad when they left.

With a scrape, Laura shoved her chair back and stood up. "You don't realize who you're playing with." She smiled and stalked away.

"Good," Sheri said. "She's gone." She scooted her chair closer to Nick and laid her head on his shoulder. "I wanted to be alone with you."

He sighed and dropped his chin to his chest, then looked at her and shook his head. Without a word he got up and started to leave.

"Nick—?"

With one hand, he made a gesture like he was brushing her away. It brought tears to her eyes. She concentrated hard on not crying and sipped her drink like she wasn't in pain, like the moon really was beautiful and she was enjoying gazing at it. Aware that everybody was leaving, she didn't even look around. Put out confidence and confidence would be there.

When the woman in the white dress started over to her—actually, more like floated, the long white skirt and tuniclike blouse shimmered around her—Sheri felt tired at what fame brought. At least, this woman's aura was peace and serenity.

She sat at Sheri's table. "I'm Raina Yancy," she said. Her dark eyes were odd, kind of luminous and—she was scary somehow. Like crazy. The big black dog paced by her side and flopped at her feet.

Sheri drew away. Big dogs frightened her, but she smiled, even if the smile was maybe a little bit strained. Always smile at the fans. "Sheri Lloyd," she said, just as though she was an ordinary person. She always did that, even though the other person obviously knew who she was. It made them feel like she wasn't setting herself above them. And she didn't want to do anything to upset this woman. You never knew what might set them off.

"'The moping owl does to the moon complain,'" Raina said.

Sheri looked around. Everybody was gone, even the kid in the corner.

"Is there anything I can do to help?" Raina said.

"How very kind of you, but I have to go now." Sheri smiled and shoved back her chair.

The noise made the dog leap to its feet and she shrank back.

"Don't mope, child. Sometimes you can't have what you want; that doesn't mean there aren't other things you can have. That are just as good."

"Excuse me." Sheri walked slowly and deliberately away. They were like dogs, the mad ones. If you didn't stare them in the eye and didn't run, maybe you could get away.

Sheri didn't look around until she had reached the door into the hallway. The woman didn't come after her. With a deep cleansing breath, Sheri let her shoulders relax, and went to complain about the vicious dog and the crazy woman. Howie—that was his name—said he'd take care of it right away. Because she felt so unnerved, she chatted with him awhile. He was really kind of sweet, in a short, stocky kind of way.

She couldn't stay long. She needed her beauty sleep. Fluttering her fingers at him, she went to the elevator that took an age to get there. It always did. One more thing about this crummy place.

On the third floor, she stuck the key in the lock and turned it. Just as she stepped inside, she felt a sharp pain in her back. She stumbled forward, and fell. Rough pile carpeting pressed against her cheek. Brown and beige. Ugly.

The door shut behind her.

Her tanned hand, nails painted red, crawled on its fingertips toward the crystal around her neck. The fingers went still, the hand fell flat and soft against the ugly carpet.

FOURTEEN

YANCY, transferring keys and change from his pockets to the chest, let the phone ring. God damn it, it's ten o'clock. I put in sixteen hours. He counted twelve rings, then with a sigh of exasperation, irritation, and downright annoyance, picked up the receiver.

"Hey, Pete."

"Hey, Howie," Yancy said. "This better be important or I'm cutting you from my will."

"Sorry. Your mother's here."

"Where?"

"The hotel."

Oh, hell. With thumb and forefinger, he squeezed the bridge of his nose. "How'd she get there?"

"How do I know?"

"Trouble?"

"No. You know I like your mother, but I had complaints about the dog."

"Elmo's there too?"

"She really did complain and, actually, dogs aren't allowed, you know."

"I'm on the way."

Yancy put keys and change back in his pockets, turned on the outside light over the stairway, and trotted down.

When Yancy came into the lobby, Howie said, "On the Patio."

With a wave of thanks, Yancy turned down the corridor and went through the doors to the glass-enclosed area at the back of the hotel. No one there. The small white lights threaded through potted shrubs twinkled on empty tables; chairs sat at angles, crumpled napkins lay on the cobblestones. Oh, Lord, she'd gone.

Back in the lobby, he said to Howie, "She's not there. You see her leave?"

"I'd have told you. Is the dog gone too? Elmo's a big dog, he can look scary."

"Who complained?"

"What difference does it make? Dogs aren't supposed to be in there."

"Come on, Howie. Who was it?"

"Don't get so short. One of the actresses—"

"Howie, I'm tired and I'm not in a very good mood and I want to be home in bed. Don't hold back on me."

"What's with you? Okay, okay. Don't get so worked up. It was Sheri Lloyd."

"She coos at you and you drop all your bones at her feet." Yancy pointed a finger. "Watch it, Howie. Haven't you heard about bad women from the big city?"

"Yeah. What I'd like is a little firsthand experience."

"You could ask the lady out."

"I did. Hey, nothing like that. I only asked her to dinner. She said no."

"Did you tell her you owned a chain of hotels and you had so much spare money lying around you were thinking of investing in a movie?"

"Of course not. It's not true."

"No wonder she turned you down. How could my mother and a big black dog get out of here without you seeing them?"

"I don't just stand here, you know. I have work to do. I have an office to do it in."

Hours for assistant hotel managers seemed even worse than hours for cops baby-sitting movie people.

"Anyway, I may have been gone for a second or two. Hey, sometimes things need to be seen to. Like seeing if everything's all right in the bar. And sending someone out to take care of drinks for the people on the Patio." Howie flushed bright pink.

Yancy hadn't seen him do that since high school when a girl looked at him. "You sent a waiter? Missed opportunity, Howie."

"Go to hell."

Before Yancy could think of a clever but no doubt equally

juvenile reply, his beeper went off. He tipped it so he could see the number and asked if he could use a phone. Without waiting for a reply, he eased around the counter and picked up the one on the desk.

"Peter," his sister said, "Mother's not here."

"Calm down. She's all right."

"How do you know?"

"What time did you last see her?"

"About seven-thirty when she went to bed. I was reading for a couple of hours and just now when I checked on her she was gone. I've looked everywhere. She's gone, Peter."

"She came to the Sunflower."

"Oh, God, is she all right? How on earth did she get there? You'll bring her home?"

"Well—she's not actually here right now."

Silence on the other end of the line. "You mean you don't know where she is."

"I'll find her. Don't worry. I'll bring her home."

"Don't worry," Serena said flatly and hung up.

Guilt reared up again. He punched in a number and told the dispatcher he'd appreciate it if the patrols would keep an eye out for his mother.

"Affirmative."

He got in his Cherokee and cruised. With the big dog at her side, she shouldn't be hard to spot. After an hour of no sign, he was getting seriously alarmed. Nothing like a shot of adrenaline to clear ideas of sleep from your mind. He widened his circles, stopped what few people were out and about at eleven o'clock at night. Nobody had seen her. Damn. By this time, a patrol should have spotted her.

When his beeper went off, he grabbed it. Serena's number. At the pay phone outside the library, he called her.

"She's back," Serena said.

Thank God. "She okay?"

"Seems to be. But, Peter—"

"I'll be right out."

"Maybe now you'll start to understand what I've been telling you," Serena said when he walked in the kitchen door. She stood by the sink with her arms crossed, a hard crust of anger under her quiet words.

"I'm tired, Serena. I need to get up early."

"You're the only one?"

"No." He gave her a one-armed hug and kissed her forehead. "But I don't want you mad at me tonight. Okay?"

She shoved him. "If I didn't love you so much, I'd yell at you. Listen, I've been trying to tell you—"

"Peter?" his mother called from her bedroom.

"Can we talk about this later?"

"Will you listen?"

"Peter—?"

"Go ahead. She thinks the moon and stars rise and set by you. See if you can find out what she did."

His mother, pillows propped against the headboard, closed the book she was reading and held out both hands. "Peter, darling. What a lovely surprise."

Elmo bumped his big head against Yancy's knee. Yancy gave him a pat, sat on the edge of the bed, and took his mother's hands. He kissed her cheek.

"Where were you, Mom?"

Elmo rested his head on the bed and she stroked it. "We went for a walk. It was a beautiful night."

"You were at the Sunflower." The book she'd been reading was *How to Recover from a Stroke*.

She smiled, slightly embarrassed. "I hoped to see an actor. I know that sounds silly, but how often are famous people in Hampstead? I saw Nick Logan. Such a handsome man. And Laura Edwards. She's very beautiful. And there was one other. What's her name? Oh, what was it? I can't think."

"Sheri Lloyd?"

"That's the one."

"How did you get there?"

"Taxi. I asked for Eddy. You know Eddy. His wife has arthritis so bad. He's the only one who doesn't fuss about Elmo."

"How'd you get home?"

"It was such a nice night I thought we'd walk. It's cooler

now. It won't be so hot tomorrow. I just can't walk like I used to. I'm afraid I pooped out before we were even halfway.''

"Then what?"

"Somebody gave me a ride." She seemed to shake a bag of suppressed memories. "Who was it?"

"I don't know, Mom."

"Sure you do, Peter. We went up by the ridge to see if we could spot bald eagles."

"At night?"

"Oh, I don't think so." She noticed his uniform. "Why are you dressed like that?"

"I've been working."

She smiled fondly and squeezed his hand. "You still want to be a policeman?"

"I am a policeman, Mom. I've been one for five years. What did you do at the hotel?"

She sang so softly he could barely hear her.

> "And it is thou art come, childe Orm,
> My youngest son so dear?
> And is it gold, or silver plate,
> Or coin, thou seekest here?"

The stroke hadn't affected her voice; it was pure and clear, but she had slipped away into whatever part of her brain waited in the shadows. He gave her a kiss, removed a couple of pillows, and said, "Good night, Mom."

Serena was still standing in the kitchen, arms crossed, hands cupping her elbows. He knew a battle stance when he saw one. "I can't throw my mother out of her home," he said.

"Peter, I've been trying to tell you. When she got home—she had blood on her hands."

FIFTEEN

MAIN STREET jumped with activity. Everybody wants to be in the movies, Susan thought. More people packed the sidewalks than would turn out for an end-of-the-world sale. College students in herds, Sophie the cat lady, Bob Haskel from heating and plumbing, Ab Perley from the hardware store. Her friend Fran Weymore from the travel agency. Kevin Murphy, high school football star and part-time gas pump jockey. Howie Gilbert, assistant hotel manager. Teens and preteens.

The director was intending to film a parade. If he didn't get it moving, his parade was going to get rained on. He stood on a camera truck speaking into a walkie-talkie, checking the status of every section along his route. Bright and sunny now, there were clouds on the horizon that might bring in thunder and lightning. One thing about Kansas, it knew how to stage a thunderstorm.

By eight, Fifer judged everything ready and a skeletally thin AD—assistant director to those who weren't in on movie lingo—alerted the crowd to put parade excitement on their faces and cheer at everything.

Fifer shouted, "Action." The cheers began. With Yancy at her side, Susan watched from the steps of city hall. The high school band played loudly, scout troops marched smartly, street clowns and jugglers did their thing. Horses stepped along, decorated flatbed trucks rolled, with drama students, tumblers, and choral groups. Hampstead could be proud.

Fifer stopped and started his parade so many times she lost count, and reshot every sequence a zillion times. The extras weren't having fun anymore. The first AD worked harder and harder getting cheers. Movie-trained horses, she noted, knew the meaning of action and cut as well as the rest of the actors.

At two, when Fifer finally finished filming his parade, the AD asked all the extras to gather by the river. Lyrics from a song? Something about gathering by the river.

"You get to gather with them," she told Yancy.

He smiled. "I thought I might get to do that very thing."

Through the milling crowd, she crossed the street to the police department. She hoped to get the work done that she'd neglected by watching the parade.

Gather, they did. For a picnic. Yancy wondered who might give him a copy of the script. So far nothing made any sense.

By now the extras were definitely not having fun and needed to be coaxed and jollied by the first AD. They milled around picnic tables brought in by the crew. Barbecue pits, also brought in, blazed and settled to low flames. Howie looked dubiously up at the sky. The AD clapped him encouragingly on a shoulder and bellowed through his megaphone, "The food is edible. Please do not eat the food unless the cameras are rolling. The food is edible. Please do not eat the food unless the cameras are rolling."

The river—sometimes slow and lazy, sometimes fast and angry after heavy rains, like now—swept by at a good clip, rippling through the reflections of trees. The building clouds overhead lent a dark ominous look to it. Yancy rested against a tree trunk on the edge of the buzzing activity. Working in the movie industry belonged to people with stamina. Nobody moved at less than a trot. He stifled a yawn. Before Hollywood came to town, he couldn't remember ever being this tired and this bored for this long. He swiped at a cloud of gnats and hoped Fifer knew rain might start pissing down anytime. Around all these trees wasn't the best place to be with lightning forking from heaven to earth.

The shouting back and forth between Fifer on dry land and two guys in a motorboat stopped; one guy in the boat inflated a raft and tossed it in the river. It darted from side to side behind the motorboat like an eager puppy. More shouting, and the guy jumped into the raft to test its seaworthiness, then clambered back into the motorboat. Much peering into cameras on the motorboat and into those planted along the river's edge.

Rescue teams set up a station, ready to race out and save anybody who fell in. Even extras and spectators? Probably not, not spectators anyway. Which left that duty to him. Promises to protect and serve, after all. He was a good strong swimmer, but more than one sinker would be a problem. With the humidity matching the temperature, the air was approaching liquid. Anybody out here for an ersatz picnic wasn't right in the head.

Although, he might be wrong about that. Laura Edwards appeared in the prow of the motorboat with a drenched T-shirt clinging to her superb body.

To be heard over the noise of the river, Fifer had to yell at Clem. Yancy could tell the director was on the thin edge of his patience.

So was Clem.

"She's not here," Clem yelled back.

"Find her."

"It's not my job."

"I need her now."

"Where's the second second?" Clem demanded. "It's her job. Why isn't she finding Sheri?"

"Get Sheri here!"

On a shoot the director was dictator and everybody did what he said, especially the director's assistant. With a look of mutiny, Clem fished keys from the large pocket of her purple tentlike thing and stomped toward the rental car parked behind all the vans used to transport cast and crew from the hotel to base camp or set. Stars had town cars—each one had hired his or her own for personal use—and the rest went by van, all piled together.

SHERI LLOYD'S honey wagon room at base camp wasn't much bigger than an overgrown closet with a bench to sit on, a rod overhead to hang clothes on, a bathroom you could get into if you weren't overweight, and a mirror with lights. No Sheri. Clem knew that she wouldn't be here; Sheri wasn't big enough to throw a temper tantrum and get away with it. Be on the set and do what you're told or there are five hundred just like you to replace you.

At the Sunflower, she called Sheri's room from the lobby and let the phone ring twelve times, then she took the elevator to the third floor and banged on the door of three-eighteen.

Heart ticking away like mad, she tried the knob. It turned

under her fingers. The room was dark. Holding her breath, she hit the light switch.

She choked on the air in her throat.

Sheri lay on the floor. Knife in her back. Blood. Looked different from the fake stuff. Dark, and sort of thin and black around the edges. It puddled out—the smell—

Oh, God. Nausea tickled her throat. She gagged, coughed. She backed against the door, swallowing hard.

Hand against her mouth, she turned and hurried down the hallway. Oh, God, let me get to my room. Please let me make it to the bathroom. Fumbling for her key, she shoved the door open and reached the toilet just in time.

Cupping her hand under the tap, she rinsed her mouth, then pawed through the bottles on the counter until she found mouthwash. She swirled it around and spit it out.

Stiff-kneed, teeth chattering, she went to the bedside table and picked up the phone.

RED. Laura my beloved. The universe is red. You belong to me. We are as one. It's his fault. I need the gun. I missed the opportunity. Your destiny is mine. The way will be shown to me. The universe will be dark. We'll be together. The knife is here. The silver blade is ready. The spirits are getting tired of waiting.

He needed another opportunity. When it came, he needed to be ready. Before the universe turned black. If that happened, Laura would choke on evil spirits and suffer a painful death.

Go deeper into the trees.

He looked at the boat that held Laura and heard it again. Go deeper into the trees.

He understood.

Lure the cop into the woods and then— His fingers curled around the knife in his pocket.

YANCY, propped against the leaning trunk, one knee bent, thought if he took up whittling that would lend a certain bucolic note of local color. He could do bats. That would be fitting and his mother would be thrilled.

The AD rushed toward him and Yancy straightened. Linsel had to be the skinniest human being still breathing; his black T-shirt that hung from chicken-bone shoulders and black shorts with wide legs didn't help. The poor guy's personality bordered on the average houseplant.

"Problem?"

"There's somebody too far back in the trees." One skeletal arm pointed. "Fifer wants you to get rid of him, so he doesn't bumble into the shoot."

Yancy tromped through layers of rotting leaves covered with tangled new vines and low-growing plants. Earthy smells of dead vegetation mingled with the sharp tangy scent of new growth. Sunlight, filtering through leafy branches overhead, dappled the brown and green footing and provided good protective coloring for snakes.

A guy thrashed around ahead, setting off a flutter of small birds from the cottonwood.

"Hey!" Yancy loped after him, tripped over a thick vine, and pitched forward. Uh-huh. He was right up there with all those other heroes. Rambo. The Terminator. Daffy Duck. Scrambling to his feet, he looked for the guy. Gone. He slapped leaves and dirt from his pants.

"Sir?" It was quiet under the trees; river sounds were muted, breezes whispered through branches. A woodpecker went to work somewhere giving him a start.

He wandered along, weaving around tree trunks. "Sir? You need to stay clear of the filming."

What the hell? This wasn't a jungle. This was a grove of trees and broad daylight. Where was the guy? Captured by aliens? Maybe it was the guy who was the alien. Beam me up.

The woodpecker stopped. An oriole sang three shrill notes. Hairs stirred on the back of his neck. He stood still and listened. On a branch overhead, a squirrel chittered, flicked its tail with irritation, and scampered away. Something had set off the squirrel. Could the guy be hiding? Waiting to ambush him? That ash over there, when Yancy went by, would the guy spring out?

Leaves and vines rustled beneath his feet. He eased one foot over a fallen limb, lifted the other—

His beeper went off.

Oh, Jesus. Heart going a mile a minute, he hauled in a barrel of air and checked the number.

"Sir," he called out, just in case the guy was hiding behind that tree and not on Mars, "this isn't a good place to be. Copperheads inhabit the area." He added, "Don't pick up any sticks until you know they won't move."

Back at the river's side, nothing had changed that he could see. Fifer still paced; cameramen still fiddled with cameras and peered through lenses. Robin hurried by at a ground-eating trot on his way to get something from the prop truck parked on the road.

"You got a phone?" Yancy yelled at him. Robin shook his head.

"Excuse me, sir." He stepped in front of Fifer midpace.

The director focused on him blankly, and had to shift through mental gears to remember who he was.

"Borrow your phone?"

Fifer made come-here motions with his fingers without even looking around. A female, obviously attuned to his every twitch, handed Yancy a flip phone. He backed off and punched the number.

On the other end of the line the phone was picked up immediately. Nobody spoke.

"Yancy," he said.

"Oh, God, what took you so long?"

"Ms. Jones?"

"Please get over here right away," Clem Jones said.

"Are you all right?"

"No! Get—"

"Calm down. What's the problem?"

"Oh, God—"

"Where are you?"

"The hotel. Please—"

"I'll be right there. Where in the hotel?"

"Room three-oh-seven."

He flipped the phone shut and returned it, then hiked the three-quarters of a mile to the road where a line of vehicles, including his squad car, were parked along the shoulder.

At the hotel, he knocked gently at Clem's door. It opened a crack and one hazel eye, black makeup smeared around it, peered out at him. The door opened wider and a hand fastened itself to his arm and hauled him in. Inside, Clem Jones fastened herself to his chest.

He patted her back. "What happened?"

"Sheri's dead and—a knife. There's blood—it's all over and—she looks so flat."

"Where is she?"

"Her room—" Clem waved awkwardly, either indicating direction or bursting with horror.

"Room number?"

"Three...I don't know. Three-eighteen. Three-eighteen."

"Stay right here."

"You think I'm going someplace?"

Eleven doors along the corridor, he tapped at 318, waited a moment, then eased the door open. Careful to avoid stepping in blood, he went to the body, knelt, and pressed his fingertips just below the point of her jaw. He knew he wouldn't find a pulse. She felt cold and clammy; her cheek, where it rested against the carpet, was dark; her neck and jaw muscles were tight with rigor.

When he got back to Clem Jones he found her sitting on the edge of a chair almost as frozen as the body.

"Fifer sent me to get her. It's not my job. It's the second second's. I didn't want to. He yelled, she was holding things up. Get her."

"Did you touch her? Move her?"

"Are you crazy?"

Putting a hand on each shoulder, he got in her face, made her look at him. "Did you touch anything?"

"No. Yes. The doorknob."

"Then what?"

"I came back here."

"Then what?"

"I called you. You're supposed to be a cop. Don't you know what to do?"

"Just relax." Using her phone, he called in and asked for the chief. She had just left; since Parkhurst was out of this one, he asked for Detective Osey Pickett.

SIXTEEN

FOOD, Susan thought. Something good. She didn't have to won-der if there was any in the house, and claiming too hot to cook wouldn't do it. She didn't cook even when it wasn't hot; she heated in the microwave. Or gave custom to Erle's Market. The deli had wonderful things, pasta salads, fruit salads, baked chicken, barbecued—

The radio, which had been mumbling to itself, caught her at-tention. She responded.

"Osey, Chief. We have us another one of those movie people dead."

No, God damn it, no. She made a U-turn. The big puffy clouds that had been piling up all day so far hadn't come to anything, but heat lightning flickered way off to the north and there seemed an increase in humidity, if that was possible; any more and they'd be swimming through the air.

Behind sawhorses and spilling into the parking lot, the media were waiting. Television crews were fixing up lights to film their correspondents' reports, print journalists shot questions at the nearest officers, and photographers waited with their cameras ready to snap pictures of anybody who might be connected with the death. When she walked up to the Sunflower, they surged around her. Was this death a homicide? Were there any suspects? Was this homicide connected to the death of the stuntwoman? Was Laura Edwards in danger? What did Chief Wren have to say about the suggestion this movie was jinxed? That Hayden Fifer was jinxed? Susan's response was, "No comment."

The lobby was empty except for the assistant manager who seemed just this side of wringing his hands, and Officer Ellis who was guarding the door. "Elevator to the third floor, ma'am, then right. Osey asked that nobody use the stairs until he can look at them."

When she got off at three, Officer White was waiting to escort her to the victim's room.

Heavy beige drapes were pulled across the windows. Overhead, a small chandelier dripped crystal tears and four flame-shaped bulbs shined dully on the congealed blood. A large brass lamp on the bedside table was also on, suggesting the attack had taken place sometime last night.

Sheri Lloyd's body lay facedown, her darkened cheek rested on pale tweed carpet, one arm was tucked under her, the other stretched ahead as though reaching for something. Long chestnut hair fell away from her face; her legs in a tight skirt were slightly bent at the knees. A bone-handled knife with an eagle emblem skewered a bright blue tank top to her back. Blood, puddled in the hollow of her spine, had run down her rib cage and soaked into the carpet.

Susan let her eyes take in the room. The bedspread, brown and beige, was crumpled and the pillows crushed; Ms. Lloyd had lain on the bed without pulling back the spread. A white skirt and a knit shirt were crumpled on the floor. Drawers were partly open with clothes spilling out, tote bag on top of the chest bulging with contents Susan couldn't see from where she stood. A pair of high-heeled sandals and a pristine pair of white Reeboks were thrown in a corner. The armchair had clothes draped over it. Not compulsively neat, Ms. Lloyd.

"She's been dead twelve to eighteen hours," Osey said. "She's cold, rigor still present, the blood's pretty much coagulated."

"You notified Dr. Fisher?"

"He's on the way."

Owen Fisher, even if he were just sitting down to dinner, would cheerfully leap up and gallop over. He was a man who deemed his profession his great good fortune; he probably sprang out of bed while it was still dark so he could get a head start on the day.

"Where's Yancy?"

"With Clem Jones in three-oh-seven."

"She found the body?"

Before he could answer, Dr. Fisher lumbered along the corridor toward them. "Another one?"

"Afraid so."

He peered at the body and told her solemnly, "My definite opinion upon superficial examination is we can almost certainly rule out accident this time."

Pathologists have a weird sense of humor. "I'll be in room three-oh-seven," she said to Osey. "Have somebody take care of these people lining the hallway. Do you have somebody going room to room on this floor?"

"Yes, ma'am."

Yancy opened the door to 307. Clem Jones sat hunched over in a padded peach chair with wooden arms. She eyed Susan warily like a frightened child on Halloween. Her pink hair stood up in spikes; the white makeup smeared with black eye shadow made it impossible to judge accurately any degree of pallor. She held herself completely still, as though if she didn't move none of this would be real.

Susan swung a chair around and sat in front of her. "Ms. Jones, would you like some water, or maybe coffee?"

"Yeah." Clem sniffled and rubbed her nose with the back of her hand. "Coffee."

"Cream? Sugar?"

Clem cleared her throat. "Yeah." A little louder this time.

Good. At least some life was returning to her face. A slack face and a weirded-out mind didn't produce answers, and Susan wanted answers. She glanced at Yancy. He nodded and left.

To start Clem talking, to keep her mind from the horror and let it ease back to functioning, Susan asked personal questions. How old was Clem? Twenty-six. Where did she live? Los Angeles. Has she always lived there? All her life. Did she go to school at UCLA? USC. How did she happen to get interested in the movie industry? Her father was an art director, she'd grown up in the business. Did she have a boyfriend? Not really. How many movies had she worked on? Shrug, lots. Did she ever work on the same movie with her father? Small shake of her head. Was her father working on this one? Another shake of her head.

After a soft tap on the door, Yancy came in bearing a tray,

with coffeepot, cream, and sugar. Bless him, he'd brought two cups. It might be a long time before she could get around to food; a little caffeine would help.

Taking the tray, she set it on a table and poured two cups. "Tell me about this afternoon." She added sugar and cream to one and handed it to Clem.

Clem held the cup against her chest with one hand under it, as though it were a puppy that might wriggle away. "She was on the floor when I went in," she whispered.

"What time was that?" Susan sat back down, keeping herself where Clem would focus on her.

"I don't know." Clem gulped hot coffee.

"Give me a guess."

"She was supposed to be on the set." Clem started breathing hard.

"Take it easy," Susan said. "Just take your time."

Clem took smaller sips. "Fifer had the second second doing something, so he yelled at me."

"Second second?"

"Second second assistant director. I called Sheri's room and she didn't answer so I went out to base camp and checked her honey wagon room, even though I knew she wouldn't be there."

"How did you know?"

"Fifer was getting ready to chop off heads. Oooh." Clem turned slightly green, clapped a hand over her mouth, and rushed to the bathroom. Sounds of retching could be clearly heard. The toilet flushed, water ran, and Clem came back patting her face with a towel.

"Sit down," Susan said. "Take it easy."

Clem sat and breathed quickly and shallowly for a few moments. "And I came back here. Something was wrong or she'd be on the set. I mean, if she wasn't there, she'd be having a tantrum and we'd hear about it. She wouldn't just—she'd be screaming to everybody and—I knocked on her door and—"

"Was the door locked?"

Clem shook her head.

"Was the light on?"

"I don't know. Yeah. No."

"Which?"

"On."

"You're sure?"

"Yeah. It gleamed on the blood—like a one K—"

"One K?"

"Light. Like a scene—kinda like from *Lethal Promise?*" Clem rubbed her face with the towel, removing much of the mess of white makeup and black mascara and further smearing around the rest. "Except the blood wasn't red enough. I thought—I thought Fifer's gonna yell about this and make them do it over. It doesn't look at all realistic. I had no idea."

"No idea about what?"

"They were so flat. Dead people. Flat—like, like—I don't know."

"What did you do yesterday evening?"

Clem pressed the towel hard against her cheeks, pulling them down and distorting her eyes. She looked like a sad clown. "What?"

"Where were you yesterday evening?"

"After wrap, you mean? Here, I think. Dinner in the coffee shop. A drink out there on that, that—" She waved her hand.

"Where was Sheri?"

Clem shrugged. "In her room. I don't know. Later she came out. She was miffed at Fifer. Saying something about she'd show him. She's not really all that swift. I didn't listen."

"What about her family?"

"We weren't buddies. I don't know anything."

"Who else was out there last night?"

Clem squeezed her eyes shut. "Robin." A tear seeped under a closed eyelid and trickled down her face.

Susan pressed a tissue in her hand. Clem took it and blew her nose.

"Who else?"

"I don't know. Some guy. Oh, and a woman."

"Describe them for me."

"The guy was medium. I don't know. He was kind of on the edge."

"What do you mean?"

"I don't know. Creepy."

"What did he look like?"

Clem's mouth turned up in a quirky smile. "Oh, wow, you're asking an awful lot." She shifted from side to side, and leaned her elbows on the chair arms. "Just a guy. Thirties? Maybe brown hair."

"Tall? Short? Fat? Thin? Skin color? Eye color? Distinguishing marks?"

Clem tugged on a tuft of pink hair. "You ever think of being a script supervisor?"

Susan smiled. "Not my field. Come through for me."

"He important?"

Probably not. Likely, he was just a guest who had a drink, then went innocently to his room. Unless he followed Sheri Lloyd and drove a knife in her back. Reason? Susan couldn't guess. A stalker, if they had one, was obsessed with a single individual. Assuming the person was Laura Edwards, why attack Sheri? He felt, somehow, she stood in his way?

Clem curled her fingers over the ends of the chair arms. "He was medium height, maybe a little stocky. That's the best I can do. Oh. He had a backpack. A little one, it was on the floor right by his feet. The only reason I noticed was he patted it now and again."

"Was anybody with him?"

"I don't think so. He was just sitting there."

"What about the woman?"

"Maybe fifty or something. Pretty. I mean for her age. She wore this long kind of skirt, white. There was something about her—I liked her and I didn't even know her."

Without looking at him, Susan was aware that Yancy, standing behind Clem near the door, tightened up like a bird dog spotting a quail.

Susan refilled both coffee cups and waited while Clem added cream and sugar. "Did Sheri mention that anyone was bothering her? That she was getting phone calls? Maybe notes or flowers?"

"Like Laura, you mean?"

"You know about that?"

"Sure. Everybody does. There are no secrets on location. Anyway, Sheri doesn't—didn't keep quiet about things. She would have gibbered on to everybody.''

''What about you? Anybody annoying you?''

Clem looked startled, then shrugged. ''Why would anybody send me flowers? I'm a nobody.''

Not in Hampstead, she wasn't, not with that hair. Susan refilled her own cup, set the pot down, and leaned back in the chair. Clem, with one forefinger made tiny rubbing movements on the chair arm, as if she were feeling for grains of sand.

''Is there anything else you can tell me?'' Susan asked.

Clem shook her head.

''Who shall I have stay with you?''

Clem propped her head on one hand and tipped it sideways to look up at Yancy. ''Him.''

Susan smiled. Sweet, handsome Yancy with his soft brown eyes and soft voice. ''Sorry. I need him.''

Clem took a breath. ''I'm okay.''

''Are you sure?''

''Yeah.''

Susan left her feeling for imaginary grains of sand. When they had gone partway along the corridor, Susan turned and faced Yancy, ''Who was the woman?'' That sounded like the lead-in to a tired joke.

He gave her a wry smile. ''My mother.''

That was unexpected. ''She's involved?''

''No.''

Stated in a nice firm tone. ''Then why are you worried?''

''She was here last night, on the Patio. Howie—the assistant manager—called me to come get her.''

''She was causing trouble?''

''The dog was with her.''

''Clem didn't mention a dog.''

''I don't know why, he's a big dog.''

''Vicious?''

''Very friendly. Sheri Lloyd complained.'' He stood squarely, feet planted at a wide stance.

''You think your mother stabbed Sheri Lloyd because Ms. Lloyd complained about her dog?''

"No, ma'am." This wasn't said with quite the same conviction.

"Then what is it?"

He hesitated. "She had blood on her hands when she got home." He spoke easily, but it came hard; ethics played hell sometimes.

"You realize I'll have to talk with her."

"Yes, ma'am."

"You wouldn't happen to know who the guy is, would you? The guy who's medium all the way around?"

"As a matter of fact, I think I might."

BROWN. Laura my beloved. The universe is brown. From the edge of the parking lot, he watched them roll the stretcher toward the ambulance. The body was all wrapped up in a black bag, like a package. They lifted the stretcher, shoved it in, and drove away. It could have been you, Laura, my darling. Don't worry. I'm coming soon. Nothing will get in the way. Until then you can be assured. She won't bother you anymore. She was a snoop, not worthy of attention. She couldn't compete with your beauty. Soon, my beloved, soon.

"HIS NAME MIGHT BE Delmar Cayliff," Yancy said.

Well now. She liked Yancy; he was easy to have around, young enough to be handy for college student problems, if necessary, and it looked like he might be coming along to being a good cop. "How do you know this?"

"A man of his description waited for the elevator with me one evening. He had a backpack that he handled like it had the combination to the safe. It had a luggage tag with his name on it."

"Do you know anything about him?"

"No, ma'am. Except he's been around watching the filming."

"Any reason why you noticed him?"

"No. Just a face I saw a lot."

They searched out Howard Gilbert in his office. When they came in he stood up from his desk and grimaced. "Don't tell me there's something else."

"I need a piece of information," Susan said.

"Oh, boy, this really isn't good for the hotel. The manager's not happy. This really isn't good. What information?"

"Have you got a Delmar Cayliff staying here?"

"I can't tell you that."

"Sure you can."

"No." Howie looked between her and Yancy and gazed somewhere in the distance. "There's privacy and confidentiality and—"

"Don't be an ass," Yancy said. "Tell her."

"Oh, God. Why do you want to know?"

"Only to talk with him," Susan said.

Howie shook his head back and forth in another "oh, boy, this isn't good for the hotel" gesture, then without sitting down tapped keys on the computer. "We have a Delmar Cayliff staying here."

"Room number?"

He sighed extravagantly. "One-oh-three."

Yancy leaned over the desk and patted Howie's cheek. Howie didn't think it was funny.

In the corridor, she asked, "Have you known him long?"

"Ever since elementary school. He's a sort-of friend."

"What kind of friend is a sort-of friend?"

Yancy smiled his enchanting smile. "The kind your mother tells you to be friends with because he's a weird kid and nobody likes him and he never gets chosen for the team and he's lonely."

Susan would have picked Howie for that kind of kid, she'd guess as an adult he was a loner. When her knock at 103 went unanswered, she tapped again. "Mr. Cayliff?" No response.

Before she could get back to check on Osey's progress, Officer Ellis said Robin McCormack wanted to see her.

SEVENTEEN

"I HEARD Sheri Lloyd was stabbed." Robin McCormack, standing at the steps to the prop truck, which was actually a long trailer, jammed his fists into shorts and directed the question at Yancy.

Susan replied in the affirmative and waited to see where this was going. The sun was riding low over the hills and mosquitoes were venturing out for the night's victims. One buzzed past her ear and she slapped at it. The ever-present wind was blowing in warm breezes.

"And the knife has a silver eagle on the handle?"

"It might be an eagle, yes."

"I think it's mine." He slapped his bare thigh leaving a bloody smear where a mosquito had landed for dinner. "I just checked. One's gone."

"Where was it kept?"

Robin, a hand raking reddish hair back, took the four steps into the trailer with two jumps.

A narrow open space ran the entire length. Tall wooden chests lined both sides, their tops covered with plastic bins and cardboard boxes, all labeled—wedding rings, eyeglasses, police hardware, earwigs, license plate screws (wherever the story was supposed to be had to have the correct license plates). "You never know what the director might call for," he said as she read labels.

He shoved a plastic basket of umbrellas closer to a phone booth and stacked a box of handbags on top of a hotel-type ice machine, handed Yancy a box of briefcases, and removed the padlock on the solid piece of metal running up the length of a stack of drawers. In the bottom drawer, knives of all shapes and sizes—curved blade, curved handle, rope handle, with silver, with turquoise, with lapis, jeweled—were wrapped in bubble packing.

"One's missing. Steel blade, bone handle with a silver eagle inset."

"These are all real?"

He nodded. "Except the gems. They're as fake as you get. But the blades are steel and I keep them sharp."

"You always keep them locked up?"

"Not always, but the truck doors are locked unless I'm here."

"You never leave without locking the door?"

"No."

"Then how did the knife get itself missing?"

"If I was going to be gone for just a second—only a second or two—I might not take the time."

"When was it taken?"

"No idea. It was there Friday morning because we used one."

"This one?"

"No." He unwrapped a black-handled knife with a six-inch blade. "But the eagle-handled knife was here then."

"How do you keep track of things?"

He looked around the solidly packed truck. "You'd be surprised how good I am at it. It's my business."

"Do you have any guns?" If a gun or two were also missing, there'd be additional worry. To use a knife, the assailant had to get close to the intended victim. With a gun that wasn't necessary.

"Yeah."

"Where are they?"

"The safe."

At the other end, surrounded by boxes, sat a tall black safe. "Who has the combination?"

"I do."

"Anybody else?"

"No."

"Blanks?"

"Yeah."

"No live bullets?"

Robin shook his head. "They're never used."

"After it's been gone over for prints, I'll have somebody show you the knife to be certain," she said. "I need to ask you a few questions."

"This hasn't been questions?"

She smiled. "A few more." She nodded at the caterer's tent. "Let's go over there."

At eight in the evening the long tables were empty. She indicated to Robin that he should sit at one and she sat across from him. Yancy stood behind him and the sunlight that angled in sketched his shadow long.

"What time did you see Sheri on the Patio?" she asked.

"I don't know. It felt late, but it probably wasn't. Putting in a long day makes you cash in early."

"Sheri was still there when you left? Who else?"

He leaned back in the folding chair and slid his feet under the table. "Some guy. Who knows."

"Have you seen him before?"

He shrugged. "Maybe."

"Where?"

"The hotel, I guess."

"What does he look like?"

He straightened, shifted from side to side, leaned forward with his elbows on the table. "Just a guy. Thirties, maybe brown hair. He was just sitting there with a glass in front of him. I was drinking club soda, that I can tell you. Nick and Laura were head to head over a table spitting at each other."

"What about?"

Robin slumped back. "You mean, this time? Who knows. They've been fighting ever since we got here. Sheri sat down with them and they both froze up with politeness." For the first time there was emotion in his voice, it was black.

"Why did you dislike Ms. Lloyd?"

"She was a pain in the butt. The only thing she had going was looks and she didn't waste them on being easy to work with. She was so dumb she couldn't cross the street by herself."

"Who killed her?"

"Hey, that's not my job, man. If you're through, I'd like to get out of here."

She let him go, stuck her notebook in her shoulder bag, and poked the pen in beside it.

"Let's go see your mother," she said to Yancy.

He was obviously uncomfortable, but he kept his eyes on the road and flicking across the mirrors, hands competent on the wheel. It was an odd situation and not one she had ever experienced before—driving your superior out to interview your mother. She knew Raina Yancy had suffered a stroke about a year ago and wasn't showing much sign of improvement. Hazel Riis, dispatcher and keeper of the flock with clucks and coos, had told her.

"She may or may not be lucid," he said.

"What is it you're worried about?"

"Uh—you mention blood and she's apt to wander off into some ballad. She knows a lot of those that deal with blood."

"You're afraid I won't be able to tell fact from fiction?"

"Uh—no, ma'am."

"Relax. I've been a cop a long time. I've even been known, once in a while, to separate fact from fancy."

"Yes, ma'am," he said, still tight as a tick.

They drove past fields of growing things, she had no idea what. Due to all the heavy rain in early spring, everywhere was lush and green. The greens were different here than in California. She didn't know exactly how—deeper, denser, richer somehow. Small hills stretched away under the endless sky, clouds, big and puffy, lazily broke apart and drifted south.

He turned down a gravel drive. Sprouting up here and there in the middle of a field of flowers were tall poles with what looked like birdhouses on top.

"Bats," Yancy said, either because he guessed her thoughts or he was accustomed to explaining. He pulled up to the garage and cut the engine. She slid from the car. Locusts were sawing away, ubiquitous sound of a Kansas summer, like the hot winds always blowing. The air smelled of honeysuckle. Yancy was looking a little apprehensive.

The screen door opened and a woman said, "Peter? Is anything wrong?" Raina Yancy, Susan assumed. A big black dog rushed out, tongue lolling.

"Nothing, Mom." He patted the dog's shoulder and then it nudged its big head up under Susan's hand.

On the porch, Yancy held the edge of the screen for Susan to enter. In the kitchen, she was introduced to his sister, Serena, slender in jeans and T-shirt, who held some sort of nonverbal communication with her brother and then excused herself, saying she'd be in her room if she was needed.

"This is my boss, Mom. Chief Wren."

Raina Yancy slid her arm through her son's, hugged it tight, and held out a hand. "I'm pleased to meet you, Ms. Wren. Let's go into the other room."

"This is fine, Mom. Sit down. She just wants to talk."

"I'll put the coffee on."

"I'll do it." Yancy steered his mother to the table.

The dog squeezed underneath and flopped down with a big sigh.

Raina smiled and Susan knew where Yancy got his sweet smile. "They don't like me using the stove," Raina said. "They think I'll set myself up in flames."

"It's happened," he said.

"Unfortunately, that's true," she admitted to Susan. "What is it you want to talk about?"

With an apologetic glance at Susan, Yancy brought two cups to the table. From the refrigerator, he took a carton of milk and poured some into a small pitcher, snatched the sugar bowl and put both on the table.

She studied Raina Yancy. Late forties, she judged. Perfect oval face, dark hair to just below the jawline. Dark eyes, clear and luminous. She was beautiful now; as a young woman she must have been stunning. Susan wondered about Yancy's father. Who was he and what happened to him?

"Mrs. Yancy—"

"Please call me Raina."

"Raina, you were at the Sunflower Hotel last night."

"Was I?" She looked at her son for the answer. "Come and sit down, love." She patted the chair to her right. "You look tired. Have you been getting enough sleep?"

"I'm fine, Mom."

"Go ahead," Susan said when he hesitated.

He pulled out the chair and sat sideways in it, then picked up his mother's hand. "What did you do at the hotel last night?"

"You think I'm nutty."

"Mom, you've always been nutty. Think about last night."

"He's right, you know," she confided to Susan.

"You were sitting out on the Patio at the hotel," he said.

"Was I?"

"Yes, you were, Mom."

"Oh dear, I don't recall—" She looked frightened.

"It's okay," Susan said. "What did you do yesterday evening?"

"I watched a movie."

"On television? What movie?"

"I usually only watch lighthearted fluff movies. This one wasn't. A woman got stabbed."

Susan felt Yancy tense. "What was the name of the movie?" she asked.

"Oh, I can't seem to remember—"

"In the movie, who did the stabbing?"

"A woman. I remember she had long blond hair."

Susan tried to get details, about the movie, about the stabber, about the victim, but got nothing. "What else did you do yesterday evening?"

"We went for a walk. Elmo and I."

The dog, under the table, hearing his name, thumped what he had for a tail.

"He likes to go out after the sun goes down, when it cools off. It's cooler today, did you notice? Much more like it should be this time of year. The heat wave's over."

Susan hoped so. Mrs. Baker had called her again today to repeat that the heat wave was because of the wicked movie people. It wouldn't cool down until they left. "Where did you go on your walk?"

"I did," Raina said as though suddenly remembering. "I went to the hotel. I sat out there on the Patio and had something to drink. Oh, what was it—?" She kept her eyes on her son as he got up to pour coffee.

"Who was there?"

"Laura Edwards and Nick Logan. Right here in Hampstead. Isn't that a hoot? Another one—I can't think of her name." She looked to Yancy for help as he set a cup in front of her. "Hair like a winter fox. Pouty expression."

"Sheri Lloyd?" Susan said.

"Yes. She didn't like Elmo. Poor Elmo, there was a man there who didn't like him either. A girl with pink hair—" Raina's voice faded out as she thought, then she said, "I talked with her."

"What about?"

"Movies, I'm sure. People who worked in the movie business." She thought, mind searching. "Clem Jones."

"Then what did you do?"

"I guess I must have come home." She sang in a clear soft voice.

> *"God give you joy, you two true lovers,*
> *In Brides-bed fast asleep;*
> *Lo I am going to my green grass grave,*
> *And am in my winding sheet."*

Susan felt goose bumps on her arms. Yancy patted his mother's hand and said, "Come back, Mom. Last night. How'd you get home?"

"We walked—no, only started. I pooped out before we got even halfway."

Susan wasn't surprised. It must be ten miles or more.

"That boy—what's his name—oh, you know, the one who works at the service station?" She looked to Yancy. "Oh, you know the one I mean."

"Kevin Murphy?"

"Yes." She turned back to Susan. "Kevin gave me a ride. He didn't mind Elmo in his car."

"How did you get blood on your hands?"

She looked at her palms, then at the backs. "Blood?

"And first came out the thick, thick blood,
And syne came out the thin,
And syne came out the bonny heart's blood;
There was nae mair within."

Raina either didn't know she'd had blood on her hands and therefore couldn't know how it had gotten there or she was deliberately sinking into vagueness. What a handy excuse, if you had something to hide. Susan drank the coffee, thanked Raina, and stood up.

"Peter—?"

"I gotta go back to work, Mom."

"Ohh, I hoped you could stay awhile."

"I'll be in the squad car," Susan said.

A minute later Yancy came out and slid under the wheel.

"Sorry," he said. He backed out and headed into town.

"Your mother is lovely," Susan said. "Does she stay by herself?"

"She shouldn't, according to my sister."

He didn't volunteer any more and she dropped it. None of her business. "Where does she get the movies she watches?"

"You're not thinking she saw Sheri Lloyd stabbed?"

"Isn't it a possibility?"

"No," he said. "You saw how she is, she's hardly coherent."

"Calm down. She's coherent. She simply can't remember things. It's unlikely. It needs to be followed up. We have a long blond-haired woman with something that could be construed as a motive."

"Laura Edwards? But—"

"I said it's unlikely. I'll put in extremely if that makes it better. Now, where does she get the movies? She owns them? Television? Video rentals?"

"My sister keeps her supplied with videos. That way, Serena hopes she'll be occupied. Look, it's not as bad as it sounds. A friend comes by in the morning and in the afternoon."

Guilt was leaking into his voice. "Yancy, I'm not making judgments here, I'm conducting an investigation."

"Yes, ma'am."

"Is Pickett's garage open this late?"

He looked at his watch. "Just barely."

"Head over there."

On Fourth Street, he pulled up to the open door of the bay at the end of the garage. At a gas pump, Kevin Murphy was checking oil for a customer. Susan and Yancy got out of the squad car and waited. Kevin slammed the hood, cleaned the windshield, and collected money, paying no attention to them beyond a sideways glance. After he'd made change and the customer drove away, he started back into the repair area. Susan called to him.

"Ma'am?" He was not quite sneering. Seventeen, high school football star, an athlete who moved with the lightness of a cat. Broad-shouldered, narrow-hipped, straight dark hair that fell into resentful dark eyes. A narrow face that would have been handsome except for the insolence that was barely hidden. A young man full of resentment, not especially of cops, or apparently even of authority, but for the entire adult world. How Charlie Pickett put up with him, she didn't know. Except that Charlie knew boys. He had five of his own, four worked with him at the garage. Osey was the youngest and a damn good detective.

"Talk to you a minute?" she said.

"Certainly, ma'am." His politeness was almost mockery.

"When did you last see Raina Yancy?"

Kevin looked at Yancy and then he looked a long time at her. He had no problem making eye contact. His self-assurance held challenge and mockery and hatred. He was not a young man any mother would like to see with her daughter.

"I saw her yesterday evening." The clear precise way he spoke was guaranteed to ruffle adult feathers, but there was nothing overt that could be pointed at, so adults were left with unfocused irritation.

"Where?"

"Mrs. Yancy and the dog were proceeding south on Massachusetts Street, approaching the city limits."

"What time?"

"Just after eleven."

No hesitation or qualifying sounds. "You seem very sure."

"Absolutely, ma'am."

"How can you be so positive?"

"The vehicle contains a digital clock."

Yancy, beside her, was getting pissed. So was she, which was, of course, Kevin's goal. She hoped Yancy kept a lid on it.

"Who owns the vehicle?"

"My father, ma'am." The guy climbing the tower with a rifle slung over his shoulder probably had the same expression. It made her pay attention.

"Did Mrs. Yancy ask you for a ride?"

"No, ma'am."

"How did it come about that you transported Mrs. Yancy and her dog in your father's vehicle?" Tiresome as he was being, she tried not to let a trace of irritation seep into her voice.

The flicker of pleasure in his dark eyes said she hadn't been successful. "She looked tired. I asked her if she'd like a ride."

"Where were you going when you saw her?"

"To see a friend."

"The friend's name?"

"He wasn't expecting me, and I decided it was too late anyway."

"Mrs. Yancy got in the car, the dog got in the car, you drove her home. Is that correct?"

"Absolutely, ma'am."

"Did you notice blood on her hands?"

For the first time, there was a hair's hesitation before he answered. She took note, but had no idea what it meant. "I had a nosebleed. She made me stop and she held a handkerchief against it."

"How'd that happen?"

"I ran into a door."

A lie. What did she have here? *Go with your instincts until you can back them up with facts.* The voice belonged to Captain Reardon, her boss in San Francisco. She took Kevin tediously through question and answer of picking up Raina Yancy, what they talked about, what time they reached her house, where he went then, what time he got home. Nothing resulted except a waste of time. Not once did his demeanor slip over into disrespect, but it always teetered right there on the edge. She had known repeat felons with less control.

"What were you doing at the Sunflower Hotel last night?"

The switch in subject didn't catch him off guard. "Who says I was there?"

"Never mind who says so, why were you there?"

"Anybody can go to a hotel. It's meant for the public."

"I see. That doesn't tell me what you were doing there."

"Do you have any reason for asking?"

He had her there. The only reason was something was going on here that she didn't understand and she wanted to find out what it was. "I'm looking for information," she said.

Mockery danced in his dark eyes. "I was working yesterday evening." He waved a hand at the garage. "I was sent over there to take care of a dead battery."

"Who had a dead battery?"

"A driver of a van used to take crew to the set."

"What time was this?"

"Eight when I left here. Eight-thirty when I returned."

A customer drove up to the gas pumps and Susan let him go. As Yancy was driving back to the hotel, she asked what he knew about Kevin Murphy.

"The Murphys moved to Hampstead last year. Kevin is the best quarterback the high school has ever had. They made state championship, and after seldom even winning a game, that's close to miraculous. The father is retired military. I heard he was a navy test pilot, and had a crash that smashed him up pretty bad."

"Mother?"

"I only know there is one."

"Why'd they come here?"

"Because this is such a great place?"

"Right."

When he parked in the hotel lot, she said, "Ask your sort-of friend Howie if Kevin's been around the hotel. Ask your movie pals if they've seen him hanging around watching."

"He's been around a lot. He was hired as an extra."

It must be because of his looks; it couldn't be his charm. "Let's go see if Delmar Cayliff, the ordinary man, is in his room."

EIGHTEEN

SUSAN KNOCKED. The room door opened.

"Yes?" Delmar Cayliff was not an ordinary man, Susan thought. Brown pants, brown shirt, medium height, medium brown hair medium length, mid-thirties, slightly stocky. All that was ordinary enough. But there was something here that set off little alarm bells. He smelled strongly of cloves—not ordinary, but not alarming. He wouldn't look her in the eye, but stared off in the distance between her and Yancy.

"Chief Wren, Mr. Cayliff." She held out her ID. "This is Officer Yancy. We'd like to ask you a few questions." She stepped forward as she spoke and he automatically moved back.

"Sure, I guess so. Is it about the actress who was killed?" His eyes strayed to the small brown backpack on the bed. The roll of clove Life Savers beside it explained the odor of cloves.

"You know about that?"

"People have been talking."

"You mind if we sit down?" Without waiting for a response, she took a chair at the small round table near the window. Yancy stood by the door.

Cayliff backed up and sat on the edge of the bed; he let one arm rest on the backpack. Those little alarm bells kept pinging. On the surface he was clean, neat, probably not wildly successful from the cut and quality of his clothes, but not unsuccessful or he couldn't afford to stay here.

"Where are you from, Mr. Cayliff?"

"Irvine. Oh, Irvine, California. You've probably never heard of it."

"You're here on vacation?"

"I suppose you could say that. A working vacation anyway. I teach history. American history. You interested in history?" Even when he asked a question, he couldn't look at her. "Fascinating. I don't understand why everybody isn't gripped like I am." A smile flicked on and off. "I've got students who actually fall asleep in class. Ha ha. Cattle trails are my interest. Every summer I pick one and go there, study the area around and the exact trail. I follow it all the way, taking note of—Well, as you can see, it's not only my occupation, it's my hobby."

"You teach at UC Irvine?"

"Yes. Did you know the Santa Fe Trail runs right near Hampstead? It goes all the way from Independence, Missouri—that's where I started—and I'm following it to the end. You know where that is?"

She was afraid she didn't.

"Santa Fe, New Mexico. William Becknell—he was a trader—opened it in 1821. They did have some trouble right around here. About 1864 Indians started attacking. The wagons would get into a circle just like you see in the movies. You'd be surprised how many things the movies get wrong."

No, she wouldn't.

"Daniel Boone, for instance, never wore a coonskin cap. But circled wagons is one thing they got right."

"Are you interested in movies, Mr. Cayliff?"

His fingers tightened on the backpack. "Only in the general way that I see one sometimes." The smile flickered on and off again.

"You've been watching the filming." She made it an accusation.

He didn't respond to her tone, simply said, "Somewhat to my surprise I'm finding it interesting."

"Sheri Lloyd, have you watched her?"

"If she's what's being filmed."

"Did you think she was pretty?"

His fingers relaxed. "Pretty, yes, very pretty."

"And Laura Edwards, is she pretty?"

"Beautiful. You have a reason for asking me these questions?"

She wondered if he had some sexual fantasy about beautiful women or thought they were evil or needed punishing. He didn't respond in any extraordinary way to the two beautiful women she'd mentioned, except he still wouldn't meet her eyes, his glance slid right past and landed somewhere over her shoulder. She wanted Parkhurst's opinion of this man. Damn it, she needed Parkhurst's help.

"You saw Ms. Lloyd last night," she said. "On the Patio. What happened there?"

Much abbreviated, he gave her the same story she'd gotten from Clem Jones and Robin McCormack. When he mentioned the dog, his breathing grew short and fast. "I don't care much for dogs."

"What else can you tell me?"

"A young person was there."

Nobody else had mentioned a young person. "Male or female?"

He shook his head. "The—uh—person was sitting way back at one side. I didn't really pay attention."

"How young?"

"Oh—teenage, I suppose."

"What was this teenager wearing?"

"I'm sorry, I simply didn't notice. I wasn't paying attention, you see."

"How did you know it was a teenager?"

He thought about that. "He had on—maybe she—shorts like they all wear, and a T-shirt. It had Wolverines in big letters and a picture of the animal."

The Wolverines were the high school football team.

"Hair color?"

"He was wearing a baseball cap. I guess that's why I thought it was a boy, but girls wear them too. Anyway, this person was writing in a notebook. Does that help?"

Susan thanked him and slung her bag over her shoulder.

"Somebody followed her out," he said as she was leaving.

"Followed who out? Ms. Lloyd?"

He nodded. "A man."

"Describe him."

"Tall. Red hair."

"Robin McCormack?" Yancy said as they waited for the elevator.

"That's the only tall, red-haired man we know of who was there last night," Susan said. "Have you any idea who this young person might be?"

"Kevin maybe? Could Cayliff be lying?"

"Anything's possible. To what end?"

Yancy's beeper sounded. She could see he wasn't enamored of the technological advancements of the telephone company.

THAT WAS SIMPLY AWFUL, Laura thought, when she left Nick's suite and trailed Mac down the hallway to her own rooms. The food hadn't been fit to eat, she couldn't even remember what it was supposed to be, they'd sniped at each other, or sat there in charged silence. He kept smoking until she thought she would choke, and drinking that ridiculous beer he always had flown in wherever he was. Dinner with Nick in the hotel had seemed better than alone in her suite. Going out was impossible. She couldn't remember the last time she'd been able to do that, people gaping at her and whispering to each other behind their hands.

Come on, Laura May. They're what make you famous. Ah, the price you pay. If you can't appreciate your fans you better get out of the business.

Yeah, right. If it just wasn't all the time.

Nick would start to talk, then she'd start to talk and it was stops and starts and stilted and careful so neither would upset the other. It wasn't like her to be concerned about upsetting anybody, but there you are, she could be nice sometimes.

Neither mentioned Sheri, and her murder was the only thing on their minds. They should have talked about her, poor little cow. How much was Nick affected? Everything was a mess. When she'd left, he'd given her a kiss with all the warmth and excitement of leftover oatmeal.

While the bodyguard checked the place, she wondered if that was an apt turn of phrase.

"Everything clear," he said. "This was slipped under the door." He held up a small white envelope. "You want me to give it to your assistant?"

"Never mind. Thank you, Mac. You can go."

Dropping it on the small writing desk, she sat down to read

the little pile of letters already waiting there. "I've seen all your movies." "I think you're wonderful." "It's so exciting that you're actually here."

She smiled, carefully folded each letter, after she read it, and stuck it back in its envelope. Her assistant would write personal replies to each and every one. Laura never got tired of them. They made her feel good all over. Okay, so she was vain and shallow, insecure even when she felt her work was good. She was never sure until it was confirmed by fans and critics. Fans liked you or they didn't. You never knew about critics. Sometimes she wondered if their reviews had anything at all to do with the movie.

She slit open the envelope Mac had handed her and unfolded the paper.

YOU WON'T GET STABBED.

Her breath caught, her heart skipped around. It took sheer force not to crumple the loathsome thing and burn it.

Okay. Calm down. Do what Ben said. Don't touch it, call the police.

The hell with that.

She picked up the receiver and punched in Ben's number. It rang and rang. Damn it, answer. She paced back and forth in half circles as far as the cord would allow. Ridiculous there wasn't a cordless phone here. She banged down the receiver and went to the little refrigerator for the bottle of white wine. She poured herself a glass.

Take a deep breath and calm down.

She tried Ben's number again, still no answer.

Okay, Laura May, what now? Be calm, be brave. She found the beeper number for that cop who was supposed to take care of things for her and punched it.

Only a minute or two went by before there was a tap on her door.

"Who is it?"

Yancy looked at Susan; she nodded.

"Police, ma'am. Officer Yancy."

The lock clicked and the door opened cautiously. Laura Edwards, a little wild-eyed, shifted her glance to Susan and her expression froze; for just an instant she looked irritated. The lady is not pleased to see me, Susan thought. She was expecting only Yancy, young and male and maybe in her mind malleable. Peter Yancy, Susan was learning, was not as malleable as he appeared.

For all Laura Edwards's look of distress she hadn't let her appearance be affected—hair artfully tousled, makeup discreet but perfect. Gold silk pants and white silk blouse with gold splashes swayed loosely but managed to cling in all the right places.

"I've been trying to call Ben," she said. "Get him for me, please."

"Is there a problem?" Susan asked.

Laura bristled, then took hold of herself and smoothed herself out. "There." She pointed to the note on the writing desk.

Susan walked over and looked at it. "When did you get this?"

"Just now. It was slipped under the door."

"Please sit down," Susan said.

Reluctantly, Laura sat on the love seat. "I want you to get Ben, please."

She surely did, she could barely stay seated. Simply to have him around? Because she thinks she can lie to him and be believed? Or could it be the lady simply doesn't like me?

"I'm sure you would, Ms. Edwards, but this is a homicide and what you've got is me. I need to ask questions."

She watched Laura consider: throw a fit, have hysterics, refuse to say a word until Parkhurst arrived? She decided on cooperation. Why, Susan couldn't guess. Fear? Playing the good citizen?

The Q and A session covered all her movements from the moment she came into the hotel this evening. Nothing startling resulted, and not because Susan didn't work at it. Laura had showered and changed and had dinner with Nick Logan in his suite, they'd ordered from room service. She'd been out of her room from seven until she came back just now.

"Mr. Logan was there the whole time?"

"Except for when he went out to get ice."

"He got his own ice?"

"Sometimes he likes to show how unaffected he is." A hint of sarcasm seeped through.

Susan went back to yesterday evening and questioned her about being on the Patio, and her encounter with Sheri. Nothing new came from that either. While answering with no hesitation, Laura Edwards was getting tired of questions and her cooperation was running a little thin.

This made Susan push harder; Laura stuck with her script, whatever it was. There was no relaxing of her guard even when Susan stood up, carefully collected the note in a plastic evidence bag, and made noises about leaving. Perhaps the lady is telling the truth. Even an actress can have a genuine emotion now and then. The lock clicked solidly behind them.

"Did you believe her?" she asked Yancy as they headed toward the end of the corridor.

"I think she's worried," he said slowly, "but she could have printed that line on the paper to reel in the lieutenant."

He wasn't Parkhurst, but he wasn't stupid.

She knocked at Nick Logan's suite. He looked a man tired after working all day, relaxing in jeans, the sleeves of his white shirt rolled up. There was no irritation on his face at seeing them, only a certain interest.

"Come on in." He gave Yancy a friendly slap on the shoulder. "Have a seat. What can I get you?"

"Nothing, thanks." She sat on the love seat opposite a flowered sofa and took in a deep breath of secondhand smoke. Ah yes.

"You mind if I have a beer?"

"Go right ahead," she said.

"Pete?"

Yancy, standing with his back to the door, shook his head. Nick in stockinged feet, a hole in one toe, padded off and returned with a bottle of Chimay and a glass. "Are you sure? It's made by Trappist monks in Belgium."

She declined again, but did wonder what the stuff tasted like.

He took a swallow and sat on the arm of the sofa. "I figured you'd be around. Fifer's got to be grateful you didn't interrupt the filming."

"Tell me what you did this evening."

He shot her a shrewd look. "Has something else happened?"

"Answer the question, please."

His story fit with Laura's except for one omission. "What reason would you have to lie, Mr. Logan?"

He flared up like a match. "You calling me a liar?"

"Are you?"

"Dinner with Laura?" Righteous indignation. "What is there to lie about?"

Dealing with these actors was exhausting. Who could tell what was real and what was acting? "You said you were here the entire time. Why didn't you mention going to get ice?"

Deep laugh rumbled. "No attempt at concealment, I assure you." He retrieved another bottle of Chimay from the small refrigerator. "I forgot," he said when he came back. "How long was I gone? Two minutes? Three? What happened this evening?"

"It's odd you get your own ice. I'd expect you would have sent a lackey or called room service. Weren't you concerned about fans?"

"The only people around are cast and crew."

That wasn't exactly true, but maybe he didn't know.

"They don't get excited on seeing me."

"Let's go back to yesterday evening."

He took a long swallow, then gave her the same story she'd heard from everybody else. Sheri was angry. When she joined them Laura got pissed. Nick himself was irritated. He mentioned Clem Jones and Robin McCormack, and Raina Yancy and Delmar Cayliff, although he hadn't known either of their names.

"I've heard Sheri Lloyd wasn't a great actress," Susan said. "So why was she hired?"

"Fifer wanted her. What the director wants, he gets. A director of his standing anyway."

"Why did he want her?"

Nick gave her a dry smile. "I'm sure you've guessed."

"He wanted to sleep with her."

"There's a Sheri in every one of his movies."

"You also had an affair with her."

"Not exactly, and to my regret."

"Enough regret to kill her when she wouldn't let it go?"

"No." Quietly said.

"How did Fifer feel about your sleeping with her?"

"He was—no longer interested." Nick chipped at the bottle label with his thumbnail. "She got ideas in her head that weren't real and—" He tipped the bottle over the glass. "She could be exasperating."

"Because she wanted love and got only sex?"

"You don't pull your punches, do you?"

"She was murdered. What kind of ideas? Marriage? She's no longer alive to be exasperating. Does that make things easier for you? Your relationship with Laura Edwards will be mended?"

He started to raise his glass, then stopped. "I didn't kill her. I felt sorry for her."

"Uh-huh. How could Fifer get away with hiring a bad actress?"

"She was okay in the right role."

"And that was—?"

"Herself. A bimbo. Not real smart. Vulnerable. Somebody you ultimately feel sorry for."

"Somebody didn't feel sorry for her. Somebody shoved a knife in her back."

"Yeah," he said softly.

Right. Couldn't be put any clearer than that. "Tell me who was on the Patio last night."

He mentioned everyone except Cayliff's young person.

"You forget anyone?"

He thought a moment, then shook his head.

"Teenager," Susan said. "Way off in the corner."

He turned his head and scratched the side of his jaw. "I didn't notice any teenager. One could have been there. I try not to look at people. That way they're not as apt to come over for an autograph."

She thanked him for his help.

In the elevator, she asked Yancy, "What do you think of Nick Logan?"

Yancy hesitated. "I like him. Except for that Trappist monk beer, which I never heard of, he seems like just an ordinary guy.

Had a hole in his sock, for God's sake. He's not even that handsome. I don't know why he's supposed to be such a great actor.''

"He's great enough that he gets paid even if this movie never gets made. And if it's washed up soon enough maybe there's still time to get the role he had to turn down. That one pays fifteen million.''

"I'm in the wrong business," Yancy said.

"Indeed.''

They took the elevator down and tracked Howie Gilbert to his office behind the registration desk. The assistant manager was looking distinctly gray around the edges.

"Who did you give Ms. Edwards's suite number to?''

"What?" He shot up. "What happened to her?''

"Nothing. She's fine.''

He deflated slowly. "You know, I think I'll be glad when they all leave. It seemed such a—so exciting, and good for the hotel, but all this—''

"Ms. Edwards's suite number?''

"Room numbers are not given out," he recited primly. "And that goes for suites. Especially suites. Never.''

Of course, just about anybody on the staff would know: housekeeping, room service, security, registration. How many spouses and friends would they have told?

After reminding Yancy to keep his mouth shut with the media, she told him to take himself home.

The media pack launched an attack on her when she came out. What kind of sentence would she get for backing them off by firing a round or two?

GRAY. Laura my beloved. The universe is gray. The spirits are getting impatient. When you know, you'll understand. If I don't get the gun, the spirits will be angry. They'll turn against us. I'll follow him until the opportunity comes. When the time is mine, I'll get it. He won't escape. I'll be there. When the world is dark.

NINETEEN

IN THE PICKUP, Susan made a note to have Osey question hotel staff, ask if any unauthorized individual was seen, if anyone had been asked to slip a note under Ms. Edwards's door. Media people had been known to pay for information, but if a large amount of money passed hands, it was very unlikely anybody would admit to anything.

She stopped at the McDonald's drive-thru and got a burger, fries, and a Coke. Popping fries in her mouth, she drove back to the department, entered by the rear door, and took the hallway to her office. The place was quiet this time of night. She flipped the light, hung her shoulder bag on the coat tree, and dropped her very late dinner on the desk. Mouth open, burger halfway there, she was aware of someone in the doorway.

"Hazel, what are you doing here? You should have left hours ago."

"Marilee's having baby-sitting problems. I said I'd cover until she found somebody." Hazel looked pointedly at the hamburger.

"One word and I'll fire you," Susan said.

Along with being dispatcher, Hazel was mother hen of the department, affectionately and behind her back called Rhode Island Red. Susan always assumed it was because Hazel had auburn hair; only recently had Osey told her a Rhode Island Red was a chicken.

"Idle threats," Hazel said airily. She ticked off on her fingers. "Cholesterol, fat, salt, caffeine—"

"The phone is ringing," Susan said. She bit off a chunk of cholesterol and fat and washed it down with a slug of caffeine. While she chewed, she searched out a pen under the folders and message slips, then she flipped pages in her notebook. To her list of suspects, she added Kevin Murphy, high school football star and summertime mechanic, and teenager, with a question mark—as in, could he be Cayliff's young person?

She tore off another chunk of the burger. He had a lot of anger packed away in a well-muscled body. Put him, for just a minute, in the shoes of a stalker. Would they fit?

They might. Sixteen, unbalanced by hormones like all teenagers. He excelled at football, a violent game and violence can spill over into the rest of life.

She leaned back and tried to remember what she knew about stalkers. Not much. She'd never worked a case with one. They were mentally or emotionally disturbed—paranoia, manic depression, schizophrenia. Did this fit Kevin? They often deluded themselves that the victim had a romantic interest in them. They were socially isolated. A football star? Possibly. Withdrawn, a loner. Again, possibly. She also thought they were usually unattractive. This didn't fit Kevin. He was very good-looking. That impenetrable air of control that she found so hair-raising would attract teenage females.

She didn't know enough about him, and made a note to ask Osey to check into Kevin Murphy.

What about Sheri Lloyd's murder? With a knife in the back, there was no question of accident. How was it connected with the death of the stuntwoman? How how how? Sheri Lloyd stood in the way of the stalker getting to his victim? Not that Susan could see, but she couldn't see into the mind of a psychotic. Could they have a killer and a stalker? Two crimes, two separate perps? An imported killer and a homegrown stalker? She read her list of suspects for Kay Bender's death. Assuming that the intended victim was not Laura, but Kay, why ice Sheri Lloyd?

Fifer: killed Sheri because she was causing trouble with his superstar Laura and/or Nick. He had to save his movie and Sheri was a thorn that could burst his expensive bubble.

Laura: jealous because Sheri was getting it on with Nick.

Nick: Sheri was causing trouble with true love Laura.

Robin: prop master, the knife came from the prop truck, thought for whatever reason Sheri killed Kay. This would tie it up. Sheri killed Kay (reason unknown) and then Robin killed

Sheri in revenge. Dust off your hands, inform the media, and go home.

Bah. Susan tossed her pen on the desk, leaned back, and sipped the Coke.

Raina: out of the mists in her mind she was confused about being in some murderous old ballad. Very weak, and Susan hoped it was as weak as it sounded for Yancy's sake.

Then we have the unknown stranger brought to town by the lure and glamour of the movie being filmed here. A stalker, a psycho, a serial killer.

She was going round and round and getting nowhere and it was making her furious. She had the same suspects for Sheri Lloyd's murder that she had with the stuntwoman's death. All she'd done was mix around motives and throw in unknown variables.

She needed a break here. Why couldn't she see one? Damn it, she wanted to discuss this with Parkhurst.

As though she'd conjured him up, he appeared in the doorway. Angry, he looked dark and dangerous; eyes cold, small muscle ticking in his jaw.

"Hi," she said.

Back straight, he sat in the wooden armchair in front of her desk. In normal circumstances, he paced until she got nuts and told him to sit, whereupon he slid low on his spine with his legs under the desk. Not since she'd first arrived had he been so still and controlled.

"There are two points of view," he said. "It's an abomination or an honor, depending on your background, education, religious leanings, and/or sense of humor."

She looked at him blankly. "What are you talking about?"

"The mad painter."

There was an edge to his voice that she didn't like. It was challenging and she didn't want to pick it up. This bit of garbage-can nonsense didn't stack up against murder. She knew it and he knew it. He was pointing out that ability and experience were being wasted here.

She grimaced and rubbed her forehead. "Have you got anywhere?"

He took out his notebook, flipped it open, and recited in a flat voice. "So far there have been eight female nudes and six male. One fish. Opinions differ as to whether the fish is supposed to be a carp or a salmon..."

She broke out laughing.

"Comach Meer, however, says that art is not merely representational..." He laid a folded newspaper on her desk.

Comach Meer, owner of a local art gallery, had gotten his picture in the *Hampstead Herald*. Kneeling, finger extended, he was quoted as saying, "There is talent here, but undisciplined." He went on to list flaws in the latest garbage-can art.

She tossed the paper to one side. "Do you know who it is?"

"Not yet. But I'm closing in. I deduce that it has to be somebody with paint on his hands."

"All right," she said. "We still have to find him."

"Yes, ma'am. I've been trying to spot a pattern. In the areas he hits, the days of the week, the length of time between hits. Nothing's showing. I escorted Professor Black of the Emerson art department out to take a look, to see if the latest painted can brought to mind the style of a particular student."

"And?"

"The work is vaguely reminiscent of Matisse. He agreed with Meer. Some talent, undisciplined. No student came to mind."

"So what are you suggesting?"

"We're not going to catch this guy except by accident. Not by fancy footwork. Unless you want to mount a gigantic stake-out."

She looked at him.

Parkhurst unbent a little. "He'll get tired and quit. He'll pick the wrong garbage can at the wrong time and get shot. We'll stumble across him on the way to something else."

Parkhurst was right, but when citizens call and make complaints, when the mayor calls and makes threats, the chief of police makes a show of being on top of the situation.

"Your point is?"

"I talked with Laura last night."

This was what she'd been expecting. The chair squeaked as she leaned forward. "And?"

"She wants my help."

"Two bodyguards and the Hampstead PD aren't enough for her?"

He said evenly, "I'm obliged to help."

"What is it you want from me?"

"You can put me on suspension. Or I can resign."

"Would Laura want that? Your throwing out your career?"

A dry smile crossed his mouth. "She wouldn't see it that way." He pushed himself up. "You want me to quit?"

Captain Reardon had once told her, "I stand behind my men."

"What about women?" she'd asked. "In case you haven't noticed, I'm a—"

"Yeah, yeah. Her too. Unless that's sexual harassment. In which case I wouldn't."

Stand behind your men. She hadn't been chief here long, a year and a half roughly, but long enough to feel Parkhurst wouldn't kill or try to kill his ex-wife, and to believe he wouldn't cover up a killing by somebody else.

"Would you give me a week to clear this?"

He took so long in answering she began to get queasy.

"Three days."

That might not be enough. "Parkhurst," she said as he was leaving, "were you at the Sunflower last night?"

Anger flashed through his dark eyes, gone immediately leaving them flat and blank.

"Don't," she said sharply.

"Ma'am?"

"React like a suspect. Just tell me."

"I was not at the hotel last night." His words were evenly spaced and clipped off at the ends.

Oh, bloody hell, she shouldn't have asked. She didn't know if she believed him.

TWENTY

THE SUN, a great red ball, rose over the horizon, streaks of pale light shot through the dark, birds rustled and twittered in the trees. A silent figure in a long coat kept to the shadows as he wound through the woods. A searching stream of light struck silver from something in his hand. On a rise above, a rider on horseback sat motionless, black against the pink and lavender light of the rising sun.

"Cut," Fifer said. "Beautiful, ladies and gentlemen, just beautiful."

Good thing, Yancy thought. Even Fifer couldn't get the sun to come up over and over until he was satisfied. Though, he might have tromped everybody out here day after day until he got what he wanted.

"Yucky, yucky," Clem mumbled to herself.

"What?" Yancy said. The scene had looked very artistic to him.

Fifer, the cameras and crew—strange shapes moving around in the dark—had set up, stumbling and cursing and had all been waiting for Fifer to get the moment when the sun came over the hill.

"Hokey," Clem said, far enough away that Fifer couldn't hear. Her bib overalls hung sacklike over a red tank top so tight Yancy wondered how she could breathe.

He'd thought there would be some acknowledgment of Sheri Lloyd's murder, but Clem had used her best face of scorn when he'd mentioned it.

"What will Fifer do about her role?" he asked.

"Fortunately, most of her scenes were already shot," she said. "For what's left he'll cut in footage of earlier pieces, use long shots, and improvise. You know, somebody else, just hands, shoulder, back of the head, that kind of thing. Same hair, same clothing. Just no close-ups on the face.''

Without a word, Fifer took off through the field toward the road about a half mile away where his town car waited to take him to the Lockett mansion. Clem was left with the crew that had to hassle equipment half a mile to the vehicles. With a lot of swearing and grousing, they managed.

''You look like shit,'' Clem said when they were inside the mansion.

''Little sleep.''

''Take a nap.''

''What, and miss all the excitement?'' The story line still eluded him, but he'd figured out the layout. Laura Edwards's character lived in the mansion that had belonged to her father; he had been killed in such a way that it looked like an accident— broken his neck in a fall from a horse. Josiah's barn was part of the property and it was all adjacent to the river. She had come back for the funeral. Nick Logan's character was a local cop she'd gone to for help because the bad guys were trying to kill her. Why wasn't made clear. Local cop was the only one, of all the people she talked to, who believed her. Or maybe he didn't believe her, only wanted to get next to her.

Currently, they were filming an indoor scene, or interior to be correct. Hero (Nick Logan) and heroine (Laura Edwards) were in the kitchen. It was late at night—this was apparent from the black duvetyn tacked over the windows—and she was fixing a snack. The kitchen had been repaired until it looked shiny bright and contained nothing but the newest and best—ovens, refrigerator, stove top, and fancy wood cabinets. One wall had been removed to accommodate the film equipment.

All the hot lights and all the people made for a room with no air flow and no oxygen. It was unbelievably stuffy. Fans or air-conditioning weren't possible, they made noise. The temperature was a hundred twenty degrees. Everybody, including Yancy, was dripping sweat. Hell couldn't be worse.

''I can't make sense of this movie,'' he said to Clem. Trying to track the plot was something to use the center of his mind for while the edges all around worried whether his mother had stumbled into a homicide.

"It doesn't need to, it's about Laura wiggling her ass."

God had been more successful with the sunrise than Fifer was with this scene. Take after take went wrong. Laura flubbed her lines, then Nick came in late on a pickup. Then it was going great and one of the crew dropped a hammer that made Laura jump. Then a camera jammed, then the sound was wrong and after that the lighting was off. Once everything was going perfectly until Laura sneezed. Everybody broke up.

"Cut," Fifer said. He spoke quietly to Laura, she nodded. He said something to Nick, then went back to his position behind the camera. "Let's try it again."

"Roll cameras."

"Speed."

The young woman with the slateboard said, "Scene ninety-two, take nine," and clapped it.

"Action."

The actors tried to figure out how to get through the night without getting killed. Take nine did it. Also take fifteen. At that point, Fifer called a lunch break; everybody split. In a hurry.

The caterer had set up in a room on the first floor, the original purpose of which Yancy couldn't figure. Library maybe, but there were no bookshelves.

A chicken sandwich and bottle of foreign water later, he stayed on his feet by moving; if he stopped he'd be gone. It was very odd to see one room all fitted out with plush furniture, thick carpets, knickknacks, sculptures, pictures, and fresh flowers, and the next was bare with cracked plaster, spiderwebs, and dirt.

Up the staircase and at the end of a hallway, voices came from the corner room. Nick Logan and Fifer were inside. Only half the room had been completed; the far end had a highly polished wood floor, floor-to-ceiling bookshelves filled with books, burgundy leather chairs around a long wooden table, and a large, highly polished wooden desk. This was the office of the head honcho in a megabucks company. In his hand, Nick had pages of the latest script changes.

He scanned them, mumbling as he did so. He put in pauses

and gestures, walked the length of the room, and leaned over the desk.

"Nick," Fifer said quietly, "this is a cop who's been framed for murder. They're tired of him bothering them, they want to get rid of him."

Nick nodded. He read the script again, then went through the scene speaking the lines carefully, using the pauses and gestures, shifting his weight and building anger. Then he did it again.

The concentration of effort showed. Yancy began to appreciate why Nick was considered a good actor.

In the afternoon when Fifer shot the scene, a rich powerful man sat behind the desk. Yancy leaning against a wall hoped he wouldn't drop over asleep and ruin the take. Nick went through the lines and moved step by step while the lighting was set up.

When Fifer got to the actual filming, Yancy felt he could do the scene himself. Nick's voice jolted Yancy wide awake. It carried such raw emotion that hairs stood up on Yancy's arms. As Nick stalked the man with white hair, every bit of him yelled *killer,* no matter how furiously he cried, "Frame up!"

The menace in his face sent the CEO cowering back. At the scene's finish, the room was absolutely silent.

Two ticks went by and then Fifer said, "Beautiful, Nick."

Beautiful, Yancy echoed in his mind and was left with the feeling Nick Logan was capable of murder if the stakes were high enough.

BLUE. Dark blue. Laura my beloved. The universe is dark blue. I'm coming. Just be patient. I'm following him. The universe will provide the right moment. I'll be ready. The gun belongs to me.

THE NEXT DAY was taken up by love scenes with Nick and Laura, both half naked, tumbling around in bed. Yancy wondered how two lovers felt portraying make-believe lovers with a roomful of people looking on. Or two ex-lovers who were feuding playing current lovers. It boggled the mind. These two did it with a lot of electricity.

By the time Fifer called wrap, it was nearly seven o'clock. Yancy was just as quick to speed off as the rest of them. A fourteen-hour day that started at five a.m. made quitting seem a fine idea.

With escape in mind, he put the squad car in reverse, had an arm over the seat back, and was looking out the rear window when he heard Clem Jones call him. Black gauze draped her from shoulders to ankles like a shawl, she was a costume who couldn't find a party.

"Hey." Both hands gripped the open window. "Would you do something for me?" A ragged note under her words didn't sound like the usual nasty Clem.

He didn't look at his watch. "If I can, certainly."

"Take me someplace for dinner. Someplace I won't be recognized."

With her appearance she'd be recognized everywhere. For a full second, he considered saying no. Then duty prevailed, it was his job, she looked right on the edge, and besides, he felt sorry for her. He tried to come up with a place that would be dark and empty.

"Please," she said, apparently thinking he was about to refuse, which with Serena waiting he'd certainly like to do. She wouldn't be happy when he was late again.

He got out of the car, went around, and opened the passenger door for her.

"I knew I could count on you. Gentleman to the core."

He sighed. "You know a whole hotel full of people. You could get any one of them to take you to dinner."

She slid in, he closed the door and went back to the driver's side. "What would you like to eat?"

"It doesn't matter. I'm not hungry."

Right. The Best Little Hare House in Kansas was loud and full of truckers. She'd probably start a riot. Poppy's Pizza? A student hangout. And she'd probably want something like kiwi and squid pizza so she could sneer when they didn't have it. The Blind Pig? He got it, Perfect Strings. He made a right, cut through town, and got on the Interstate.

"Everybody's looking at me," Clem said darkly when they walked in.

"Nah." Of course, she was right. Locals didn't see very many people with purple hair decked out in black gauze and white face paint. Nonlocals were media folks and they were on the lookout for somebody like her. This place had been a mistake.

A waitress with a long black skirt seated them in a booth and handed them each a menu.

"I need to make a phone call," he said.

"You need somebody's permission?"

"You need to change your attitude or I'll leave you right here."

"Sorry." She opened the menu and stuck her face in it.

She really was feeling low. Sorry wasn't in her vocabulary. He found the phone and called his sister.

"Let me guess," she said. "You're not coming. You have to work."

"I'll be a little later is all."

"Sure."

"I'll be there as soon as I can."

"Sure."

"Espresso," Clem said with disgust when he slid into the booth.

"What did you want? Moonshine?"

"Yeah. Local color."

"Wrong color. You're sixty years too late."

She asked the waitress for a glass of wine. He ordered iced tea.

"You don't even drink?" Clem sneered.

"Shove it."

"You aren't your usual sweet self. Phone call go badly? Who was it? Girlfriend?"

The drinks arrived and he took a gulp. "Why do you do that?"

"What?"

"Deliberately irritate people."

"Oh, that. It's just my personality. It goes with funny faces." She crossed her eyes and made her mouth go up and down like a retarded fish.

He smiled. "Good for a laugh, and it keeps people standing on one foot."

"What?"

"They never put the other one down to get a step closer."

"What are you? Some kind of closet psychiatrist?" She glared at him, started to make some smart remark, then just sat there with her priorities all confused.

"Want to try a little dinner talk? Did you go to California to get into the movie business?"

"We call it the industry. I'm an only child. My mother was a housewife. They don't make them much anymore. You know, at home baking cookies when you get there from school. Dad out in the big world earning a living."

When the waitress came for their order, Clem asked for another glass of wine.

"What do you want to eat?" he said. She looked on the way to getting drunk and he wanted to get food down her.

She picked up the menu. "I don't know. Anything."

"Bring her spaghetti and meatballs," he said.

"I'm a vegetarian."

"Bring me spaghetti and meatballs. Bring her spaghetti." He handed back the menus.

"What did your father do?" He eyed the media people. So far none had approached.

"Movies. What else?"

"Actor?"

"Art director."

Before she finished answering his question about what that was, big platters of spaghetti arrived with Clem's wine and a refill of iced tea.

"Did you ever want to be somebody else?" Clem poked a fork at her spaghetti.

"Like who?"

She shrugged. "I don't know. Anybody who seems to have it all in control." She broke off a chunk of bread and crumpled it on her plate. She sipped wine. "Life's a bitch and then you die." She started to laugh and it got caught somewhere.

"Were you a close friend of Sheri Lloyd's?"

"No. She had a hard time when she was growing up. I know that because she was always wanting to 'dialogue.' Get it out in the open. Huh. She was always trying to be somebody else, because her life was so yucky. She wasn't very smart."

Clem's eyes got blurry; she pressed the heels of her palms against them as though to hold back tears. "She probably didn't even know why."

Reporters at the next table were comparing information. One asked, "Did you get a picture of the hotel room?"

"No. Cops wouldn't let me in. I got an interview with a local though. She said the death was God's punishment. Have you ever noticed the people on God's side like lots of blood with His punishment?"

Clem placed her fork on her plate, folded her napkin carefully and placed it neatly beside her fork, and said in a very soft and careful voice, "I have to get out of here."

He took one look at her, beckoned the waitress, and mimed scribbling on his hand. When the check came, he threw money down, got up, and took her elbow. She held herself totally stiff, as though one misstep and she'd shatter like fine china. He steered her to the squad car and helped her in.

"To the hotel?"

"No. Drive."

With longing regrets for his spaghetti, he drove north and kept going. The sky was getting darker, stars were beginning to pop out and the moon, just past full, was covered by thin clouds. He took back roads, past barbed-wire-fenced fields of wheat and milo, over easy hills and down to the river at a spot three miles below where they'd been filming. He stopped and cut the motor.

For a second quiet took over, then sounds filtered in, the rush of water, the *tick-tick* of cooling metal, and the rustle of wind through the trees. The water, a dark slick endlessly moving, reflected a veiled moon, and minutes later a bright moon when clouds slid on. His mother always said this spot was magic, a place of healing. He didn't know about healing, but it did provide a spot to catch up and regroup, gather the wherewithal to carry on.

Clem sat motionless, looking down at the water. Abruptly she hit the door handle and jumped out. She moved so fast, he was left scrambling and cursing. If she fell, hurt herself—

She simply stood on the bank gazing up at the night sky. "She was just a joke to them, those reporters. They just—" Clem shook herself like Elmo after a bath. "I didn't even like her, but at least I knew her—" She looked at him and smiled, a crooked little smile of sadness.

In a second misery took over and she wrapped her arms around his neck, gulping and booing all over his uniform shirt. He let her sob, didn't say a word, didn't give encouraging pats on the shoulder. When she was done, she'd be mad at him, but right now she needed something to cling to and he obliged, holding her tight to let her know she wasn't alone, but not intruding on the spasms of damp misery.

When it ended, she was quiet with her arms around his neck, face on his chest, leaning heavily against him, all energy spent. Occasionally a ghost of a hiccup escaped. The night sounds crept around them, tree leaves tossed as the wind picked up, the heedless river rippled on. There was an eerie cry of an owl, the whine of mosquitoes, and the rustle of small hunters in the low ground growth.

TWENTY-ONE

WIND BLEW IN from the north pushing a bank of clouds and bringing the temperature down so fast Yancy could almost feel it drop. Rain was coming. He could smell it. Wind whipped through the Cherokee's windows as he goosed the accelerator to take the hill, trying to catch up for being two hours late. Lightning flickered behind the clouds, too far away to hear thunder, making the radio crackle.

As soon as the Cherokee's nose hit the driveway, Serena appeared in the doorway, a silhouette against the kitchen light. "I was afraid you wouldn't come."

"I told you I'd be here." Heavy lazy drops slapped down as he trotted to the house; they felt good on his face and arms. The rain wasn't ready yet; it would take its own good time.

"You've also been known to call and say you can't make it."

"I'm here. Go."

In the dark living room, his mother sat at the window with Elmo at her feet. When he bent down to kiss her cheek, the dog extended a friendly poke with his muzzle.

"Peter." Her fingertips gently ran down his cheek.

"Don't you want some light?"

"I suppose." The sudden light made her blink. "You look tired."

"It's been a long day." He jerked off his tie and unbuttoned the top button.

"You and Serena have had a lot to cope with over the years."

Dropping to the couch, he rested his head back. "What are you talking about?"

"I wasn't exactly a conventional mother."

"That's true."

She was silent for a long moment. "I've been thinking—trying to think. It's so hard when I can't concentrate. A few seconds and then my mind—skitters. Remember when you used to skip rocks on the pond? It's like that. Jumping around so I never get anyplace. Frustrating—''

He pulled himself forward and leaned his arms on his knees to study her face—tears glistened in her eyes. "Hey," he said softly. "What's wrong?"

"I'm sorry, Peter. All those years—when you were little, you and Serena. I'm sorry it was so hard for you. I was selfish. When you're young, you don't think. I never had any relatives. My parents died, and then I didn't have any family at all. I decided to make my own. I never thought how hard it would be for you and Serena."

Elmo, hearing the sad tinge in her voice, whimpered and put his head in her lap. She stroked his ears and eyebrows. "It's still hard for you."

"What are you talking about?"

"Your crazy mother, that's what I'm talking about. I don't know how I could have been so selfish."

"I've always been proud of my crazy mother." For the most part that was true.

She smiled. "Well, Serena hasn't."

"Girls are more delicate."

"Both of you put up with so much. Don't think I don't know."

"We had everything we needed." Except for food, he thought, and some way to fit in with other kids. That was hard, being different, being laughed at. It got him in a lot of fights, which she never could understand, but there were things he had that they didn't. Through her eyes, he was given magic. He had Shakespeare for breakfast, and flowers unfolding in the moonlight, saw birds and animals living lives of heroism.

"Will you take care of Elmo, Peter? I wouldn't want anything to happen to him."

"Nothing's going to happen to Elmo."

"Promise?"

"Yes." This mood worried him. She'd always been loony, but she was happy with it, not despairing like this. "Don't worry."

"Poor Peter. You always had to take care of things."

"Mom, what—?"

She dropped her hand over the arm of the chair and Elmo laid back down, planting himself just under her fingertips. "He's been restless this evening. I don't know what's bothering him. He keeps pacing around, and barking."

Her mood, Yancy thought.

"Tell me what happened in the movie business today," she said.

He gave her an account of his day, starting at five a.m. at the river.

"The actress who got killed—I can't remember her name. Who killed her?"

"No solution yet. The chief is walking around with fire in her eyes and ice in her voice."

"What's the name of the movie?"

"*Lethal Promise*. Don't ask what it's about because I don't really know."

"A promise that shouldn't be made? Which you should never do, by the way. I hereby absolve you of any promise which shouldn't have been made. Except the one about Elmo."

"I'll keep only promises that need keeping."

She smiled. "You're a good boy, Peter. You deserved better, you and Serena. I love you and your sister more than life itself. I didn't know— Only looking back do I realize—"

Her voice was so thin with sorrow he wondered if she were seeing a particular memory.

"Don't look so worried, Peter. I'm all right. Anyway, as all right as I ever get."

An echo of his own voice resonated in these words and he felt like he maybe shouldn't be so flippant.

She kissed him, squeezed his hands, and said she should get herself to bed. He kicked off his shoes and stretched out on the couch, trying to figure out what her regrets had been all about. An hour later something woke him.

He swung his feet to the floor and rubbed his grainy eyes. His teeth felt like green fuzz. Elmo barked. Yancy plodded into the kitchen where Elmo had his nose against the door. He barked again.

"I'm coming, I'm coming."

Head low, Elmo growled deep in his throat. Yancy fumbled with the lock, half-asleep.

The dog's toenails scrambled on the linoleum as the door opened. He shoved his muzzle through and took off, barking furiously.

Oh, Christ. What was the dumb dog after? He never learned about skunks. Yancy took off in stockinged feet, wincing and limping as gravel cut into them. The rain had fizzled to mist blown by the wind so that he had to turn his head to one side and blink as he peered into the darkness.

"Elmo!"

The dog skidded to a stop and looked uncertainly at Yancy.

"Come!"

Elmo looked in the direction of his prey, looked at Yancy, seemed undecided, then galumped toward Yancy, leaped up, and tried to lick his face.

"What's the matter with you, you stupid mutt?" Yancy grabbed his collar. "Hey! Anybody there?"

No answer but the wind fanning mist in his face. Whoever or whatever it was had fled from the hound of hell who didn't want to be dragged back inside.

Yancy limped over to the couch and stripped off his damp socks. When Serena got home an hour later, Yancy shoved bare feet, horrible as that was, into his shoes and took himself off.

The mist, thinned to not much more than an occasional fat drop from wet trees, made muzzy halos around streetlights. As he pulled in at the old Victorian, movement flickered across the side mirror. Somebody had slipped down the driveway of the house across the street. The moon glowing behind clouds and the moisture in the air put him right into a spy movie. Except for a light over the front door, the house was dark. The owners were away and he'd been asked to keep an eye out. "If this mad painter should strike," Mr. Fandor had said with an impish smile, "let him finish the picture before you arrest him."

Yancy wasn't waiting for anything. He grabbed his flashlight and loped across the street. The shiny slick drive reflected the light. "Police! Come out with your hands up."

No response.

At the far end, he swung the beam in a wide arc through the rear yard. Nothing.

Behind him, he heard a shoe slide on wet concrete. Before he could turn, somebody barreled into him. Stumbling forward, he landed on one knee, lost his balance, and fell hard on his left side. His breath caught on the sharp pain.

Oh, shit.

He'd been stabbed. And if that wasn't enough, he'd fallen on the knife and forced it in farther.

TWENTY-TWO

LIGHTNING SPLIT THE SKY. Thunder crashed. With his face against damp cement, Yancy stared at the fan of light from his flashlight a couple feet ahead where it had rolled when he'd dropped it. Whoever had stabbed him had taken his gun. He waited for a shot in the back. His heartbeat thudded in his ears.

He was clammy, shivering, but didn't seem to be lying in a pool of vital fluid. His breathing didn't crackle from blood in his lungs.

He heard a whisper, "Oh, God. Oh, God."

Heart banging nightmare time. A hulking form materialized above him, bent to pick up the flash, and ran the beam over him. He flinched; the pain made him clench his teeth.

"You got a knife in your side."

"Don't touch it!"

"No way, man. I'm not getting near it." The light lit up the lower half of Kevin Murphy's face.

"Why'd you do it?" Not coughing. Good sign, still no blood in his lungs.

"Uh-uh, not me."

"Bleeding?"

"Yeah."

"How much?"

"Your shirt soaked around the knife."

"Keys. Left pocket. Go up to my place. Call for help."

"Right." Kevin didn't move.

"Do it!"

"Right. Yeah. Okay." Gingerly, Kevin eased his hand in Yancy's pocket and, in sliding the keys out, jiggled Yancy slightly. Yancy clamped down on his back teeth.

"You got sweat all over your forehead," Kevin said.

"Phone."

"Yeah, I'm going." Kevin hesitated, then sprinted down the driveway.

Lightning split the sky, thunder rolled over it, and cold drops of rain pattered on Yancy's face.

Some minutes later—two? Five? Yancy couldn't judge time—Kevin sprinted back. "Okay," breathless, like he'd been running miles, rain dripping down his face. "They'll be right here. You all right? Oh, God, come on, man, don't die."

Somewhere in Yancy's mind there were words to respond, but they were far back. When he tried to reach them, they went farther back, until there was nothing but velvet blackness.

Overheads on the squad car bled red, blue, and red into the rain-slick street and across faces of neighbors clustered on porches. EMTs slipped an oxygen tube under Yancy's nose, started IV fluids, and kept checking his blood pressure. Parkhurst stood around like excess baggage, and kept out of the way while they strapped Yancy on a stretcher and loaded him into the ambulance. It took off with the siren competing with thunder.

"His sister."

Parkhurst turned.

Mrs. Blakeley, Yancy's landlady, held the ends of a scarf together around her chin. "Would you like me to call her?"

"I'll take care of it," he said. "Are you all right?" She looked a little wobbly. "I'll have somebody see you get back to the house."

"I'm fine. Just—" She breathed in. "Will he be all right?"

"I hope so."

The small group of neighbors, stunned by what had happened, hadn't seen or heard anything until they'd heard the ambulance. Parkhurst had Kevin Murphy taken in, then sent White and Ellis on a door-to-door. What were the chances some individual was home, knew something, and hadn't rushed out to check the action?

Windshield wipers humming back and forth, he drove ten miles south to Raina Yancy's home. Bringing bad news to a family was the worst of it. At least, the current duty wasn't bringing death. It was just past two a.m. when he got there. Using his flashlight to avoid puddles, he trotted through the rain to the rear porch.

Inside, the dog barked; outside, the light came on, and the kitchen door opened. Serena, white-faced, robe thrown over pajamas, had one hand on the dog's collar. "What happened?"

"May I come in, Serena?"

"Is he dead?"

"No, Serena. He's been hurt. He's at the emergency room."

Her knees loosened. Parkhurst grabbed for her and the dog came at him with all its teeth hanging out.

"Elmo!"

"Easy. Okay." Parkhurst released her and stepped back.

Serena caught the dog around its shoulders and let it slink under the table. "I'm sorry about that. He's been weird this evening. I don't know what's wrong with him. He's really a very sweet dog."

Sure he is. Parkhurst eyed the beast warily and guided Serena to a chair. "Your brother's been stabbed. We don't know yet what happened."

"How bad?"

"Until I get in and talk with the doctor, I don't know."

She shot up. "I have to go."

Toenails scrapping, the dog got out from under the table. Parkhurst remained sitting, not wanting to set him off again. "I'll take you. You might want to get dressed."

In confusion, she looked down at herself. "Yes. Oh, yes. Of course."

"Leaving you with me," he said to the dog.

Elmo padded over to him, placed his big head on Parkhurst's knee, and peered up at him through bushy eyebrows.

"Does this mean we're friends?"

Elmo wiggled his eyebrows. Parkhurst gave him a careful pat and the dog snuggled closer, squashing one foot with a large paw.

Five minutes later, Serena came back wearing jeans and a blue blouse, carrying a raincoat that she slipped on.

Parkhurst stood carefully. Elmo, now that they were friends

and all, just seemed sorry to see him go. "What about your mother?"

"She's asleep. I'll leave her a note in case she wakes up. First I'll see how bad—how he is and if—if I need to I'll come back and get her."

With a hand on her elbow, Parkhurst guided her to the Bronco, turned it around, and headed back to town.

Eyes fixed on the silver strands of rain caught in the headlights, Serena said, "I've been nagging at him."

It was a confession in a voice laden with guilt and remorse. A common occurrence, from a family member or loved one. Regrets. People don't seem to live with love uppermost in their lives, or they don't remember it. They remember the anger and sharp words they can't take back.

When they got to the hospital, he parked in a loading zone, careful not to block entrances or emergency vehicles, and they went inside.

"Where is he?" she asked the emergency room nurse.

"Don't worry." The nurse, Mary Mason, gave her a reassuring smile. "He's fine. We're working on him. He's in the last room."

Working on him didn't sound so reassuring to Parkhurst. He shepherded Serena in the direction indicated.

"Hey," Mary said.

He turned.

"Peter's had a big shock to the body. He's also had morphine. He is not to be pestered with questions."

"Yes, ma'am. All right if I take a look at him?"

"No. You're not family. And I know you, you'll ask questions."

"The doctor? All right if I see him?"

"He's busy. You wait right over there and I'll let you know when he's free."

Parkhurst paced the waiting area until Dr. Sheffield appeared in scrub greens and booties.

"How is he?"

"Stable."

Parkhurst crossed his arms and said evenly, "This is me you're talking to. Tell me what's going on with that officer, or I'll shoot your foot off.''

A smile crossed Sheffield's tired face. Padding to a yellow plastic chair, he plopped down. "He's fine. Young, fit, healthy. Barring complications, he'll be good as new in a day or two. He was lucky. The knife was rammed into his side approximately here." Sheffield bent his right elbow and placed a thumb against his side about halfway between waist and armpit. "The knife point hit a rib and went skating along the bone. It's cracked, either from the blow or from the force of his fall. But it didn't go straight in between ribs and puncture a lung."

Parkhurst felt his shoulders ease. "How much strength did it take? Was the assailant male?"

"I suppose a woman could have done it. He did most of the damage himself when he fell."

"I need to talk to him."

"Tomorrow."

Parkhurst stared.

"He's not Superman, for God's sake. He's a kid who's just had a hell of a traumatic insult to his body. He's not on the critical list, but that doesn't mean it's just a scratch. He's got a cracked rib and a stab wound. He's in pain, and in shock. He's also lost some blood. Give him time to rebound. This is my domain and I'm telling you to stay away from him." Sheffield started to stride off.

"A couple of questions."

Sheffield threw up his hands. "Go. Just don't stress him out."

Shirt off, rib cage wrapped, Yancy lay on a bed, Serena at his side, and a young nurse making notes on a chart. Seeing Parkhurst, he tried to get up.

"Hey," the nurse said, "you want to fall?"

"They gave me something," Yancy said apologetically.

Parkhurst could see that they had. Yancy's eyes didn't quite focus. "What happened?"

Considering the drugs, Yancy related the incident clearly.

"What did you see?"

"Nothing. A shove. Next, I'm on the ground, waiting to meet my maker. He took my gun."

"He?"

"I don't even know that."

Parkhurst collected the bloody shirt, asked the nurse to date and initial the tag after he did. He told Serena he'd have somebody take her home when she was ready.

He went back to Baylor Street to make sure Osey was working the scene and find out what the neighbors might know. He told White to get back over to the hospital and look after Yancy's sister.

ROSE. Laura my beloved. The universe is rose. He held the gun in his hand and tested the weight, looked down the sights and gently put a finger around the trigger. Beautiful. It won't be long, Laura, my sweet, my love. It won't be long. We'll be together. Forever.

IT WAS THREE A.M. when Parkhurst called the chief. Her voice was clogged with sleep.

She'd been dreaming. Down jacket blowing around her, she was running along the beach, trying to catch the man ahead. Cold wind clawed her face and whipped her hair. Her bare feet made sucking hollows in the sand, waves rolled in and washed the sand clean as they rolled out. Seagulls wheeled overhead in a gray sky, their high plaintive mews grew shrill, then dissolved into the ringing of the telephone.

Snaking out a hand, she groped at the bedside table, turned over, and cleared her throat. Rain pattered against the roof like tears she had to grieve. "Wren."

"Parkhurst." He told her what had gone down.

Dregs of sleep wiped from her mind, she told him what little she knew about Kevin Murphy. An only child, his father a navy test pilot who'd smashed himself up in an accident, now retired and moved to Hampstead with his family. Then she said, "I'll be right down."

While he waited for her, Parkhurst watched Kevin through the one-way mirrored glass. From the kid's manners, Parkhurst could have guessed the military father. Years ago, Parkhurst knew a military brat. Parkhurst was twelve, Noah a couple years older. At fourteen Noah had that same outward respect of authority, posture straight, stance at attention with adults, and the same self-assurance a kid might get from living all over the world, being transplanted every couple years and asked to survive.

Noah knew four languages, and even in English he could talk rings around Parkhurst. He called everybody *sir*, even Parkhurst's drunken, abusive father. At fourteen, he'd lived places Parkhurst had never even heard of.

They'd met one hot summer day. Noah, flying down a hill on his skateboard, was heading right into an ambush. Four local kids had decided to take the skateboard. Noah—hair short, clothes clean, matchstick arms, expensive shoes—looked like easy fun. They shouldn't have been so confident. Like a dancer, he stepped off the board, picked it up, and smashed one kid across the face. A broken nose with gushing blood put him out of commission. The other three, with just enough brain power combined to know one heavy offensive would take him, came in a flying wedge.

Parkhurst lent a hand, or rather both fists, and his knowledge of street fighting. Even so it wasn't a walk over. All six were bloody and bruised before it was finished, but by God he and Noah won. They grinned at each other, chests filled with the pride of young males walking away from battle as victors.

Skateboard under one arm, Noah turned to him. "I suppose you think we're going to be friends."

Parkhurst, nonplussed, hadn't given it a thought. "Why not?" Even in preadolescence the battlefield made fast friends.

"I don't have friends," Noah said in that tight-assed way he had of showing he was better.

"How come?"

"Who needs them?" This was said with jaw firm, shoulders back. "Keep moving. No baggage."

Wow. A motto. Like the Three Musketeers, one for all and all for one. Noah didn't need anybody. Keep moving, no baggage.

Despite Noah's motto, the distances when he was off in some country Parkhurst couldn't even spell, and the time between Noah's visits to his grandmother, they did become friends.

Years later, in a bar, late one night with both of them slightly squiffed, Parkhurst asked why.

"You were the only person who ever came into a fight on my side," Noah said. "A new school every year. You walk into a classroom and every face stares at you. There's never time to make friends because you're always packing up and moving on. Next class, different faces stare at you, but they're the same damn faces. You learn to fight your own fights. You learn to live as a loner and you're lonely. Jesus God, are you lonely," he said to his vodka.

He drained the glass. "The only person in the entire world who ever came into a fight on my side." He swiveled the bar stool and punched Parkhurst's shoulder. "You, my friend, are the only reason I'm not in a nuthouse."

In those days Parkhurst was packed with gunpowder waiting to explode. He was always looking for a fight, any fight would do.

Susan came up beside him and they both looked at Kevin in the interview room, seated in a brown plastic chair at the long wooden table, face worried and young. They stood side by side for a minute or two. She'd obviously dressed in a hurry, but she looked as cool and poised as always. Without taking her eyes from Kevin, she said, "You take this on."

He didn't know what she'd based her decision on, but he was glad. He wanted a go at this kid. When he stepped into the room, Kevin's head whipped up with insolent, thin-lipped assurance and a reckless air of being ready to stand his ground, no matter the consequences.

"Why'd you stab him, Kevin?"

"Sir?"

The *sir*, drilled into him by his military father, had the same hard spin as fuck you. He had a calm self-confidence seldom seen in a seventeen-year-old kid. Forced into being a loner either created self-assurance or sent a kid straight down the tubes.

A natural athlete, with reactions the speed of a prairie rattler, this kid was a miracle for the high school Wolverines; it was the only time in the history of Hampstead High School that they had a team to be reckoned with. A lot of newspaper space got devoted to him at every game.

"You got a score to settle with Officer Yancy?" Parkhurst asked.

"Sir?"

Staring got no more than amused contempt. Of cops? All adults? Susan was probably right. He was at war with the adult world, and that made Parkhurst think. He just might know what made this kid tick. As a teenager, Parkhurst had zeroed his hatred in on cops, because he was constantly hassled. Back in the days before there was so much noise about illegal search and seizure, he'd be netted on the street during routine hauls and dragged in for questioning. Once in high school, between classes a plain-clothes man had slammed him against his locker, crushed a fore-arm against his throat, and said, "You're coming with me." No fooling around with Miranda, he was thrown in a lineup. He never knew what he was suspected of. The witness didn't come through with an ID and the cop grudgingly dropped him back at school. He'd swaggered into English class. Most likely, nothing like that had ever happened to this kid, not a kid who had a father who knew how to raise hell if it did.

"Why'd you do it?"

Kevin, back straight, both hands lying loosely on his lap, had no trouble looking Parkhurst in the eye. "You'll have to be more specific," he said.

"What'd you do with the gun?"

"I thought he was stabbed."

"Where'd you get the knife?"

"You don't hear very well. I said I didn't do it."

"You didn't, huh? Why you protecting the bastard who did?"

"I don't know anything about it."

Parkhurst walked around behind the kid, rested a shoulder against the door frame, and crossed his arms. "You were there." He spoke softly because he didn't want Susan, watching on the other side of that glass, to know how near he was at slamming this kid against the wall.

If Kevin had a nerve anywhere it was under control. He hadn't said anything about an attorney, or a parent. Parkhurst wondered why. "What were you doing there?"

"Passing by."

Parkhurst walked around and leaned forward, hands on the table. "You a pretty smart kid?"

"Genius range."

"What kind of grades you make in school?"

"C's and D's."

"What kind of genius gets C's and D's?"

"I know more than the teachers. They're so boring they could stop birds from singing."

"These poor grades, they annoy your father?"

Kevin grinned.

Now Parkhurst was getting someplace. "He ever hit you?"

"No."

Bingo. "Ever hit your mother?"

"Of course not."

He lied with conviction. "What interests you?"

"That have anything to do with the subject at hand?" Kevin said.

"What is the subject at hand?"

"This is your show, don't you know?"

Parkhurst smiled. Kevin didn't know it, but Parkhurst now knew a lot about him, could describe the home atmosphere and the despair he lived with. Parkhurst knew because he'd been there, the yelling, the backhanding, the fists. The misery was constant, unless the old man was gone; then the air was poisoned with dread of his return. "You trying to say you didn't stab that police officer and you don't know anything about who did?"

"You finally got it. Congratulations."

"Maybe you can tell me why I should believe you when you're a liar."

That got to him. Kevin stiffened, clenched his jaw, and made a fist of the hand in his pocket. "You don't know anything about me."

"I know more than you think."

"When did I lie?"

"You said your father never hit you, never hit your mother."

"He never laid a hand on either of us."

"Right. You were on the Fandors' driveway. What were you doing there?"

Good as this kid was at hiding whatever went on in his mind, he couldn't suppress a flicker across his eyes of I'm-so-smart-and-you're-so-dumb. It was an expression any cop knew well, the expression of somebody who thinks he's getting away with something. What was it that Parkhurst was missing here? He wondered if Susan knew.

"I thought I heard a noise."

"Officer Yancy isn't dead. That means a witness."

"Why don't you ask him then?"

Oh, for God's sake. Maybe he was as dumb as the kid thought. The Fandors were away. Yancy had heard something suspicious, he went to check. "You went in that yard to paint another garbage can. Officer Yancy caught you and you stabbed him."

Kevin went dead still, bright mind calculating whether he'd admit it or not. He'd know there was no evidence. If he decided to deny it, the cops might believe he was guilty, but they couldn't prove anything.

"Why the artwork? To make your father mad?"

In a split second, Kevin made his decision. Parkhurst caught a glimpse of a seventeen-year-old kid under the smooth exterior. "It drives him nuts. I got an offer for a football scholarship. I want to study art. 'Art is for wimps and queers. You'll never make a name for yourself with art.'" He folded his hands on the table. "Did I make a name for myself?"

He had at that. First the *Hampstead Herald* and then, because it was so odd, it was picked up by a wire service, even mentioned as the final note on network television news. The kid was no coward; when his father found out, he'd beat the hell out of him.

"What'd you see?"

"Nothing. I heard the commotion. And I waited. I figured he'd be after me and I'd have to go over the fence."

"Why didn't you?"

"I don't know exactly. He didn't yell, 'Freeze! Police!' All that. It made me nervous. I waited and when nothing happened I went to take a look. He was on the ground, I thought he was dead. I picked up his flashlight to look and he talked to me. He gave me his keys. Anyway told me to take them. I didn't touch anything in the house but his phone. I did the nine-one-one bit.''

"Was his gun missing when you found him?"

"I don't know. I didn't notice anything but that knife. Shoved in his side that way, I've never seen anything like it. I was afraid he'd croak before the ambulance guys got there.''

"You could have taken the gun.''

"Yeah. But I didn't.''

Whether Kevin was lying or not, Yancy's gun was floating around. "What did you do with all the paint paraphernalia?"

"It's under the sink in Yancy's kitchen, with the cleaning supplies.''

Parkhurst looked at the kid a long minute, then stepped out to talk with Susan. "We've caught us the mad painter. I don't know what else.''

"You think he stabbed Yancy?"

"I could use some breakfast.''

TWENTY-THREE

FOOD. Susan considered. At five a.m.? Coffee, now there's an idea.

One of the few places open this early was The Best Little Hare House in Kansas out on the Interstate that catered to truckers. Was she strong enough to withstand a jukebox issuing forth country and western philosophy at this hour?

"Let's go," she said.

Breakfast wasn't the only thing he could use, she noted. Sleep was in order, fatigue showed in his face. Unshaven, with dark circles around his eyes, he looked sinister.

A trucker, hunched over the counter, peered into his mug of coffee, either estimating his chances or contemplating the meaning of life. A nasal voice mused musically that the only way to go is past where you've been. At five in the morning even that made sense. She and Parkhurst took a booth. Two men in the next booth were telling jokes.

The waitress, middle-aged and friendly, brought two mugs of steaming coffee and the menus. Rain splattered against the window, washing flickering streams of red and blue down the glass from the neon sign outside. Smells of frying onions fought with frying bacon for first place. Susan's stomach set up a protest. How soft she'd gotten; it used to be, she could snatch anything on the run. Just to prove she still had it, she ordered sausage and eggs.

"You think he did it?" she asked.

"Stabbed Yancy?" Parkhurst ripped open a packet of sugar and dumped it in his coffee. "I don't know."

"The reason being to get the gun?"

"Why else would anybody go after Yancy?"

Yancy was a sweetheart, but that didn't mean somebody

couldn't have a reason. "Kevin Murphy stabs Yancy and then calls nine-one-one to get help," she said.

"He didn't want a dead cop, only a live gun."

"For what purpose?"

The waitress slid filled platters in front of them. Susan eyed hers warily. Aha, now there's food. All on an empty stomach. She shouldn't have been so rash. Starting slow, she sipped coffee.

"That's the question." He sprinkled pepper on his eggs. "I think we can rule out target practice."

She forked off a sliver of sausage and nibbled it. Spicy! Oh, yes, hot. Hot hot. Taste buds now awake, eyes watering. Orange juice helped. "What did he do with it?"

"Hid it somewhere."

"You did look."

Parkhurst raised an eyebrow. At the next booth, one of the men said, "There was this eighty-six-year-old man who married this eighty-four-year-old woman. And they were happy and traveling and doing all these things..."

"Okay, so why didn't you find it?" Susan said. "He ran across the street, used the phone, ran back. How long was he gone? Two minutes?"

"That's what he says. Yancy concurs."

"Hardly time for anything complicated."

The waitress came by and refilled coffee mugs.

"...and then one day the woman wasn't feeling well. And she thought it was just the flu. Except she didn't get better and she didn't get better until finally the man told her to go to the doctor and so..."

"Yancy wasn't exactly clearheaded," Parkhurst said. "Kevin got rid of the gun, stashed the paints, called nine-one-one, sprinted back. It took longer, five minutes. Yancy maybe didn't know the difference."

She held her mug in both hands. "Why would he want Yancy's gun?"

"To blow away his old man. He hates the bastard with the intensity of tornado winds." Parkhurst's voice was easy, but there was something cold as dry ice underneath.

"That's a lot of hate."

"Murphy Senior is a handy man with his fists."

"You can't know that."

"Trust me, I know. The kid is brave, I'll give him that. Stupid, but brave. That's how he got the bloody nose. I'll lay a year's salary on it. The bastard belted him." Parkhurst laughed without humor. "Picking up Mrs. Yancy had more to do with getting a big dirty dog in his father's shiny new car than with neighborliness."

"Before you jump to conclusions—"

"I'll run a check—emergency rooms, physicians, teachers. I'll find broken bones, bruises, contusions, accidents all over the place."

Victims of abuse commonly explained injuries by saying how clumsy they were; they fell and broke arms, tripped and broke jaws, slipped and got bruises.

"...and the doctor took all different kinds of tests. X-rays and blood tests and EKGs and EEGs and MRIs and every other initials he could think of. And he couldn't find anything wrong with her. So he said, 'There's just one other test I want to do and the results will be ready on Monday.' "

"You never say the old man beats the shit out of you, and never admit he does the same to your mother, but you think about killing him, and you plan."

"Painting garbage cans ties in with this?"

"Ingenious, this kid. He's dancing on the back of an alligator. I hope Murphy Senior doesn't kill him. I'll have a talk with the navy test pilot, retired. Man to man." Parkhurst's smile was so tight it was nothing more than his top lip flattening against his teeth.

"...and so on Monday the woman went back to the doctor and he told her. 'I finally figured out what's wrong with you. You're pregnant.' The woman thought about that for a minute and then she called her husband and she said, 'You got me pregnant, you old goat.'

"There was this silence on the other end of the line, and he said...'Who is this?'"

"If you're right, we've exchanged a mad painter for a potential killer. Is he our stalker?"

Parkhurst leaned forward and picked up his coffee mug. Holding it between both hands, he spoke over the rim, "I flat out don't know. The kid is accustomed to lying, he's done it all his life, and he's good at it."

Parkhurst sipped, then sipped again. "He could be. Stalkers grow up in families that are physically and emotionally abusive. Not always, but often enough to throw it into a profile. They're loners. Our boy fits there. Angry. Mentally or emotionally disturbed. Insecure. Unattractive."

"That doesn't fit. Kevin has self-confidence all over the place and he's very good-looking. He's the high school football hero. Much adulation, even from adults."

"Yeah. He is a loner though."

They were into the easy back and forth of an ongoing case, but he was slightly defensive, his shoulders tensed, and she was slightly brittle. Both were pretending there wasn't a big swamp of emotions swimming around underneath them.

"What does any of this have to do with the stabbing of Sheri Lloyd?" she said.

"Yeah."

"...so there was this guy and for his birthday his wife..."

"Hey, Ben." A trucker came up and slapped Parkhurst on the shoulder, in that half challenging, half playful way that passes for friendship in males. "We have a bet going." He nodded at the counter where two beefy males in jeans and checked shirts sat sideways on stools.

"I said you were married to that movie star that's here. The one that's"—he glanced at Susan—"so pretty. Eddie said you wasn't."

"You lose."

"Damn." The trucker went back to pay up.

"*Was* means used to be," Susan pointed out.

"I have also been known to lie. Let's get out of here." He slid from the booth and grabbed the check.

They trotted through rain to the pickup. She started it. "Parkhurst?"

"Yeah?" Impatient. Cautionary.

She wanted to say something like "I'm sorry." For what, she

wasn't quite sure. That memories, when they got loose, had thorns, and you got hurt when you tried to pick them up? "Nothing."

Hampstead, just waking up, stirred with people getting off to work.

WHAT WOULD the rain do to Fifer's schedule?

INT. YANCY'S BEDROOM.

Yancy, lying in his own bed, frets because he isn't there.

A mocking smile would go well here. Rain pelted against the skylight, very artistic. Somewhere along the line he'd developed a stake in this movie. It was good to be home anyway, even if he did have Demarco guard-dogging because the chief was protecting him from assassins. Demarco only made one crack about baby cops losing guns, then sat around looking alert.

Dozing took up most of the morning while Demarco sat in the kitchen and read the paper, then Yancy washed as well as he could without getting bandages wet, dressed and shaved and dozed some more. Whatever they'd given him at the hospital had a hell of an afterlife.

In the easy chair, he was dozing over a book on Quantrill's raiders...slipping in from the east, hidden by the predawn sky and the seven-foot-high corn in the field, they approached the rural home of John L. Crane. Before sunup Crane was dead, his house burning, and William Quantrill was leading his raiders to Lawrence. The date was August 21, 1863...when a knock brought him up with a start. Demarco let in Stephanie Blakeley, ever-present notebook clutched to her chest, plastic container in her other hand. She came in dripping water. Rain spilled over the wrought iron and ran down through the wooden steps.

"Mother sent this." She thrust the container at him. "Bean soup. It's actually pretty good," she added. Stephanie, at thirteen, didn't always see eye to eye with her mother, but she believed in being fair. She'd been eight, sporting two new permanent front teeth when he had moved in, and had told him astonishing facts about the world as she'd seen it. Now she was a solemn, serious thirteen-year-old who was going to be an author, hence the notebook—to write down important or profound thoughts.

"If you're not busy, I'd like to talk."

Uh-huh. Her questions could get sticky, like Do you believe in God, or What is it like to be in a fistfight. These things were of significance to an author. He shoved the soup in the refrigerator and asked if she'd like a beer.

She gave him a look of withering scorn. "I'm not still eight, you know. That's no longer funny."

Sometimes he didn't remember to respect her thirteen-year-old dignity, which she was quick to point out.

"Coke?"

"Yes, thank you."

Demarco kept himself out of the way at the kitchen table with his paper. Sitting cross-legged on the living-room floor, bony knees poking out of blue shorts, she opened the can and sipped, studying him thoughtfully. "Does it hurt?"

He always answered her questions as well as he could. Not knowing how her mother would feel about these discussions, he tried to walk a fine line between honesty and what his landlady might get upset about if she knew her thirteen-year-old daughter was getting answers from him. "Not a lot."

She tucked a strand of brown hair behind her ear, opened the notebook, and wrote in a tiny, precise hand. "Did it hurt when you got stabbed?"

"Some. But mostly, it was scary."

She thought about that and then nodded as though that made sense. "Did you think you were going to die?"

"I sure thought I might." He hoped she wasn't going to ask his opinions about an afterlife; that was something he didn't feel equipped to handle. He popped the tab on his Coke and took a gulp.

"Some people die and it's a blessing."

"Who told you that?"

"Nobody tells me anything. I'm treated like a child with no intelligence. And I'm neither." Her mouth tightened and she twitched it back and forth. "You, at least, think I have brains."

"Who died going out with a blessing?"

She shrugged. "That's what the women at church were saying about Mrs. Evanosky's husband."

"Did I know Mr. Evanosky?"

She shrugged again. "He's been sick for ages and ages and now he's dead and Mrs. Evanosky doesn't have a penny to live on. That doesn't sound like much of a blessing to me."

Evanosky. The woman in the hospital courtyard keeping a death watch? Her vigil was finally over then.

"Do you know who murdered that actress?" Like a pushy reporter, she had her notebook and pen ready.

"Not yet."

"Why did the murderer try to kill you? Because you were getting too close?"

"Naw."

She made notes. "Maybe you know something you don't know you know."

"That's only on television, Steph."

"Have you been interrogating suspects?"

"Why are you so interested?"

"You're the only one who ever tells me anything. I'm figuring out who did it."

"I'm a flunky who goes where I'm sent to stand around all day and watch other people film a scene."

"Did you ever go anywhere your mother didn't want you to go?"

Uh-oh. "Where'd you go, Steph?"

"Well, the thing is, she doesn't know, and actually she told me not to, but—" She glanced at Demarco.

Narrow face, crew cut, and square chin, he looked like a drill sergeant, which is what he had been before he came to HPD.

"Well, anyway—never mind. I have something important to ask."

She let it sit there until he said, "What do you want to ask?"

"Will you tell me about sex?"

He choked on the cold liquid he'd been tipping down his throat. "Uh—Steph—I don't think your mother—"

She grinned, gotcha. "Well then, will you teach me how to shoot a gun?"

That didn't exactly have an easy answer either, given the way her mother felt about guns. Before he could launch into qualifiers all around a response, there was a knock on the door.

"I'll get it." Stephanie unfolded herself and started for the door.

Demarco beat her to it. Stephanie studied Clem Jones as she came in, glanced at Yancy, and used "Don't forget to eat your soup" as an exit line.

The director's assistant was her usual nightmare vision, only this time her hair was green, but her face was the usual white and her eyes black, she looked like a rakish raccoon. Three painted green teardrops glistened on her left cheek. She wore no coat to keep the rain off; her overalls had rips in knees and the butt, they looked like she'd just shaken out the wino and pulled them on. The sleeveless T-shirt matched her hair. Demarco gave her a hard stare.

"You dead yet?" she asked Yancy.

"No. Would you care to sit down?" He offered her the easy chair.

She ignored the offer and prowled. "You really sick or just malingering?"

"With your great sympathetic manner, you ever think of going into nursing? Can I get you something to drink?"

She shook her head. "We heard you'd been shot."

"I fell and cracked a rib." He took the chair she'd rejected.

"Sure you did." She plucked a book from the shelf, riffled pages, and put it back.

"Small matter of a knife wound. Was it you? A knife in the back seems just your style."

Edging to the couch, she perched. "Is that what happened? Does it hurt? Can I see it?"

"Yes, yes, and no."

"I brought you some magazines, but I left them in the car." As jittery as a prairie dog with a hawk overhead, she reached for the television remote, looked at it front and back, pushed a button, watched the television flicker on, then pushed the off button. "Was it Laura?"

"Laura what?"

"Who stabbed you."

"Why would she do that?"

"I don't know. There have been a lot of weird things that I don't know. I wish I'd never come to work on this movie. What kind of soup?"

"What?"

"The kid"—Clem gestured with her thumb—"she said eat your soup."

"Bean. Would you care for some?"

"I guess not. I'll get the magazines." She darted out, leaving the door open.

The rain had slacked off to a misty drizzle with an occasional fat drop falling from the eaves.

Minutes later, heavy footfalls pounded up the steps. Unless Clem bought a ton of magazines, this wasn't her returning. Demarco got to the door just as Mac, Yancy's teamster buddy, ducked in with a vaseful of roses in one huge paw.

"Clem said give you these." He dumped an armload of magazines and tossed a small white envelope on the coffee table.

"Sweet of you to bring me flowers," Yancy said.

"Ha. If I cared, I'd bring you a six-pack of Millers. These are from Ms. Laura herself." Mac plunked the vase next to the magazines; jostled roses sprayed rainwater on the table. "I just pick up and deliver. You got any Millers?"

"Budweiser?"

"Bah, bad stuff. If that's all you got." He shrugged off his jacket and handed it over. Yancy passed it on to Demarco.

"Why is Ms. Edwards sending me flowers?" Yancy snatched a beer from the refrigerator.

"To show she's all heart." Mac opened and swallowed. "You don't look all that delicate. Aren't you supposed to have pale skin and shaky breathing, long-faced nurses standing by?"

He drank his beer, told a string of corny jokes, some of which were funny and didn't do Yancy's cracked rib any good, and when he left, gave Yancy a pat on the back that his rib took personally.

Just as Yancy picked up the cans to toss them, there was another knock on the door. And he'd thought making movies was tiring.

Demarco ushered in Serena, still dressed from work in green skirt and print blouse, and said he'd split for a few.

"How are you?" Serena sounded tightly wound and her face was a careful mask.

"Fine."

"I brought Mom."

"Hey, Serena, this is your brother speaking. Did you get dipped in brine on the way over?"

Her face crumpled. "You could have been killed."

"No, Serena, no. I'm fine, going back to work tomorrow. It's just a scratch. Nothing to get uptight about."

"Now look what you did. When Mom sees me, she's going to be upset." She made quick jabs in her purse for tissues, dabbed at her eyes, and blew her nose. "I wish you'd quit this job."

"I can't."

"It's too dangerous."

He took her hand and threaded his fingers through hers. "It was an accident. Accidents can happen anywhere."

"It wasn't an accident. Somebody tried to kill you. Why do you have Demarco watching over you, if it was just an accident?"

"Serena—" He searched for the right words. All through their childhood they'd depended on each other for survival. If they hadn't stuck together, with their Looney Tunes mother they wouldn't have made it out as normal as they had. They were two halves. If one was gone, the other would be just that—a half.

"You duck out on me by getting yourself killed and I'll never speak to you again. You hear me? Mom's waiting. I wanted to see how bad off you looked before I brought her in." She blew her nose again. "Where'd you get the flowers?"

"The famous and beautiful Ms. Laura Edwards."

"You're kidding. Just a scratch, huh? Why then is she sending flowers?"

"Serena—"

"Yeah, yeah."

His mother rushed in, hugged him—too tight for his rib—and

ran her hand down his cheek. "Didn't I tell you not to climb the apple tree?"

Over her shoulder, he sent Serena a look. Serena shrugged.

"Does your arm hurt?" His mother sat on the couch and pulled him down beside her. With a feather touch, she stroked his left arm.

She was back sixteen years to when he'd fallen and broken it. "You're a brave boy." She noticed the flowers. "I knew you'd like the roses. Serena said bring pansies."

Serena smiled sweetly at him and crossed her eyes.

"It's okay." His mother placed a hand on his face and looked puzzled.

"We need to go," Serena said. "Dallas is coming for dinner."

"You might see what's in the locket," his mother said. "That could be the answer."

"I'll do that, Mom."

She kissed his forehead.

As soon as they were out the door, Demarco came back. He was taking this guard dog stuff a little seriously. Yancy picked up the envelope Mac had delivered for Clem and opened it, assuming it would say something like "Get well soon."

Wrong.

Printed in block letters:

WHAT WAS YOURS IS NOW MINE.
WAITING FOR THE SUN TO SHINE.
THE LOVELY BEAUTY.
WHEN IT'S RIGHT
THIS WILL BRING THE END OF TIME.

TWENTY-FOUR

CAREFULLY, Susan inserted the poem in a plastic envelope. "When did this come?"

Yancy shifted uncomfortably in the chair. Patrol officers didn't like to be interrogated by the chief when they were sitting down; they preferred to be on their feet, even standing at attention.

"A couple of movie people were here," he said.

"Who?"

"Clem Jones. She's the one who takes care of everything for the director, requests and complaints, whatever he needs or wants. Mac Royce. He's Laura Edwards's driver."

"You must have made a great impression if the megastar sent flowers. Who else was here?"

"My mother and Serena."

"And the kid," Demarco said.

"Right. Stephanie Blakeley, the landlady's daughter."

"Mac Royce brought the note?"

"He dropped it on the table. I didn't open it until after he'd gone."

She sat down on the couch. "Now that you've had time to think about it, is there anything you can add to what happened last night?"

"Uh—no." He looked embarrassed. "I saw an individual— To be accurate, I saw movement I *thought* was an individual go into the rear of the property at twenty-one twenty-nine Taylor. I knew the residents were away. I thought it was the mad painter at it again."

"You went after him."

"Yes, ma'am."

"You were intent on catching him and didn't watch your back."

"Yeah—yes, ma'am. I felt a push. Like someone was—like

somebody had shoved me hard. I went down on one knee, lost my balance or got shoved again, and fell on the damn knife. That's when I knew this was not a good situation. I wasn't thinking about much else for a second or two. Then I realized my gun was missing. I expected to be shot. I heard my heart beat. Loud and clear.''

Either the assailant thought Yancy was as good as dead or he was after the gun and didn't care whether he had a dead cop or not. The note indicated the gun was the target. "What else?"

He gave her a half smile. "On that bright and cloudless morning.''

"What?"

"It zinged through my mind. 'When the roll is called up yonder, I'll be there.'''

"Anything else?"

"Footsteps."

"Which direction?"

"Retreating."

She closed her notebook and dropped it in her shoulder bag. "Well, you did catch the mad painter."

Yancy gave her a humorless smile. "He more or less caught himself when he crept up to see if I was dead."

"Could he be your assailant?"

"Possibly. He'd have to go through the rear of the property and around to the front to come up at me from behind. If he did, why would he come back and call for help? Oh.''

"What?"

"I gave him my house key."

"Parkhurst has it. He checked the place out. As near as he could tell, nothing was missing. Unless you had valuable silver or stamp collections."

"The most valuable thing I own is a T-bone steak in the freezer. Is it still there?"

"I'll ask Parkhurst. He did send someone to collect Kevin's paint stuff. What's the poetry all about?" she said, circling around to where she came in. "Who's the lovely beauty?"

"Laura Edwards, I would guess."

"Why would you guess that?"

He looked at her like this might be some trick question. "I'm aware a nutzoid has been sending her threats. I assumed this was more of the same."

"Anybody come to mind? Always hanging around, getting too close? Someone who just doesn't smell right?"

"Smell," he said.

She waited.

"Why did I think of pumpkin bread?"

"When?"

"Just as I was stabbed."

"What do you associate with pumpkin bread?"

"Thanksgiving. Childhood." He thought. "Sophie the cat lady."

Susan smiled. Sophie baked pumpkin bread and brought it to those in trouble or grieving or feeling low. Or to people she wanted to find out more about. Snooping was almost as big a passion as cats. "Anything else?"

"Only that whoever wrote it is a bad poet."

"You know good poetry from bad?" That sounded surprised and horribly patronizing, which she could see he picked up on.

"Yes, ma'am, I do," he said with no hint of sarcasm. "My mother may be odd in many ways, but she knows poetry and she made me learn."

"If you think of anything else let me know. Otherwise, take it easy. Take a few days sick leave—"

"No, ma'am."

She raised an eyebrow.

"Uh—with your permission, I mean. I'd just as soon go back. If one of those movie people shoved a shiv in me, I'd like to know who. And—" He gave her a cockeyed grin. "This is hard to admit, but I feel a proprietary interest in this movie."

"You're not exactly one hundred percent tiptop."

"Close enough."

"I'll check with Sheffield and let you know."

Officer Demarco, trying to stifle a yawn, swallowed it when she looked at him. "Ma'am," he said.

A body could get used to all this instant respect. She reminded herself, before she got too carried away, that she didn't know what they said behind her back. "You've been here all day?"

"Since oh six hundred."

Overtime. Never did she expect to be concerned about overtime, except her own. "I'll see you get relieved."

"No problem. I'd just as soon see he's taken care of."

"Anything Yancy left out?"

"No, ma'am. I assumed the roses weren't dusted with deadly poison so I let them come in."

Ex-military, Demarco wasn't thrilled by a female superior; by playing single-minded, he got away with snide comments. One day, she was afraid she'd have trouble from Demarco.

SINCE SHE PASSED the hospital on her way to the department, she swung into the parking lot and went inside. At the nurses' station, she asked a young red-haired nurse to page Dr. Sheffield. Seconds later, the PA system announced, "Dr. Sheffield? Dr. Adam Sheffield."

A man with muscles, dark curly hair, and a day's growth of beard burst through the stairway door. "You wanted to see me?"

"About Officer Yancy," she said. "Is he okay to return to duty?"

"You gonna have him doing sit-ups and fistfights?"

"I didn't have that in mind, no."

"As long as he keeps his ribs taped and doesn't try to run marathons, he should be fine."

Before she even got the pickup out of the hospital parking lot, the radio was chattering at her. "Yes, Hazel?"

"There seems to be a problem with Laura Edwards. She called in hysterics, demanding to see Ben."

"Where is she?"

"In her trailer out there on old Josiah's property."

"I'm on my way."

At base camp, rain soaked into the ground beneath all the trailers, trucks, cars, and vans. California summers didn't include rain; surely, whoever scouted this location had known it rained in Kansas at any time of year. The ground was already soft underfoot when she slid from the pickup.

"Where's Ben?" Laura demanded.

For someone who'd been having hysterics, Laura Edwards looked remarkably unhysterical; what she looked was pissed. Dressed in a tidy little black number that fit like skin, she stalked toward Susan on four-inch heels, a diamond—or what looked like a diamond—pendant hung on her creamy bosom. An exotic sight for a Kansas afternoon. Platinum hair was swept up with wispy tendrils on the sides of her beautiful face, now artfully made-up. She whirled and stalked away, giving them the backless view.

"I'm due on the set," she said.

Directors didn't simply sit around and wait for the sun to shine. Electricians, carpenters, drivers, props, makeup, wardrobe, and everybody else got paid whether they worked or not. After eight hours they got time and a half; after twelve, double time. And that was the least of it; car and van rentals, security guards, hotel rooms, catering. Every day of filming was horrendously expensive. Each day over schedule meant that much over budget, which explained why Fifer couldn't afford to stop shooting for somebody's murder. It cost too much. What little Susan knew about the movie industry came from occasionally working movie detail in San Francisco. She used to have a friend who'd become an entertainment lawyer and defected to Los Angeles.

"Ms. Edwards, could we sit down?"

Laura took in deep breaths, heaving bosom and all. Or tried. The dress was so tight, there wasn't much room for expansion. Susan hoped she wouldn't faint.

Laura debated, seemed about to keep stalking, then went to the couch where she was forced to perch.

"What's the problem?" Susan sat facing her and spoke softly.

"Mac."

The teamster handed Susan a Ziploc bag, inside was a piece of white five-by-seven paper that had been folded in half. Printed in block letters:

MY LOVE, YOUR HEART WILL FEEL NO PAIN
AND YOUR DEVOTION IS MINE TO GAIN.
THERE IS NO WAY TO REST OR SLEEP

UNTIL I COME FOR YOU TO KEEP.
WHEN YOU KNOW YOU LOVE ME BEST
THEN YOU'LL FIND BOTH PEACE AND REST.

A second plastic bag held the envelope it came in with Laura Edwards's name printed on it also in block letters.

And so we learn why the gun was taken. "Where did you get this?"

"Somebody gave it to me."

"Who?"

"Mac." It was more a snapping of her fingers than a question.

"It was handed to me by a kid on a bicycle. Girl. Thirteen, fourteen."

"What did she look like?"

"Skinny. Tan raincoat, hat pulled down. She said a cop asked her to give it to Laura."

"Did she say Laura? Not Ms. Edwards, or Laura Edwards?"

He chewed that over. "I think she said Laura Edwards."

Not that it meant much, but the more formal might mean an individual who didn't know her. "Would you recognize her?"

"Naw. Kids hang around here all the time."

Right. If Laura Edwards didn't draw them in, Nick Logan would.

"I thought it was from Ben," Laura said.

"Why would he send you a note?"

"I didn't give it much thought," Laura snapped. "I was dressing, going through the scene in my mind."

"What does it mean?" Susan tapped the note.

"Isn't that your job?"

It was, indeed. Yancy's gun, the note he received, and now this. Added up, they gave notice of a serious threat to Ms. Edwards's life. Strong indication she was the intended victim and Yancy only a means to that end. Time to circle the wagons. A thought darted across her mind like a bright fish: Delmar Cayliff and his wagon trains. "Who put this in plastic?"

"I did," Mac said. "The kid handled it, I handled it, and Ms. Edwards took it and opened it, but when she—"

Screamed?

"...I put them in bags, for what it's worth."

Fingerprints needed to be taken for elimination purposes. Susan would send Osey. Taking prints was his idea of fun.

A knock, followed by a damp-looking second assistant saying Laura was wanted on the set, brought an end to the questioning.

"How many notes have you received today?" Susan asked Mac.

"What?"

"You claim you received this from a young female with a request to give it to Ms. Edwards. Earlier this afternoon you brought flowers to Officer Yancy with a note."

"Oh, that. Clem gave it to me with a stack of magazines. She said since I was going up, I might as well take them, she had to split."

To be certain she understood correctly, Susan repeated, "Ms. Jones gave you a note and asked that you give it to Officer Yancy."

Susan tracked down Clem Jones inside the mansion where the filming was going on. Distracted, paying close attention to the director and none to Susan, Clem said the kid asked her to bring the note to Yancy. What kid? The one who lives there. Lives where? Where Yancy lives.

And some days you just go round in circles. The *swipe-swipe* of the windshield wiper kept background rhythm as Susan tried to chivvy pieces along so they'd form some shape. Did these recent events clear Laura Edwards of suspicion? Nearly. Susan couldn't see her skulking around in the rain, skewering Yancy to lift his gun and hightailing it back to the hotel. One thing was clear. The intended victim was Laura, not Yancy.

These notes put another plus on the side of Parkhurst's non-involvement; he wasn't silly enough to be writing bad poetry, even on his day off. Where was he when Laura tried to get him? He had a perfect right to go wherever he wanted. Except in the vicinity of Laura Edwards. And that, of course, was the worry; he was out there somewhere, like the Lone Ranger, keeping guard.

The lady had been royally pissed because she couldn't get him. A suspicious person might suspect Laura didn't care, or maybe—

for some reason of her own—actually wanted him to lose his job. Stupid of her. He was good at this job, and more than that, it gave him substance.

A leggy female, early teens, but tall for her age with straight brown hair to just past her ears, stepped out on the porch. "You mind talking out here? Mom's giving a lesson."

In the background, Susan could hear the piano being attacked by heavy hands. Lessons were definitely needed. Black clouds and off-and-on drizzle had turned summer daylight gray, drops hit the shrubbery around the porch with a *pit-pat, pit-pat.*

Stephanie, clearly excited by a cop asking questions, wasn't about to let it show. Cool was her stance. She was a typical small-town teenager, lovingly cared for, educated, with a bright future. Her worn shorts and droopy shirt didn't hide glowing health and good grooming. Less worldly, innocent even, in comparison with her big-city counterpart, and how could it be otherwise? In San Francisco, mothers got knifed in front of their kids, friends got mowed down in school yards, baby brothers or sisters asleep in their strollers got shot in the cross fire between drug dealers.

Stephanie was disappointed to be asked only about notes. "Oh, those. I gave one to that chauffeur guy just like the cop told me, and the other to that weird movie person to give to Peter."

"A cop told you to deliver the notes? How do you know he was a cop?"

Stephanie shrugged. "He said he was."

And this child wouldn't ask a cop for identification. "A police officer gave you two notes and asked you to deliver one to Ms. Edwards's driver and one to Officer Yancy," Susan said, making sure she got it straight.

"Yes. Actually, he said one to Laura, but people were all around, security guards and everybody, so I couldn't give it to her. I gave it to her driver."

"He said Laura? Not Laura Edwards or Ms. Edwards?"

"Yes."

"Where was this?"

"At the barn, this morning. They were filming inside. And of course they wouldn't let me in."

"How did you know her driver?"

"I've watched. You know, making the movie. Actually, it's mostly bor-ing. He brings her and takes her and everything."

"This cop. Did you know him? Was he wearing a uniform? What was he wearing?"

"A black raincoat. He was in a hurry, gave me the notes, and rushed off."

I'll bet he did. "Describe him for me."

"Hat. One of those floppy kinds, and he kept ducking his head and looking the other way. I don't even know if he was fat or anything because the raincoat was loose. He had on black shoes, they were getting all wet. He was about your height."

Since Susan was five eight and wearing two-inch heels, that made him around five ten. Maybe.

"You didn't take the note to Yancy yourself. Why was that?"

Stephanie stuck a cupped hand over the porch railing and caught drops of rain. "She came—the one with the funny clothes and white makeup—while I was there. And I forgot to give it to him. When I left, she came back down for the magazines in her car, so I thought—as long as she was going back up, she might as well take it."

Ah, Susan thought. Stephanie had a crush on Yancy and felt jealous when Ms. Jones trotted up to see him.

"Let me make sure I've got this right," she said. "A cop gave you two notes. One for Laura Edwards, one for Yancy. You gave Ms. Edwards's note to her driver and Yancy's to Ms. Jones? Is that right?"

Stephanie nodded.

Like the emperor said to Mozart, Susan thought, there are too many notes. She asked Stephanie to come in at some time and have her fingerprints taken.

"Cool."

TWENTY-FIVE

YANCY WAS THINKING he shouldn't have been so eager about telling the chief he was great, rarin' to get back to movie duty. He felt stiff as day-old toast, and trying to shower without getting bandages wet was a joke. A good hard run was what he needed, work the kinks out. No running, no workouts, until the rib knit.

Stepping into uniform pants, he buttoned and zipped, buttoned up his shirt and buckled on his belt with the unfamiliar gun. Nothing better happen to this one or he'd never hear the end of it.

Stephanie, at four p.m., was sitting on the bottom porch step looking woebegone. "Hi," she said. The air was sticky hot with the worst of the day's heat.

"Hi, Steph. Anything wrong?"

She shook her head. "How come you're going to work when you're sick?"

"I'm not sick."

She scowled just like Serena used to when she was a kid. "You should be staying home."

"I can't do that. I'll see you later." From the Cherokee, he gave her a wave as he backed out the driveway. Adolescents, who knew what went on in their minds. Even themselves.

At the department, he picked up a radio, got a squad car, and set out for the mansion. As usual people stood around watching even when they should have been home eating their suppers. He got a call sheet from Clem Jones and ran his eye over SET/DESCR.

EXT. TREES BEHIND BARN

Billy fires at Sara.

Billy, of course, was the hit man hired by the bad guys, and Sara was Laura, the heroine who stumbled across the information that the bad guys had killed her father because he was going to turn them in for using banned pesticides.

Cover Set:

INT. JEFF'S OFFICE

Jeff was the hero cop.

Yancy didn't like this "Billy fires at Sara" stuff. He hied himself over to the prop truck in search of Robin McCormack.

"I told you," Robin said. "All firearms are kept locked in the safe."

"Bullets."

"IN THE SAFE." Robin sighed. "Look, this isn't the first shoot I've been on, no pun intended, and I've got nothing but blanks."

"Let me see them."

"Oh, man, I've got things to do."

"I can shut you down, which will give you lots of time. Now, open up that safe and show me everything you've got in there."

"This is really stupid, man. You think I don't know what I'm doing? You think everything isn't checked and rechecked before it's used? What's got in your soup?"

Robin dialed the safe's combination number, 5-7-3. Yancy, standing beside him, had no trouble seeing what he was doing. If this was how careful Robin was, no telling who had the combination.

"This is what he's going to use." Robin handed him a scope-mounted rifle. "And this is what he's going to be firing." Robin handed over the shells. "If you worried this much about who killed Kay maybe you'd have the bastard by now."

Yancy examined the stock, the trigger, the hand guard, and looked through the scope. He looked at each bullet, definitely blanks.

The Starbucks coffee he'd picked up from the caterer sent fully alerted nerves zinging to attention throughout his body. He moved around and got in everybody's way.

Billy, the villain, was getting some last-minute instructions from the director. Robin handed him the rifle. A black armed condor (metal structure painted black) stood taller than the barn with the light on top blazing. Yancy judged it could be seen four miles in all directions. Probably like the light God had used to shine down on Adam when He asked where the apple came from.

Yancy kept reminding himself Billy had a blank, he probably didn't know shit about rifles, and couldn't hit what he was aiming at in any case.

That went up in smoke when Billy took the rifle and handled it like he'd gone deer hunting all his life. Yancy's adrenaline level kept rising.

Sara/Laura, in a filmy white thing that Yancy assumed was a nightgown, stood by a tree waiting for the director's word. When he gave it, she ran. A path had been semicleared, at least enough so she could run among the trees. If it hadn't been, the chase would have ended about three steps after it began. There was too much in the way, fallen branches, dead leaves, and new growth covering the ground.

Sara/Laura, following the path marked out for her, crept down a rise, darting from tree to tree. Billy, the villain, stalked. As fetching a sight as the heroine was in her nightgown, or whatever it was—peignoir?—Yancy kept his eyes on the rifle. Occasionally it glinted in the beam of light. Otherwise, it was simply a menacing shadow. Periodically, Billy brought it to his shoulder and looked through the scope.

Jeff/Nick, automatic in hand, was creeping after the bad guy trying to off him before he could put a round smack in the middle of the heroine's beautiful back. Standard movie stuff.

Every time Billy brought the rifle to his shoulder, Yancy's teeth clenched. He'd need a trip to the dentist if this went on much longer. Billy curled a finger around the trigger.

Yancy held his breath.

Billy brought the rifle down and stalked on.

The whole routine again. Stalking, sighting, finger around trigger. Finger tightening.

Yancy discovered it was impossible to take a deep breath with your ribs strapped.

Billy fired.

No recoil on the rifle. Yancy relaxed. Billy had fired a blank. That didn't mean that the rest of them wouldn't be live.

Two more shots. Blanks.

This bit of rifle to shoulder, fire, was repeated over and over. Yancy assumed bullets gouging chunks from trees, boulders, and the very ground beside the heroine would be added at some time, along with close-up views through crosshairs.

Right. They're making a movie here. All make-believe. Nobody's getting shot.

Sara/Laura, face frozen in fear, kept just one step ahead of the bullets. Billy, the villain, expression of a job to be done, relentlessly followed.

Jeff/Nick, the hero, expression of worry, was just a bit too far behind to be of any use. Bit by bit, he was gaining. Finally he fired his automatic. He wasn't close enough to hit anybody and he wasn't aiming, but hey, he was firing like all good heroes.

Fifer kept shooting the scene, even after the pink light of dawn bled into the clouds. Yancy paid close attention to the villain's rifle and the hero's handgun. Sara/Laura shivered realistically with cold and fear, and maybe for real. Early morning chill hung in the air, but wouldn't go on much longer. With yesterday's rain feeding the humidity, it would be humid in spades when the sun got going.

Coffee in hand, Yancy moved around, getting dirty looks from the crew.

"Hey!"

A shot. Two more in rapid succession.

Yancy was a split second slow in responding. He was still in fantasyland.

Oh, Christ!

He tossed the coffee cup and ran.

The spectators scattered. People screamed. Mac, trying to shield Laura Edwards, hustled her toward her town car. People ducked, crouched, darted. Or just looked around in confusion as though they were uninformed of this change in script.

Like a Keystone Kop, Yancy waded into the middle of it, gun in hand. A guy with a handgun was aiming at Laura.

"No!"

The guy fired.

Like a movie scene, Mac looked at his arm in surprise, clapped a hand around it, and watched blood seep through his fingers.

"Put the gun down! NOW!"

Sun, tipping over the rise, spilled golden light into the hollow. Looking directly into it, Yancy saw little more than a silhouette.

"NOW!"

The sniper ran.

Yancy chased. "Police! Stop!"

The gunman ran straight into the sunlight. Yancy stumbled over the rocky, uneven ground.

The guy tried to run uphill, slipped on wet grass, and almost fell. He recovered and dashed left.

With no breath to yell, Yancy kept after him. The sniper ran flat out. Not a smart thing to do on this terrain: holes, rocks, and pockets of rainwater waited to trip up the unsuspecting.

Yancy slowed, fighting for air.

The gunman stumbled, sprawled on the ground.

Yancy sprinted. "Don't move! Stay right where you are!"

One knee on the back of the guy's neck, Yancy grabbed the gun. "One...twitch..." he panted, "you're...dead..."

Yancy's lungs felt on fire.

"You're hurting me."

Yancy holstered his gun and fumbled for cuffs, got one wrist cuffed, and thought he'd expire before he got the other. Finally, he managed to bring the other arm around.

Head hanging like a spent horse, Yancy worked on getting air without breathing deeply.

"Could you get off now?"

Wondering how he was going to get himself upright, Yancy eased pressure from the guy's neck.

"How am I going to get up?"

"Well, pal, you're on your own." Yancy could almost breathe again, but fire still locked his chest. "At least till I know whether I'm going to die."

"The grass is wet."

This was true. Yancy could feel it through the knee of his pants. "Roll over and sit up."

"I can't."

"Hold on." Yancy pulled out his radio and spoke to the dispatcher.

"Okay, pal, let's go." Yancy flipped the gunman over. It was the weird history teacher from the hotel. Delmar Cayliff.

With a little help, Cayliff managed to sit. Cracked rib protesting, Yancy got him to his feet.

The gun was his, Yancy was glad to see, but after this, no telling how long before he'd get it back. They went down the rise a whole lot slower than they'd gone up.

Everybody watched, spectators, crew, actors, directors, and probably the squirrels in the trees.

Fifer said quietly, "Cut."

Everybody clapped. Yancy felt like a complete ass.

TWENTY-SIX

WERE YOU TRYING to be a hero?'' What was it about cops? Like teenagers, they thought they were invincible.

Yancy stood more or less at attention in front of her desk. He wasn't ramrod stiff, she thought, only because of pain. At least he wasn't turning pale from hemorrhage caused by a rib puncturing a lung.

"No, ma'am."

She thought he was more embarrassed than anything, but that didn't mean he wouldn't do the same thing again.

"Get yourself over to the hospital and have Dr. Sheffield take a look at you?" She sat down in her chair and made a shooing motion. "And, Yancy—?"

He turned.

"Good work, but if you've done any damage to yourself..." She let it hang.

"I don't think I would have been so stupid..."

The expression on her face stopped him and he put a lid on it. After she called the hospital to check on Laura Edwards's driver, alerted them Yancy was coming, and went down the hallway.

Delmar Cayliff waited, sitting in a molded plastic chair in the interview room. Parkhurst stood outside looking through the glass. "He hasn't moved."

"He ask for an attorney?"

"He refuses one. He's going to be his own attorney. He's more intelligent, according to him, than any attorney he could hire."

"Oh, boy." Why couldn't the guy just make it easy on everybody and agree to an attorney? He was a lunatic who should be locked away but care had to be taken so they didn't trample on any civil rights. It might be claimed he wasn't able to make this decision for himself. If they didn't get this one put away, he'd kill somebody.

When she opened the door, Delmar Cayliff looked up and smiled. "I've been here two hours, forty-five minutes, and sixteen seconds," he said. Not angry, not threatening, simply matter-of-fact as though she'd asked and he wanted to be accurate.

"Do you know where you are, Mr. Cayliff?" She went around the table and sat down across from him.

Parkhurst, arms loose at his sides, stood behind.

Delmar gave her a superior smile. "The Hampstead Police Department. Hampstead, Kansas. Two miles from the Sante Fe Trail."

She turned on the cassette recorder, stated her name, the date and time, mentioned Parkhurst was in the room, and stated Cayliff's name and read him his constitutional rights. "Do you understand these rights?"

"Yes, I do."

"Do you know why you're here, Mr. Cayliff?"

"I'm not stupid, Ms.—excuse me, *Chief*—Wren. You don't have to talk to me in words of one syllable. I'm educated and I'm intelligent. I have a doctorate in American history. So many people—Americans—don't know anything about their own country. The Sante Fe Trail runs not five miles from where we're sitting. How many people know? How many people even know what it was for? Do you know?"

His eyes stared down at the table or gazed past her shoulder.

"Why did you come to Hampstead?"

"Laura my beloved, of course. The princess of heaven in my heart and the desire of my dreams. Our love in the spring holds enchanting visions of our walking together through the gardens of magnificent palaces."

"You assaulted a police officer."

"The spirits guided me. The most humane way to kill her."

"Kill who?"

"Laura my beloved. We are one. She is mine and I am hers. Hand in hand, we will walk through the flowers of all colors. They helped by telling me where."

"Who helped?"

"The colors." Short, sharp, as though he'd been perfectly clear and she was slow.

"Are you married, Mr. Cayliff?"

"No."

"Ever had a girlfriend?"

"Only Laura my beloved. She is my soulmate."

"How did you know Laura would be working in Hampstead?"

His smile flickered on and off. "*Variety,* of course. Filming on location in Hampstead, Kansas. I had to make sure we'd be together, but I didn't know how until the spirits told me."

"They told you to kill Officer Yancy?"

"To get his gun, so she wouldn't suffer."

"You understand you've been arrested?"

"Yes, yes, read my rights. Mirandized. Isn't that what you call it?"

"You understand what that means?"

"I just said so."

"At any time during this interview, you can stop and ask for an attorney. Do you understand?"

"I don't need an attorney. The plan is finished." Loud, irritated.

Parkhurst, behind him, straightened, alert and ready.

"Tell me the plan," she invited.

"I've already confessed," he said. "Freely, with no coercion. I stabbed the police officer to obtain his gun." Delmar wanted to make that clear. He had no animosity toward the police, he simply had to have the gun. "I shot Laura. Now." He looked around. "I need my backpack. It's all in there. It's perfectly clear." He was getting agitated.

"We have it, it's safe. Tell me your plan."

His eyes flicked over her rapidly and found a spot on the wall behind her. "First, I need surgery for correcting nearsightedness. That's very important. Eyes are the mirror to the soul. Glass— or plastic, even polycarbonate—disfigure the soul. Why aren't you taking notes?"

"You said you had it all written down."

He nodded. "I don't know if I can remember every detail."

"You're doing fine."

"This mole must be removed." He rubbed his wrist. "It saps my strength. You see the color? Brown. Brown allows all the inner strength to flow from the body."

"I see."

"I've thought this out very carefully, and the spirits have guided me. I could have committed suicide, but that wasn't right. In court, my plea will be justifiable homicide, and I'll ask for the death penalty. The only stipulation is, I must choose the prison. Our new life has to start correctly. I haven't decided yet. I have a list. It's in my backpack. I really need my backpack."

"You can give me the list later."

"It's very important." He clenched and unclenched his hands. "It's the beginning of phase two."

"What was phase one?"

"Laura's death," he said sharply. "I confirmed my love for her by her death. I have to follow the plan exactly. Arrest..." He nodded at Susan. "Prison..." He was getting agitated again.

Parkhurst watched closely.

"...my trial..." He calmed down. "I will act as my own attorney, and I will be convicted." He took a breath and his eyes darted around the room.

"I understand," Susan said.

"You don't understand." Voice raised.

Parkhurst took a step nearer.

"That's only the end of phase one. It's all in my notebook. I have to have my notebook."

"Don't worry, Mr. Cayliff. The notebook is being kept in a safe place."

"I have to have it."

"Tell me more of your plan," she said.

"It isn't my plan." He was losing patience with her stupidity. "It's the universe. I had to figure out what the universe wanted. It took a long time and the spirits got angry if I got it wrong. After I'm convicted, I have to be executed by firing squad. One expert marksman with a Springfield 30.06. Facing me, he'll put a bullet just above my right eye, then one above the left eye. He will move to my right side and place one just above the ear. Two in the back of the head, and the final bullet on the left side just above the ear."

"Tell me about Kay Bender," Susan said.

"I don't know anyone by that name."

"She fell from the hayloft and—"

"I killed her." Hands against his face, his fingertips rubbed his temples. "She looked like Laura my beloved. The spirits were confused. I had to remove her."

"How did you kill her?"

"The railing. I cut through it. And put the pitchfork where she could fall on it. It had to be done."

"Why did you kill her?"

"She was trying to be Laura my beloved, invading her soul."

"Where did you get the saw?"

"One of those trucks," he said.

"Who was there while you cut the railing?"

"The spirits wanted me to be alone." He leaned forward and whispered to the table, "I know he's there."

"Who?"

"The officer standing right behind me. I can sense him."

That may be the only sane comment Delmar had made since he was brought in. "He's there to listen to this interview. What else can you tell me?"

"The actress who was stabbed."

"You know her name?"

"Of course, I know her name. I told you I'm not stupid."

Susan had deliberately waited to ask about Sheri Lloyd, wondering if he would mention her.

He gave another one of his small superior smiles. "Are you going to ask me if I killed her?"

"Did you?"

"Yes. It had to be done."

"Why did it have to be done?"

"She was making Laura unhappy. That would have messed up the plans. Laura had to be happy when she died."

"Where did you get the knife?"

He thought a long moment. "I don't want to talk anymore. I have a headache. Would you get me some aspirin, please?"

Susan leaned back and let Parkhurst ask questions. Delmar Cayliff refused to say anything more. He refused the help of an attorney. Earlier, he'd been eager to make her understand his plan; now he was through talking. He didn't want to waste any more time. He wanted to join his hand with Laura's in heaven. He wanted his backpack with his notebook.

Susan had Ellis and White take him away. Her mind playing over Cayliff's statement, she wandered along the corridor to the soft drink machine before realizing she had no change with her. Parkhurst stuck a hand in his pocket, brought out a handful of change, and held it out to her.

"You want one?" she asked.

"Sure."

She took enough coins and thumbed them in the slot. One can rumbled down, she gave it to him and collected the second. A few weeks ago, it would have been nothing; now it was awkward. Stupid. There was no emotional significance in taking quarters from his palm. Yeah? Then why did she feel stiff, why did he look stiff?

"Have you seen his backpack?" she asked.

"Not yet."

"Let's take a look."

Five minutes later she dropped Cayliff's backpack on her desk. The front pocket held a topographical map, a hardback, and a paperback both about the Sante Fe Trail. Inside the main section, there was an album with pictures—news photos, glossy studio giveaways, and snapshots, some blurred and grainy, some clear, taken without permission with a zoom lens, clippings, articles about Laura and reviews of the movies she'd been in. There was a bag of trail mix, a roll of clove Life Savers, a pair of white socks, two bottles of water, and a notebook, bluish gray, a three-ring binder like kids used for their homework, filled with ruled paper. In tiny, neat script, he'd written minutiae of his daily existence and the cosmic meaning of it all. On the day he'd gone to the bank, he'd endorsed a check with the bank's pen, it had black ink. Later he'd seen a movie with a character named Black. Black was a murky color meaning the universe wasn't pleased with him, he wasn't trying hard enough. Another movie, a western, had a Wells Fargo stagecoach. His bank was Wells Fargo. The evening news reported a child had fallen into an abandoned well. This meant the spirits were with him and wished him well. Stopping at a red light behind a red car was a double warning; the spirits were angry. A right turn followed by spotting the street sign Golden Avenue appeased the spirits.

Susan flipped pages until she came to the third of June, the day of the stuntwoman's accident. "She had to die. She looked too much like Laura my beloved. The spirits were confused." Three pages of colors with the descriptions these colors meant for the moods of the spirits, and explanations of why these moods affected the universe. Many pages of detailed plans to kill Yancy and take his gun, all to remove Laura my beloved from this world with the least suffering.

Susan quickly scanned pages and found, "She's stabbed. She can't upset Laura my beloved now."

And June 7. "It's done. The gun's mine. The time is now. I'm coming, Laura my beloved."

"The mayor will be happy," Parkhurst said.

"Yeah," Susan said.

"You can have Osey get on television and tell the world how we captured this guy with diligence and careful police work."

"Yeah."

"He confessed."

"Yeah, he did. Did you think there was anything odd about his confession?"

"The man is a nutcake. Everything about him is odd."

"Yeah."

"You don't sound overjoyed considering you just cleared a very high-profile case."

She wasn't. She was uneasy about Cayliff's confession. Inconsistencies abounded.

"You inform Ms. Edwards," she said. "I'll handle the press."

TWENTY-SEVEN

As Parkhurst shifted the Bronco into gear and pulled out of the lot, he glanced at his watch. Four o'clock. Laura was probably at the hotel. He felt guilty about her and guilty about Susan. Susan had said stay out of it. He'd been as much as lying to her and she knew it. Disobeying a superior hadn't ever been a conscience-heavy matter. Going soft?

Going stupid. Being his superior wasn't the half of it, being Susan got all tangled in there. He could hear his father say, "Hey, chickenshit for brains, you a coward too?" A real sweetheart, his old man. "If you're not man enough to go for it, you're no son of mine."

Aw, Laurie, what are you doing back in my life?

Leaving the Bronco in the hotel parking lot, he weaved through cars and went inside the Sunflower. On the fourth floor, he got off and went to Laura's suite.

Before he could knock, the door opened and Nick Logan stormed out. Seeing Parkhurst, Nick turned and called into the suite, "Your Mountie's here."

Parkhurst thought throwing him against the wall with a forearm across his throat and jabbing one quick punch to the gut was just the thing to let out a shitload of frustration.

"Ben—?" Laura, face shiny clean like she'd just taken a shower, started toward him, arms extended, then hesitated. "What's the matter? You look ready to punch someone. What is it with the male sex? You always want to hit each other."

He half smiled. There was something very clear and pure about rage. You knew what it was and you knew what to do with it. You hit someone. If you were like the old man, you battered your wife and beat up your children. If you were one of the children, you told yourself you were better than he was. You might even have believed it until an ex-wife came along and reminded you you weren't better, simply not a drunk and you had better control.

Laura laughed, a light sweet sound, and walked into his arms, put her hands on his face, and kissed him softly. He was wrong about the control.

"Laura—"

Her arms slipped around his neck, and she breathed into his throat. "I see you haven't forgotten me."

An inner voice ordered: throw her over your shoulder, march into the bedroom, and toss her on the bed. He cupped a hand behind her head and kissed her soft lips. Lightly. Control. Oh, yeah.

"You want to hear the latest from the cop shop?" His voice was hoarse.

Anger flashed up in her blue eyes so quickly, he thought she'd yell at him. She didn't, she slapped him. Not a ladylike tap or a choreographed move, she hauled off and landed a flat palm across his face hard enough to make his teeth clack.

"Hey. What was that for?"

"You know what it was for. For being a prick, for pulling away like you always did, for hiding under your cop shell." Tears filled her eyes.

"Laurie—" He gathered her in his arms again, smoothed back her gold hair, and murmured apologies.

She smiled up at him. Awareness, forgiveness, promise—all in a three-cornered smile. The inner voice again. Throw caution to the winds.

IN FRONT of the police department, Susan looked, she hoped, suitably serious and spoke, she hoped, with suitable solemnness. Lights blinded her, mikes bristled in her face.

"Have you arrested the killer?"

"Who is he?"

"What's his name?"

"We have a man in custody," she said.

"Did he kill two people?"

"Does he know Laura Edwards?"

"What do you know about him?"

"Why did he want to kill Laura Edwards?"

"Would you describe him as a stalker?"

"We're not releasing his name at this time," she said.

"Does Laura Edwards know him?"

"Is he a friend?"

"A boyfriend?"

"At this point, we haven't interviewed Ms. Edwards. She is shaken up over the incident. We'll have a great deal more information after we've spoken with her." Susan slipped back inside, as questions were shouted and microphones shaken.

At her desk Delmar Cayliff's notebook waited and she went back to it. By seven o'clock, she was still at it. She squinted, rubbed her eyes, and leaned back, then leaned forward, snapped on the desk lamp, and kept reading. Where was Parkhurst when she needed him? Probably having a jolly little reunion with his ex-wife.

Susan wanted a cigarette. Come on now. No reason he couldn't do anything he wanted, reunite with anyone he pleased. So get your mind where it belongs.

Every entry was dated and the time noted. The first rambled on about Laura Edwards, the movie being filmed in Hampstead, and the many instances that the universe was with him. When he made the decision to come to Hampstead, he wore a blue shirt and saw a blue car with the letter B on the license plate. These were important signs that told him the universe approved his decision. Whatever he did, wherever he went, he made these minute little connections.

In Hampstead, he watched all the outdoor filming; indoor shots, he got as near as he could and watched from there. Getting hired as an extra was big proof the universe applauded his venture.

On Monday, June 3, the day the stuntwoman had died, Delmar had been with other spectators outside old Josiah's barn. Even though he couldn't see any of the filming, it was enough for him to see Laura arriving. He went on for several pages about her love for him and how she looked at him and her plea that he make it possible for them to be together.

The stuntwoman received a brief mention; her attempt to look like Laura upset the spirits.

Susan couldn't define the difference between spirits and universe, except spirits tended toward bad and the universe toward good. The spirits brought fear when the universe wasn't pleased. The entries were hard to read: rambling, convoluted sentences started with one subject, then shot off onto something else. A single sentence was often more than a page in length. Pronouns were used without thought to antecedents, and much of the time only Delmar could possibly know what he was writing about.

In the middle of the next page, she found, "The impostor is dead." That was all, unless "like the sounds of locusts" had reference to sawing through the loft railing. In Delmar's world everything symbolized something. What a very exhausting world he must live in.

She tried to scan pages, but the smallness of the writing and the crowding of words made it impossible. There were a dozen or more pages on the decision that Laura Edwards must be shot, that being "the most humane" death. Pages on the decision to kill Yancy to obtain his gun, and how this would be done.

Pages of despair when he'd not succeeded in killing Yancy in the trees by the river, fear that the universe had turned against him. How in the hell could this man hold down a job? And isn't it grand that someone like him is teaching our college students? Detailed account of Delmar following Yancy, being chased by the dog, pages of the actual stabbing and taking of the gun.

The labyrinthian paths of a psychotic mind were awesome to behold.

On the night of Sheri Lloyd's murder, he wrote about being on the Patio. Yancy's mother, "the quiet woman with knowing eyes," several paragraphs about the "vicious, dangerous dog," pages about Laura and Nick Logan, and Sheri joining them. Imagined looks of love and pledging eternal fidelity from Laura. Her anger at Sheri Lloyd had been twisted into anger at Delmar for taking so long to claim her. No mention of a teenager. The following day, he wrote, "She can no longer upset Laura my beloved."

They could get him for assault, attempted murder, stalking,

and a number of other things, and a damn good thing to get him off the street, but—never mind his confession—he hadn't killed the stuntwoman and Sheri Lloyd. Forget the questions about how he could have known where to find the saw and the knife, and forget that he thought he'd killed two people—Laura and Yancy—who were still alive, every tiny detail as mundane as what he ate for breakfast while he was planning to kill them was written about. One line about the stuntwoman and one line about Sheri Lloyd? No way. If he'd killed them, he would have written pages and pages before he did it, and pages and pages afterward.

They still had a killer out there.

YANCY TRACKED DOWN Dr. Sheffield in the ER. Midmorning on a Sunday, the place was almost deserted. All the bad folks were sleeping it off and all the good folks were in church. The doc was sewing up a little boy who had fallen on some pieces of broken glass. When the boy was handed back to his mother, Sheffield turned to Yancy.

"Does this hurt?"

"No."

"How about this?"

"Yes."

"Any fever?"

"No."

"Bleeding?"

"No."

With a warning to avoid mad sprints until the rib healed, Sheffield scribbled a prescription for pain, told Yancy he was allowed limited duty, and rushed back into the fray.

Yancy was curiously relieved. After seeing this movie through two murders and the stalking of its star, he felt entitled to see it through to the end. He wanted, with his thumbs hooked in his belt, to watch the whole caravan leave town.

After tracking down Mac's room number, he dropped in. Mac, hands behind his head, left biceps bandaged, ankles crossed, was stretched out on the bed watching a soccer game on the television mounted on the wall.

"Well, well," Mac said. "The walking wounded." He clicked off the television. "What? No flowers? No grapes?"

"I thought I'd see how bad off you were before I spent my money."

"Huh. That quack down there in the emergency room claimed the bullet only grazed the skin. Didn't even tear up a muscle. Now, how am I going to get sympathy and workman's comp with that?"

"Isn't it a fine movie tradition that it only hurts when you laugh?"

"As a comedian," Mac said, "you might be a good cop. I keep telling them I'm in terrible pain, but they're going to boot me out of here tomorrow morning anyway."

"As a patient, you'll never get compassion."

"Oh, ha ha. The soccer game was better than this."

Yancy left him to it and headed back to the department to turn in the squad car and pick up his Cherokee. Since the chief's light was on, he went in to relay the news that the doctor had given him a halfway clean bill of health.

Susan threw her pen on the desk and leaned back. "Changed your mind about giving anything to get out of this assignment?"

He smiled, his sweet soft smile. "I think I might miss them when they're gone. I did talk to Howie—uh, he's the assistant manager at the hotel—"

"And?"

"Well, I don't know if it's of any interest at this point, Kevin Murphy—"

"Garbage-can-painting high school football star. What about him?"

"He's been hanging around the hotel. He replaced the battery, like he said. Once he jump-started a van when the lights had been left on all night. But he's been there other times, just to be there."

A seventeen-year-old kid, football star or not, might be interested in the glamorous movie people. Anything more than that? Maybe it was time to go home. She couldn't get her mind interested in picking at ideas.

"Put yourself to bed, Yancy. I can't help wondering if Dr.

Sheffield is an idiot, but if he says you can report for duty, who am I to argue?''

She gathered her scattered thoughts and Delmar Cayliff's notebook. The notebook she took to the evidence room, the thoughts she took out to her pickup. The air was velvet and fresh. She rolled down the windows and let the night blow in around her. In San Francisco, darkness could be an enemy, hiding danger. Deep blackness gathered in narrow streets, inside sad houses, and around cluttered corners. Desires and frustrations mingled like explosive chemicals and traces hung in the night air. Given the propensity of fellow cops for twisted humor, Susan had never admitted to fear, especially fear of the dark, but had used her facade of cool poise to carry her through. Even more than a year here didn't let her accept thick darkness as benign.

This damn case. Back to the beginning. God damn it. She smacked the steering wheel hard with her palm. Someone wanting to kill Laura? Stuntwoman and Ms. Lloyd got in the way. Laura wanting to kill stuntwoman or Sheri Lloyd?

The kitten was glad to see her when she opened the kitchen door. Perissa, twisting around her ankles, nattered about neglect. She dumped fishy-smelling stuff in a clean bowl and set it on the floor by the refrigerator. As is often the case with love, the kitten left her for something better, food in this instance.

The answering machine blinked about messages; Susan ignored it. She felt two steps behind; this was not a feeling she liked. We've collared a stalker, she consoled herself. He's confessed. Yeah, yeah, I've been all through that. I don't think he did it.

So now what? Back to the beginning. Start over. Yeah, I've been through that too.

Well then, how about a drink? The sharp bite of alcohol to cool the frustrated brain. A bottle of chardonnay stood in the refrigerator. Naw. In vino, muddled mind. She passed up the tall cool bottle and moved on to leftover pizza. She never was much of a drinker; her drug of choice was nicotine, and she'd given that up. Sometimes, like now, she wondered why. The microwave beeped a summons and she put steaming pizza next to the *Herald* that she unfolded on the table. The state of the wheat crop didn't hold her attention, nor did the quilting exhibition or the proper feeder for purple martens.

Laura Edwards in close proximity to Lieutenant Parkhurst kept bringing images to mind. Ah yes, well. None of her business. If she ignored famous actresses with cop ex-husbands and the ties that bind, Kevin Murphy was something to think about.

Sullen, angry young man. Impeccable manners, polite to parody. Complex, filled with hatred for the entire adult world. High school football hero. Beaten by his father—according to Parkhurst—retired test pilot. Smart. Poor grades. An extra in *Lethal Promise*. Is any of this interesting? He'd made a name for himself with his garbage-can art and getting dubbed the mad painter. How much more of a name would he make by murdering Laura Edwards? He might have been at the hotel the night Sheri Lloyd was stabbed. Somebody was—a young person, a teenager. It could have been Kevin. Why had Sheri been killed? The answer might shed light.

Yancy's mother had also been there. Raina had left with her dog and started walking home. She'd been picked up by Kevin Murphy. If Kevin had just killed a woman would he stop to pick up Raina and her dog? Unless Parkhurst's instincts were off, Kevin had picked them up to irritate his father—big hairy dog in pristine car.

She scooped up strings of cheese and popped them in her mouth, swallowed and took a swig of orange juice. Her watch said eight-thirty. Too late to drive out and talk with Raina Yancy?

Yes. She was going anyway. Raina probably wouldn't remember the young person/teenager, but Susan intended to ask.

The little brown Fiat, sitting in the garage next to the pickup, could use a wash; it was so covered in dust, the paint didn't even gleam under the light. She drove it barely enough to keep the battery charged and didn't know why she didn't get rid of it; a reminder of another life maybe. She climbed in the pickup.

The just-past-full-moon poured silver light on fields of wheat that rippled in the wind like the sleek muscles of a running predator. The stars blinked in and out of slow drifting clouds. A jackrabbit on the side of the road sat up on its haunches and turned its large ears like antennae, listening for enemies or judging the safety of crossing the road. She slowed and watched it bound past on its powerful hind legs.

Beyond her headlights, moonlight softened the night. The dense darkness out here on moonless nights made her uneasy. A city creature, she felt safer with neon and two-legged animals than with darkness and four-legged ones.

After more than a year here, she was getting better at finding rural places. Having been to the Yancy house before helped, but even so she missed a turn and had to backtrack.

The house, on a rise with a pale glow inside, sat in an island of darkness. Little house on the prairie. The dog barked, and an outside light came on. She cut the engine, but sat where she was as the dog streaked like a demon toward the truck. It danced around, leaping up to stare her in the eye.

Yancy's sister, standing at the kitchen door with the screen open, called to the dog. It gave one last menacing leap and galloped back to the house. Susan slid from the truck, hoping the hound had been fed.

"Chief Wren?" Serena came toward her, dog at her side. "What's wrong?"

"Nothing. I'm sorry, I didn't mean to frighten you. I know it's a little late, but—" The dog came at her. She froze, understanding very well why Delmar Cayliff was afraid of the beast.

"He's very friendly," Serena said.

Right. Elmo shuffled up to her, licked her hand with a soft tongue, and led her into the kitchen. Maybe he was friendly. "I wanted to ask your mother a few questions, if she's still up."

"Oh, sure, she's reading."

"Pretending to read, more like," Raina said. She sat in the overstuffed chair by the window. "Reading isn't what it used to be when you can't remember what you read on the page before." Fear and frustration sat just below the light words.

"You remember Chief Wren," Serena said.

"Please sit down. I'll get some iced tea."

"No. Thank you." Susan sat on the couch and dropped her shoulder bag at her feet. "I'm sorry to disturb you, but I have a couple questions to ask."

With a great sigh Elmo spread himself at Raina's feet; she reached down and smoothed his ears.

"I was here around four days ago."

Raina nodded. "The young actress who got killed."

"You saw her earlier in the evening, before she was stabbed."

Raina reached up and turned off the lamp on the end table. "Look," she said.

Out the window, Susan saw a jackrabbit, ears visible over the flowers. She wondered if it was the same one she'd seen on the road. If so it had gotten here almost as quickly as she had.

"They're timid," Raina said. "When they're frightened, they run. They've got long teeth for eating plants—they're—oh, what is that word—"

"Herbivores?"

"Yes. They're not rabbits really, you know, they're hares. Those teeth are made for tackling plants. They've got long claws on their front feet, to pull plants and strip them. They move fast, but if they're trapped, they're not bunnies. Foxes have been known to make that mistake and gotten blinded and gutted. Even a mountain lion has lost its life by trapping one in its lair."

Raina sat in shadow, her profile highlighted by light coming from the kitchen. She looked young and beautiful, her voice soft. She might have been telling a fairy tale to a child, or a witch weaving a spell. "That's what it was, don't you think? Desperation."

Susan shook herself back to her purpose here. "Do you remember being at the hotel?"

Raina blinked, then said, "I've been there many times. Peter says watching the movie being made is boring. Maybe, but it's interesting."

"Do you remember Tuesday evening?"

Raina smiled. "Sometimes I can barely remember my name."

Susan felt a rush of liking and respect for this woman. No wonder Yancy was bent on protecting her. She was charming in what must be to her a devastating situation. "You were on the Patio. Sheri Lloyd was there."

"She was angry, poor little thing. To get her own way, she threatened someone."

"Who?"

"Vengeance was in the air."

"Vengeance?"

> *"Vengeance is in my heart, death in my hand,*
> *Blood and revenge are hammering in my head."*

"Kevin Murphy," Susan said. "Did he have vengefulness in his heart?"

"Oh, yes. Definitely." Raina reached down to stroke the dog's shoulder. "He offered us a ride. Nice of him, even though his purpose wasn't to be nice."

"Was he on the Patio that night?"

"No."

Raina was certain, but how much reliance could be placed on her memory? "Who else was there beside the actors?"

"A very troubled young man. He was afraid of Elmo."

"Anybody else?"

"Not that I can think of."

"Was there a young person there? Maybe teenaged?" Leading the witness, Susan.

Raina thought. "You know I believe there was."

"Who was it?"

"That girl, the one who lives where Peter does. I forget her name."

"Stephanie Blakeley?"

TWENTY-EIGHT

YANCY PULLED HIMSELF out of bed Monday morning, sat on the edge, and let his hands prop up his head. Why, having been given the opportunity, did he not snap to and take some days off. What? And leave show business?

After an unsatisfactory shower, he pulled on his uniform pants, shrugged into a shirt, buckled on his belt, and went stiffly and creakily down to his Cherokee. At the department, he turned it in for a squad car and set out for...

He didn't know where they were filming this morning. That information was on the call sheet, which he'd left at home. He had the feeling this wasn't going to be a great day. He went back to retrieve it. The crew call was six a.m. His watch said 5:45.

Location for shooting was the stable at the Lockett mansion. Fifer had Kevin Murphy, shirtless, mucking out a stall, the muscles showing off nicely in his back and shoulders. He did a good acting job, Yancy thought, didn't look at the camera, didn't ogle the stuntwoman, did exactly what he was told. Sullen expression perfect for a kid who has to work when he'd rather be swimming with his girlfriend. He led a horse from the stall, tied it to a ring, then loaded dirty straw in a wheelbarrow. Howie, however, should stick to the hotel business. He was supposed to drive up and park. That's all. Except he couldn't seem to stop the car at the right spot. After several tries, Fifer dismissed him. Yancy was afraid his friend Howie's movie career was over.

Fifer filmed the new stunt double leading a horse from the stable and tossing on a saddle. As she reached under the horse's belly for the girth, footsteps were heard. She straightened. Guess what? The villain. The stunt double cinched up, leaped on the horse, and galloped away.

That sequence was filmed over and over. Then Fifer did some shots of Laura Edwards standing by the horse, curry brush in hand. It was obvious she wasn't happy to be there. Any actual brushing was done by the stuntwoman, long shots and close-ups of hands and the horse's glossy hide. Even then only the neck and shoulders were touched, the hindquarters were left strictly alone. The horse looked bored.

The morning dragged on with the horse brought out of the stall, taken back in, and brought out repeatedly. No wonder it was bored. It seemed an amiable chestnut who knew his part well, until Laura got near; her tension made the horse uneasy and it continuously stepped away. Either that or the horse had a sense of humor.

When Fifer judged the light was wrong, he called a halt. The predicted twenty percent cloud cover had him in short temper, and he made changes in the schedule and shifted everybody inside the mansion for interior scenes. The crew followed orders without chitchat, praying for the clouds to dissipate. Yancy snagged coffee from the caterer. There was nothing wimpy about California coffee. If it didn't jolt him into serious clear-mindedness, nothing would.

That wasn't cloud cover up there; it was the beginnings of rain clouds. Most likely another thunderstorm was on the way before the skies got brighter. Whether Fifer knew or not Yancy had no idea, but Yancy wasn't going to tell him.

"Gotta talk to you," Robin said to Yancy on one of his trips back and forth to fetch props.

Fifer snapped at Clem because the AD—not Clem's fault—had herded Laura onto her mark instead of the stand-in. Laura threw a fit, went back to her trailer, and wouldn't come out.

Nick, the unflappable professional, flubbed lines over and over on a scene Fifer was trying to shoot without Laura. Robin McCormack forgot a vital prop and had to go back for it. A light blew with a pop that sent everybody six inches off the floor. One take was going along fine, cast and crew just beginning to relax, when a camera jammed.

Fifer went very still, his face hardly moved when he spoke and his voice held the menace of a disturbed rattler. Everybody immediately got so tense a pin dropping would have shattered them like a footstep on thin ice. Yancy, caught up in the tension hanging like low-lying fog, was soaked with sweat, oppressed by the humidity, and limp as a rag. His rib hurt. Fifer called an early lunch break and everybody split like lightning.

In the caterer's tent, Yancy slid next to Mac, who had his left sleeve rolled up above the bandage on his biceps. A plate piled with ravioli, salad, and chunks of bread sat in front of him.

"How's the arm?"

"Hurts," Mac said.

"You couldn't wrangle a few days off?"

"I'd rather keep an eye on things." Mac tore off a chunk of bread and shoved it in his mouth.

Odd, Yancy was under the impression Mac didn't like Laura Edwards. What did he want to keep an eye on? "What's wrong with everybody today?"

After washing down a mouthful of ravioli, Mac said ominously, "Jinx."

"What?"

"Movie people are suckers for superstition. All of them; cast, crew, hired hands, above the line, below the line. They believe this movie is jinxed and they all tiptoe along looking over their shoulders waiting for the crouched beast to spring."

Yancy hadn't known Mac was so poetic. "You too?"

"Naw. I do my job, get paid. Don't have my ego nailed to the floor."

"Unless something happens to Laura Edwards while you're driving her somewhere."

"Better me than her." Mac tapped the gauze on his arm. "Fifer, who knows what that one thinks. He's spooky, is what he is."

Yancy circled the tent looking for Clem. He found her in the rear, drinking lemonade and looking miserable.

"You okay?" he asked.

She spun around, face shutting down like a window closing. "Don't creep up on me like that."

"I wondered if you were all right?"

"Why wouldn't I be?"

"Some people get upset," he said mildly, "when they get yelled at for something that wasn't their fault."

"I'm used to it." She stomped off.

Filming in the afternoon was a repeat of the morning—scene after scene went wrong, lines were forgotten, words were garbled, doors wouldn't open, or wouldn't stay closed. Fifer got more and more deadly quiet, which rippled out to cast and crew until everybody was ready to run shrieking into the woods. Yancy included.

There was no chance to talk with Robin, and when Fifer finally called a halt Robin couldn't be found. Yancy decided to try base camp.

Robin was waiting at the prop trailer. "Listen," he said, "there's something you should know. A pair of handcuffs is missing."

"Handcuffs are missing," Yancy repeated.

"Yeah. You deaf or something?"

Yancy looked around at the long, crowded prop trailer. "You're sure?" He found it hard to believe that Robin knew anything was missing.

"It's my job to know," Robin said, a mite irritated.

"Guns missing?"

"Hell, no. All you people ever think about are guns. Guns are locked in the safe. None missing."

"Why would anyone steal a pair of handcuffs?"

"People are nuts. Some actor uses it, they want it. Don't ask me why. We can't even have snapshots developed at the local quick photo place, because some jerk off says, 'Hey, that's Nick Logan' and prints up two dozen extra copies to pass out to his friends."

"What can anybody do with handcuffs?" Yancy was talking more to himself than to Robin.

"Handcuff someone. Hang the cuffs on the wall, put them in a box under the bed. Who the hell knows."

"Where do you keep them?"

Robin opened a chest drawer, five pairs of cuffs lay inside.

"When were they taken?"

"I can't tell you. I had them in a bag with a bunch of other stuff we were using. Sometime this afternoon, I noticed they were gone."

Yancy walked up and back looking at boxes and bins of props, chewing over missing handcuffs.

"I just wanted to let you know. Could you ruminate somewhere else? I'd like to lock up and get out of here?"

"Sure." Yancy clattered down the metal stairs. Nobody was left except the security guys. He nodded to them and wandered around stepping over electrical cables. Something was nagging at him.

"THE BLAKELEY GIRL'S in the interview room," White said.

Susan looked up from her desk. "Her mother with her?"

White smiled. "Stephanie was playing tennis at Broken Arrow Park. I asked her if she'd like to come with me."

White, with his blond hair, round face, and apple cheeks, looked like a Boy Scout. Even his severe crew cut didn't detract from the image. He wouldn't scare anybody.

Susan tucked in her blouse and went down the corridor. "I need to ask you some questions, Stephanie." She put an edge in her voice.

Stephanie Blakeley turned from the mirrored glass that she'd been studying. At thirteen, she was tall for her age, almost as tall as Susan, and it was easy to see how, in a dimly lit area, she could look in her late teens. A loose T-shirt covered a thin boyish figure. Her brown hair with tawny streaks reached just past her ears, and could be worn by either male or female. Hazel eyes, clear and intelligent, were right now wary and frightened.

"Sit down, please," Susan said.

Stephanie slid onto a chair, and turned wide-eyed when the Miranda rights were read to her.

"Why didn't you tell me you were at the hotel the evening Ms. Lloyd was killed?"

The girl pushed her hands through her hair. "I know I should have." A basically truthful child, this one, and relieved to be clearing her conscience. "I tried to tell Peter. Two days ago. But he looked so—you know, not feeling good and that other cop was there."

Demarco looked like a marine with matters of national security on his mind. No teenage girl would be quick to confide in him.

"Tell me now."

"I was there. Does my mother have to know?"

"You were there without permission?"

Stephanie stared straight ahead like a cadet being disciplined. "Worse. She said I couldn't go."

"Why did you?"

Stephanie sniffed and rubbed a finger under her nose. "There was no reason why I shouldn't. I wouldn't be late, it wasn't a school night. How many times will a movie be made here? I wanted to be around where the actors might be. I wasn't going to talk to anybody, or ask for an autograph or anything. That would be exceptionally gross."

"Then why go?"

"You'll think I'm silly. Childish."

To a teenager, there was nothing worse than being thought childish.

"I'm going to be an author." There, she'd said it. Make ridiculing remarks if you want.

"And?" Susan carefully kept the word neutral.

"I wanted to observe. See what they were like."

Susan put her through questions. When Stephanie accepted that she wasn't being thought childish, she answered easily, but she didn't have anything to add to what Susan already knew. She sketched out the scene with colorful detail. This girl might, indeed, be a writer. Unlike the others, she didn't think Delmar Cayliff was ordinary. She thought he was creepy.

"How did you get to the hotel?"

"I rode my bike. Mom doesn't want me to ride it after dark. It's got lights," she hastened to add.

At that point, Susan would have let her go, except something still sat on her mind, something that wasn't going to be volunteered and Susan wasn't quite sure how to get at it. "What happened on your way home?"

"Well—"

Right question.

"You know that curve on Arbor Street down by the quarry?"

Susan nodded.

"It's sharp, and right there where it sort of bends there's that flat field behind the fence before you come to where it drops off. Anyway, I was riding right at that bend when a car came roaring straight at me. I got pinned in the headlights. All I could think, I'm going to be killed and my mother will know I went out.''

"Who was driving?"

Stephanie hesitated.

Susan let her struggle with it.

"I'm sure he just didn't realize how—" She let that trail off, not even believing it herself. "Anyway, when he saw me, he jumped on the brakes, they screamed, and the car fishtailed all over the place.''

"Who was it?"

"Kevin," she said after another struggle. "Then he kind of got control and drove off and I came home.''

Stephanie sighed. "I figured maybe I'd just stay home next time.''

After she let Stephanie go, Susan sent White out to bring in Kevin Murphy.

IN THE INTERVIEW ROOM, Kevin slouched in a plastic chair, hands in his pockets. He smelled faintly of horses, having been picked up at the Lockett stables where he'd just finished making his movie debut. He'd pulled on a tank top, tight enough to outline the muscles in his chest. Not nervous, not scared and maintaining his parody of politeness, he looked at her with faint mockery.

"What happened to your eye?" She leaned against the wall, one knee bent.

With fingertips, he touched the fading bruise by his left eye. "I ran into a door.''

"Again? First a nosebleed, now a black eye. Clumsy.''

"Yes, ma'am, I certainly am.''

"On the night Sheri Lloyd was murdered, you were driving your father's car. Tell me again what you did.''

"I got off work and went home to shower. Later I started out to see a friend, and then decided not to.''

"When you got home from work, you had an argument with your father." She made it a statement, not a question. "He struck you. You took his car. You weren't going to see a friend. Where were you going?''

He raked hair from his eyes. ''Just driving.''

''With your father's permission?''

Amusement flickered in his eyes. ''Not exactly.''

She sat down across from him. He drew back and hung an elbow over the chair.

She leaned forward. ''He hit you, you got angry and drove away in his car. Weren't you afraid he'd report it stolen? Your emotions were so intense you nearly killed a girl on a bicycle.''

''I never got near her.''

Due to his young and extraordinary reflexes. ''What were you trying to do?''

''See how fast I could take the curve.''

''The girl says you weren't trying to make the curve, you were coming head-on.''

''She's mistaken.''

The kid had been going to kill himself. Susan was at a loss about what to do.

She looked at him. ''He would have wept,'' she said softly. ''And everybody would have believed him.''

She waited, then went back to it. ''You drove around, picked up Raina Yancy and her dog, got blood on the steering wheel and the gearshift.'' Osey'd also found blood on the door handle and the driver's seat. The shirt Kevin had worn was splattered down the front and there'd been blood on Raina's white skirt—even though it had been washed—as well as on Kevin's handkerchief. It was all his blood. At least, it was all the same type as his. It wasn't Raina Yancy's type and it wasn't Sheri Lloyd's.

He looked at her, no squirming, no blustering. A bright young man with looks, artistic talent, athletic ability.

''You're free to go,'' she said.

He stood, pushed the chair back up to the table, and walked out.

There might have been time for him to follow Sheri Lloyd to her room and stab her, then go home, get smacked around by his father, and drive off. Except. Except. Why? Sheri might have been snooty to him; she was snooty to everybody she felt beneath her.

And the stuntwoman? A mistake, an attempt at Laura Edwards. Why would he want to kill Ms. Edwards? Well now, let's see here. Perhaps Laura Edwards killed the stuntwoman and Kevin killed Sheri Lloyd. And the stalker stalked.

Sure.

Sitting at her desk, she let her mind drift, coaxing thoughts from the murk on the bottom to float up. She wasn't one fact closer to a solution. One person dead, perhaps by mistaken identity. Another stabbed. Nothing mistaken about that. A stalker who confessed to both deaths. She shuffled papers until she found the autopsy report on Ms. Lloyd. Except for being dead, she was in great shape. Heart and lungs perfect. Kidneys and liver perfect. No diseased tissues anywhere. No traces of drugs beyond a small amount of alcohol in the stomach. The phone rang.

"Yes, Hazel?"

"The mayor is on the line."

"Tell him I'm not in. I'm not available, unless it's important. In which case I'll be at home watching movies."

"Excuse me?"

"Keep it to yourself."

At the video rental place, Susan picked up *When the Rose Blooms* and *Family Style* and *My Sister's Friend*, the movies Raina Yancy had watched on Wednesday. Popcorn? Sure. What's a movie without popcorn. She threw in a box of micro-wavable popcorn and two Hersheys with almonds.

At home, Perissa, rapidly becoming more cat than kitten, greeted her with loud complaints of neglect and hunger.

"No way," Susan said. "It's not even two o'clock."

She zapped the popcorn, stacked pillows on the couch, slid in *Family Style* starring Laura Edwards and Nick Logan, and settled the bowl on her stomach. Katie/Laura goes home for parents' anniversary. Runs into old boyfriend Greg/Nick. Lots of unfinished family business, snappy dialogue, and touching moments of reality, happy ending.

Where the Rose Blooms, a thriller, also starred Laura Edwards and Nick Logan. Julie/Laura, your normal everyday fabulous

beauty, gets threatening messages via her computer. Fast-paced
with heart-stopping moments and car chases. Julia/Laura does
have long blond hair and somebody does try to stab her. Could
this have been the basis for Raina's comment about the woman
stabbed?

The third movie had Ms. Edwards but not Nick Logan. Hear-
twarming with social significance and tear-jerking scenes. Just as
it came to an end, the kitten leaped on her stomach, knocking
over the bowl and sending popcorn flying. Susan yelled, the cat
got frightened, the remote got lost, and popcorn got all over the
carpet.

On hands and knees, Susan gathered kernels and flung them
in the bowl. Perissa, thinking this great fun, scooped them out
and batted them across the floor.

"That's it, cat. You're an orphan."

The credits were rolling before Susan rescued the remote from
under the couch. She watched the names scroll by and told the
cat. "Oh, my. Art director."

Perissa approached her sideways, back arched.

"Just kidding," Susan said.

TWENTY-NINE

JUSTIN WESLEY KIDDERING the Third. The only person Susan knew down there in Los Angeles living shoulder to shoulder, or maybe acre to acre, with the rich and famous. It had been over ten years since they'd spoken, and in fact, it was entirely possible he wouldn't want to talk with her now.

His father, Justin Wesley Kiddering the Second, was the owner of everything that made money, shipping, land, fishing, stocks. His mother, in pearls and silk blouses, always had her picture in the paper on behalf of every charitable organization worth its name.

The Kidderings lived several blocks up in class, status, and size of residence from Susan's family. He was a rich kid whose father gave him everything the wealthy are entitled to by birthright. Susan was the one who had first started calling him Just Kidding. They were buddies from the time they were eleven. He was tall, blond, and square-jawed, as befitted the heir to the throne.

In high school English class, she wrote his papers. Kiddering the Second wanted him to go to Brown, but he held out for UC Berkeley to be with her.

He went to law school because she did and he didn't have any burning desire to study something else. It wasn't as though he had to earn a living. They studied together, shared notes, and divided topics for research. They hung out in coffee shops that stayed open late, impressing each other with their intelligence, their grasp of humankind, and their free-thinking ability to get to the heart of the problem.

The Big Plan was to open a law firm together and take on causes, raise banners for the underdog and downtrodden. Even at their most committed, she thought they were only playing a fantasy. Shortly before graduation, they had a fight. She told him she was chucking it all to be a cop. A shouting fight followed; he stomped off. She felt he was secretly relieved; he wasn't cut out to take care of the poor. That was the last time she saw him. She signed on with the San Francisco police force and he took his law degree down to southern California and made his name recognized in the entertainment industry.

It was 7:30 here, that meant 5:30 in California. Possibly still in his office. She couldn't believe how shaky her hand was when she picked up the phone. Information gave her an office listing. That number gave her a secretary with a British accent who said Mr. Kiddering was not available, she would be pleased to take a message.

"I'm a police officer investigating a homicide. Tell him I'd greatly appreciate a few moments of his time."

"That's a new approach," she said in her bored, high-toned voice. "I'll pass your message to him."

Even after all these years, Susan recognized his voice with no trouble. "This is Susan Wren," she said.

"Yes?" His voice was cool, approaching Siberian borders. She didn't know if it was because he didn't recognize her or because he did. Oh, hell, why did she use that name? Of course, he didn't recognize it.

Nervously, she cleared her throat. "Susan Donovan."

There was dead silence on the other end of the line. Maybe he didn't want to talk to her, maybe he was still angry.

"The thud you heard," he said, "was my mouth dropping. This is the time for some devastatingly clever remark, but damned if I can think of one. Damned if I can think, actually. How long has it been?"

"Ten years."

"Didn't I stomp out saying something embarrassing like you'll regret this?"

"Something like that."

There was an awkward silence.

"Jesus. Susan. Could you call back tomorrow? Give me time to work up some great lines?"

"Same old Just. Too much class to ask right out, What the

hell do you want? You think I called for something deplorable like Mel Gibson's autograph.''

He laughed. ''You would never be so mundane.''

There was another silence.

''To get this conversation rolling, fill me in on the last ten years.'' He sounded so Hollywood, she would have laughed, except she was afraid it might sound too high-pitched. ''Aw, come on,'' he urged. ''To make it easier, pretend like you're giving me a pitch for a new sitcom.''

''Well, the night after graduation—''

''Not scene by scene. Just give me the story line.''

''I thought you should see motivation to get the essence—''

''Nobody in the Industry talks about essence. We deal strictly in T and A or violence. You got married?''

''You connect violence with marriage?''

''Ex-wife number one did. But not till we got into the divorce.''

''How many wives have there been?''

''Only two. The second was very civilized about the divorce.''

''Children?''

''Let me think. Yeah. Two, I believe, the first time and one the next time. Does that make three? With a little more thought I could give you their ages. It gets confusing because the ex-wives came with their own. When you jumble them together, you have a hard time remembering which ones are which. You said you were married.''

''Yes.''

''He died?'' Just asked softly.

''How did you know?''

''I still know you. You froze when I asked about marriage. I'm sorry.''

''Thank you. Actually, I called for a reason.''

He gave a theatrical sigh. ''Not just to talk over old times? Are you still one of those''—he lowered his voice and spoke like a broadcaster—''men and women in law enforcement.''

''I'm the chief of police.''

''No shit? Congratulations. That's terrific. Not San Francisco, or I would have heard.''

"Hampstead, Kansas."

"Where?"

She laughed, then told him about *Lethal Promise* being filmed in Hampstead. "I called for information: fact, fiction, conjecture, and gossip. Do you know the director Hayden Fifer?"

"Everybody knows who he is, of course."

"Of course."

He laughed. "Was that a nasty crack?"

"No. Well, maybe a small one." It was difficult talking with a long-ago lover and she suddenly had more sympathy for Parkhurst. You fell right back into the old patterns and then you remembered. What a mess. She shouldn't have called. "Do you know anything about this movie?"

"As a matter of fact, I do. I was involved at the beginning on behalf of some of the moneylenders. Big budget film that keeps getting more and more over the huge budget it started with. A not-very-original script. A thriller-love story about a beautiful sophisticated woman who came from farming stock. Her father, the farmer who has some poetic affinity for the wonderfulness of the land and growing things on it, is killed. Woman finds out an evil agribusiness is destroying local flora and fauna by whatever destroys these things—unsafe and unlawful pesticides probably. Evil agribusiness types have to kill her too. She goes to local law enforcement who say she's nuts. Except for one guy who doesn't really believe her, but falls in love with her. She gets hunted down, chased, shot at, a gratuitous car chase or two. Somewhere she realizes the land, or maybe it's the prairie—I forget—is a sacred trust and must be preserved. The bad guys are about to win. The local cop risks life, limb, and career to save her. End on a romancy shot which suggests happily ever after."

"Romantic walks through the wheat fields?"

"It's probably in there somewhere. I only hit the high spots. Or maybe it's horseback rides through the meadows."

"Is it a good movie?"

"Depends what you mean by good. Will it be intellectually stimulating, full of socially significant questions with or without answers? No. But it should be exciting, funny, moving, and—

above all—entertaining. That's the kind of film Fifer does. His last two weren't successes, so he has a lot riding on this. The man himself—"

"What are you thinking? Anything might help."

"For a hotshot director, Fifer has a reputation for being anxious. He's known for his retakes, and not keeping track of dollars. With so much riding on this movie, I'd say he must be *really* anxious and ready to do anything to make it work. Three or four marriages, the usual."

"How did he come to direct this film?"

"Two reasons. Laura Edwards and Nick Logan. Both top of the heap big box office. They have a love affair that's been given much play. Investors were elbowing each other out of the way to get in line."

"Is Laura Edwards good?"

"Have you read a paper in the last five years? Don't they have movies there? Yes, she's good, but she has a tendency to over-emote. The director needs to sit on her, make her do what he wants."

"Personal life?"

"Actors—the big ones—don't have a personal life. The public wants to know when she eats, where she frolics on the beach, and who she sleeps with. She's been married a couple of times. Once, come to think of it, to some hometown boy."

She wondered what Parkhurst would think of being referred to as a hometown boy.

"...childhood sweetheart, or something. Married a penny-weight agent whose name escapes me. I'll bet he drinks himself to sleep every night for letting her get away. He never had or ever will have somebody of her stature. The usual scandals about happily married male throws away wife and family for her. *National Enquirer* stuff."

"Nick Logan?"

"He can act. The viewing public may not know it because he isn't doing Shakespeare or Ibsen."

"Why isn't he, if he's good?"

"Money, darling."

"Rumor, gossip, innuendo?"

"He gives the impression he's an easygoing man, but he's got a temper like a killer bee. He's pushed around a few media people. Smashed cameras. Doesn't like to hear the word *no*. Got a divorce to engage in the romance with Laura."

"His wife upset?"

"It's all very civilized here. We're all still good friends who love each other. She's a model, says the accepted thing, it wasn't working out, she still loves him."

His voice faded and she heard Ms. British Secretary in the background, saying Mr. Anklet was asking how long it would be.

Justin said, "Tell him I'll be right with him."

"You have a client waiting?"

"Naw. I just told Phoebe to say that so you'd be impressed. Are you impressed?"

"Is his name really Anklet?"

"He's changing it from Bracelet. What do you think?"

"I think you haven't changed. Your kids must find you a riot."

"They're great. When can you come meet them?"

"Next time I come to L.A. Right now there's an art director I want to ask you about."

YANCY'S RIB began to pinch a little as he tromped around base camp. He was telling himself to go home, uneasiness was for movie heroes. *Hear that? I don't hear anything, it's quiet. Yeah, too quiet.*

He was headed over to his squad car before he realized it wasn't quiet. The air-conditioning in Laura Edwards's trailer gave out a monotonous hum. She could have neglected to turn it off. If so, it was apt to overload and give out.

Her town car was gone, all the vehicles were gone except the van belonging to security. Yancy knocked on the trailer door. He knocked louder, at the risk of disturbing the female star, if she were inside and busy, like getting it off with a dear friend. Nick Logan's car was also gone, but who knew.

No answer. The air-conditioning droned away. He tracked down the security guy. "You know if Laura Edwards is still in her trailer?"

"Not to my knowledge. Far as I know nobody here but me and my partner."

Yancy would have thought it was his job to know these things.

"What're you doing here?" the guard asked.

Wandering around when I should be home. "The air-conditioning's on. That happen often?"

"Not to my knowledge."

"You got a key for these trailers?" Yancy asked.

"You think they'd just hand out keys to Laura Edwards's trailer? You been smoking something funny?"

With the guard dogging his heels, Yancy checked every trailer, all quiet and locked.

"You report in at certain times?" Yancy asked.

"Sure. Every two hours. I have an hour and a half to go."

"Call your boss. Let me talk to him."

"I can't do that."

Yancy rubbed a knuckle up and down his forehead. "You see this uniform? See any difference between yours and mine? Right. If it helps you any, you can say I've got you at gun point."

The guard sighed, to show he wasn't doing this willingly, took the cell phone from its holster and punched a number. Yancy was beginning to be a believer in cell phones; they surely were handy.

The security guy handed it over to him. Yancy explained his problem.

"You might have a problem, but I don't. Maybe she wants it cool when she comes in," and hung up.

Maybe he was right. Go home. Yancy went to the Sunflower instead.

"Howie, I'm looking for Ms. Edwards. Is she in her room?"

"I don't know. Why?"

"Put me through to her room."

"We're not supposed to—"

"Just do it, okay?"

Howie started to argue, gave it up and a few seconds later said, "There's no answer."

"Try Nick Logan."

No answer there either. They probably went out together. Oh

hell, forget it. He took the elevator to the fourth floor and rapped on the door of Ms. Edwards's suite, then he tried Nick Logan's.

He was overreacting here. There was no reason Ms. Edwards had to be in her suite, or answer phones or knocks even if she was in. He went back down the elevator and hiked along the corridor to the coffee shop.

"One?" The waitress was a college student with an inviting summer smile.

"I'm looking for someone?"

"Who?"

"Famous movie stars."

"They're not here." She waved her arm to indicate the almost empty room.

He could see that. He checked out the Patio; nobody there either. In the lobby, he left a message with Howie to have Mac call him, then headed for the department to turn in the squad car and pick up his Cherokee.

If the Lieutenant or Osey had been in, Yancy might have mentioned it to them. Might have. Even he was beginning to think he was stirring up a bunch of nothing. He took himself home.

Stephanie was sitting on the steps looking morose.

"Hi, Steph." He sat next to her. "What's the matter?"

"I wish I were older."

"Why? Thirteen's a good age."

"Don't patronize me."

"I'm sorry. Tell me what your problem is."

"You wouldn't understand."

"I might. You could give me a try."

She drew up her long legs and rested her chin on one knee. "Do you like living here?"

"Sure," he said, wondering where this was going.

"You think you could like my mother?"

"I do like her."

"You know what I mean."

"It doesn't work that way, Steph."

"How does it work?"

"Poets have been writing about it forever, right?"

"She's older than you are anyway," Stephanie said glumly.

"She's overprotective. If she had somebody else to focus on, she wouldn't sit on me so much."

"What is it you want to do that she won't let you?"

"Have you teach me to shoot a gun."

Oh. He wasn't surprised Mrs. Blakely wouldn't allow it. She was totally against firearms.

"Could you ask her for me?" Stephanie asked.

"Oh, Steph, I don't know about that."

"See, I told you you wouldn't understand."

Upstairs, he phoned Mac, who didn't know where Ms. Edwards was. She'd dismissed him earlier this afternoon.

"She told you she didn't need you?"

"That's right. Why?"

"She told you herself? Didn't ask one of her flunkies to tell you?"

"Her assistant. What are you getting at?"

"Probably nothing." Yancy hung up and rubbed the back of his neck. He was getting all worked up over air-conditioning. Ms. Edwards might claim all sorts of concern about the environment, but when it came to her own comfort, she might not give a damn, like the guard said, left it on so the trailer would be cool when she came back.

He sat in the overstuffed chair, untied a shoelace, and slipped off the shoe. He hesitated, blew out a gust of air, and put the shoe back on.

"Got a date?" Stephanie asked as he trotted down the steps.

"Cop stuff."

"Take me along. Maybe I can help."

"You'd be bored. I'm just going to check out the mansion."

Another waste of time, he figured, but he was making sure Ms. Edwards wasn't on a set working with Nick on a scene before he laid this in Osey's lap and listened to Osey laugh.

The place was locked up tight. He walked the outside perimeter, nothing out of the way. Locusts were warming up for the evening. A red-tailed hawk made lazy circles in the blue sky. His rib was beginning to remind him it didn't like all this activity.

Okay, that's it, go home.

He tramped around toward the squad car, then looked over at

the stables. Oh, hell, being this far, he might as well give a look there too. Gravel crunched under his feet as he followed the path.

He slid back a door and stared right into the barrel of an old Colt .45.

THIRTY

You couldn't mind your own business.''

He couldn't, and that was a fact. Nor was he totally surprised to see who was pointing a revolver at him.

Another thing he couldn't do was draw his eyes from the barrel. It wasn't steady. It downright wavered. Nerves wriggled in his chest like a sackful of garter snakes. Stomach muscles tensed in a futile attempt to deflect a bullet. His rib didn't bother him a bit.

"Help me!" Laura Edwards, hanging with hands cuffed to a metal ring affixed to the wall, twisted and struggled. She still had on the leather pants and vest she'd worn for the filming earlier.

"Come on," Yancy said. "Don't do this. Give me the gun."

"Shut up!"

"Let her go."

"Shut UP!"

"Okay." He held his hands up, palms forward.

"Take out your gun. Slowly! Lay it on the floor." The barrel of the .45 nuzzled up against Laura's neck. "Do it! I'll shoot her."

Laura, face white, eyes wide with fear, froze.

Fancy thoughts tumbled through his mind. Draw and fire. Movie-style stuff. Laura'd be dead before his finger reached the trigger. "Okay. Stay calm. What are you doing? Tell me what's going on." Gingerly, he laid down his gun. This was the second one he'd given up. If he lived through this, he'd never live it down.

"Step away from it."

He took one step to the side.

The .45 gestured.

He took another. Laura whimpered.

"Now your radio."

He hesitated.

"Do it!"

He unclipped the two-way radio from his shoulder and set it on the floor.

"Take it easy now," he said.

The .45 boomed like a cannon.

THIRTY-ONE

HE LEFT HIS WIFE to be with Laura and the wife killed herself in the best movie tradition,'' Justin said.

"I believe you have cleared up a very puzzling homicide." Susan shifted the phone receiver to her other ear.

"You mean all that was true about murder investigations? It wasn't just a ploy to get me interested?"

The irritating *click-click* of an incoming call broke in, she asked Justin if he could hold a second.

The call was dispatch. "Yancy just requested backup."

"What's going on?"

"I don't know. Too much static interference."

She better send somebody up to check that birds weren't sitting on the communications tower again.

"I couldn't make out more than who was calling before there was a gunshot."

"Where is he?"

"Unknown. Osey's going out to scout."

"Tell him to pick me up. Stat." She got back to Justin. "Thanks," she said. "I have to go, something's come up."

"Hey, you're not going to leave me hanging, are you? The least you could do is let me know what this is all about."

"When it's cleared."

A phone call to Yancy's place got no response. She checked her gun, slid it in the holster, and clipped it to her belt. She was waiting on the curb when Osey pulled up in a squad car.

"Anything?" she asked.

"No. I'd like to hit the overheads and the floorboard, but I don't know where to hare off to."

"Any filming going on at the moment?"

"I don't know."

"Go out to the base camp."

Even without the lights, he zig-zagged through town and churned up mud on country roads. Base camp was quiet, Yancy's Cherokee wasn't around, the security guard came ambling toward them when they slid to a halt.

"Help you?" he said.

Susan asked about Yancy.

"Well, he was here, back maybe an hour. He got a nut in a vise about air-conditioning being on. Used my phone and didn't give it back."

Susan looked around at the trailers. "What air-conditioning?"

"Ms. Edwards's trailer, over there."

Sure enough, the air-conditioning on Ms. Edwards's trailer was humming away, only hers; the rest were silent.

"Is it often left on?" she asked.

"Tell you the truth, I don't know, but your cop didn't think so. He thought there was something fishy about it." He related Yancy's actions.

Like Yancy, she wanted his boss. Unlike Yancy she was insistent, and more clout got the guard's employer chasing out a skinny, worried production assistant with keys to the trailers. Susan tried Ms. Edwards's first. It was cool inside, but otherwise uninteresting. No tables knocked aside or chairs tipped over. No blood spatters.

Much to the disapproval of the PA, she made him open all of them. While some were messier than others, none had been tossed, nothing indicated a struggle. She thanked him.

"Old Josiah's barn," she told Osey when they got back in the squad. She picked up the mike and told dispatch to send a unit to the Sunflower to ask questions of guests, staff, movie people, hangers-around, ask if anyone had seen Yancy, when they had last seen him, if they knew or had any idea where he had gone. Ditto for Laura Edwards.

The barn stood tall and solid, a monument to the past. Empty, quiet, except for the whisper of ghosts of Josiah's ancestors. Neither Osey, nor she, could find evidence of blood.

"Where now?" Osey said, his face tight with anxiety.

"His apartment. Maybe we can *detect* something."

Mrs. Blakeley refused to unlock the door for them. Osey, with country-boy charm, convinced her, without saying why, that they had a reason. Reluctantly, she agreed. Susan wanted to shake some speed into her as the woman slowly climbed the outside stairs and opened the door. She stood aside to let them in, and watched while they did a quick walk-through and then a closer look.

For all the good it did them. Nothing, not a hint, not a scrap, not a smell of where Yancy was, or the trouble he was in.

"Thank you," Susan told Mrs. Blakeley who carefully locked up behind them.

As they were crossing the sidewalk toward the squad, Stephanie came rolling up on her bicycle.

"Is something wrong?" She propped the bike with one foot on the ground.

"We're looking for Officer Yancy," Susan said.

"Is he hurt again?"

"We just need to talk to him."

"You know where he is?" Osey asked.

"Have you tried the mansion?"

"Why there?"

"That's where he said he was going."

To SUSAN'S EARS, she sounded like an elephant thrashing through the woods.

Osey had dropped her a mile away, and though she was hardly mountain climbing, the hill was thick with trees, the footing covered with fallen limbs and dead vegetation made slippery by recent rain. New growth covered whatever she might be stepping on. The air was damp and sticky.

From the crest of the hill, she had a partially obscured view of the back of the mansion about fifty yards straight below, and to her left an even more obstructed view of the front of the stables approximately a hundred yards west. She breathed heavily.

A gravel path about a half mile long led from the stables to the road. It was shortly past eight-thirty, and not quite dusk, but soon it would be. Mosquitoes hovered. She stumbled over a hidden root and the crushed plant sent up a pungent odor that cut through the earthy smell of rotting leaves.

Damn Yancy for going off without backup. With Justin's information, she'd finally worked out what was going on and before she could move on it, Yancy had walked right in.

Oh, Christ, don't let him be dead. Not Yancy with his sweet smile and soft voice. Not Yancy, young and idealistic. Smart and quick and sensitive. And inexperienced. If she'd been sharper and faster—what happened to all her experience?—Yancy wouldn't be in trouble.

She was afraid to use time working out a plan. She couldn't get hold of Parkhurst, and none of her officers were experienced in hostage situations. She didn't dare risk radio communication in case the suspect had Yancy's radio.

A stable door slid slowly back. Whoever had opened it was caught in interior shadows and she couldn't see who it was. She eased her gun up, eyes fixed on the door.

Nothing happened. Dusk was creeping in.

A jeans-clad figure with a denim shirt led a chestnut horse with white stockings from the stable. Saddle and halter, no bridle.

Susan squinted, straining to see.

The figure retreated into the stable and the light went on. The horse stood patiently, ears flicking, looking around as though trying to determine what he was supposed to do. The figure came out again, took the horse by the halter and started walking, then stepped aside and let the horse continued on his own.

Oh, for heaven's sake. Somebody was going through training sessions with the horse. She had come tearing out here, sneaked through a wilderness with lethal mosquitoes, gotten snags in her shirt, twigs in her hair, and mud on her shoes to creep up, gun drawn, on a horse trainer.

And they still didn't know where Yancy was.

In the act of reholstering her gun, she froze.

Oh, dear God.

The horse walked along the gravel path with the trainer walking beside it. A rope, tied to the saddle horn, stretched back to Laura Edwards's neck; a light shone on her face, set with terror. Hands cuffed in front of her, Laura had no choice but to walk along behind the animal.

This was so much a movie scene that Susan simply gaped in disbelief. With a sense of unreality, she watched.

The trainer yelled. Then reality hit. She didn't know what to do. The horse quickened to a trot. Laura, cuffed hands grabbing the rope, staggered after him.

If Susan did the wrong thing, made a wrong decision, Laura would be strangled. Almost anything Susan did would be wrong. Yell, "Freeze! Police!" and the trainer might have the horse tear down the path and hit the road in a flat-out run. How long would Laura survive?

Think. Think.

Shoot the trainer? Unless she hit the target smack on and killed with one bullet—not a sure thing—the trainer could still yell and make the horse move to a gallop.

Oh, Jesus. How long could Laura stay on her feet?

Shoot the horse? A guarantee to spook him unless one bullet dropped him. Where would she have to put a bullet so he would fall in his tracks?

The brain? Horses had large bony skulls, and with the head in constant motion, she wasn't sure she could hit the exact spot. Even a sharpshooter would have trouble and she wasn't a sharpshooter.

She didn't even consider what the gravel would do to Laura's vulnerable flesh. The pain would be agonizing. The horse trotted sedately. Laura kept on her feet. The trainer jogged alongside.

By going straight down, past the mansion, Susan might reach the road first.

She scrambled, hoping clopping hooves would camouflage any noise she made. She prayed nobody would come streaking up the road, sirens screaming, lights flashing. If the horse took off cross-country, he could bash Laura's head against a tree and split it like a watermelon.

Oh, Jesus.

When she reached the mansion grounds, the trees were thinner and there was no brush to snag her feet, but she had very little cover. If the trainer turned, she'd be seen.

On the path off to the left, the horse trotted along, its white stockings clear in the dusk. So far, Laura had managed to stay on her feet.

Thoughts and rebuttals zinged through Susan's mind. She had no plan. A movie hero would race out, grab the saddle horn, swing astride, and bring the horse to a stop.

The trainer ran up behind the horse, shouted, and clapped. He broke into a gallop. Laura took two or three staggering steps, then fell. The rope tightened around her neck. Her hands clung to it. The galloping horse dragged her.

NO!

Going downhill wasn't easier. Momentum carried Susan too fast to keep her balance. She slid on a pocket of wet leaves, caught herself, took a lurching step, and tripped.

She grabbed at a tree and scraped her hands, but got herself upright.

Oh, Jesus, Laura was being pulled over gravel with a rope around her neck. Hurry!

Susan scurried. The gathering dusk made it hard to see. She pounded along the side of the house, then plunged downhill.

Thick weeds waited to snag her ankles. She fought through them, fell, and tumbled down inside the ditch along the road. Scrambling for the other side, she grabbed at weeds to pull herself up.

On the road, the horse thundered past.

"Cut!" she yelled.

The horse—movie-trained animal that he was—slowed, stopped, looked around, then lowered his head to crop weeds at the edge of the road.

Thank God thank God thank God.

Moving easy, she approached him. He raised his head and eyed her, ears twitching.

"Okay, okay, let's be real careful. You're a good boy."

The horse stepped away.

"Don't do this to me. You don't want to be a killer."

He sidestepped. She stopped. He dropped his head and tore at the weeds. Moving up calmly, she grabbed his halter. He raised his head and chewed placidly.

The trainer had disappeared.

Osey, with White and Ellis right behind him, came running up the road.

"What were you waiting for?" she said. "The credits?"

With a pocketknife, Osey cut through the rope. Susan released the horse and knelt to tug at the section biting into Laura's throat. That famous beautiful face was cyanotic, the leather pants torn and bloody.

Susan pressed fingertips under the corner of Laura's jaw. The pulse was thready and fast, but it was there.

A motor roared. A black pickup with a roll bar jounced toward them, tires spinning in the gravel.

All hands grabbed Laura and dragged her out of the way.

The driver stomped the brakes. The truck fishtailed, the back end slid in the ditch on Susan's side of the road. She grabbed the side rail to keep from getting smashed. Her hands slipped, she struggled to hold on. As the truck bounced back on the road, it made a wide arc. Her legs swung out.

As the truck straightened, she hoisted herself over the rail and fell into the bed. She landed on an elbow; pain shot up her arm. Rolling toward the cab, she drew her gun, grabbed the roll bar with her injured arm.

"Police! Stop!"

The driver cut the steering wheel hard right, throwing Susan back. A left cut tossed her the other direction.

She hooked her arm around the roll bar. "Stop! You're under arrest!"

The driver twisted and fired. Susan crouched. The back window cracked into a weblike maze, a small round hole in the center. The truck swerved erratically back and forth.

Holding on to the roll bar, she smashed at the glass with the butt of her gun. "Stop the truck! Now!"

The truck roared off the road, hit the ditch, faltered, and then bucked and bounced up the other side. It slid sideways out of control down a rise. Susan hugged the roll bar. The truck slammed into a maple tree.

Susan was torn loose. Tree branches spun above as she tumbled over the tailgate. She landed hard on her left side, her gun went flying. Her vision wobbled, had black edges.

Scrambling to hands and knees, she scrabbled through leaves and vines for her gun. Just as she spotted it, two shots made her grab it and scuttle for a tree.

Breathing hard, she sat with her back against the tree trunk and rubbed an arm across her forehead. Jesus, what did she think she was doing? Making a movie?

Her left shoulder felt like sledgehammers had been at it. Served her right if something was broken. You're a cop, not a stuntwoman.

Crouching, she tried to catch a glimpse of movement through branches. Dusk had fallen, and it was too dark to see. Staying low, she eased from pine to ash moving toward the pickup. It sat in a small group of maples with open space all around and directly behind, fifty yards up a rise, the thick trees covered the hill.

She eyed the pickup.

"Get out of the truck!"

Silence. Rustle of tree leaves. Croak of frogs.

Pulling in air, she ran low for the passenger side and pressed her injured shoulder against the door. No sound but the hiss of the radiator and *ping-ping* of cooling metal. Slowly, she raised to look in.

Empty.

Through the driver's window she saw a dark shape streaking up the rise for the woods. Shit. Rounding the pickup, she charged uphill, running at an angle at her suspect, hoping like hell she wasn't going to be picked off like a rookie in a drug bust.

She plunged into the trees, stumbling through brush. A shadow of movement ahead on her right lured her that direction. A bullet bit into a tree at her shoulder. She dropped back, listened, heard thrashing through brush. She caught another glimpse, then the shadow disappeared.

Damn it.

She was making just as much noise, giving away her position. Her leg muscles screamed, her lungs felt on fire. A bullet nicked a tree a foot from her head. Ducking off at an angle, she strained to listen over her own heartbeat. She moved parallel with the shooter using trees to stay out of the way of bullets.

On the crest of the hill, trees stood black against the slate sky. Stars glittered. The moon was bright.

Movement slipped through moonlight. Susan ran, keeping her eyes on her suspect racing toward the mansion.

"Stop! Now!"

She put on a burst of speed. Lowering her shoulder, she rammed into the suspect with an explosive grunt. Her weight brought them both down hard, they skidded a few inches.

Lungs dragging at air that was too thin, she stuck her gun an inch from Clem Jones's throat. "It's a wrap," she said.

THIRTY-TWO

YOU'RE LATE AGAIN.'' Susan, breathing hard, stood back and let Osey help a cuffed Clem Jones to her feet.

"Take her in." Susan's leg muscles were beginning to spasm.

"Yes, ma'am." He took Clem's elbow.

"Yancy?" Susan asked.

"Okay. He was locked in a stall with the security guy who was supposed to be taking care of the place."

And very embarrassed about it, she realized when she got back to the stable. The wide sliding door stood open and he waited like a recruit before the drill sergeant, standing in the large rectangle of light reaching out to the gravel path.

"You make a habit of getting yourself in trouble?" she asked.

"I sure hope not," he said fervently, and when he saw her face, added, "ma'am."

EMTs loaded a drugged security guard—a young college student with a summer job—into the ambulance. They pronounced him okay, only sleepy.

"TELL ME WHAT HAPPENED?" she said to Yancy as she drove them to the department.

He related his vague thoughts about the trailer's air-conditioning and not being able to locate Laura Edwards.

About the time he was talking with Laura's driver, Susan was learning from Justin Kiddering information that had her zeroed in on Clem Jones.

"You gave up another gun," she said.

"Yes, ma'am."

"How did you expect to get out of this one?"

He didn't say he hadn't expected to need getting out of anything, but she could see him thinking it.

"The mansion is kind of far. I figured it might be out of range. I borrowed the security guard's cell phone. It was in my pocket."

"Dispatch heard a gunshot."

"I punched nine-one-one and hoped they could hear what was going on. That was Clem convincing me she'd shoot Ms. Edwards."

"WHY COULDN'T YOU mind your own business," Clem said sorrowfully to Yancy when he came into the interview room with Susan.

She was so ready to explain, it had taken some doing to stick Miranda in there before she started.

"For my mother," Clem said. Her fingers found the locket hanging on a chain around her neck and opened it. One side held a picture of herself. She indicated the other. "This is her." Blond hair, pretty oval face.

"At her funeral, I promised her Laura wouldn't get away with it."

The Laura Edwards's character in *Lethal Promise* had made a promise to a dead father. Susan wondered if that had affected Clem.

"Laura deserved to die." Bitterness curled the words up at the edges. "Lie in a coffin of dark shiny wood with satin pillows under her head. She killed my mother."

Clem twisted around to see if Yancy understood. "Your mother was at the barn."

He stiffened.

It was him she was explaining to, wanting him to understand. She'd refused to say anything at all unless he was present. Under different circumstances, she'd have been a young woman in love.

"I sawed partway through the railing and somehow I lost this." She touched the locket. "The clasp had broken. I was frantic, but it was right there lying on the straw. I grabbed it and kissed it and slipped it in my pocket. When I looked down your mother was watching. I wouldn't have hurt her."

Yancy gave her a stare of top-grade disbelief.

She blinked furiously as tears pooled in her eyes. Susan

thought she was trying desperately to hold on, as though she'd reached the brink of some inner precipice.

"I got it fixed first thing," Clem said. "I wear it always. On the Patio that night before—before Sheri—I kissed it then too." Clem seemed mortified at the tears, and wanting some pride to cling to. Despair settled over her slumped shoulders along with an impotent anger that he was seeing both. "Your mother," Clem said to Yancy, "looked at me with the strangest look."

"What about your father?" Susan said.

"I don't have a father," Clem replied with porcupine reflexes. "He left us. She killed herself." Clem could barely say the words. Her hands clasped and reclasped, meshing her fingers together. "Hanged herself. I was eighteen."

Clem's throat worked. "She couldn't go on without him."

"Why did he leave her?"

Fierce hatred flashed in Clem's eyes. "To be with Laura. He thought she was going to marry him. Would you like to hear something funny? She never wanted to marry him. He was in love." Heavy sarcasm. "Everybody falls in love with Laura. He destroyed my mother and Laura didn't even love him back."

Clem leaned forward across the table. "And would you like to hear something funnier? She didn't even know who I was and I have the very same name as my father."

The look she wore was defiant, tempered with toughness, a look of desperation trying to say, I can nail anybody's ass to the wall.

"What about Kay Bender?" Susan said.

"Kay was an accident. Laura was supposed to be up there. She never pays for what she does, somebody else always pays."

"And Sheri Lloyd?"

"She wouldn't let it alone. I told her and told her, but she was such a flake."

"Is that why you killed her?"

Clem shook her head impatiently. "She saw me come back from the barn. I said I was getting something for Fifer, but she kept threatening me. She wanted me to do things to Laura so Fifer would get mad at her. She babbled on about her astrologer.

'Help will be available from an unlikely source. The color pink is important.'''

Clem rubbed the heels of her palms over her eyes. "The idiot decided I was the help because of my hair color. It didn't even matter when I changed the color, she still—I was afraid she'd say something to somebody with brains and—"

Clem talked to her hands. "And get me caught before—" She looked at Susan. "I wanted Laura to die like my mother."

IN HER DREAM, Laura could see Clem's vicious, white face, eyes ringed with black. *You didn't care...* The voice was eerie with echoing menace. She wanted to scream, to beg. Hands tied. Rope on her throat squeezing. She trembled, felt herself falling, spinning in black pain. Helpless. Choking.

She jerked awake. The hospital gown felt clammy. She stared up at the tile ceiling, took a breath, working through terror, remembering. She was safe, in a cool white hospital room.

She remembered images, a muscular man with dark curls asking questions and giving orders. Nurses with soft voices. *Take a deep breath. Hold it.* Pain. Needles. Losing consciousness... Visions of Ben looking down at her. A dream?

Her mind felt fuzzy. She slept. How long? Hours? Days? Pain made its way through whatever she'd been given. Her head ached, her legs, arms, and stomach felt on fire. Bandages. She worried about her face.

Dr. Sheffield, of the muscles and curls, had been back—when?—and listened to her chest, looked at her throat, peered in her ears, shined lights in her eyes. He'd also checked dressings. Everywhere pain. Pain pain pain.

Resting a hip against the bed, he crossed his arms. "Contusions and abrasions. You're going to feel it for some time. Infection is something that needs to be watched for. But you're going to be fine."

"My face?" She was almost afraid to ask.

He smiled. "Just as beautiful as ever. A scratch or two. Nothing. You're very lucky. If you hadn't grabbed the rope like you did—" She listened in horror at him drop grizzly comments. "...dislocate the neck between first and second vertebrae...fracture of odontoid process...sever spinal chord ...medulla oblongata...outright decapitation.

"The leather helped," he said. "It isn't for show that motorcyclists cover themselves in it."

On those words of information, he strode off and she could imagine him leather-clad and straddling a noisy aggressive machine.

She hadn't been trying to save her life so much as save her face. Pain the length of her body and in her arms had removed even that desire. It had wiped out all thought except how much she hurt.

Tears ran down her face. Everything, it seemed, made her cry. Covered in bandages. *Now Laura May,* she heard her father's voice, *you always do exaggerate.* She reached for a tissue and blew her nose. Why couldn't she cry like she did in films. Tears glistening, a trickle down a cheek. Blah, nose running all over the place.

She was an actress, her face was her biggest asset. With it damaged permanently, what kind of roles would she get? Her whole life, everyone she knew, everything she did, work, play, revolved around movies. What would happen if she lost it? She wouldn't have a life. She wouldn't get a roomful of flowers; nobody would care she was almost killed.

And balloons, and cards. Nick had sent a bouquet of red roses.

She mopped her face and blew. Mopped and blew. To stop all this, she groped for the remote control, clicked on the wall-mounted television, and surfed through channels. The runaway stagecoach with a cowboy hanging between galloping horses plunged her slipping and tumbling down a long black tunnel. She punched the control.

"...and now our top news story from Bob Randall in Hampstead, Kansas. Bob?"

"It's an incredible story, Jerry. Here in the quiet little town of Hampstead, Kansas, in the middle of wheat fields, actress Laura Edwards came to make a movie. What happened was even more dramatic than the story she was filming. It had everything: suspense, terror, misdirection, a cliff-hanger ending. Even a runaway horse."

Cut to visual of horse looking noble, deigning to accept an equine nugget.

Jerry: "He'll probably be approached with movie offers." Chuckle. "Maybe even a television series. I hope he has a good agent." Serious. "I understand there is a suspect in custody. Can you tell us anything about that, Bob?"

"There is a suspect, Jerry. The police are not releasing any information about him yet."

"Thanks, Bob. And now we take you to the press conference videotaped earlier."

Cut to: conference room. SRO. Chief Wren at a podium, cool and poised. On her right, looking handsome and heroic, Officer Yancy. On her left, looking important, the mayor.

In a dry voice, the chief related the events of Laura's harrowing ordeal. A little expression wouldn't have hurt any, Laura thought irritably. For all the emotion this woman was putting out, Laura might have stumbled stepping off the curb.

Chief Wren fielded questions, refusing to answer most, not even giving out the suspect's name "while the case is still active."

"What about the stalker?"

"Is he involved?"

"I can't comment on that at this time."

"Is it true the suspect you have in custody is a member of the film crew?"

"No comment at this time."

"How badly was Ms. Edwards hurt?"

"I'm not a physician, I can't answer that."

"Will she be able to finish this movie?"

"Is she expected to recover fully?"

Laura thought Fifer must be gloating. He'd see that information and innuendo got spread around, truths and falsehoods and anything else he could throw in. All that free publicity. Star threatened by deranged crew member. There might even be front-page headlines.

"Is it true you personally captured the suspect after a dramatic chase that rivals a movie climax?"

Dry, level voice. "The suspect in custody was brought in through the combined efforts of the officers of the Hampstead police department." Chief Wren stepped down, cameras flashed, motors whirred, mikes were thrust at her. Laura clicked off the TV.

"Terrible performance."

"You could have done better?" Startled, she turned her head. Ben stood in the doorway, looking tight and invulnerable.

"Oh, Ben—" She held out her arms and hugged him awkwardly. Tears started again and for once in her life she didn't want to cry.

"How are you?" he asked.

"Which reply do you want? The one Fifer will give the investors or the real one? 'Ms. Edwards is doing great. A few scratches and a bruise or two. She's shaken up, but she's a great lady and she'll be back at work tomorrow.'"

He sat on the edge of the bed.

"I didn't know I could hurt in so many places at the same time." Damn it, would she ever stop crying.

He lifted her chin with a knuckle and tipped her head to one side, then the other. "You look in good shape for someone who got involved with a runaway horse."

"You wouldn't lie to me, would you, Ben?"

"Have I ever?" He handed her a tissue.

"No, you haven't." She blotted her face. "It's so upsetting to think someone could hate me that much. Clem Jones? I hardly know who she is—" Laura examined his face, trying to see behind his shuttered exterior. "You going to tell me that's why she hated me? I'm so self-centered, I don't see anybody else?"

He smiled.

Tears again. He looked so damn good when he smiled. "You're really arrogant. You know that?"

"So you always told me."

True. He wrapped himself up in so many macho defenses, his armor clanked when he walked. She didn't know that when they were married; she was a lot smarter now. "Do you hate me, Ben?"

"No."

"Did you ever?"

"Maybe. When you left. It's been a long time."

"I was so scared," she said in a small voice. "The rope kept getting tighter and tighter. I couldn't breathe—"

He ran a hand gently down her cheek. "Hey, you came through with barely a scratch."

She pressed her face against his throat and cried. He stroked her hair and murmured, "It's okay, Laurie. It's okay." She heard his heart beat.

He tipped her chin up and she looked into eyes that were softer and, for the first time that she could remember, understanding.

"Are you happy, Ben?"

"Happy?"

"Content, fulfilled, ready to spend the rest of your life here?"

"It's Californians who talk about contentment and fulfillment. In Kansas we talk about humidity and whether it's going to rain."

She put a finger on his mouth to stop him talking. "Twelve more days of filming here. Assuming there are no more interruptions like murder, kidnapping, and—is there anything else?"

"Assault with intent to kill, reckless endangerment—"

She kissed him, sweetly, with promise. "After the filming, do you think you could change your mind and we could go somewhere? You and me? Please?"

THIRTY-THREE

IT WAS JUST DUSK. From the kitchen window, Yancy watched the bats swoop and arc against the gray sky as they left their houses for the evening hunt.

"What is all this?" Serena said warily as he poured coffee into mugs and asked her to sit down.

"Come on. Don't be so suspicious." He cut two pieces of the apple pie he'd bought on the way over, slid them to plates, and pushed one across the table to her.

"You're trying to soften me up for something, Peter. I know you." Her joking tone didn't hide the hint of exasperation underneath. "That stuff may work with Mom, but—" She forked off the end of the pie and stuck it in her mouth. "Uh-huh, good. We better eat before we fight." She took another bite. "We are going to fight, aren't we?"

He sipped coffee. "I have a plan."

She started to say something.

"Wait. Mrs. Evanosky's husband died."

"Who's Mrs. Evanosky?"

"I met her at the hospital. She was trying to survive the vigil of his death."

"So?"

"She has no money."

"Ah."

"You see where I'm going with this?"

"We couldn't afford her."

"We could afford something, and she could live here."

Serena eyed him with her head tilted to one side. "Have you talked with Mom about this?"

"I wanted to run it by you first."

"You think she'll like it?"

"She feels guilty about you, Serena. Like she's depriving you of a life."

Tears came to her eyes. "I know. I love her, Peter, and sometimes I want—and then I'd like—and—"

"Hey—"

"I feel like such a terrible person. And I've been yelling at you and—"

"Serena," he said softly. "Don't get in a knot. You're entitled to a life. It's just that sometimes I forget. This might work."

THIRTY-FOUR

...AND ALL in the name of love.

"Storm's coming," the waitress said as she refilled Susan's coffee mug. "Electricity in the air."

Words of prophecy. She'd barely spoken when the café lights dimmed, then brightened again. Thunder rumbled. In the blink of an eye, rain washed down the windowpane.

A rainy evening for musing over the vagaries of life. Writing to Justin Kiddering had her wondering what might have been. If they had married, if they had opened their own law firm. Two or three children and a divorce? Certainly not a seat in the last booth of a coffee shop in Kansas.

Clem loved her mother who loved her father who loved Laura Edwards who loved... And that was the house that Jack built.

They've all returned to Hollywood. Maybe now those of us out here on the prairie can go back to our buckskins and buckboards. Nothing at all pertaining to the subject at hand, but did you know that Daniel Boone never wore a coonskin hat? An entire country believes he did. Just shows the power of Hollywood.

We had it. That power, I mean. It swept through town like the plague. Infected my department. Would you believe even I wasn't immune? True, I'm sorry to say.

All these good solid folks behaving like they were in a movie. I stayed cool until the last reel, then the fever seized me.

I had one officer stabbed. Inexperienced, trusting. He's not as much of either anymore. Although he was on the right track. I called Sophie the cat lady who makes pumpkin bread. Clove is one of the ingredients. No wonder he thought of pumpkin bread when he was stabbed, Delmar constantly ate clove Life Savers.

I think the officer was on the way to being in love with Clem. She loved him, that I do know. He's the hero type. You know, rescue the damsel from the burning tower. One thing, he'd never seen anything like her before.

Another officer—well, I'm not sure what happened to him. Stabbed in the heart maybe. Not literally, of course.

Rumors are rife through the department that he will pack up and take of with Ms. Edwards. His status has never been higher in the eyes of the male officers. If he'll get over it, I have no clue.

Somebody slid into the booth across from her. She felt that electricity in the air and raised her head.

Parkhurst, slightly damp around the edges. Putting down her pen, she leaned back. "Weren't you invited to the promised land?"

He half-smiled. "Sharks stay in familiar waters."

THE HUMPHREY BOGART MURDER CASE
by George Baxt

ONE

EVELYN WOOD, A HANDSOME woman in her mid-sixties, was furious. Not because she was a woman scorned, but because her apartment had been ransacked. She was a successful, highly respected freelance newspaperwoman here in her hometown of Portland, Oregon. She dwelled fondly on the memory of her late husband, Jack Methot. He had been a sea captain on the Orient run, away for months at a time, which didn't seem to bother Evelyn. She never referred to herself as Mrs. Methot. Evelyn Wood had a certain celebrity. Evelyn Methot was nobody. They did manage to produce an only child, a daughter who was christened Mayo, presumably after the county in Ireland where Jack Methot was born.

Mayo was a precocious child and while still in her teens, announced to her mother she was off to New York to become an actress. Evelyn wished her Godspeed and good luck, and saw her off at the train station, after which she ate lunch in a coffee shop where she flirted with an army officer. Usually petite, smartly dressed and coiffured, now, thirty-five years later, she was still smartly dressed and coiffured, but in a rage. The two detectives, Marley and Gross, sympathized with her but were surprised when she told them nothing was stolen. They were not too concerned with Evelyn's break-in. Within the past two weeks both had received greetings from their Uncle Sam and knew they'd soon be inducted into the army. There was a glorious Second World War raging in Europe and they knew it was only a matter of time before the United States would be involved. 1941 would hold little promise for either one of them.

Evelyn led them from the living room to her bedroom and then to what had been Mayo's bedroom where, now that Mayo was long departed, there was precious little to ransack. She then led them to the den which also served as her office where havoc had truly been created.

"This is a disgrace!" said Evelyn.

"Yeah," agreed Gross, "a real disgrace." Eyes narrowed, Marley shot his partner a look. Gross caught it but ignored it.

"You must do something! I have been vandalised! I feel as though I've been raped!" Now both detectives shot her a look. "Well?" Her hands were on her hips and her eyes were ablaze. Gross thought she looked kind of sexy for an old broad. "What are you going to do about this?"

"Well, Miss Wood," said Gross, "if you say nothing was stolen, then that leaves us with the crime of breaking and entering. You're sure nothing was stolen?"

She was breathing heavily, her bosom rising and falling like a small craft in a troubled sea. "There's really nothing much to steal. I own very little jewelry, but it's been undisturbed. I showed you my bedroom. Nothing's missing. The radio is still here. My silverware was handed down from several generations back but has only sentimental value." Gross found it difficult to think of waxing sentimental over some knives and forks. She indicated the desk at which she worked. "They left my typewriter. You might have thought they would have stolen that." Now she sounded indignant. The fact that the thieves thought she possessed nothing of value to steal was beginning to pain her.

"This looks to me like a case of mischief," said Marley.

Evelyn stared at him. "Mischief? What do you mean by mischief?"

"A practical joke in very bad taste," he replied.

"Nonsense! Look at the drawers spilled open. My papers scattered all over the place. Whoever it was was looking for something. Isn't that obvious?"

Marley asked, "Can you think of something you own that somebody might be looking for?" He waited. The look on her face discomforted him. He knew she was thinking they were morons. That was certainly what she was thinking. Throughout her career she'd had occasion to deal with the police, and they were rarely satisfactory. Marley decided Evelyn needed some prompting. "Stocks? Bonds? Bank certificates?"

"They're in a safety-deposit box."

Gross had a thought and expressed it. "Love letters?"

"Who from?" she snapped.

"Miss Wood," asked Marley, "does anyone else have a key to your apartment?"

"My daughter. She's in Los Angeles."

Marley continued, "No special person?"

Evelyn Wood permitted a trace of a smile. "I don't indulge in special persons. There's a woman who comes in to tidy up twice a week but she doesn't have a key. I'm usually in when she arrives. If I'm to be out, I leave the key for her at the desk."

"The door hasn't been forced," said Marley.

"And the window opening on the fire escape," said Gross.

"Oh this is hopeless!" cried Evelyn. "I shall speak to the chief about this."

"Miss Wood, I doubt if there's much he can do under the circumstances. We can arrange to have your place dusted for fingerprints. But I doubt if there'll be much of a yield other than yours and the cleaning woman's."

Gross said, "Perhaps your daughter can think of something. Why don't you tell her about the break-in?"

"My daughter hasn't lived here in over twelve years. She hasn't visited in over five. She's in the movies."

Marley's eyes lit up. "Oh yeah? Maybe I seen her in something."

"Her name is Mayo Methot." Her face hardened. "She's married to a bum named Humphrey Bogart."

Gross's eyebrows went up. "Miss Wood, by you he may be a bum, but by me, he's one hell of a good actor. He was sure swell in *High Sierra*. Didn't you think he was terrific in that one?"

"I never see Mr. Bogart's films. He's my daughter's concern, not mine." The ice in her voice might have given them frostbite.

Marley handed her a card. "If you think of something, Miss Wood, you can reach us at this number. We'll file our report and confer with the chief. There's little else we can do."

"Don't you realize had I been home when the break-in occurred, I might have been injured? I might have been killed?"

"Miss Wood," Marley said her name with exaggerated patience, "criminals who break into homes usually know when the victim will be away from home. Or make sure the victim will be out of the way."

"Oh."

"Yes?" asked Marley.

"I was tricked into leaving the house this morning. A man phoned. Said he was Salvador Dali." She was sure they'd never heard the name before. "The Spanish surrealist. The artist."

"We recognize the name, Miss Wood," said Marley, now with added exaggerated patience. He wished he could contact Humphrey Bogart to tell him what an overbearing bitch his mother-in-law was, though it immediately occurred to him that Bogart was probably well aware of it.

"A few years ago I interviewed Pablo Picasso and this man who said he was Dali said he'd be pleased to be interviewed by me. Well, he's such a notorious publicity hound that I was delighted to make a date to meet him." She mentioned one of Portland's better restaurants. "It was to be an early lunch. I waited almost an hour. He didn't show up. I realize now, of course, I was duped." She made a small, futile gesture. "He did have an accent." She sat. "What the hell could he have been after? I own a few good antique pieces but they're at a shop being cleaned. They're not very valuable so I discount them. This is so frustrating! So maddening!" She arose. "I apologize, gentlemen. I realize there's nothing you can do. It's all so baffling." She added, "And I'm frightened."

"Miss Wood," said Marley, "whoever it was won't be returning. I'd suggest you change the lock on your door except this professional is an exceptional professional. His skeleton key could probably get him into Fort Knox. You should speak to the management about the security in this building."

"I shall." The face was hard again. "I most certainly shall."

A few minutes later after the detectives had gone, Evelyn Wood poured herself some scotch whiskey, lit a cigarette and sat on the sofa. She plagued herself with questions. What was he or they after? It couldn't be anything of Mayo's because all her possessions were in the house in Beverly Hills. She thought of something else. She thought of Jack Methot, her late husband. He had plied the seas of the Orient, a fit setting for all manner of intrigues. But after his death, she had disposed of everything. His clothes went to the Salvation Army. Mayo collected his papers in a large carton and they were now stored in the basement of the Beverly Hills house. There had been some discussion three years earlier, when Mayo entered into her unholy alliance with Bogart, of the possibility of Evelyn relocating to Los Angeles, but Evelyn preferred to remain a big fish in a little pond.

Mayo Methot, the third Mrs. Humphrey Bogart. Bogie, Spencer Tracy dubbed him that when both made their feature-length film debuts back in 1930 in John Ford's prison comedy, *Up the River*. Tracy did well after it, Bogie didn't. He floundered around in small parts, mostly as gangsters until the opportunity to portray Duke Mantee on Broadway in *The Petrified Forest*, a thinly disguised character inspired by 1934's public enemy number one, John Dillinger. Leslie Howard starred in the play and when Jack Warner asked him to re-create the role on film refused to do so unless Bogart was signed for Mantee. Bogart stole the film from its costars, Howard and the volatile Bette Davis. Bogie didn't look back after that though he often wanted to. Warner's kept him in supporting roles with an occasional lead in a B low-budget film. Bogart with his complaints for better treatment joined Miss Davis and Jimmy Cagney as major thorns in Jack Warner's side. Bogart soon graduated to accepting other stars' rejects. When Paul Muni and George Raft refused *High Sierra*, Bogart inherited it. It was a surprise success. Only a few days ago Mayo had told Evelyn that Bogie was rehearsing another George Raft reject, *The Maltese Falcon*. Bogie. Heavy drinker. Wife beater, though Mayo assured her mother she gave as good as she got. This had to be true. Bogie called her Slugger, a tribute to her left uppercut.

Evelyn was back pouring herself another drink. To hell with Bogie. Who was the Dali impersonator? What did he want? Why hadn't he thought of phoning and saying something to the effect that he thought she might have something belonging to him and might he drop by to discuss it? She snorted. That would be damned stupid of him. Whatever he was after, she did not know she had it. It had to be something connected to Jack Methot. Jack

Methot. Why ever had she married him? That's unfair. He was handsome and dashing and romantic. A sea captain. A girl didn't get many opportunities to land one of those back in 1902. Bogie. Why did Mayo marry Bogie? His first marriage to actress Helen Menken had lasted less than a year. Then another actress, Mary Phillips. How many years did that one last? Not many. And now Mayo. Christ, shouldn't he have built up an immunity to actresses by now?

And who the hell was this smoothie who passed himself off as Salvador Dali?

HIS NAME was Marcelo Amati. He was Italian. In international circles he was a notorious playboy supported on various occasions by wealthy women and wealthier women attached to royal houses. He was, when it suited him, which was fairly frequently, a cheat and a swindler. He blackmailed and was twice suspected of murdering or attempting to murder lovers, but not his. He claimed to be descended from the Amati violin family but that was because he had difficulty spelling *Stradivarius*. He was, of course, breathtakingly handsome with a slim and muscular body. He spoke many languages and lied in all of them. He now sat in the drawing room of a train making its way from Portland, Oregon, south to Los Angeles, California. He was not alone. His companions were two women.

La Contessa di Marcopolo was a large woman who carried a great deal of weight. She had remarkably beautiful skin and her last encounter with plastic surgery at a clinic in Switzerland had successfully eliminated her latest cache of facial wrinkles, so that one would never guess her age was closer to sixty than to forty. The outbreak of war had forced her to flee Italy after being warned her estates were to be confiscated and she faced imprisonment having been suspected of secreting some Jewish blood in her veins. She had no idea what brand of blood Marcelo had in his veins; she knew only that it was hot when passionate and cold when homicidal. But Marcelo was quite affably agreeable about fleeing with her and her secretary, Violetta Cenci, who was the other woman in the compartment. La Contessa had rescued her jewelry, and it was several of these valuable pieces that had paid for their flight to freedom. How long the money would last was a matter of conjecture. La Contessa stayed in the best hotels and in the best accommodations befitting a contessa. She traveled first-class and ate first-class. She amused Marcelo and browbeat Violetta who saw herself as Cinderella though minus either housekeeping assignments or a prince toting a glass slipper. Violetta, although well into her thirties, looked much younger and knew in her heart that as the train drew closer to Los Angeles so would her ambition to be a movie star ripen and blossom. She would marry a rich producer, lord it over many servants in a mansion in Bel Air, and give lavish and much-talked about dinner parties to which she would never invite la Contessa. She loathed the fat one, but disguised it brilliantly. Violetta lowered the copy of *Screen Romances* she had bought at the railroad station in Portland. La Contessa, after a long silence, was speaking, and when la Contessa spoke, she demanded undivided attention, or else.

"Portland was a great disappointment." Little did she know there were others who shared the sentiment.

"My darling, I thoroughly ransacked the place. Why must I repeat myself? I left no drawer unturned. I even ransacked her refrigerator." He added with a smile, "I helped myself to a cold chicken leg. Quite tasty."

"You're laughing at me," said la Contessa.

"I never laugh at you, Contessa." Only on occasion when I'm soaking in a hot tub and think of you huffing and puffing in bed and making those obscene noises that are supposed to be synonymous with passion.

"Are you mocking me?" She was jamming a cigarette into another one of her hockables, a cigarette holder studded with ruby and emerald chips.

He imitated her voice mercilessly. "'You're laughing at me. You're mocking me.' I'm beginning to wonder if you're not paranoid."

"Violetta!"

Violetta looked up. "Yes, Contessa?"

"My cigarette!" Violetta reached down the seat for her handbag from which she produced a cigarette lighter and a flame. La

Contessa inhaled, followed by the usual fit of coughing, while Marcelo stared out the window and Violetta returned to her fantasies. The coughing abated; la Contessa was exhausted.

"How many times do I have to beg you to give up smoking?"

She ignored the question. She always did. "If the mother didn't have the letter, then the daughter has to have it."

"Perhaps there was no letter," suggested Marcelo.

"My father wrote me from Hong Kong that he would entrust a letter with Captain Methot to be delivered to me. He had a premonition he was dying, I'm sure of that. Premonitions are the family curse. One day I'll have a premonition and then I'll be gone."

"Without having sent a letter."

"You're mocking me again!"

"Cara mia, what has happened to you? You've become so grim and somber. You used to laugh and be gay, you bubbled like vintage champagne. But since you've become obsessed with the letter…"

She leaned forward. "The letter will lead us to the cornucopia, my father's cornucopia. His precious horn of plenty. He always told me about it. I grew up on the legend. Marco Polo's cornucopia! A valued gift from the emperor of China. Handed down for six centuries. How often it was stolen and recovered."

Marcelo stifled a yawn. How often had he heard the story. She even repeated it in her sleep. The Baron di Marcopolo's cornucopia. Stuffed to the brim with precious jewels worth millions of dollars. Millions that could keep them in a bountiful existence in Hollywood where the film population were suckers for royalty and foreign accents. How often she reminded him that silent stars Gloria Swanson, Pola Negri, and Mae Murray had purchased royalty as husbands. Constance Bennett bought herself a marquis. They were all penniless but titled. Royal titles! Worth a fortune. Horns of plenty. He realized the countess had ceased her droning.

Her head drooped. She was dozing. Marcelo nudged Violetta with a foot. He indicated the cigarette in the old lady's hand. Violetta removed it to an ashtray and then blew Marcelo a kiss. Violetta settled back on the comfortable seat and stared out the window. She believed la Contessa. There was a cornucopia stuffed with jewels. There was a letter entrusted by the Baron di Marcopolo to Jack Methot, the sea captain. It was romantic and intriguing. She gazed at Marcelo as he looked out the window, admiring again his magnificent profile. He should have been an actor. A swashbuckler, a brilliant swordsman. Zorro. D'Artagnan. Captain Blood. Marcelo yawned, closed his eyes, and settled back for a nap. Violetta's thoughts turned to Mayo Methot. Mrs. Humphrey Bogart. How she longed to meet the movie star. How she longed to meet all movie stars. How wonderful it must be to be Mrs. Humphrey Bogart.

WHILE VIOLETTA fantasized on the bliss of being Mrs. Humphrey Bogart, Mrs. Humphrey Bogart was in the middle of her living room in Beverly Hills exercising her pitching arm. Her target, her husband the movie star, was too quick for her. He had successfully dodged a number of wedding gifts he loathed. There was a vase that he thought had been a gift from actor Barton MacLaine. It was painted with little bare-assed cherubs connected by a daisy chain. There was a candelabra he recalled came from Mr. and Mrs. Jack Warner. Then there was an oversize ashtray, the selection of comedian Frank McHugh and his wife. The vase had shattered against a wall. The candelabra tore a hole in a Renoir print that he loathed. The ashtray came perilously close to concussing him and Bogie shouted, "Close but no cigar, Slugger. But you're improving!"

"You coldhearted brute! You miserable son of a bitch! Mother might have been murdered!"

"I'm not interested in what might have been!"

She sent a metal pitcher that she picked off the sideboard hurtling toward him. He leaped out of its path shouting, "No wonder I keep losing weight!" The pitcher shattered a window pane. "I thought we agreed no more breaking windows! You gave me your word!"

"She said the police were of no damned use either." Her hands dropped to her side, then she sagged into an easy chair. "What the hell could they have been after?"

Bogie leaned against a wall, eyeing his wife with suspicion. This suddenly sinking into an easy chair could be the warning of a sneak attack. Not too long ago she'd stabbed him in the shoulder with a steak knife and he was now reluctantly entertaining the notion that she might have recently bought a snub-nosed automatic, having heard her admiring one that Joan Crawford kept on her bedside table.

"It might have been the work of some neighborhood kids. What did the cops call it?"

"Mischief. They called it mischief." She thought for a moment as she applied a lighter to a cigarette. "Neighborhood kids don't lay their hands on skeleton keys. There's something very nasty about that break-in."

"Say listen, Slugger," said Bogart warily, ready to duck and dodge if she made a false move. "Your mother being all this frightened and upset, maybe you ought to go up there and spend a few days with her."

Her eyes were narrowed into slits. "You'd love to be rid of me, wouldn't you." Very prescient, thought Bogart. "You'd love me out of the way while you're having your affair with Mary Astor."

He exploded. "I am not having an affair with Mary Astor! She's fully booked!"

Mayo rubbed the cigarette out in an ashtray and then jumped to her feet, fists clenched. "Don't you think I know what this whole *Maltese Falcon* movie is all about?"

"Sure you do. You read the script."

"*I* should be playing Astor's part!"

"Now come on, Slugger. Let's not go through that routine again. It's getting pretty tired. I suggested you to Jack Warner..."

"Halfheartedly!"

"Goddamn you, I'm always sticking my neck out for you and what do I get for it? Do I get any gratitude? All I get is the chop! I got you into *Marked Woman*, didn't I?"

"Four years ago! And playing an over-the-hill whore!"

"Typecasting," he said without thinking and to his immediate regret. Between her hands over her head she held a flowerpot, and sent it flying like a basketball player targeting a hoop. Bogart ducked behind a couch. The flowerpot crashed into a mirror hanging on the wall, a wedding gift from the Pat O'Briens. "Ha!" yelled Bogart triumphantly. "Seven years bad luck!"

In the kitchen, Hannah Darrow, their housekeeper and cook, leaned against the sink, arms folded, clucking her tongue. Hannah was a tongue clucker of the old school. Her tongue didn't make little clicking noises; it rose and fell against her hard palate with all the vigor and force of a suction pump. The Battling Bogarts, as they were affectionately known in the movie colony, had earned their reputation. They had neither shame nor discretion. Their battles were not confined to the domicile. They had ferocious scrapes in restaurants, movie theaters, department stores, bowling alleys, and were especially adept at maneuvers in parking lots. Once Mayo had tried to run Bogart down, but he somehow managed to outrun her. Their sadomasochistic union was a joy to the gossip columnists. Why they continued to remain chained in wedlock was a puzzle their friends had long ago ceased trying to solve. Most of the sympathy was on Bogart's side. He was a charmer with a good nature and an affable disposition. He did frequent battle with Jack Warner over better parts and better money because he felt he owed it to himself. He certainly couldn't depend on his agent, who was one of Warner's cronies. This had been a good year for him. After the surprise success of *High Sierra* he went into a circus movie, *The Wagons Roll at Night*, with Sylvia Sidney starting a screen comeback after several years away in the theater. Bogie had balked at doing this one, not because of the actress, whom he had supported in *Dead End* four years earlier, but because *Wagons* was a remake of the Edward G. Robinson and Bette Davis melodrama of four years earlier, *Kid Galahad*, in which Bogart had been the villain. Now he was playing Robinson's role. Bogart thought there was something incestuous about it. But the film did well, and now he was rehearsing *The Maltese Falcon*, the third version of Dashiell Hammett's successful novel. True, he was second or maybe third or even fourth choice for the part, and it would be the directorial debut of John Huston, who had also written the script. And a new director and an old story could be a fatal combination. Bogart didn't care. Bogart believed in Huston, who was a friend, a poker-playing buddy, and a fellow skirt-chaser.

Mary Astor was something else. She had survived an ugly scandal in 1936 when she had divorced Dr. Franklin Thorpe and fought for the custody of her daughter Marilyn. Thorpe's attorney produced her private diary in which she discussed playwright George S. Kaufman's privates most indiscreetly, striking envy in the hearts of millions of readers around the world and sending Kaufman into temporary seclusion. Mary Astor was a fighter. She fought for her daughter and won her and she fought to retain her status as a star. Fortunately, she was extremely well liked in the industry and had powerful allies in most movie moguls. Now she was under contract to Warner Brothers for three features, and John Huston wanted her for *Falcon*. Bogart's pitch for Mayo was made in a whisper that could barely be heard. Mayo was not a star. She would never be a star. She had no charisma whatsoever.

Hannah Darrow hadn't been told yet if the Bogarts were dining in or out or at all. She was doing an inventory of what was stocked in the refrigerator when she realized a rare silence had settled in the house.

In the living room, Bogie had made a flying leap at Mayo and wrestled her to the floor. She was struggling ferociously, face down with Bogart holding her hands behind her in a tight grip. "You give up?" he shouted, knowing full well not to trust her if she did. She peppered the room with a series of expletives that both dazed and dazzled Bogart. Finally, she was exhausted. She was staring at Hannah Darrow who had entered the room with two raw filet mignons on a plate.

"Excuse me," she asked sweetly, "are these steaks for dinner or for your eyes?"

TWO

HAZEL DICKSON STEERED HER five-year-old Studebaker with her usual panache and joie de vivre toward the very swank Hotel Ambassador in the downtown area of Wilshire Boulevard. Her dented fenders and shattered left headlight were a testimony to her indifference to the safety of either herself or other drivers. Behind the wheel of her car as in life, Hazel's philosophy was every man for himself and the devil take the hindmost. She was in her twelfth year of waiting for Detective Herbert Villon of the Los Angeles police force to declare himself and make her an honest woman. On the other hand, if he ever got around to popping the question, she was terrified she might say "Yes" and give up her long fought for and treasured independence. She recognized Herb as a satisfactory boyfriend and lover, but saw a grim prognostication for his qualifications as a husband.

Hazel was one of those rare creatures indigenous to the film industry. She gathered gossip and news items about celebrities and peddled them at fancy prices to gossip columnists and the Hollywood correspondents from all over the world assigned to the glamour capitol. More people swore by her than swore at her, which was a rare accomplishment in this treacherous town. She had friends in high places and very important contacts in low places. There wasn't an unlisted number she didn't know and she had a legion of faithful spies who supplied her with invaluable tips. One of the desk clerks at the Ambassador Hotel tipped her of the arrival of la Contessa di Marcopolo, a direct descendant of the famed Italian explorer, or so emphasized la Contessa tirelessly and tiresomely. Hazel knew better than to ignore the arrival of a fresh title in town. And the contessa and her entourage of two had commandeered one of the most expensive suites at the Ambassador. Hazel lost no time phoning la Contessa, explaining she had access to such powerful columnists as Louella Parsons,

Hedda Hopper, Sidney Skolsky, Jimmy Fidler, and Harrison Carroll to drop the names of the five leading dispensers of gossip, mostly vicious. She also promised invitations to private screenings and world premieres. La Contessa was interested indeed in meeting some famous movie stars, to be invited to their homes and their parties. La Contessa did not express over the phone an ardent desire to meet Mayo Methot, Mrs. Humphrey Bogart. Subtlety was in order here, and if Hazel Dickson was to prove a powerful friend and ally, la Contessa must move carefully into her good graces. If necessary, she'd lend her Marcelo Amati. And if her pendulum swung in the opposite direction, Violetta Cenci was hers.

At the Ambassador, Hazel turned her miserable Studebaker over to a parking attendant she'd known and liked for years. He asked her his usual question about the auto, "When are you going to shoot this thing and put it out of its misery?" and was rewarded with her usual reply, "I'd sooner shoot you. Don't park it next to any limousines. It has enough of an inferiority complex."

In la Contessa's suite, her highness was prepared to enchant and captivate Hazel Dickson. She wore her most alluring Coco Chanel hostess gown despite the fact it was three years old (how would the Dickson woman know?), and had room service stock the suite with liquors and liqeurs and a tray groaning under the weight of some beautifully arranged hors d'oeuvres. (Easy on the anchovies, she cautioned; la Contessa had a sodium problem.) Violetta was smartly dressed in the one suit she owned and Marcelo Amati had positioned himself against a French window leading to an American balcony, the sunlight behind him giving him a radiant halo that proclaimed here indeed sits a golden boy.

The desk announced Hazel Dickson, and Violetta told the clerk to send her right up. La Contessa settled onto the couch, cigarette smoldering in its holder. She instructed Marcelo, "You'll see to the drinks, mi amore. Violetta, you'll pass the refreshments. They do them much more creatively at the Hotel Flora in Rome." She sighed. "How I wish I was having an aperitif at the Flora right now with Edda Ciano." Marcelo advised her not to name-drop

Mussolini's daughter in the United States, and la Contessa said, "Oh dear, you're right. One has to make so many adjustments."

The doorbell buzzed and Violetta counted ten and then crossed to the door and opened it, favoring Hazel Dickson with what she hoped was an enchanting smile despite one discolored front tooth. "Miss Dickson?"

"Yes, I'm Hazel Dickson," said Hazel briskly, with her own brand of enchanting smile.

Violetta closed the door and led Hazel across the foyer and into the sitting room where la Contessa sat in all her Coco Chanel glory, aided by strings of pearls around her neck and across her bosom. She lifted her right hand, a ring on every finger except the thumb, and around her wrist a display of bracelets that almost blinded a very impressed Hazel Dickson. Hazel held la Contessa's hand as they exchanged greetings and then was introduced to Violetta and Marcelo Amati.

Hazel smiled at Amati while thinking, movie-star material. He's gorgeous. I could eat him with a spoon. She and Marcelo shook hands and he offered her a drink. Hazel asked for a ginger ale, knowing if she started the gin martinis they'd be hauling her out of the suite on a stretcher.

Once all were seated and settled with drinks and hors d'oeuvres, Hazel said smartly, "So I'm the first to welcome you. I indeed feel privileged. Tell me, Contessa, are you just visiting or perhaps planning on settling here? We have so many refugees from the horrors in Europe." She rattled off the names of directors, writers, and actors, and la Contessa acted suitably impressed. When Hazel paused to take a much-needed breath, la Contessa spoke, Hazel finding her accent more thick than charming. "I have always wanted to visit this famous city. And when circumstances made it necessary to flee my beloved homeland, we were most fortunate to receive visas and passage here." She refrained from mentioning Edda Ciano's assistance in securing the necessities.

"Have you seen much of America?" asked Hazel while sneaking looks at Marcelo Amati, who seemed to be wearing a permanent smile. His teeth were porcelain white and Hazel wondered if she was too old for him. Then in a flash she realized she wasn't, not if he was la Contessa's lover. God, she thought. Not really. But what the hell.

"Just a week in New York City and then directly here by train. That was a nightmare. So much shunting onto sidings to let troop and supply trains through. One would think this country was also at war."

"We will be," said Hazel matter-of-factly, "it's unavoidable."

"Oh, really?" said Marcelo. "What about your isolationists?"

"A minority. There'll be a war. War means big bucks and we're struggling out of the Depression and we need big bucks. Tell me, Marcelo, are you an actor?" La Contessa smiled a very small smile. The fish had taken the bait.

"Interesting you should ask. I have at times in the past given it some thought. You have heard of the actress Isa Miranda?"

Hazel acted startled. "Heard of her? Why she was a buddy of mine when she was at Paramount a couple of years ago making a pair of stinkeroos. Forgive me. I mean failures."

"Isa was also a friend of mine," said Marcelo warmly while la Contessa's eyes were veiled with jealousy at the mention of Miranda's name. "She made with me...oh how do you call it..."

I'd call it "whoopee," thought Hazel.

"Ah yes...a screen test."

"How'd it come out?"

"I never found out. With the confusing first days of the outbreak of war, I lost all contact with Isa. Anyway, I don't think the time was appropriate to inquire as to the outcome of a screen test."

Hazel gushed, "I'll bet you photograph divinely. Now, I must interview la Contessa. Tell me, Contessa, are you truly descended from Marco Polo?"

"Indeed I am."

"But you spell the name as one word."

"It saves time."

Marcelo explained, "The names were joined over a century ago by la Contessa's grandfather."

"Did you see Sam Goldwyn's movie about Marco Polo? It came out three years ago."

La Contessa said with distaste, "I saw it out of curiosity. Absolute nonsense."

"But he did go to China, didn't he?"

"Oh that's quite true. And he brought back the first samples of what the Chinese called Spa Get Ti. And now it is spaghetti!"

"Well, how about that! And I suppose he brought back all sorts of treasures. Jewels, tapestries, and all that jazz."

"Oh, yes," said la Contessa. "He returned to Venice with great wealth. Over the years, much of it was stolen, and equally, much of it was recovered. There are still certain items we are trying to trace."

"Oh, really. Say, you're not here on a treasure hunt, are you? This town goes looney over treasure hunts."

"Does it really?" La Contessa and Marcelo exchanged looks. Violetta passed around the hors d'oeuvres tray. "Actually, there is one interesting object I would love to recover for my family."

Hazel crossed her legs and leaned forward with interest. Marcelo wondered why she wasn't taking notes. He didn't know Hazel had a memory like a steel trap.

La Contessa continued. "It's a cornucopia."

"A what?"

"A cornucopia. It is shaped like a conical horn. Not too large, but big enough to hold a wealth of valuable jewels." Hazel whistled. "Cornucopias are also known as The Horn of Plenty."

"That's a horn I wouldn't mind blowing," said Hazel. "What's become of it?"

"It has disappeared. It was a gift to Marco from the emperor of China. It was stolen shortly after Marco's death. Later it was recovered and the thief's hands were severed at the wrists and his eyes burnt out with hot pokers. Then he was tortured. For centuries there has been a game of cat and mouse thievery until it finally was recovered by my father, the Baron di Marcopolo."

"And where's your father?"

"He's dead. He died on a ship making its way to China where my father rather generously was preparing to return the cornucopia to the Chinese government."

Hazel looked and sounded perplexed. "Wasn't that a bit rash of him?"

"We thought so. It killed my mother. She had a heart attack. When my father's ship docked, there was no sign of the cornucopia. My father was supposed to entrust a letter with the ship's captain explaining the cornucopia's fate. The captain was to have then delivered the letter to me. I never received the letter."

"I see," said Hazel. "Dirty work at the crossroads."

Marcelo spoke. "Of course, there is the possibility there was no such letter. That it didn't exist. And perhaps the cornucopia was not on board the ship."

"Don't be such a fool, Marcelo. My father was seen carrying the cornucopia on board. His intention was to entrust it to the captain for safekeeping in the ship's vault."

Hazel asked, "Are you suggesting the captain might have made off with this treasure?"

La Contessa said, "The ship's personnel, you understand, also had access to the vault. The purser, for example. I never met the captain but my father considered him a very honorable man. My father took many voyages with Captain Methot. One of his hobbies was collecting Oriental art."

Hazel's face was slightly screwed. "Captain who?"

"Methot. Captain Methot."

"Really! I wonder if he's any relation of Mayo Methot. It's a most unusual name." She explained, "Mayo Methot is the wife of the movie star Humphrey Bogart. Surely you've heard of him in Italy."

"Indeed I have."

Violetta found her tongue and gushed, "I adore Humphrey Bogart. He is one of my favorites."

"This is really such a coincidence. If Mrs. Bogart is related in some way to Captain Methot, I'd be most interested in meeting her."

Hazel stood up. "I'll phone her right now. She just might be at home." She dug into her handbag for her address book. "Here it is. The Bogarts." She crossed to a desk on which rested a phone and dialed.

IN THE BOGART living room, Hannah kept a tight grip on the plate holding the steaks while making an assessment of the damage wrought by her employers. Mrs. Bogart was so charming when she interviewed Hannah, and then her Mrs. Hyde personality slowly emerged. It was Hannah's personal opinion that Bogart was too good for her. She'd read somewhere he came from a very upper-class New York family. Real high society. Not as high as it could get but impressively high enough.

Mayo said to the housekeeper, "We're dining out." She directed her mouth at Bogart, "Dinner at seven at the Brown Derby with Dash and Lily."

"I haven't forgotten," said Bogart. He was fond of Dashiell Hammett and Hammett's lover, the playwright Lillian Hellman who had scored a huge Broadway success in 1934 with her play, *The Children's Hour.*

"I'll save the steaks for tomorrow," said Hannah. And that was when the phone rang. Hannah answered. "Bogart residence."

"Hannah?" chirruped Hazel Dickson at the other end. "It's Hazel Dickson. Is Mrs. Bogart in?"

"I'll see, Miss Dickson." Bogart groaned on hearing the name. He pantomimed to Hannah that he wasn't in but Hannah squelched the movement with "It's for Mrs. Bogart."

Mayo snapped, "You keep forgetting there's another star in the house." Bogart said nothing. Mayo took the phone. "How are you, Hazel?"

"I'm just dandy. Mayo, I'm at the Ambassador in the suite of la Contessa di Marcopolo."

"Sounds real grand."

"Mayo sweetie, was your father a sea captain?"

"It's no secret. It's in my bio on file with my agent."

"Oh how marvelous! Hold on, Mayo." She said to the fat woman on the couch, "It's her father!"

La Contessa was delighted. "We must get together!"

"Mayo, you'll never believe this. But La Contessa's father, the Baron di Marcopolo was a friend of your father's. In fact, he died on one of your father's voyages in the Orient!"

Mayo commented wryly, "I'd say that's carrying friendship a bit far, even for my father." She thought for a moment. "The Baron di Marcopolo. Come to think of it, Jack mentioned him a couple of times. As I recall, there was something about a cornucopia filled with jewels. One of them stories out of the *Arabian Nights*."

Bogart chuckled. "I remember that one. It took your father about half a dozen Boilermakers to tell it all."

Hazel persisted. "It's not a fairy tale. It's the truth. I think it's a great story. Won't you come and meet la Contessa?"

Mayo would have preferred to wipe the smirk off her husband's face. Bogart and her parents didn't like each other. Bogart referred to Evelyn as the Empress and to the captain as Captain Bligh. Jack Methot was dead of a heart attack shortly after the Bogarts married and Evelyn rarely visited them. It was the way Bogart liked it. He heard Mayo say, "Sure I'd like to meet her. Then I can drop in at Magnin's and run up some bills." Bogart winced. Hannah had departed for the kitchen after handing the phone to Mayo. In the kitchen she gently lifted the phone extension and heard the rest of the conversation between Mayo and Hazel. Hannah and the other housekeepers in the neighborhood met daily for coffee, cake, and gossip in somebody's kitchen while their employers were engaged at their studios. This was how, as Hannah put it, they remained au courant. She'd learned the expression from Charles Boyer's housekeeper.

Bogart said to Mayo as he straightened his tie without needing a mirror, "Go easy at Magnin's."

"Why? Are we poverty-stricken?"

"Let's not get into another battle. As far as I'm concerned we've had ours for today. We're not poverty-stricken but you're going a little too heavy on the shopping sprees."

"I'm Mrs. Humphrey Bogart!"

"Well, *I* ain't!" snapped Bogart.

"I have to keep up appearances. If we're so hard up for money why don't you help me get some jobs!"

"Why doesn't your agent get off his ass and get you some jobs?" He raised his hands defensively. "Don't you throw that book!"

She slammed the book back on the table. "You know, with a little more practice, I could really loathe you."

"Naw, Slugger. You could never loathe me. Like I could never loathe you. Be patient, babe, one of these days you might meet Mister Right."

"Go to hell."

"I'm going to rehearsal. I don't know how long it'll be, so let's meet at the Brown Derby at seven. And when you get there, try to be on your best behavior. No pushing your food on the fork with your fingers." The book flew past his head and landed in the foyer. Laughing, he left the house and went to the driveway where his car was parked. He reflected upon his wife as he started the ignition, put the car into gear, and set off to the Warner Studio in the valley.

Mayo.

When did he fall in love with her and why? It was when he saw her on Broadway in *Torch Song*. She'd gotten great reviews and everybody was talking about this exciting new actress so he decided to check her out. She'd gotten the reviews but the play hadn't, so it was playing to half houses, forcing the management to paper performances with free passes. Bogie got himself one for a matinee. It was Saturday, and Bogart recognized and acknowledged many of his fellow actors who were also unemployed and seeing a show for free. Mayo was no great beauty but she could act. Her technique was good and the way she underplayed the rest of the cast was something she might have learned from his second wife, Mary Phillips. Mary was no great beauty either, but she was a superb actress. She was memorable in Kaufman and Hart's *Merrily We Roll Along* in a part based on Dorothy Parker, the Algonquin wit and character assassin. Bogart's first wife, Helen Menken, was a true star given to frequent bouts of indigestion from chewing so much scenery, though she held her own opposite Helen Hayes in *Mary of Scotland*.

Mayo was something else. But her features were mismatched. She had the body of a star but the face of a character actress. It didn't matter in the theater but was a detriment on screen, where the face was magnified over a hundred times. Still, Harry Cohen brought Mayo to Hollywood when her play folded and gave her the lead at Columbia in *The Murder of the Night Club Lady* with Adolphe Menjou as Detective Thatcher Colt. Unfortunately,

Mayo didn't have enough footage in which to make much of an impression because as the nightclub lady in question, she was dispatched in reel one which gave audiences plenty of time to forget her.

When the Bogarts met, they had heavy drinking as well as acting in common. They laughed a lot together and were incredibly lonely. So booze, laughter, and loneliness led to marriage, and the marriage soon evolved into disillusions and recriminations. As Bogart became more successful, Mayo felt herself slowly but surely shunted to the background. As Bette Davis had told her when they were filming *Marked Woman*, "There's nothing more unnecessary than a Hollywood wife."

Mayo had repeated the line to Bogart after they were married. Bogart remembered his response, "A Hollywood wife carries more weight than a Hollywood mistress"—this at a time when Mayo was dieting strenuously, which won him his first bruised chin and a begrudging respect for his wife's right uppercut.

At Warners, he found Mary Astor reading the script of *The Maltese Falcon* aloud to herself in one of the conference rooms occasionally used for rehearsals. Most directors rehearsed on the set and then ordered a take, but John Huston was taking no chances with his first film. The script was an ensemble piece, and he had pleaded with Jack Warner for extended rehearsal time. Warner gave it to him because the film's budget was half that of other "A" features. Warner referred to this one as a nervous "A." Almost everyone in the cast was under contract and those who were not contracted were hired on daily rates that were usually cheap. There was a comparatively short shooting schedule; Bogart knew Huston was planning to shoot at a fast clip to give the picture the kind of pacing the previous versions lacked.

"Hello, beautiful, where's the rest of the company?"

"I think they're out scrounging cocaine for Peter Lorre. The war seems to have played havoc with his European connections. How'd you bruise your eye?"

He sank into a chair. "Need you ask? Another scuffle with my bitter half."

She liked and admired Bogart and was sympathetic to his domestic difficulties, having suffered a plethora of her own. "Bogie, sometimes I think there's a touch of madness in you."

"If there is," he said while lighting a cigarette, "there's Methot to my madness."

She smiled. "This is a terrific script. There isn't a poor line of dialogue or a superfluous one. John's done a terrific job with it."

"Let me let you in on a little secret. He stuck to the book."

"I know. I read the book. Hammett is brilliant." She crossed her legs. "He hasn't written anything in a long time. I wonder why."

"I'll ask him tonight. We're having dinner with him and Lily Hellman at the Brown Derby. I'd ask you to join us except I'm hoping Mayo will be on her best behavior and she's already accused me of having an affair with you."

"Christ. About the only actor I haven't been suspected of having an affair with is Alfalfa Switzer and I'm wondering if he's terribly hurt about that. I read that article on you in this month's *Photoplay* magazine. I'm terribly impressed."

"Oh, yeah? What does it say? I never read that crap."

"I'm really impressed your mother was Maude Bogart, the famous illustrator."

"Well, how about that? Yeah, when I was an infant, I was her favorite model. Mostly because she didn't have to pay me anything." Mary smiled. "I was the Mellon's Baby Food baby. Is that in the article?"

"Yes, and that you were Baby Dimple in *Sleepytime Stories*."

"Christ, I forgot about that one. Yeah, Maude was pretty good with illustrations. She was pretty lousy with her husband and her kids. I had two sisters. Kay died young. Pat had a mental breakdown so maybe there's something to your madness theory."

"Oh, please, come on," she demurred as a blush came to her cheeks.

"My mother could make an iceberg seem like an oasis. What a cold and unfeeling bitch."

"And yet she gave birth to three children?"

"Mary, I get the feeling all three times she wasn't looking. You should have met my father. Doctor Belmont DeForest Bogart. How's that for a fancy mouthful? Mary, I don't know how I got to be a product of that union. I was a real mean kid."

"Stop being so hard on yourself."

"I was! I was a real mean kid." He was warming up to himself, usually his least favorite subject. "I went to this very exclusive private school. Trinity. It was so exclusive, I think it didn't have an address. The kids used to beat me up." He laughed. "I suppose I wasn't exactly a charmer, what with my kind of parents and my poor sisters terrified of both of them. Poor Pat. How she suffered. I think her breakdown was a blessing."

Mary shook her head from side to side. "Isn't there anyone in this town who loves their mother?"

"Yeah. Ginger Rogers." He was on his feet with impatience. "Say, where the hell are the rest of them? We're supposed to be rehearsing. Otherwise I might have gone with Mayo to meet this Contessa di Marcopolo."

"A contessa, no less. Mayo's moving up in the world. Sounds like one of Hazel Dickson's trophies."

"Right on the nose. Sayyy..."

"What?"

He snapped his fingers. "I thought that cornucopia sounded familiar. First cousin to *The Maltese Falcon*."

"Come off the wall, Bogie. What cornucopia?"

"Listen to this." He sat down again. He told her what little he knew of the Baron di Marcopolo's cornucopia and the involvement of Mayo's father. He knew he'd get the rest from Mayo, but what he told Mary she found fascinating.

At the conclusion, she said, "Say, that *is* the Maltese Falcon's twin brother. Bogie, do you suppose Hammett knew the cornucopia story and refashioned the cornucopia into the statuette of the falcon?"

"It's a possibility. Aren't writers supposed to write what they know about?"

"They're supposed to, but they don't always."

Bogart was chain-smoking. "You know, I'm going to spring this on Hammett at dinner. If Lily Hellman lets me get a word in edgewise." He lowered his voice. "Who's the fat guy? Is he playing Casper Guttman?"

Mary smiled at the huge, white-haired man in his sixties who approached them with a delightful smile. "Sidney, come meet Bogie."

"Ah, Bogie. At last!" He and Bogart shook hands. "I'm Sidney Greenstreet, the villain of the piece. I believe in a previous incarnation the part was written for a woman. Perhaps I'll use a subtle touch of effeminacy."

Mary Astor said, "You'll have a hard time getting that past the censors."

Said Bogart, "Sure, it'll pass. It's already in the script. Huston's used it the way Hammett wrote it in the book. The kid traveling with Greenstreet and Joel Cairo, Lorre's part. He's obviously Guttman's lover."

"But he's a killer!" exclaimed Mary.

"But aren't most lovers?" asked Greenstreet.

"Sidney," said Mary, "you are a card."

"Oh, my dear," said Greenstreet aware of the actress's scandalous past and possibly a scandalous future, "no offense intended, I assure you."

"No offense taken," she said with a laugh. "Bogie, tell Sidney about the cornucopia. I'm sure he'll be fascinated."

"Cornucopia? A horn of plenty?" He had sat on a hard-backed chair after testing two canvas director's chairs which seemed too risky for his tremendous weight. "Am I about to be regaled with a tale of adventure and intrigue?"

"Well, frankly, Sidney, it depends on how you swallow it. Now then..."

THREE

FOR HER MEETING WITH la Contessa, Mayo changed into a diaphanous dress with a flowery print and wore a Lily Dache hat that would have been more appropriate to a garden party. Hazel Dickson thought she should have carried a tasseled parasol in her left hand, and her right hand holding two leashes at the end of which were a pair of borzois. Mayo and la Contessa didn't quite outdo each other in the gushing department though each gave it her best effort. Marcelo almost succeeded in drowning her in Mediterranean charm and sexy innuendo while Mayo accepted Violetta's excessive admiration of Bogart's persona with a polite smile and a suppressed sneeze.

"So our fathers were friends," said Mayo as she refused an hors d'oeuvre and accepted a gin and grapefruit juice. After some chitchat which was the usual time waster and made Mayo wonder if she should consult a psychiatrist (as Bogie so frequently urged her), la Contessa with exquisite timing said, "There is the letter my father entrusted to yours shortly before he died."

"What letter?" asked Mayo with sincere innocence.

"The letter that tells who was in possession of the cornucopia," insisted the Contessa while dabbing at beads of perspiration on her upper lip.

"Search me," said Mayo with an expressive shrug, little knowing la Contessa wished they could. "Why was a letter necessary if the cornucopia was nowhere to be found when the ship docked?"

"My theory is that my father assigned someone to smuggle the cornucopia ashore."

"Why would he have done that?"

"Perhaps it was a matter of distrust."

Mayo's voice hardened. "You mean for some reason he'd grown to distrust my father."

"Oh no no no," said la Contessa so musically Hazel Dickson feared she was about to break into song. "But you see, my dear Miss Methot, in the past people have been killed for this treasure."

"Do you think your father was murdered?"

"I'll never know. He was buried at sea."

Mayo said, "Well, that's what's usually done when someone dies aboard ship in midocean."

"It wasn't in midocean. It was a little over a day away from port."

"Have you any idea how intense the heat is on the Orient run?" Mayo sipped her drink. "My father's ship wasn't equipped with the proper refrigeration for a corpse. So your father presumably wrote a letter to you identifying the possessor of the cornucopia and entrusted the letter to my father whom he no longer trusted." She said to Hazel Dickson, "This one should star Laurel and Hardy."

Marcelo interjected. "I still don't think there was a letter."

"You hush!" said the countess sharply. She told Mayo, "I received a phone call from someone who said he had been on board the ship and my father confided in him the letter existed and to call me to make sure I got the letter from Captain Methot."

"How long ago was this?" asked Mayo.

"Five years ago."

"My father's been dead for three years or thereabouts. My mother and I went through his effects before disposing of most of them. I assure you there was no such letter. Contessa, do you know the name of this mysterious person who phoned you?"

"I shall never forget. His name was George Spelvin."

Mayo's eyes widened and then she exploded with laughter. La Contessa was bewildered. She looked at Hazel who was equally mystified by the eruption and Marcelo and Violetta exchanged shrugs.

Mayo put her drink on a table, opened her handbag, extracted a tissue and dabbed at her eyes. "Contessa," she said after a few more moments, "I am very well acquainted with George Spelvin."

"Aha!" shouted la Contessa. "Where is he? Where can I find him?"

"Where is he? Find him? Oh Contessa, he is up there in the heavens..."

La Contessa was aghast. "He is dead?"

Mayo was laughing again. "He is out there somewhere in New York, or Detroit, or possibly Philadelphia and St. Louis, anywhere there's a play to be seen." She sipped her drink again. "Contessa, you've been had."

"I beg your pardon?"

"George Spelvin is a theatrical tradition. It is a name cloaked in anonymity. It is a name used by actors who don't want their own names printed in the playbill or the program, as you better know it. Usually it's an actor down on his luck, once well known, now relegated to playing a bit or a walk-on. You'd be surprised how often in a theatrical season George Spelvin trods the boards."

"You are saying I was duped."

"Very. Boy, wait till I tell Bogie about this one."

The countess barked at Violetta to fling open the French windows, which the young woman did with alacrity. The welcome breeze upset Marcelo's immaculately coiffured hair and he sought refuge in a chair next to Mayo. La Contessa said, "You and your husband will laugh at me."

"Not at all. We will laugh at George Spelvin. You see, in a way he's such an old friend. Bogie was George Spelvin a few times early in his career. It's nostalgic."

La Contessa was playing with her pearls, staring at Mayo with hooded eyelids. "Has your husband ever sailed with your father?"

Mayo smiled. "No, Contessa. My husband has never been to the Far East. Not even on location."

Hazel informed la Contessa brightly, "But they do own a boat. The *Slugger*. Named for Mayo who..."

Mayo interrupted her. "Hazel, a most unnecessary non sequitur. Contessa, my husband and I are dining with a famous mystery writer, Dashiell Hammett."

"What's up?" asked Hazel.

"Oh, can it, Hazel. It's just your ordinary run-of-the-mill non-gourmet dinner at the Brown Derby. As I was saying, Contessa, Mr. Hammett has written a book whose story is similar to that of the cornucopia."

"The cornucopia is not a story. It is a fact. It is the truth."

"Don't fret needlessly, Contessa, I see now you were anxious to meet me hoping I had your father's letter in my possession. And," she added, subtly suspicious, "neither does my mother. At least not to my knowledge. Funny, her apartment in Portland...that's up north in Oregon...was ransacked this morning. Nothing was stolen. You people haven't been in Portland lately, by any chance?"

"How dare you!" bristled la Contessa.

"How dare I what?"

"Insinuate we were in Portland and ransacked your mother's apartment!"

"Now really, Mayo," said Hazel.

Mayo had risen. "The party's turning sour and I have a date with some sales people at Magnin's. Don't see me to the door, Marcelo. I know how to make an exit." Within moments, she was gone.

In the hallway, Mayo paused to repair her face. She examined herself in the compact mirror and decided all she needed was some lipstick. She applied the special brand prepared for her by makeup expert Perc Westmore who with his brothers catered exclusively to the Hollywood elite. Moments later, waiting for an elevator, she thought about her father. She'd always suspected there was some larceny in her father's soul. It went with the territory, the Oriental route. Drug smuggling. Gun smuggling. Developed by some more unscrupulous seafarers into a sophisticated high art. He had entertained and sometimes frightened her with tales of piracy in the Oriental waters. Had he stolen the cornucopia? Was he capable of such treachery?

George Spelvin.

Her father knew the origin of George Spelvin. He'd heard it from Mayo and Bogie. He could have used the letter and George Spelvin to mislead la Contessa. And taken the cornucopia for himself. She was now descending in the elevator. He'd suddenly been talking about retirement those months before his death. Her mother hated the word. Retirement. Jack at home, underfoot, his constant presence annoying her while she tried to entertain her muse. Leaving the elevator, she entered the hotel bar, sat at an isolated table, and ordered a gin martini. She knew she shouldn't, but she did. There was plenty of time before she was due to meet the others at the Brown Derby. Plenty of time to tank up on gin martinis. She'd better not. She'd better have just this one and get on to I. Magnin's. She could use another pair of shoes. She always needed another pair of shoes. She had almost as many pairs of shoes as Joan Crawford. The martini arrived and Mayo stared at it as though it might have been an ocean in the Far East. She had never seen her father's ship, but it didn't matter. She had a vivid imagination. His ship was right here in front of her eyes. It was circumnavigating the martini, her father leaning over the rail and plotting the future of the cornucopia. It was warm but she felt a sudden chill. Had the Baron di Marcopolo been murdered? By her father?

"What's wrong, sweetie?"

Mayo's head turned to the sound of the voice on her right. She had neither heard nor seen Hazel Dickson sitting opposite her. "Oh. Hazel. You startled me."

"Didn't mean to. I'm glad I found you. I'd like to discuss the cast of characters upstairs. Is that a gin martini I see? It's inspirational. I think I'll have one."

"Take mine. I shouldn't have ordered it. Go ahead, Hazel. Take it. I don't want to show at dinner a bit squiffed. Bogie wouldn't like that."

"If you insist," said Hazel as she moved the gin martini in front of her. "Twist of lemon. Just how I like it. I loved the George Spelvin bit. You had la Contessa going around in circles."

"She's awful fat. Is Marcelo her lover?"

Hazel made a face. "What a repulsive thought. He probably is because he's probably penniless and any port in a storm. And she's quite a port."

"Are you going to peddle the cornucopia story?"

Hazel airily flipped a wrist. "Isn't it a hoot? I think it's a damned good story."

"You know the plot of *The Maltese Falcon*."

"Sure."

"It's a cousin of the cornucopia."

"Say! You're right! Sidney Skolsky will love it!"

"Why not shoot for the big time? Louella."

"I suppose I should, but I owe Sidney." She downed a healthy swig of martini, and commented, "Could be colder. Mayo, aren't you feeling well?"

"Do I look ill?"

"You have this strange look. Something's bothering you."

"George Spelvin is bothering me."

"Now that was an inspiration, Mayo. You sure knocked la Contessa on her backside." She thought for a moment. "I'm not so sure I like her very much. I could go for the boyfriend though. Couldn't you?"

"I'm a married woman."

"So?" Hazel downed the rest of the drink.

I'm a married woman. So? That's Hollywood.

At Warner Brothers, the rehearsal had still not gotten underway. Bogie, Mary Astor, and Sidney Greenstreet were joined by director John Huston, son of actor Walter Huston and three other important cast members, Peter Lorre, Gladys George, and Elisha Cook Jr. Miss George was looking painfully thin, and Bogie wondered if she was hooked on drugs as the rumor had it. In 1935, she'd been brought from Broadway to Paramount Pictures for the starring role in *Valiant Is the Word for Carrie* and was then signed by M-G-M, who soon had her playing supporting roles because no magic of a makeup man or a special camera lens could hide the fact that she was middle-aged. They'd found cocaine for Lorre in the Mexican barrio in downtown L.A. He was now as dapper and jovial as always. Gladys George kept dabbing at her nose with a handkerchief, a sure sign she was hooked on the funny powder, too.

Mary Astor urged Bogart to tell the late arrivals the story of the cornucopia. "Sure," agreed Bogie, "I especially want John to hear it."

Huston's curiosity was piqued. "Is it dirty? Does it have a great punch line?"

"It's dirty, but not in the way you'd prefer it. As for the punch line, it's waiting to be written." Bogart told the story straightforwardly with Mary occasionally prompting him when she thought he was leaving out an important fact. He didn't, at the time, have all that much story to tell, but what he did tell he told provocatively and colorfully and had everyone's undivided attention. He signaled he was finished when he lit a cigarette.

Huston slapped his knee and roared with laughter. "Why, you slimy son of a bitch, that's a variation on the *Falcon!*"

"I'm glad you noticed," said Bogart, sending a smoke ring past Peter Lorre's left ear.

"Is it supposed to be true?" Huston was openly skeptical.

"Mayo's over at the Ambassador having tea, I hope, with the lady who claims the thing belongs to her if it's ever found. La Contessa di Marcopolo."

"Oh sure," said Gladys George and all eyes centered on her.

"You know her?" asked Bogart.

"Indirectly. I met her father years ago in London when I was an ingenue and looked it. The Baron di Marcopolo. Very rich and very much taken with himself." She closed her eyes. "Let me think if I still remember." Her eyes flew open. "Oh yeah. I remember." Now she was smiling. "He had so many lovers, he was known as the Machiavelli of Mistresses. Quite a horseman, if you know what I mean." She winked at Mary Astor who blushed. She knew what Gladys meant and would never regret that she did.

Peter Lorre had a wicked look on his face. "Gladys, did you ever come down the home stretch with him?"

"He didn't interest me that way," she said coolly. "But I could appreciate what the ladies saw in him. So he died on an ocean liner captained by Mayo's father."

"They were good friends," said Bogart, "or that's what la Contessa says."

Huston said, "I don't buy the letter. That one needs a rewrite."

"You're probably right," said Bogart. "And I find myself not buying the cornucopia when I give it some sensible thought. After all, the *Falcon* never materializes. What we do find is a fake.''

"'Such stuff as dreams are made on,'" said Greenstreet solemnly.

"Sidney, you're stealing my line," admonished Bogart.

"It's such a lovely line. I find it irresistible." He sat with his hands folded across his formidable stomach. "Mr. Hammett, bless him, is no slouch at good lines of dialogue."

Huston wondered aloud, "Do you suppose Hammett at some point was privy to the cornucopia story?"

"Seems to me, John," said Bogart, "there have been all sorts of stories handed down through the ages about priceless articles that have gone lost and are still being sought. The silver chalice of the Crusades, Christ's cloak when he was crucified, the lost city of Atlantis…"

"My option at renewal time," said Lorre wistfully.

Bogart told Huston and the others that he and Mayo had a dinner date with Hammett and Lillian Hellman and he had every intention of questioning the author on the subject.

"Okay. Let's get back to our own legend, Bogie, I'd like to start with your first meeting, when Mary comes to your office with a trumped up story about a missing sister…"

While a troubled Mayo Methot drove several sales clerks at I. Magnin's to the brink of insanity, Hazel Dickson steered her sad excuse of a car downtown to Detective Herbert Villon's precinct. She wanted to see what he made of the cornucopia story. Darling Herb, longtime detective, longtime lover, longtime name-dropper known as The Detective of the Stars. Hazel looked in the rearview mirror, not to see if she was being followed but to check her face, which was still a rather attractive one.

She drove into the precinct's parking lot, which she wasn't supposed to do. But there'd be no squawk. Everybody in the precinct recognized Hazel's Studebaker with its dents and bruises and gallant defiance of any form of destruction. She turned off the motor while wondering if Hitler had invaded another country this morning. The son of a bitch was gobbling countries as fast as la Contessa gobbled hors d'oeuvres. She locked the car despite its being on a police lot. Hazel Dickson trusted nobody. Had she been a man, she would have sported both belt and suspenders. She breezed into the precinct with a proprietary air, greeted the desk sergeant like a long lost brother, and without bothering to have herself announced marched down the long corridor to Herb Villon's untidy office.

She opened the door briskly and saw Villon and his young partner, Jim Mallory, shuffling photographs. They didn't look up. She hadn't disturbed them. They were too engrossed in the photographs.

"Dirty pictures?" asked Hazel.

"Filthy," said Villon without bothering to look up. Hazel crossed to the desk, looked over Jim Mallory's shoulder, and let out a yelp.

"You son of a bitch, I feel like throwing up!"

"You know where the toilet is," said Villon. Then he sighed with defeat, "Jim, we still have a leg left over."

Mallory straightened up and with hands on hips said, "This isn't a dismembered body; it's a jigsaw puzzle."

"Who is it?" asked Hazel in a small voice.

"We're assuming she was a prostitute. We were able to fingerprint her and we are waiting for the answers, but we couldn't find her head."

"Oh God!" wailed Hazel. "What sort of maniac would do such a thing to a person!"

Villon finally looked up. "Someone, I should think, who has gone to pieces." He added glumly, "You're wearing that hat."

Her eyes narrowed. "*I* happen to like this hat. It was a gift from an old admirer. My grandmother."

"Tell your grandmother to wear it. It would suit the old bat. She still cheating at pinochle?"

"Of course. It's all she lives for. Listen, Herb, I just spent some time with la Contessa di Marcopolo at the Ambassador and..."

"Oh, for crying out loud! Not more of those phony European titles of yours!"

"She's not phony, she's authentic and she's got the royal rocks to prove it. Will you *please* pay attention? She's here on some kind of a treasure hunt."

Villon sank into his swivel chair. Jim Mallory folded his arms and leaned against a wall. He thought of lighting his pipe but remembered his dentist's warning his teeth were eroding from biting down on the stem. Hazel sat in a chair opposite them and placed her handbag on the desk, crossed her legs, and warned them, "Now no interruptions. I'm giving this one to Sidney Skolsky." She told the cornucopia story without embellishments but with a kind of intensity that had them more or less believing it. "Well? Do you think la Contessa has something or she belongs in a loony bin?"

"I've heard crazier ones. In fact I've read one similar to it."

"The Maltese Falcon," said Hazel.

"Right on the nose. You think Mayo Methot's father pulled a fast one?"

"I prefer to think not. I'm very fond of Mayo despite that time at Mocambo she threw a highball at Bogie, who ducked and it hit me."

Jim Mallory said, "I like that bit about George Spelvin. I wonder who invented George Spelvin?"

"Don't open that can of peas," cautioned Hazel. "But if the story is at all true, then I think Captain Methot took off with the thing and then pulled the Spelvin thing to mislead the contessa, who, as you gather, is not easily misled."

"Tell me, Hazel," asked Villon, "if you were a stuffed cornucopia, where would you be hidden?"

"How the hell should I know? I've never been a stuffed cornucopia."

Mallory asked, "The baron was buried at sea?"

"Yes, that's part of the plot."

"And the captain remained on board for the return voyage?"

"Isn't that what captains are supposed to do?"

"Not necessarily," said Villon. "He could have arranged for someone else to supervise the return voyage. They sometimes do that."

Mallory said, "I don't think the thing left the ship. I think Methot ran the return voyage and from wherever it docked, he brought the cornucopia back with him. It's more logical."

Villon threw up his hands. "Who needs logic in this illogical world! Anyway, how do we know there really was a cornucopia?''

"Because my woman's intuition, my gut instinct, tells me there is a cornucopia lurking in some dark, sequestered corner.''

Villon asked, "You leaving town, Hazel?''

"What the hell for?''

"To hunt for the cornucopia.''

"Why would I leave town? If la Contessa is here, then she thinks it's here. And what about that ransacked apartment of Mayo's mother? Mayo practically accused them of doing the job though she'd have a hard time proving they were in Portland.''

Said Villon, "The countess sounds too fat to do any ransacking.''

"If they were in Portland and did the ransacking, then my finger would point at Marcelo.''

Villon asked, "What about this Marcelo?''

"He's her lapdog.''

"Oh. One of those.''

"Very sexy.''

"How would you know?'' asked Villon as he applied a match to a cigarette.

"I'm not blind and you know my vivid imagination.''

Villon said to Mallory, "I wonder what Bogie makes of all this?''

"Don't ask him, ask me,'' insisted Hazel. She told him about the dinner date at the Brown Derby. "Maybe you feel like taking me to dinner at the Brown Derby?''

FOUR

A FINANCIER NAMED Herbert Sonnenberg conceived the idea of the Brown Derby restaurant, on Vine Street just off Hollywood Boulevard. It was a restaurant built and shaped like a Brown Derby. In no time at all, it was one of Hollywood's favorite playrooms, the food of secondary importance and rightly so. Sonnenberg had been silent screen queen Gloria Swanson's second husband and thanks to her had instant access to all Hollywood. The walls were decorated with caricatures of Hollywood celebrities, an inspiration borrowed from the famed Sardi's restaurant in New York whose walls were adorned with caricatures of leading Broadway lights. The restaurant consisted mainly of booths so situated that they afforded a certain amount of unwanted privacy to their occupants. Actors ate in public not merely to satisfy their appetites but to be seen and recognized and adored. Upon entering the place one had to make one's way through a sea of gaping tourists and an army of autograph hounds who through some strange and mystical grapevine seemed to know which celebrities were in temporary residence. The bar was a magnet for Hollywood's drinkers and they were legion. If there was a stray husband or lover or boyfriend on the loose, a call to the Derby usually found him and sent him on his way.

On this particular night that the Bogarts were dining with Dashiell Hammett and Lillian Hellman, the place was hopping, an autograph seeker's dream or nightmare, depending on how they were treated by the celebrated. Everyone remembered with relish when silent star Norma Talmadge, a very wealthy woman who had failed to make it in talkies, shouted at an autograph seeker, "Get the hell away from me! I don't need you anymore!" Hollywood's frequent cruelty was also remembered, especially the time when silent-screen comic Roscoe "Fatty" Arbuckle, having won a justly deserved acquittal after three trials for murder, nevertheless sat alone in a booth, chagrined at being unacknowledged, ostracized forever.

Dashiell Hammett and Lillian Hellman were the first to arrive and ordered scotch highballs. They both drank too much and swore too much and were presumably the models for Nick and Nora Charles in Hammett's brilliant novel, *The Thin Man,* immortalized on the screen by William Powell and Myrna Loy. Hammett was tall and urbane and cadaverously thin and it was his portrait that graced the jacket of the book when it was published in 1932. Lillian Hellman was urbane, too, and a very gifted playwright. She was also very mean and very rude and did not suffer fools gladly. She was incredibly homely. She had a nose that only Jimmy Durante and W. C. Fields could appreciate. Hellman's very good friend, Dorothy Parker, usually explained it was her intellect that had captured the much pursued (by women) Hammett. There had been a husband in her life, a playwright named Arthur Kober who'd written a Broadway success several years earlier, *Having Wonderful Time,* and contributed humorous pieces frequently to *The New Yorker.* It was said that Hammett had his undying gratitude after Miss Hellman bounced Kober for the novelist.

"I hate this town," said Hellman.

"You just said that," said Hammett nibbling a peanut.

"I can't say it often enough."

"Don't knock it too loudly," cautioned Hammett, "or they might stop paying you all that money you demand and get."

"I'm worth every nickel." She looked at her wristwatch. "What the hell's keeping the Bogarts?"

"The Brothers Warner. Bogie told me they pay him one hundred and fourteen thousand dollars a year."

"Peanuts. Bette Davis gets over two hundred and fifty thousand dollars."

Hammett winked. "He knows that. It's eating away at him like a cancer."

Hellman sat up. "Here comes Mayo. Christ, that getup. You'd think she's planning to be entertained by Queen Mary."

"Keep a civil tongue in your mouth. You know she packs a hefty wallop. Hello Mayo, darling. Where's Bogie?"

"Hello dear. Hello Lily. Waiter, a very dry gin martini with a lemon twist." She moved into the booth next to Hellman, leaving room for Bogart.

"Where's Bogie?" asked Hellman.

"Huston was holding a rehearsal of *Falcon.* Shouldn't you have been there, Dash?"

"What for? I only wrote the book. You know that means less than nothing in this town."

"Come off it, Dash," said Hellman, "they did a great job on *The Thin Man.*"

"What about those awful sequels?"

"Oh, come on," said Mayo, "I thought *After the Thin Man* was just plain darling."

"That's just what it was," said Hammett glumly, "just plain darling."

Mayo asked Hellman, "What are you working on now?"

"More money."

"Lily never gets paid enough money," said Hammett. "Ever since Sam Goldwyn filmed her *Children's Hour,* she's been one of his favorite scripters. And he pays her plenty."

"What's wrong with that?" asked Mayo as the waiter served her martini.

"Goldwyn."

Bogart had arrived and was greeting friends at the bar. He waved at the booth indicating he'd be joining them momentarily. For the first time in a long time, Mayo couldn't wait to tell him something.

She raised her glass to propose a toast. "To absent friends."

"Which ones?" asked Hellman.

"Don't be surly, Lily," cautioned Hammett. "The night is young."

"We're not and I'm hungry." She said to Mayo, "Do you think your husband will ever tear himself away from the bar?"

"He just did. Here he comes."

Bogart arrived at the table and demanded of Mayo, "Where's my drink?" He sat next to her and shook hands with Hammett and Hellman.

"I wasn't sure what you might have wanted. I'm not a mind reader."

Bogart signaled a waiter and ordered a gin martini. Hellman added, "And menus and bread and butter. How I miss Sardi's. The service is impeccable."

Bogie wondered why Mayo was dressed like a bridesmaid, but said nothing. "How'd you make out with the countess?"

"It was very very interesting. She's a rather large woman who favors rather large jewelry and worth plenty."

"They could be paste," said Hellman.

"They could be, but they aren't. I know the real thing when I see it. I once had a boyfriend who worked at Tiffany's. He taught me plenty until they sent him up the river for stealing some diamond rings. Anyway, the contessa has a playmate. One hell of a good looker named Marcelo Amati. And there's a pretty secretary, Violetta Cenci. And almost from the minute I got there, the countess began carrying on about the cornucopia."

Bogart interrupted. "Dash?" Hammett turned to him. "You ever hear a story about a lost cornucopia, a horn of plenty stuffed with a fortune in jewels? I thought maybe you did because it's so much like *The Maltese Falcon.*"

"The *Falcon* is an absolute fabrication, so help me God. What about this cornucopia?"

"It belonged to the countess's father, Baron di Marcopolo, a descendant of the original Marco Polo."

"Oh, go away," said Hellman as the waiter arrived with a tray that held Bogart's martini, a basket of bread, and a dish of butter. A second waiter accompanied him and distributed the menus. Hellman began reading hers immediately.

Hammett said to her, "You're being rude, Lily."

"No, I'm not," she contradicted, "I'm being hungry. I've had no lunch."

"Bogie is telling us a story."

"Well, you listen and I'll read."

Bogart had always wondered what had attracted Hammett to Hellman. She was homely and disagreeable. A brilliant mind but so what? The story was bruited about that he edited her plays for her yet had never written one of his own. Bogart expressed no opinion of his own about the woman. He liked Hammett and wanted to continue their friendship. He knew Mayo wasn't crazy about her but then, Mayo was crazy about very few people of either sex. Hellman looked up from the menu.

"It's gotten awful quiet around here," she said.

"We're waiting for you to join us," said Hammett in a tone of voice that could easily be taken as a threat. She flashed him a look and Bogart waited to see if she would challenge Hammett. She put the menu down and lit a cigarette. There would be no challenge.

Bogart continued. "Mayo spent some time with the countess this afternoon."

"With Hazel Dickson, who's sitting in a booth over there with Herb Villon and trying to attract our attention," said Mayo.

Hellman said, "Miss Dickson's hands are rather frantic. Why doesn't she throw bread?"

Bogart and Mayo waved back at Hazel who was telling Villon, "Maybe we can have a nightcap with them later."

Villon didn't like Lillian Hellman. He wished hers was the dismembered body that he and Jim Mallory were trying to piece together.

Hammett asked, "What about the countess?"

"Tell us, Slugger. Let's hear it all."

It wasn't often that Mayo Methot was given the opportunity to glow in a spotlight and she took every advantage of the chance. She had their undivided attention, even Hellman's. She left nothing out, even the hint of suspicion that her father might have helped the baron along the trail to his final reward in order to appropriate the cornucopia for himself.

"You ever notice one around the house, Slugger?" asked Bogart.

"I was long gone and in New York. As a matter of fact, I was long gone and right here in Hollywood." She then launched into the George Spelvin incident which delighted Bogart and the others. All agreed there was the probability that la Contessa's George Spelvin was Jack Methot leading her astray.

"Why bother leading her astray at all?" asked Hellman with her usual probing mind.

"Simple," said Hammett. "She knew the thing existed and so where had it disappeared to? Thanks to Spelvin it's disappeared into thin air and we know how thin thin air can be. There never was a letter, there was only the baron entrusting the thing into the care of his good and trusted friend Captain Methot who may not have been very good and probably shouldn't have been trusted with anything. I hope I haven't hurt your feelings, Mayo."

"Not at all. I liked my father. I had no reason to dislike him. He was rarely in residence. I think my mother suspected he was a bit of a scoundrel, though she always spoke well of him. Mother was and still is a newspaperwoman and the profession meant more to her than he or I did."

Hammett smiled and said, "The victim of another miserable childhood."

"Who said I had a miserable childhood?" as Bogart signalled for a fresh round of drinks.

Bogart told them Gladys George had known the baron, who was famed as a bedroom swordsman, in London a couple of decades earlier.

"That's heartening," said Hellman. "So where is all this getting us?"

"Into a very interesting puzzle involving a cornucopia," said Hammett. He added as an afterthought, "Say Bogie, this isn't a press agent's nightmare to spark interest in the *Falcon?*"

"No way. Scout's honor."

"Scouts have no honor," growled Hellman. "It's all a myth perpetuated by den mothers. When I was a kid, a Boy Scout tried to rape me."

"Did you help?" asked Hammett.

"Now that's not funny," raged Hellman, "and I'm going to order my dinner. Waiter!" she shouted, attracting the attention of everybody on her side of the room except a waiter.

Hammett said to Bogart, "Too bad we don't have a bullhorn." He caught a waiter's eye. The waiter hurried to the table with pad and pencil at the ready and took their orders. They all wanted steak, fries, and salad, and the waiter, a recent arrival from war-torn Paris, felt they were barbarians. Had no one in Hollywood a sophisticated palate?

The fresh round of drinks was served as Hammett stroked his chin and asked, "Do you think the cornucopia exists?"

Bogart shrugged. "God knows, antique shops are up to their belly buttons in them. I've seen some at the Old Curiosity Shop."

Hellman squinted at him. "The Old Curiosity Shop? You mean as in Charles Dickens's *The Old Curiosity Shop?*"

Bogart laughed. "It's out in Venice. Slugger and I check it out every so often. Especially when she gets this yen to get to the pier for a ride on the carousel."

Hellman stared at Mayo and said, "He's kidding, right?"

"Not at all," said Mayo, chewing on her martini's lemon peel, "I adore carousels. It's a late in life fetish. I never saw one as a child."

"Amazing," murmured Hellman and sipped her drink.

Hammett's words prodded Bogart. "Well, Bogie, do you think the cornucopia's a phantom? Like the baron's letter?"

"I'm a sucker for stories like this. I really am. Yes, I do believe there's a cornucopia because of la Contessa."

"Meaning?" asked Hammett.

"That broad hasn't traveled halfway around the world in pursuit of some ephemera."

Hellman said, "She traveled halfway around the world to seek refuge."

Bogart countered, "She could have settled into Switzerland. It's neutral and just across the border from Italy."

"It is also a very dull country," said Hellman. "All it's got is cheese, chocolate, and cuckoo clocks. And consider the boyfriend. I'm sure he's one of those gigolo types that gets bored easily."

Mayo said with a wicked glance at Bogart, "He's an outrageous flirt."

Bogart grinned. "Oh yeah? How'd you make out?"

Mayo said coldly, "I wasn't looking to make out."

Bogart shook his head from side to side. "Can you beat this broad?"

"I hear you do," said Hellman sweetly followed by "Ow!" as Hammett kicked her under the table.

Bogart rode past her ill-natured statement while Mayo stared across the room at Hazel Dickson and Herb Villon who were absorbed in conversation the way she and Bogart rarely were. Bogart said, "I give her every opportunity to cheat on me but she remains ever faithful."

Hellman was about to say, "Maybe she gets no offers" but thought better of it, reminding herself she was damned lucky there was Dashiell Hammett in her life.

Hammett steered the conversation back to the cornucopia. "I think it exists. And I think the countess might have been behind the raid at Mrs. Methot's apartment."

"That's what I thought after I left her suite," said Mayo.

"Over a dry gin martini in the bar downstairs," said Bogart, grinning again.

"Well, actually, beloved, I did order one but Hazel Dickson drank it. She joined me in the bar and I decided I needed a clear head when I tried on shoes at Magnin's." The grin disappeared from Bogart's face. Mayo said to Hellman, "I never seem to have enough shoes. Are you as crazy about shoes as I am?"

"I am crazy about money and Clark Gable in no particular order," replied Hellman.

"Gable has false teeth," said Mayo.

"So did George Washington," said Hellman.

"Ladies, please," said Hammett, "our salads have arrived and the trip from the kitchen seems to have exhausted them."

"Well, I'm putting mine out of its misery," said Hellman as she doomed a piece of tomato to her yawning mouth.

Hammett got back on track. "If the countess and her gang were in Portland this morning, they made good time getting here."

"They had plenty of time," explained Mayo. "My mother was lured out of the apartment for a seven-thirty breakfast with a man who claimed to be Salvador Dali."

"For crying out loud! What the hell would Salvador Dali be doing in Portland, Oregon?" asked Hellman.

Mayo replied haughtily. "Pablo Picasso was once in Portland

and my mother interviewed him. He was there for an exhibition of his work at the art museum. And it so happens a Dali exhibit opened this week so Mother had every reason to believe it was the actual artist. Anyway, it wasn't, probably Marcelo Amati imitating him.''

"Makes sense," said Bogart, "good thinking, Slugger. Am I the only one who thinks this salad dressing is rancid?''

"Mine's fine," said Hellman.

"Yours is all gone," said Hammett.

"Well, I'm hungry, for crying out loud!''

Mayo resumed her timetable. "There's the Portland express to L.A. with just a brief stop in Frisco. It gets in at one-thirty. It's the one I take after I visit my mother. They're at the hotel within half an hour to forty-five minutes depending on downtown traffic and then Hazel contacts them, having been tipped by one of her many spies that they're in residence, and then I'm brought in to meet them because if Mother hasn't got that nonexistent letter then it stands to reason the daughter might have.''

"Sure," said Bogart, "there's that carton with his papers in the basement." He said to Hammett, "We've been through them. Nothing." He pushed his salad aside, and lit a cigarette.

Hammett asked, "What about this Old Curiosity Shop?''

"It's run by this eccentric and his daughter.''

"He's not eccentric, he's nuts," said Mayo, passing sentence with alacrity.

"I like old Edgar, he's got a great sense of humor. It's his daughter Nell I wouldn't turn my back on. Edgar and Nell Dickens.''

"Oh come on!" said Hellman. "Dickens! Old Curiosity Shop! Little Nell!''

"She's not so little." He winked at Hammett. "She's how do we say in the old country, very zoftig.''

"Which old country is that?" asked Hellman.

Bogart ignored the statement. "There's also a clerk named Sidney Heep.''

"Ha!" said Hammett as a busboy cleared the salad plates and a waiter served the steak and french fries.

"The steaks look great," said Mayo.

"I think mine just moved," said Hellman.

"Lily," asked Hammett, "why don't you ever enjoy yourself?"

"Who says I'm not enjoying myself," fork and knife poised for a fatal attack.

"Lily," said Bogart, "if it moved, kill it."

"Sidney Heep!" exclaimed Hammett as he trimmed his steak of its fat. "Except in *David Copperfield* it's Uriah Heep. The shop is a setup, right?"

"Of course," said Bogart as he chewed with contentment. "It's Hollywood. It's the pier at Venice. It's all for the tourists."

"We go there and we're not tourists," said Mayo defensively.

"I don't care who it's for," said Bogart, "I like the place. It's great for Christmas presents."

"And the prices are reasonable," added Mayo, "and for Bogie, therein lies its charm."

"You insinuating I'm a cheapskate?" He said this with rare warmth. Hellman looked at him and then at Mayo. The Battling Bogarts? It's got to be a sham. He loves her, for crying out loud, and she'd kill for him. I think they beat up on each other because it's their perverted way of expressing love. She looked at Hammett. If he ever laid a finger on her other than erotically she'd cut off his essentials.

"What are you thinking, Lily," asked Hammett.

"Better you shouldn't know."

"You know, the funny thing about Dickens and his daughter is there's absolutely no resemblance."

"Come to think of it, you're right," agreed Mayo.

Bogart continued, "Maybe Edgar's a stepfather, or maybe she's adopted."

"Or maybe she's not a daughter," suggested Hellman.

Hammett said, "There you go, Lily. Always looking for the seamy side of things."

"They're the most fun and the most interesting. What makes my *Little Foxes* so fascinating to audiences, thank God. Most of my characters are rats."

Bogart couldn't resist. "Didn't I read somewhere they were based on your own family?"

"That's right. They were. Thought you'd upset me, Bogie?"

"No, I was just looking for confirmation. That's your best play, Lily."

"How nice of you, Bogie, how very nice."

"And that's all the nice you're going to get out of me tonight. You know, Mayo. We might take a drive out to Venice Beach tomorrow. See what's with the Dickens and cornucopias. There's no rehearsal tomorrow, Mary's doing a radio show and that ties her up all day. Dash? Lily? You want to join us?"

"Do I have to ride the carousel?" asked Hellman.

Bogart said, "Hazel Dickson's been abandoned. Her boyfriend's deserted her."

"No, he hasn't," said Mayo. "A waiter called him to the phone."

"Terrific guy, Herb Villon. And a damned good detective," said Bogart.

"We've met him," said Hellman. "Sam Spade he isn't."

"Sam Spade's fiction," said Bogart. "Herb's for real. He's headed this way. I don't like the look on his face. Something's wrong."

Hazel left her table and hurried after Villon. She could sense something was up that could prove profitable for her.

Villon said to Bogart and Mayo, "Sorry to break up the party, folks, but I just spoke to my partner, Jim Mallory. Bogie, Mayo, your house was broken into. Your neighbor out walking his dog saw the front door open. He investigated. The place has been ransacked."

"Our housekeeper! Hannah! What about Hannah!"

"Now take it easy, Slugger," said Bogart. He asked Villon, "She's okay, isn't she?"

Villon would always remember this moment and the pain it caused the Bogarts. "She's been murdered. A knife in her chest."

"Oh my God!" cried Mayo, "Oh my God!"

And at the next table somebody said, "The Battling Bogarts are at it again!"

FIVE

HANNAH DARROW LAY ON HER back on the foyer floor, the subject of the police photographer's camera. She had never received this much attention in life. The Bogarts came into the house through the back door. Turning into their usually quiet street, Bogart saw in addition to patrol cars a swarm of reporters and photographers and exploded with a series of expletives. He maneuvered the car into an alley that led to the rear of his house, followed by Hammett and Hellman in Hammett's unprepossessing roadster. Villon with Hazel at his side drove right up to the front of the house and immediately fielded a barrage of questions from the newsmen. "Men and ladies, you know as much as I do. I just got here. Let me through, damn it!" He elbowed his way through the mass of reporters while Hazel paused to tell a sob sister she knew, "Love your hat."

Inside the house, Mayo stared down at Hannah with a pained and sorrowful expression. Bogart gently patted Mayo's shoulder and she heaved a dry sob. Hellman stared at the sorrowful tableau in the foyer and then switched her attention to the mess in the living room. The overturned chairs, the open drawers with contents spilled out on the floor, the broken wall mirror—which Lillian didn't know was not the fault of the ransacker—a sideboard from which had spilled a variety of dinner linens. Hellman said to Hammett, "Mayo's one hell of a housekeeper."

"Come off it, Lily. Save the wisecracks for the gang back at the Garden of Allah," meaning the small hotel on Sunset Boulevard that mostly housed refugees from New York and had once been the elegant residence of silent star Alla Nazimova. Bogart joined Hammett.

"What an effing mess. Jack Warner ain't gonna like the attendant publicity. I wonder if the countess and her help have solid alibis. Mayo! Don't go upstairs alone! There might be somebody up there."

"Just me," said Jim Mallory as he appeared on the top landing. "Come on up, Mrs. Bogart, and check if anything's missing."

"That's just what I intend to do." She hurried up the stairs followed by Hazel Dickson.

Hellman said in an aside to Hammett, "I don't suppose she had much in the way of expensive jewelry."

"Why not?"

"Well, that story of the boyfriend who worked at Tiffany's. It sounded a bit wistful to me. I don't see Bogie as being a man who showers a beloved with expensive gems."

"I see Bogart as a man who's practical enough to keep from drowning in a sea of unnecessary debts." He reintroduced himself to Herb Villon, having met him several weeks earlier when there were several break-ins at the Garden of Allah, but Villon most assuredly remembered him. Bogart was at the desk checking for damage. It was one of the few good antiques in the room and he envisioned a good price for it if he should ever have the misfortune to liquidate, something to contemplate if Mayo continued her spending sprees. He saw a man kneeling and examining Hannah Darrow. Obviously a medical examiner. Bogart turned his face away as the examiner removed the knife from Hannah's chest. The knife was placed in a plastic bag and as far as Bogart and his weak stomach were concerned would forever remain in exile. Bogart joined Hammett and Villon and asked Villon, "You know about the countess?"

"From Hazel."

"Then you know everything."

"When Jim Mallory paged me at the restaurant I had him ring the Ambassador at once. The secretary answered the phone. Then the boyfriend got on the phone and last but not least, the kid herself, la Contessa. All present and accounted for."

"How convenient," said Bogart while Hammett wished Lillian would get off her knees and stop nosing about in the Bogarts' dinner linens. God forbid there should be no damask napkins. Apparently there was. Hellman was holding one up to the light with a look of surprise on her face, and then rubbing the napkin with her fingers to test the quality of the material. From the look on her face, it was a damned good and expensive cut of damask. Poor Lily. Foiled at last.

Mayo came marching down the stairs with Hazel in tow. "Nothing's missing. Everything's there, including my good Cartier earrings."

Damn fool, thought Hellman, she could have lied through her teeth and collected some insurance.

Mayo said to Bogart, "I think we'd better check into a hotel tonight. Upstairs it's a nightmare."

Bogart suggested roguishly, "I'm sure we could get into the Ambassador."

"Why not our place?" asked Hammett.

"Allah be praised," said Hellman, joining them and lighting a cigarette. "Poor Mayo. This is just awful. It'll be on every front page across the world in the morning."

"Oh, no, it won't!" The one and only, the inimitable Jack Warner had entered unseen by his star, the star's wife, and their friends. He stepped over the corpse to enter from the foyer and the coroner gave him a sharp and unpleasant look. Two of Warner's high powered publicity men accompanied the mogul and also hopscotched over the body. Warner said to Hazel, "Thanks for phoning me, Hazel. It's worth five exclusives."

"Ten," countered Hazel. Warner ignored her.

"Come off it, Jack," said Bogart, "what makes you think you can keep this out of the papers? Murder in Humphrey Bogart's house."

"If it was Humphrey Bogart who was murdered, I'd have a lot of trouble," said Warner, "in fact, I'd cause a lot of trouble, wouldn't I boys," this addressed to his press reps, who had brought their cameras and were photographing everything in sight including keyholes. "But when the corpse is only a housekeeper..."

"What an epitaph," murmured Hellman, who made a mental note never to work for Jack Warner no matter how much money he offered, even if he threw in the services of Errol Flynn.

Mayo had built up a full head of steam. "Only a housekeeper! She was a person! A human being! She was our friend!"

"No offense meant," said Warner amiably and then he exploded. "I've got hundreds of thousands of dollars invested in Humphrey Bogart! He starts a major motion picture in a couple of weeks and there's three more lined up for him!"

"What three more?" asked Bogart.

"They're a surprise," swiftied Warner.

"Sure. Like a big increase in my take home."

Warner asked winsomely, "Are you referring to salami sandwiches?"

"No, I'm referring to cheese."

Warner glared at him and then asked, "Who's in charge of the investigation?"

"You've got to be kidding," said Herb Villon. "I'm not window dressing."

"Oh, of course! Herb!" He crossed to Villon and put an arm around his shoulder. He said to the room, "L.A.'s greatest detective! Say, Herb! Why don't you collaborate with Hazel on your autobiography? I'll buy it for Bogie."

Bogie said, "He'll pay you in salami sandwiches."

"I don't like salami," said Herb Villon, and refrained from adding, and I also don't like Jack Warner and if he doesn't get his arm from around my shoulder I just might be tempted to break it.

"Say, Jack," said Bogart, a quixotic tone to his voice, "how do you plan to keep this quiet? Cross everybody's palm with silver, and I mean cash, not the Lone Ranger's horse."

"Just leave it to me and my boys!" To an amused Hammett he sounded like W. C. Fields describing how he cut his way "through a solid wall of Indian flesh." Hammett, like everyone with Hollywood connections, knew Jack Warner considered himself sophisticated and urbane and possessed of a distinct and unusual wit. But like most of his peers, he was crass, vulgar, and about as funny as an infant's funeral.

"Not so fast, Jack. You may be losing out on yards of free publicity for *The Maltese Falcon*."

Warner raged, "This kind of publicity we don't need and I won't have."

"Supposing I tell you the subplot of this murder case is practically synonymous with Dash's story."

"How so?"

Bogart told him of the pursuit of the mysterious cornucopia.

"That's plagiarism!" shouted Warner.

"It's cold facts," said Bogart. "That's why our place was destroyed and poor Hannah murdered, and the least you can do is send lots of lilies to Hannah's funeral."

"She liked gladiolas," said Mayo.

"You!" cried Warner. "You and your father!"

"Go no further with my father," warned Mayo. "And my mother and I are just innocent victims."

Warner's publicity men took him to one side for a conference.

Bogart said to Villon, "If Warner ever bought the rights to your life story, the son of a bitch would assign it to Jimmy Cagney. Don't you write it!"

Warner emerged from the brief huddle with his toadies. "Maybe this is a blessing in disguise. As my blessed mother used to say, "Every cloud has a silver lining.' "

"If it was your mother, I'm sure she said velvet," said Bogart.

"I'm going to hire Adela Rogers St. John to write our news releases!"

"That figures," said Bogart. Miss St. John was Hollywood's most respected, most prolific dispenser of news and gossip. Even the major columnists deferred to her. Her father had been the notorious, hard drinking criminal lawyer Earl St. John. Adela fashioned a story about herself and her father into *A Free Soul*, starring Norma Shearer and Lionel Barrymore and a young Clark Gable whose impact as a sadistic gangster made him an "overnight" success after seven years of struggles.

"Adela has class and respect. She'll make sure this isn't turned into a three-ring circus." Hannah Darrow's body was being removed from the premises, covered with a sheet and strapped to a stretcher.

"Say Jack," said Bogart impishly, "why don't you consider the life of Hannah Darrow?"

"Hannah Darrow? Any relation to Clarence Darrow?"

"That might be arranged." Hammett's expression openly admired Bogart and his total lack of respect for his employer. Lillian Hellman was busy hunting for the Bogart's obviously secret stash of liquor which apparently hadn't interested the intruder.

"Who is Hannah Darrow?" asked Warner.

Bogart pointed to the stretcher being carried out of the house. "There goes Hannah Darrow. Our housekeeper. A hell of a part for Marjorie Rambeau."

"Bogie," said Warner with a sudden attack of piety, "that's sacrilegious."

"How would you know? You never met her."

"Let's get out of here!" Warner barked at his press reps. "And you," pointing a finger at Bogart," tomorrow you rehearse."

"Tomorrow I don't rehearse. Huston cancelled it. Tomorrow I take my wife for a ride on a carousel. Want to join us? Maybe you'll catch the brass ring." Warner advised him to do something both unprintable and physically impossible and then left the house with his flunkies in his wake. Outside, he paused to pose for the photographers and let himself be questioned by the reporters. Bogart appeared in the doorway. "Hey, Jack!" he yelled, "tomorrow send over a crew to straighten out my place! If Mayo and I have to do it, I'll be too tired to rehearse the day after tomorrow!" He shut the door while Warner's face reddened and he clenched his fists.

In the house, Bogart returned to the living room. The indestructible Lillian Hellman had found a bottle of scotch and glasses in a kitchen cabinet and had poured for herself and Hammett. Mayo was in the kitchen fixing a pitcher of gin martinis with Jim Mallory and Hazel Dickson aiding and abetting. A crew of plainclothes officers and forensics experts were dusting down the room and would spend the better part of the night and possibly the next day working on the rest of the house.

Bogart said to Villon, "I don't suppose the countess and her supporting players did the actual ransacking. It's a long schlepp from the Ambassador to here and then back again. I don't think they could have managed it."

"It's an even longer schlepp from Venice Beach," said Villon.

"What do you mean?"

"The countess said they were out visiting the Old Curiosity Shop."

"Well, what do you know about that!" He stopped to think. "I wonder if old man Dickens and Nell know the cornucopia story."

"By tomorrow or the day after, the whole world's going to know it. Miss St. John packs a mean typewriter. Say, Hazel, are you going to let her scoop you?"

Hazel smiled and fluttered her eyelashes. "You may not have noticed, but I have been on the phone with Louella and Hedda and Jimmy and Sidney and Harrison and my sister Clara to tell her I won't be home tonight."

"Why? Where you shacking up?"

She glared at him. He said, "Oh," and returned his attention to Bogart. He took him by the arm and away from the others as Mayo returned with a pitcher of martinis and Jim holding a tray of glasses. Mayo said to Hazel, "Where'd you disappear to?"

"I had some phone calls to make."

Mayo shouted, "Bogie! Martinis!"

"In a minute," he shouted back.

"Why are you two shouting?" asked Lillian Hellman as she added more scotch to her glass.

"It goes with the territory," said Mayo.

Villon said to Bogart, "It's my theory the countess isn't the only one hunting for the whatchamacallit."

"I'm glad you said it. I've been thinking the same thing but couldn't figure out who it might be."

"It could be any number of people," said Villon. "Collectors, dealers, all very unscrupulous people. Like autograph hounds. You know what they're like."

"Vultures with fountain pens and autograph albums. But to commit murder!"

Villon's hands were outstretched with palms open and facing upward. "So what? Maybe the killer thought the house was empty. She didn't live in, did she?"

"No. She has an apartment in West Hollywood. Lives with an

unmarried daughter. Christ. She's got to be notified. Mayo! Where's Hannah's home number? Call her daughter before she reads it in the papers. She's probably worried Hannah's not home by now." Mayo went to the desk where she kept their personal phone book. It was an assignment she didn't relish.

Bogart resumed with Villon. "Sometimes Hannah stayed late to do some chores she couldn't do if we were at home. That's what she probably did tonight, poor soul, working in the kitchen, the rest of the house dark. She probably heard the bastard breaking in..."

"Skeleton key," corrected Villon. "She probably heard the racket and ransackers make one hell of a racket. It's my guess she came into this room, made a racket of her own and then started for the front door, got caught in the foyer and you know the rest."

"I know the rest. I wish I didn't, but I know the rest."

They heard Mayo talking on the phone. "Call your aunt, honey. Tell her to come stay with you. I'm so sorry, darling." She listened. "They've taken her to the morgue." She listened. She put her hand over the mouthpiece and said to Bogart. "This is sheer agony." She removed her hand from the mouthpiece. "What, darling? Her purse?"

Jim Mallory said, "There's a handbag on the counter next to the refrigerator."

Mayo said into the phone, "It's in the kitchen. It's safe." She listened. "We won't be here in the morning. We're staying at a hotel tonight. Wait a minute." She asked Bogie if they were staying at the Garden of Allah or the Ambassador.

"Allah," shouted Hellman, "the apartment next to us is vacant. And why am I shouting?"

Mayo instructed the daughter to come to the Garden of Allah for her mother's handbag as it was conveniently located in West Hollywood near her apartment. When she hung up, she said to anyone who might hear her, "That was so awful. That poor woman. She was devoted to Hannah."

Bogart said to Villon, "Slugger and I are going out to Venice tomorrow, I think with Hammett and Hellman. Care to join us?"

"Why, Mr. Bogart," said Villon cozily, "I don't mind if I do."

SIX

WHILE THE MELODRAMA WAS being played in the Bogart house, la Contessa di Marcopolo, wearing a housecoat decorated with peacock feathers, stormed back and forth in the living room of her suite shouting epithets in Italian, French, English, and a few in Lithuanian which she had picked up during a brief affair with an ambassador from that country. "The housekeeper should not have been killed!" Neither Marcelo nor Violetta agreed or disagreed. They were playing Chinese checkers. "Clever burglars never commit murder. Now this catastrophe at the Bogarts will be headlines! Headlines! Do you hear me? Headlines!"

"I'm sure they hear you in Pasadena," said Marcelo.

"Don't mock me!"

"Don't shout. We're just a few feet away from you. My nerves are frayed. I need champagne." He reached out to a bottle in a metal bucket and poured some bubbly into the glass at his elbow. He sipped and then studied the label. "Presumptuous. But it will serve until champagnes can come flowing again from Europe."

The contessa sank onto the couch, which groaned for mercy. "A treasure hunt! Hollywood loves a treasure hunt! Ha!"

"Hysteria dulls the mind, cara."

"So now you're a philosopher!"

"You're not thinking clearly. If we can't locate the cornucopia, let someone else locate it for us. And then we step in and appropriate it."

"I can't claim it's mine without the letter!"

"There is no letter. It does not exist. My instinct tells me it is a fabrication of Captain Methot's. If there is a cornucopia, it will surface. Remember what this Dickens person told us. This city crawls with dealers and collectors. This is a country in which everything is collected and treasured. Baseball cards! Can you believe that? Baseball cards! Movie star autographs! Some said to be worth hundreds of dollars! Comic books! They collect everything!''

"Including wives," said Violetta, a student of fan magazines.

Marcelo asked la Contessa, "Have you ever seen a baseball game?"

"As a matter of fact, on several occasions." She was holding a cigarette. "Violetta!" The secretary crossed the room, lit the cigarette and then returned to the Chinese checkers. La Contessa was still ruminating about baseball. She said, "Loathe the game." A small smile. "*Adore* the players." Then her face darkened. "Do you suppose this Dickson person deliberately sent us on a wild goose chase to Venice?"

Marcelo said, "I think not. I think she sincerely was trying to be of service."

"That was certainly a strange lot," said Violetta.

La Contessa said thoughtfully, "There was something familiar about the proprietor, Mr. Dickens. I don't think he is descended from the Dickens family as he so flagrantly claims. I think I've seen him before."

"Possibly in England when you lived there as a young girl," said Violetta.

"We did not rub shoulders with literary people. The only people welcome in our mansion were the Woolfs, Virginia and Leonard. They bored me." She was deep in thought for a moment. "Dickens's look is very Mediterranean," she sighed. "It will come to me. It always does." A stricken wail escaped her mouth.

"Now what?" asked Marcelo.

"Nobody murders a housekeeper! You fire a housekeeper! But murder one! Oh God, what is the world coming to?"

As VILLON intimated he'd be joining the excursion to Venice, Bogart snapped his fingers. "The basement! That's where we've got the captain's papers." He hurried into the kitchen where there was the door leading to the basement. Hammett, Villon, Hazel, and Jim Mallory were close on his heels. Mayo remained in the living room with her martini and Lillian Hellman.

Hellman asked in a monotone, "Aren't you joining them in the basement?"

"I've seen the basement."

Hellman studied the sad face and the way she hungered for the martini and then asked, "Why don't you get out of it?"

"Out of what?"

"Your marriage."

"It's the only marriage I've got."

"You can tell me it's none of my business, but it won't help. Why don't you go back to Broadway?"

"Nobody's asked me."

"Go back and make them know you're back, I saw you in *Torch Song*. You're a good actress."

"Why Miss Lillian Hellman, there does exist a kind word in your vocabulary."

Hellman sat up. "I simply don't understand my reputation for being a flaming bitch on wheels!"

"Because you are, dear. You are."

In the basement, Jim Mallory looked with interest at the wall decorations. Posters of all of Bogart's films to date, including the ones in which he had minimal billing. Mallory couldn't figure out what Gary Cooper's *Mr. Deeds Goes to Town* was doing there and asked Hazel. She told him Mayo had a small role in it, but Mallory couldn't place it.

There was a bar with wicker stools and a Ping-Pong table and over the bar was a large photograph of the Bogart's boat, *Slugger,* with the Bogarts at the rail. They both wore sailor suits and were laughing and waving and looked genuinely happy unless they were even better actors then he knew them to be. Behind him Hazel Dickson said, "Four short years can make a century of a difference."

There was a storage space to the right of the bar. The door was open and Bogart stood in the center of the room with his hands on his hips. "Doesn't look as though the place has been disturbed." He knelt beside the large carton that contained Jack Methot's papers. The strong cord with which the carton was bound was undisturbed. There was no sign of an attempt to cut it. Hammett was at a shelf examining scripts of Bogart's earlier films. "For crying out loud, did you really do something called *The Return of Dr X?*"

"Yeah. I was a ghoul back from the dead. It died." He smiled. "I did a Western with Cagney that year. *The Oklahoma Kid*. Can you imagine me on horseback popping a six-shooter? Scared hell out of the horse. Scared hell out of Cagney, too." He surveyed the rest of the room. "Nothing's been touched here."

Hammett stared at his fingertips. "Nothing's been dusted here either."

"Don't be a fussbudget. We rarely come down here." He exhaled. "I don't know why, but this space always gives me the creeps. I don't like this house." He led Hammett back to Villon and the other two. Villon was behind the bar while Mallory and Hazel were still occupied with the photograph of the *Slugger*. "Never did like this house. Never knew what attracted Mayo to it. It's got no personality."

Hazel turned on hearing Bogart's voice, "You both look so happy and content here, Bogie."

"That's history. What have you found, Herb?"

The detective held up a faded St. Valentine's Day card. "This relic."

Bogart took it and read it. "I remember this. I sent it to Slugger the year we were married. When I was still sentimental." He placed it on top of the bar. "Let's get out of here. I wonder if the press creeps are still hanging around outside."

Upstairs in the living room, Mayo was saying to Hellman, "Might there be something for me in your new play?"

"What you should be asking is, is there a new play? I've just finished one. Something about a liberal on the run from the Nazis."

"Sounds grim."

"These are grim times." Bogart and the others entered from the kitchen. "Find anything of interest?"

Hammett said, "A lot of well organized dust."

Bogart said, "Let's get out of here. I'm parked behind the house. If the creeps are out front, Herb, keep them amused until Mayo and I make our escape. Dash, Lily, see you at the Allah. Come on, Slugger."

"Wait a minute! I need some things. Don't you want your pajamas? Your shaving things?

"Be a sport, kid. Pack them for me." She looked on the verge of saying something nasty, but then thought better of it and hurried up the stairs. He asked Villon, "Your forensic guys find anything interesting?"

Villon held up a cellophane bag in which nothing appeared visible. "A long, blonde woman's hair. Single strand. Not visible to the naked eye."

"Can't be Mae West's. She does another kind of ransacking. Besides, she's never been to the house."

Villon said, "It doesn't mean it belongs to the ransacker. Mayo's hair is blonde."

"Occasionally."

Hellman said as she applied a lipstick to her petulant mouth, "Bogart, you're all heart."

Hammett was at a window that looked out at the front of the house. Two fingers separated two slats of the venetian blind. "The dogs are still baying around a dead carcass."

"That's pretty good, Dash," said Hellman, "why don't you use it?"

"I have."

Mayo came hurrying down the stairs carrying an overnight bag.

"That was pretty quick, Slugger," said Bogart.

"I needed to get out of there fast. It was giving me the creeps. I don't like this house. I never did like this house."

"Then why'd you urge me to buy it!" shouted Bogart.

"Because it was a bargain!"

"There's no such thing as a bargain!" countered Bogart.

"Oh God, let me out of here!" cried Hellman and headed for the front door. Bogart shoved his hands into his jacket pockets and hurried to the kitchen and the back door while Mayo exchanged a hasty good-bye with Hazel and the detectives.

Hellman opened the front door and stared down at the reporters and photographers. Hands on hips, she asked, "I suppose you're wondering why we asked you all here?" Hammett came out behind her and then Villon, Hazel, and Mallory. The detectives were under siege from a barrage of questions. Any leads? Any clues? Any suspects? Anything stolen? Where're the Bogarts?

Lillian Hellman preceded Hammett to his roadster slowly and with difficulty. Flashbulbs blinded her eyes and several members of the press tried to block their escape. She shouted, "I don't know anything! I'm just a friend of the Bogarts."

"Say where the hell *are* the Bogarts?" cried a reporter.

Hammett said, "I think those are their taillights disappearing in the distance." Villon growled orders to some of his men assigned to guard the exterior of the house to make sure none of the press would enter the house. While some people were ransackers, others were scavengers and the contents of the interior were sufficiently damaged that there was no need to add insult to injury. He hoped Mayo had remembered to pack her jewelry in the overnight bag.

Hammett and Hellman finally made it to the roadster. "Christ," said Hellman, "I hope they don't follow us."

"If they do, I can lose them," he reassured her. "Jackals and hyenas. I've seen nothing like them before. Not even in New York."

"When we get to the Allah, drive straight into the bar." Hellman looked out the rear window as they drove off. "Who said Hollywood goes to sleep early?"

Hammett turned on the radio and found a news program. The newscaster didn't tell them anything they didn't already know. Hellman asked, "Can't you find something cheerful? Like the invasion of Paris?"

Bogart finally parked the car in the Garden of Allah lot. Across Sunset Boulevard from the Allah was director Preston Sturges's Players Club but the Bogarts were in no mood for it. They made their way into the hotel and to the front desk. Lillian Hellman had thoughtfully phoned ahead and the suite next to hers and Hammett's was awaiting them. The lobby was quiet, unusually so at 11 p.m. Hollywood might go to bed early but the Garden of Allah didn't. Bogart wasn't ready for either the arms of Morpheus or his wife. After he signed them in and a bellboy captured the overnight bag, Bogie said, "You go ahead, Slugger, I'm going to case the bar."

"And case a case?"

"You can always join me there once you've used the john.

Here, take my hat.'' She snatched it and followed the bellboy down the hall. Bogart hoped she had some silver with which to either tip the bellboy or betray him.

The bar wasn't as lively as Bogart expected to find it, but there was a pleasant array of familiar and friendly faces. The first person he encountered was Sidney Greenstreet seated at the bar on a stool that seemed inadequate to his size. Greenstreet was with comedian Charles Butterworth who spotted Bogart first. ''Ah! Here's Bogie! Why'd you do it?''

Bogie cracked a grin for this droll and loveable little man as Greenstreet beckoned to him. ''Come closer. I want to talk to you.''

''Be gentle, Sidney. I'm feeling a bit delicate. It's been quite a night.''

''This murder at your house. Is it a setup?''

''You don't use a genuine corpse in a setup, Sidney.'' He ordered a dry gin martini. ''And no garbage, bartender. It leaves more room for gin.'' The bartender understood. Mr. Bogart wanted a glass of iced gin and may the Lord have mercy on his head tomorrow morning.

''How bizarre,'' said Greenstreet, ''and how tragic. I'm glad we're not working tomorrow, it'll give you the chance to rest and compose yourself.''

''You might never see me as composed as I am right now. If you see Dash Hammett and Lily Hellman, Charlie, point them in my direction.''

''Point them yourself,'' said Butterworth, ''they're right behind you.''

''Bartender,'' shouted Hellman, ''I'll drink anything. It's been a rough night.''

''She'll have the same as me,'' said Bogart. ''And Mr. Hammett, too. And keep one in reserve for my wife.''

Hellman said, ''There's Dotty Parker. She looks very sloppy.''

''Not as sloppy as usual at this hour,'' said Hammett. ''We're not sitting up all night with her and the husband.''

''Hell no. We've got a rendezvous in Venice tomorrow. The wrong Venice, but nevertheless, Venice. I don't see her less-than-better half. Probably out cruising Hollywood Boulevard. That looks like Bob Benchley with Dotty.''

"It looks like Bob Benchley," said Hammett, "because it is Bob Benchley. I'm not in the mood for him."

"Who are you in the mood for?" asked Hellman.

"Marcel Proust."

"You don't speak French."

"Sure I do."

"Baloney! I've never heard you speak French."

"There's never been an occasion for me to speak French."

"Dash Hammett, you're so full of it it's coming out of your ears!"

"Lily!" shouted Dorothy Parker, "Don't you agree with me? Aren't men a load of horseshit?"

"It's going to be one of those nights," said Hammett to Bogart. "Look at Benchley. To quote nobody in particular, probably myself, his eyes are stagnant pools of despair."

"I hear he's not been well."

"He's making pots of money."

"What's that got to do with the state of his health?"

A waiter said to Bogart, "You're wanted on the phone, Mr. Bogart. At the bar."

"Thanks," said Bogart, excused himself and went to the bar. It was Mayo and she was upset. "I'm coming to the room. Tell me the number again."

In the room, Mayo had laid out Bogart's pajamas and a change of shirt, underwear, and socks. "Bogie, I'm going to Portland."

"How come all of a sudden?"

"I just spoke to Mother. I had this feeling something might be wrong. She's very upset and frightened. I told her I'd come up and stay with her. Anyway, she said she'd feel better if I was out of this town. Hannah's murder and the break-in were on the radio and she's fearful of my life."

"You really want to go?"

"She's my mother."

"I'm your husband."

"You can take care of yourself."

"So can she, for crying out loud."

Mayo was firm. "I'm going to her. She's all the mother I've got."

"And I'm all the husband you've got."

"Please drive me to the house. Or else give me the keys and I'll go alone."

Expletive followed expletive and then Bogart snapped, "Come on!" She followed him out of the room. In the lobby, they met Hellman on her way to the ladies'.

"What's going on?" she asked.

"My wife is going home to Mother." Hellman watched the Bogarts hurry out the door, shook her head from side to side, and then hurried to the ladies' room to avoid embarrassment.

Shortly before midnight, the Bogarts hurried to the platform where the last express to Portland was ready to depart. At the gateway, Bogart said "Here" and pressed what cash he had into her hand. "I'll wire you some more tomorrow."

"You don't have to. I'll get it from my mother."

"Get going or you'll get it from me."

She smiled. They kissed. She picked up the suitcase she had none too carefully packed and hurried down the platform and boarded the train. A conductor shouted "All aboard!" and the engineer blew his whistle. Steam began to cloud the platform and the attendant at the gate recognized Bogart as the actor was lighting a cigarette.

"Mr. Bogart?"

"Yeah?" one eye cocked in the attendant's direction and waiting for the expected request for an autograph.

"In the immortal words of the Bard," said the attendant mellifluously, "'Parting is such sweet sorrow, until we meet again on the morrow'."

"Oh yeah? I don't think we'll be in the same vicinity tomorrow. I'll be out in Venice Beach."

The attendant smiled. "I'll be at my mother-in-law's funeral."

"Some guys have all the luck."

Back at the bar in the Garden of Allah, Dorothy Parker announced it was time to go to bed. "Every Cinderella has her midnight."

"Where's Prince Charming?" asked Hellman referring to Parker's husband, Alan Campbell.

"Out somewhere getting himself beat up, I suppose. He's going into the army." She didn't notice the variety of upraised eyebrows. "And I'm sure vice versa." Nobody understood why so womanly a woman as Dorothy Parker chose to marry a homosexual. "He supposes he'll be assigned to the Signal Corps. I hope he is. He's awfully good at giving signals."

Parker along with Hammett and Hellman, Charles Butterworth, Sidney Greenstreet, and Robert Benchley were seated at a round table. It in no way duplicated Parker and Benchley's long departed, infamous Algonquin Round Table back in New York, but there was enough wit and bitchery to stir dormant memories.

"I'm glad Alan's been conscripted," said Mrs. Parker as she signaled for a fresh drink, conveniently forgetting her midnight had paused briefly and then passed on. "I'm real glad the army's taking him. Now I can get to wear my dresses again." This convulsed her and nobody else. Then came the fit of coughing accompanied by soothing noises from Benchley, the one man Dorothy Parker had ever really loved. Hellman stared at the two of them with undisguised disapproval. She didn't believe in unrequited love. It was a bore, just as the Ira Gershwin lyric had claimed back in 1930 in *Girl Crazy*. Hellman went after what she wanted tenaciously, and so she was in full possession of Dashiell Hammett despite his wife and daughter cooling their heels in parts unknown.

Charles Butterworth asked with his usual fey cock of the head, "Has anyone noticed Bogie is missing?"

"Over an hour ago," said Greenstreet. "He was called to the phone and then hurried away."

Hellman said, "Mayo is going home to Mother," she pondered. "Maybe it was something to do with his housekeeper's murder."

"I've had a few housekeepers I'd like to have had murdered," said Mrs. Parker. Then, "When was Bogie's housekeeper murdered?" Hellman told her. "Dash and I saw the body."

Parker said smartly, "The privileged few. How come you get to get invited to places that I never do?"

Hammett recapped the evening for the benefit of those of his companions interested in listening. All were interested. By the time he reached the conclusion, Bogart returned and picked himself up a martini at the bar before joining them.

Hellman asked, "Mayo safely on her way home to Mother?"

"Yeah," said Bogart, "the return of the native. But Venice is still on for tomorrow, at least for me."

Said Hellman, "I wouldn't miss it for the world. I can't wait to explore this Old Curiosity Shop."

"I've been there," said Charles Butterworth, "it's awfully coy."

Mrs. Parker interrupted, "Your poor housekeeper. What an awful way to die."

"Is there a good way to die?" asked Bogart.

"I haven't found it yet," said Mrs. Parker, "and nobody's attempted suicide as often as I have. So some burglar did it."

Hammett said softly, "Burglars never commit murder. In my years as a private dick, I've seen this proven too often to refute." He repeated, "Burglars never commit murder." Little realizing this would be all he would ever have in common with la Contessa di Marcopolo, not that he would ever give a damn. "A burglar might hit you over the head."

"Charming," said Mrs. Parker.

"But that's only if you walked in on him and surprised him."

"And burglars loathe surprises," commented Hellman.

"Burglars are very clever and very ingenious. I'm not discussing the ordinary upstart breakings and entries, small-timers who have neither taste nor finesse, you know, the window smashers, the lock pickers. The professional has his selection of skeleton keys. He knows how to smartly unseal a window. He plans his burglary very carefully. He cases his victim for days before pulling the job. He knows his victim's habits. When he comes and when he goes. I've dealt with a lot of burglars in my time and most of them have my deepest respect."

"Dash, you're a pervert," said Mrs. Parker.

"Mind your tongue, Dottie," said Hellman with a loving look at Hammett who cared less about Parker's comment than the look on his paramour's face.

"What we've got here is a classic case of a hunt for treasure," said Hammett, "and treasure hunters are a very mean-spirited lot. They're obsessed with greediness."

"Well aren't burglars?" asked Greenstreet.

"Hell no," said Hammett. "Burglars are out making a living. They know exactly what to steal. You notice when you read in the papers the police are perplexed the burglars left untouched a stash of diamonds or some emerald earrings. Well if they'd learn to check the marketplace in the demand and supply of diamonds and emeralds, they'd find there's little demand and too much supply and the burglar only takes what he's pretty sure he can fence."

Bogart said, "I read someplace that there are unscrupulous dealers and collectors who hire burglars to pick up some things they're after."

Benchley said wistfully and from out of an alcoholic haze, "Doesn't anyone care to steal Mrs. Benchley?"

Mrs. Parker patted his hand. And returned her attention to Hammett.

"As I said, treasure hunters are a mean-spirited lot obsessed with greediness."

"Like archeologists," insisted Mrs. Parker.

"Well they can hide behind the respectability of historical research," said Hammett. "But archeologists don't kill."

"Not that we know of," said Hellman. "I don't trust any of them."

"They're pretty trustworthy, Lily. Anyway, Bogie. There's more bloodshed ahead."

Bogie had lit a cigarette and was fanning the smoke from his eyes. "You think so?"

"Inevitable."

Parker rejoined, "As death and taxes." She smiled, "Which, as you will all recall, was the title of one of my collections of poetry, now available in a Modern Library edition."

"I'm chilled," said Hellman eerily.

"Maybe somebody walked over your grave," said Bogart.

Hellman embraced herself and said, "Damn rude of them."

SEVEN

AT NINE IN THE MORNING, there weren't many patrons in the Garden of Allah's coffee shop. Those who were indentured to the studios had driven to work and those who were unemployed lay in bed, staring at the ceiling and wondering if the phone would ever ring with a promise of employment. Bogie's coffee was growing cold, his toast was largely untouched, and the eggs sunny-side up stared at the actor with yellow, runny eyes. Bogart was engrossed in the *Los Angeles Times* and the front page story of Hannah Darrow's murder. It was illustrated with a recent photograph of Bogart and a not so recent one of Mayo. There was a bonus photograph of Hannah Darrow's body after the knife had been removed. Bogart thought it was obscene and in bad taste. The story was fairly accurate and there was a boxed story devoted exclusively to the legend of the cornucopia. Bogart folded the newspaper and put it aside. He looked at his wristwatch and then got the waitress's attention. He asked for a fresh cup of black coffee. He also asked if she knew Hammett and Hellman and had they been in for breakfast yet. She knew them and they hadn't, adding it was a tad early for them. It was a tad early for Bogart, too, but Mayo awakened him at eight to let him know she had arrived safely and having thought it over, decided maybe she should return to L.A. and her husband and resume the role of dutiful wife. Bogart suppressed a guffaw and urged her to stay with Evelyn. Mayo seemed relieved and said she and her mother were going shopping. Bogart's eyes crossed and then they said their good-byes.

Bogart picked up the newspaper and found yesterday's racing results, pleased to see he had had a couple of winners and wondered if it was too early to phone his bookie. It could wait. He hadn't won a phenominal sum. Lillian Hellman entered briskly wearing white slacks and a blue blouse, a jaunty sailor's cap

perched perkily on her head and dangling from a chain around
her wrist, a blue and white handbag. Bogart eyed the getup and
said, "I don't know whether to salute or to kneel."

"Just get me some OJ and coffee, lots of coffee." Bogart
repeated her request to the waitress who brought his coffee and
then asked, "How's Dash?"

"Dashed." She had seated herself across from Bogart who
wondered if the lines under his eyes were as unhealthy looking
as those under hers. "Whatever you do, don't tell me I look well.
I couldn't tolerate dishonesty at this ungodly hour." She rummaged in her handbag and found a pair of dark glasses which
she promptly secured to her nose and ears. "Why did we stay
up so late and drink so much?"

"Force of habit. Here's Dash. He seems to be walking at a
very strange angle. Good morning, Dash, or do you prefer not to
be spoken to."

"Not at all," he said huskily. "Tell me, Bogie, is this still the
Garden of Allah?"

"Oh yes." Without being instructed, the waitress brought two
orders of orange juice and black coffee and placed them before
Hellman and Hammett. Hammett gently patted her backside in
gratitude and then recognized Hellman. "Lily, is that you?"

"It's not Dietrich."

"Why Lily, my dear, you look like the finale of *Hit the Deck*."
He stared down at his coffee. "This coffee is black."

"You prefer it black," Hellman reminded him.

"Yes. Of course. I prefer it black." He took a sip. "I'd prefer
it hot, too. But oh well, mine not to reason why. Anything special
in the paper?"

"My house was ransacked and my housekeeper was murdered.
And here comes Lucy Darrow."

"Ingenue?" asked Hammett.

"My housekeeper's daughter. I've got her mother's handbag
in my room. Good morning Lucy." He introduced Hammett and
Hellman who expressed condolences. Lucy thanked them and
Bogart hugged her. "Sit down. Have some coffee."

"No thanks, Mr. Bogart. I have to shop for Mother's laying
out." She didn't notice Hellman shudder. Lucy was a spinster in

her mid-thirties who while not unattractive, wasn't attractive enough. Bogart asked the waitress to get a bellboy which she promptly did. Bogart gave him the key to his room and instructions to bring him the blue handbag on the coffee table. Lucy continued, "They're performing an autopsy this morning which I think is so completely unnecessary. I mean she was only stabbed to death, wasn't she? There was nothing elaborate like maybe she was raped or something." She found a tissue in her handbag as her eyes began to dampen. Bogart assured her her mother hadn't been raped. Lucy said to Bogart, "You saw her body, didn't you?"

"The three of us saw her body."

"Oh I'm so glad she was in such good company." She sniffled and dabbed. "Oh Mr. Bogart, she absolutely adored you and your wife. She was sorry there was only one cup left in the tea set but she said it was an ugly tea set to begin with."

Hellman said in an aside to Hammett, "I haven't felt this touched since Little Eva was hauled up to heaven."

Bogart said to the woman, "Lucy, I'm taking care of everything."

"What do you mean?"

"I'm paying for everything. The casket, the flowers, the grave site, everything."

"Now that's damned decent of you," said Hellman.

"It's more than decent," said Lucy, "it's Christian. But it's not necessary, Mr. Bogart. Mother arranged everything for herself only last year, like I'm beginning to think she might have had a premonition or something." She said to Hellman and Hammett, "Mother was very psychic and had visions."

"I can believe that," said Hellman, "working for the Bogarts."

"You see, Mr. Bogart, mother bought a family plot and arranged her own funeral and paid for it. The only thing she didn't prearrange was what she would wear as she predicted styles would change and they sure have, so I have to go choose one for the laying out."

The bellboy returned with the blue handbag, returned Bogart's key and Bogart slipped him a couple of dollars.

Lucy took the handbag and opened it. She was sniffling again and dabbing at her eyes. "It's all here. Her keys and all. Would you recognize the one to your house, Mr. Bogart? You should take it. She'll never need it again." Hellman resisted the urge to suggest burying the key with Mother by way of tribute to the Bogarts but was sure the suggestion might be taken as thoughtless frivolity. Bogart retrieved the key and Lucy retrieved the handbag. "When the services are set, Mr. Bogart, I'll let you know."

"You be sure to do that. My wife's up in Portland but I'll positively be there."

Lucy asked shyly, "Mr. Bogart, would you perhaps say a few words? I know it would mean so much to Mother."

"Sure, Lucy. If Mayo was here, we'd arrange a fight for old time's sake."

"Oh wouldn't that be splendid!" said Lucy. "I'd better be going. It takes me forever to pick out a dress for myself. God knows how long it'll take me to pick out one for Mother." She was standing, Bogart standing with her.

He said to Lucy, "Too bad there's not enough time to get Orry-Kelly at the studio to design one."

"Oh wouldn't that have been wonderful. But, we can't have everything, can we?" She said her good-byes to Hellman and Hammett and confirmed to Bogart she'd be in touch and then compulsively threw her arms around him and kissed his cheek and then hurried out of the coffee shop.

Bogart sat as the waitress poured fresh coffee for the three of them. Hammett announced he was suddenly hungry and wanted a bowtie Danish, Hellman spoke up for a prune Danish, and Bogart asked for some aspirin. He looked at his wristwatch. "I wonder what time the shop opens. It's about an hour's drive out there and it'll be another half hour before we finish here."

"When we're ready to go, why don't I lead and Dash, you follow me."

"Blindly," said Hammett. "Bogie, from the look on your face you're having maudlin thoughts."

"Didn't you know that under this tough exterior there lies a sentimental slob? I was thinking of Lucy Darrow and her having

to do all the arrangements on her own. Hannah has a sister somewhere downtown. Mayo tried to get Lucy to get hold of her last
night. I guess she didn't.''

"Bogie, has it occurred to you that our Lucy absolutely revels
in all her tragedy? She is the bereaved and therefore the center
of attention. How often do you think she's been the center of
attention. She'll hold the spotlight until the last mourner has departed, and then back into the oblivion of spinsterhood. That's
the fate of all the Lucys of this world. Sad. She has excellent
features. If she'd only learn how to do her face correctly, she'd
be very attractive.''

It fascinated Bogart, how anyone as homely as Lillian Hellman
could dare suggest improvements to another woman. He caught
Hammett's eye. Hammett winked, Bogart grinned and Hellman's
eyes darted back and forth between the two men. "What's going
on here?''

"Why what do you mean, Lily?'' asked Hammett innocently.

"That look that just passed between the two of you.''

"Why Lily,'' said Hammett, "we realized we've fallen in
love.''

"Go to hell!'' cried Hellman.

The waitress was distributing the pastries and the aspirins.
"Will there be anything else?'' she asked.

Hellman said, "Some artificial respiration for my two friends
here.'' She poked her prune Danish with an index finger. "This
thing looks stale.''

"Lily,'' said Hammett wearily.

"What?''

"Shut up and eat.''

HERB VILLON AND Jim Mallory were on their way to Venice
Beach in an unmarked police car. Jim was driving while Villon
read the morning newspaper. Jim asked Villon, "What happened
to Hazel? I thought she'd be tagging along this morning.''

"Don't we get enough of Hazel?''

"You getting bored with her?''

"It's not a matter of being bored with her, it's just that there
are times when one needs a rest from Hazel. She's at the beauty

parlor. An earthquake couldn't tear her away from the beauty parlor. Especially when the roots are beginning to show. I'm not happy with what forensics turned up at the Bogarts.''

"They didn't turn up much."

"That's why I'm not happy."

"I wonder why they didn't rummage through the basement."

"Probably discouraged by what they found in the rest of the house." He whistled atonally for a few moments which meant Villon was thinking. "Christ but detective work is boring. It's even worse when we don't have a clue except for that strand of blonde hair." His voice went up an octave. "We don't even have a decent set of suspects. An adipose countess, her gigolo, and something that passes for a secretary."

"What's an adipose countess?"

"A big fat slob."

"Where do you find words like *adipose?*"

"First in a crossword puzzle and then in the dictionary." He resumed whistling. Jim thought he detected a tune that sounded like it might be ''The Music Goes 'Round and 'Round'' but then he thought it might be "America the Beautiful." "You ever been to the Old Curiosity Shop?"

"Haven't even read it."

"Prepare yourself for eccentrics. I don't mean movie type eccentrics I mean eccentrics so far out they're on another planet."

"I've drunk at the Garden of Allah's bar."

"That's rehearsed eccentrics. New York transplants. Dottie and Alan and Lily and Dash and Prancer and Dancer and Donder and Blitzen. An endangered species. They're getting old which is unavoidable. What's sad is there's no new generation to provide replacements. The war's going to thin the herd. Some awfully talented kids are going to be robbed of their chance to be heard from.''

Somewhat shyly, Mallory said, "I wish I had a gift."

"Why? It's your birthday?"

"A talent. Something special."

"For crying out loud, you're a good detective. And by the time you retire, you might be a great one. And in my books that's one hell of a gift.''

"Sometimes I want to write a screenplay."

"Why bother? It'll only be rewritten. Let's talk about the ransacking murderer. We can discount a professional burglar. This one's a mean killer and has bad manners. The very idea of murdering Hannah Darrow. So damned unnecessary."

"Maybe it was someone she recognized."

Villon smiled. It was his first smile of the day. It pleased him. It was a very welcome smile. *Maybe it was someone she recognized.*

"Jim, I could kiss you," said Villon.

"Please don't. I promised my father I'd stay heterosexual."

"Who the hell could she have recognized? She never met the countess and her motley crew. The Bogarts have airtight alibis and are hardly about to wreck their own place. Any number of celebrities have been to the house but who among them ever heard of a cornucopia?"

"Or can spell it."

"Right. Now where does that leave us?"

Jim Mallory stared ahead, deep in thought, his hands relaxed on the wheel. "For starters, it leaves us with dealers and collectors..."

Villon sang, "Alive alive oh!" He sank into thought and almost immediately reemerged. "I wonder if Hannah Darrow had any occasion to visit art galleries or meet some dealers. What art I saw on the Bogart walls wasn't exactly Matisse or Modigliani."

Mallory was impressed. "You know Matisse and Modigliani?"

"Not personally. But I get around to museums and exhibits. Hazel scrounges a lot of invitations to opening night cocktail parties. Especially when that crazy antenna of hers tells her there'll be lots of celebrities and lots of gossip."

Mallory had been thinking. "I'll bet the Bogarts have had the Edward G. Robinsons to the house."

"Probably. So what?"

"Robinson's supposed to have a great art collection, worth millions."

"So?"

"So he's a collector. Hannah Darrow would have recognized him."

"Oh for crying out loud. Robinson a ransacker? A killer? What the hell would he want with a cornucopia?"

"If it's our cornucopia he'd want what everybody else wants, the jewels inside."

"Scrub Robinson. He doesn't have a drop of ransacker killer's blood in him."

"There's Hearst."

"Let him stay where he is. Let's consider the more likely candidates."

"Such as?" asked Villon.

"Collectors. Dealers." And after a pause. "Fences. And we've got a lot of fences in L.A. who need mending. Aren't we in Venice yet? I see nothing but ramshackle huts and broken down shacks."

"We're in Venice. Forgive me for not taking the scenic route, but this is faster." In the distance they heard the calliope strains of Venice's celebrated carousel playing "On the Good Ship Lollipop."

Herb Villon scratched his jaw. "Hazel might come in handy after all. She knows lots of dealers and collectors. I'm sure she knows who are the shady ones. Hazel is a connoisseur where that sort of thing is concerned. Why you making a turn?"

"You can't drive on Ocean Front Walk. I'm taking a wild stab that this is the area of the Curiosity Shop."

HAMMETT AND HELLMAN tailed Bogart in his car. Bogart was listening to the news on the radio and liking none of what he heard. Britain under bombardment, the U.S. escalating conscription. In World War I Bogart had been in the navy. He hated it. He was a seaman second class on the *Leviathan* and became a master at swabbing decks. An accident scarred his upper lip resulting in his slight lisp which had already become his trademark. Now he was just past forty and didn't think he'd be called up. The country was not yet at war but it was inevitable. There were rumors that President Roosevelt was listening with interest to the overtures of the British to come on in, the water's just fine. But there were the isolationists in D.C. who promised their constituents that they would see to it the United States would never participate. Let the Brits and the Axis fight it out between them. There was already Bundles for Britain and Battleships for Britain though these were just a few steps away from being condemned as scrap metal. Bogart thought about his fellow actors at Warner Brothers. He couldn't see Cagney, Paul Muni, George Raft, Pat O'Brien, Alan Hale bearing arms. The younger ones would be called. Bill Lundigan, Herb Anderson, and, with any luck, that pain in the backside Reagan who kept insisting one day he'd be president of the United States. Bogart had advised him, "First learn how to act. The presidency is a great part. It's almost as good as *Hamlet*." Next he tried to envision Mayo as a war wife. It wasn't easy. Mayo baking him cookies? She'd need a compass to find the oven. Mayo knitting him sweaters. It was easier envisioning her shearing sheep for the wool. Mayo collecting his life insurance accompanied by a swelling score by Max Steiner or Erich Wolfgang Korngold. From behind, he heard Hammett bearing down on his horn. Bogart looked to the right and saw a street that led to Ocean Front Walk. He beeped in reply to Hammett and then swerved to make the turn. He'd been advised there was a small parking lot at the end of the road on the left. The Old Curiosity Shop was to the right. The parking lot was empty. Villon and Mallory had not yet arrived. Bogart and Hammett pulled into the lot and parked adjacent to each other. Hellman emerged from the roadster and inhaled luxuriously. "Ah! That magnificent sea air! The Pacific Ocean!"

Hammett said to Bogart, "She will now erupt into a fit of coughing."

Hellman erupted into a fit of coughing. Tears welled up and she struggled in her handbag for a tissue. Hammett said to Bogart, "By law there should be a large billboard erected here, proclaiming breathing fresh sea air can be injurious to your health. I just might write to the Chamber of Commerce."

"If you do," said Bogart leading the way to the Old Curiosity Shop, "don't take any bets there'll be somebody there who can read."

EIGHT

THE OLD CURIOSITY SHOP was two stories high. The store occupied the bottom half and the top half contained the living quarters. The entrance was centered between two large display windows that contained relics and curios and various assortments of oddments that would probably bring a paean of joy to the lips of a pack rat. On the walk in front of the store, there was a variety of junk furniture, bins with used books and magazines and a rack of T-shirts, one of which appealed to Hammett. On it was the legend: I OWE, I OWE, SO OFF TO WORK I GO. Hellman was several feet away from Bogart and Hammett, still recovering from her fit of coughing. She did not hear Hammett's comment as he and Bogart admired a cigar store Indian. "Startling resemblance to Lily, don't you think?" The facade of the store was a fair replica of the Old Curiosity Shop in London near the Tower of London. Bogart hoped it hadn't been bombed out of existence.

Hammett was asking, "Lily, you all right?"

"I'm just dandy." She slowly walked in their direction while rudely staring at the variety of Venice denizens that were at large. There were the ever-present body builders with their abnormally developed pectorals and biceps. There was an assortment of women, young and old, in various stages of undress and overdress. Some girls wore bathing outfits that emphasized their humongous breasts, while others emphasized their oversize buttocks. Legs ran the gamut of unusually shapely to varicose veins. Peddlers hawked souvenirs or ice cream or custard or cold drinks. One could purchase souvenir scarves and gloves and anklets. There were any number of shops and cafes along the sea front and there were wooden tables and benches for picnickers. There was the usual quota of musicians, some playing reeds, some playing accordions, and one sturdy individualist sat at a portable organ belting out hymn after hymn, with a female companion banging a tambourine and a small boy, presumably their son, worked the strollers with hat in hand soliciting contributions.

Bogart was the first to enter the Old Curiosity Shop. The doorbell chimed the opening bars of "The Land of Hope and Glory." Bogart left the door open for Hellman and Hammett who were slow in joining him, so caught up were they in the spectacle outdoors. Bogart was captivated by the charm of the premises, the thousands of items on display, their tackiness. There was a lot of art work and referring to most of it as art was an uncommon generosity. There were lots of Indian heads painted on wooden boards; there were lots of bad copies of a variety of the masters; there was a plethora of Art Deco items that Bogart figured were of value to certain collectors. He remembered as a child a woman friend of his mother's who collected salt shakers, one of which was decidedly obscene. There was a tray of Indian arrowheads and a display of old weapons; knives, pistols, swords, sabers, and cutlasses. Behind the display stood an elderly man who was Bogart's height. He had a voluminous shock of white hair and a white goatee. Bogart guessed his age as anywhere from the late sixties to the mid-seventies. On the bridge of his nose was a pince-nez attached on each end to a ribbon that hung around his neck. He wore a sleeveless shirt and slacks tied around his waist with a rope. There was certainly nothing ostentatious about this person, thought Bogart, so he must be terribly rich. Bogart indicated the weapons on display.

"That's quite an arsenal you've got here, sir."

"These? A mere bagatelle. I've many more impressive items in the basement."

"Oh? Some really good stuff?"

"All my stuff, as you put it, is good stuff." He removed the pince-nez. "It's been a long time since you've honored us with a visit, Mr. Bogart. Where's your delightful wife?"

"This week she's doing her shopping in another city. You might have heard about the recent unpleasantness we've suffered."

"I have indeed. So tragic about Miss Darrow."

"You knew her?" It was Villon who had just entered with

Mallory. Hammett and Hellman were still, outside, Hellman suffering from a slight case of biceps fever.

"Hello Herb," said Bogart, "meet Edgar Dickens. Edgar, this is Detective Villon and Detective Mallory of the downtown precinct."

"How do you do," said Dickens affably. "Yes I did know Hannah Darrow. A lovely person. Terribly tragic, her death. I must remember to phone her daughter Lucy and commiserate."

Hellman and Hammett had entered. Bogart introduced them to Edgar Dickens. Hellman gave Dickens a thorough going over. "Perfect type," she said to Hammett.

"For what?"

"Courtly Southern gentleman, what else?"

Bogart reminded them, "Mr. Dickens is of British descent, isn't that right?"

"Most assuredly," said Dickens. Hellman wondered why did so many British sound so affected. It seemed that everytime they left the United Kingdom for destinations overseas, their accents became more pronounced and exaggerated, especially actors. Then she said under her breath, "Jesus Christ, now what?"

From the rear of the store, through a set of beaded curtains that tinkled softly as she rustled through, there arrived Nell Dickens. Bogart had commented when he first encountered her that to fully appreciate Nell Dickens one had to be perfectly sober. She was five or six inches over five feet in height. She wore a calico dirndl that revealed surprisingly shapely legs. Her shoes were a simple variation of ballet slippers, laced at the ankles. Her blouse was a frilly piece of froufrou that Hellman decided had once wrapped a large box of imported fancy candies. But the face. The hair. On each of her cheeks was a perfect circle of blood red rouge. Her lips matched her cheeks in color. Hellman thought she'd been slaking her thirst at somebody's neck. Her eyelids were outlined with heavy black kohl. The lids were painted a deep blue and her eyebrows were two slashes of black mascara. They looked like they had been shaved. Her hair was something else. It was egg yolk yellow and carefully coiffured long, thick curls hung down to her shoulders. More thick curls crowned her head. She looked like the sort of dolls they gave away as prizes at sideshows. Hellman didn't even try to guess her age.

"Aha! My Nell!" Dickens voice had turned even fruitier. "My enchanting daughter. You remember Mr. Bogart."

Nell advanced toward them slowly. "Of course," she said in a voice surprisingly husky. Hellman had expected the sounds of a lute. "Mr. Bogart is unforgettable. I'm so sorry about what happened in your house last night. We are entering an era of anarchy. The brutes are taking control of the world. I feel the coming of Armageddon. The destruction of the world."

"I hope not too soon, my dear," said Hellman, "I've got a screenplay to finish."

Nell's eyes embraced Hellman, and it made the writer uncomfortable. Dickens introduced Nell to the others. "Ah! Detectives! It's been so long since we've had detectives." Nell's curls shook and it seemed to Hellman they had lives of their own. She wondered if they had ever suffocated anyone Nell had slept with. Nell seated herself at what was purportedly an antique desk, and found a cigarette in a musical box that played "Yes! We Have No Bananas." Mallory hurried to her with his lighter at the ready and prayed it wouldn't betray him. As he lit her cigarette, she said seductively, "I am always looking to the comfort of strangers, Mr. Detective."

Villon interjected, "How long's it been since you've had detectives?"

"You mean in the store?" she asked alluringly to the accompaniment of fluttering eyelashes, also coal black.

Villon chose to ignore the double entendre, while Hammett and Hellman exchanged glances. They'd be dining off little Nell Dickens for many nights to come. Hellman couldn't wait to describe her to Dorothy Parker. "Do detectives visit here often?"

"Every time there's a robbery of any consequence," said Dickens. "After all, I buy. I don't ask where the object for sale originated unless it arouses my suspicion. But according to reports, Mr. Bogart, nothing was stolen from your place."

"Only its dignity. And a good person was murdered."

A tragic wail enveloped them. Little Nell was clutching her

ample bosom. "Our poor Hannah! How could this have happened to our poor benighted Hannah?"

Hellman whispered to Hammett, "I may scream."

He replied, "If you don't, I will."

Villon said, "Have you got much in the way of cornucopias?"

"Oh not again!" It was an unfamiliar voice coming from the back of the store. From a wing chair there arose a slender man of slight height, with squinty eyes protected by rimless glasses and crew cut hair that made him look like a military brush. He wore a blue apron over faded blue jeans and a brown tee shirt.

"My God," said Hellman, "could it be Roland Young?"

Edgar Dickens laughed. "A reasonable assumption as Mr. Young portrayed Uriah Heep in *David Copperfield* and this is my shop assistant who laughingly enough is called Sidney Heep."

"I'm sure no relation," said Hellman, "as Uriah Heep was fictional."

Sidney Heep laughed. "There are those who think *I* am too. Ha ha ha. Actually, I'm the only Heep on this side of the ocean. There's a heap of Heeps back in Blighty. We're not in touch." He came closer to Villon and Mallory. "You're detectives. I can tell by the way you slouch." He turned to Hammett and Hellman. "You're both literary. I can tell by the snide asides." Hammett introduced himself and Hellman to Sidney Heep who recognized the names with delight. "Capital! Capital! Two fine writers!" He concentrated on Hellman. "I didn't much like your lesbian play. I don't like lesbians. They worry me. They make me feel weak and ineffectual. You're not a lesbian, are you?"

"Not lately," said Hellman wishing for a breath of fresh air despite the possible threat of a coughing fit.

Sidney Heep turned to Villon and Mallory. "Yes we have cornucopias, but not the one you're looking for. Heh heh heh." He sidled to a space next to Nell Dickens. "A crazy fat lady was here yesterday with two minions looking for cornucopias. We showed her everything we had, didn't we Nell?"

"Well yes," said Nell on the verge of another double entendre, "we showed her everything we had in the way of cornucopias, that is. Her boyfriend should have a frame built around him and be put on exhibit. He's the sort of man who makes a woman glad she's a woman, if you know what I mean.''

Bogart was wondering if that strand of hair Villon found in the house might be one of Nell's. Villon was apparently reading his mind. Bogart heard him asking Nell, ''Were you by any chance in the vicinity of Mr. Bogart's house last night?''

She smiled a rather vague smile. ''There's nothing very subtle about you, is there Mr. Villain.''

''Villon. As in François Villon.''

''The poet?'' asked Sidney Heep somewhat shrilly.

''The poet,'' said Villon.

''Well there's nothing very poetic about you, sir. There's never anything poetic about detectives. At least not the ones we've been getting. They're poor imitations of Tommy Dugan and Fred Kelcey.''

Bogart explained Dugan and Kelcey were actors who specialized in fumbling comedy detectives.

Villon repeated his question to Nell.

''We shut the shop a little before ten and went upstairs for some supper and a couple of rounds of Monopoly.''

Villon indicated Heep. ''He live here, too?''

Edgar Dickens said, ''And most welcome. He's an old friend and associate and there's plenty of room.''

Villon asked Nell, ''Miss Dickens, have you ever acted anywhere beside this store?''

For a moment her face froze. Then it relaxed as she rubbed out her cigarette in a tray. ''Years ago, I was with a stock company back East. It was just a whim. I can't act.''

Oh yes you can, thought Bogart, you're doing one hell of a job right now. If I could see what you've got under all that makeup, I might recommend you to Jack Warner.

''I don't trust that fat thing,'' said Sidney Heep, ''claimed she was some kind of contessa.''

''La Contessa di Marcopolo,'' said Bogart.

''You've met her?'' screeched Heep.

''No, but my wife has. Seems her father and the contessa's father were buddies some time back.'' He quickly recapped the story of the Baron di Marcopolo's fatal voyage.

Villon said to Edgar Dickens, "Sound familiar?"

Edgar Dickens replied, "Actually yes. The hunt for the cornucopia is an old story. It's been dormant for quite a while. Actually Mr. Bogart, I thought its revival might be a publicity ploy for your new version of Mr. Hammett's old story."

"Now don't be mean," said Bogart affably, "Mr. Hammett's old story is a hell of a lot better then any so-called new stories I've read in the past ten years." He said to Villon, "If the countess has already examined their cornucopias, no need for us to waste any time."

Edgar Dickens interrupted. "Surely you mean to speak to other collectors? There are several unscrupulous scoundrels at large in this city."

"Yeah. Mostly they produce movies," said Bogart.

Villon asked Dickens, "Any suggestions?"

"Well sir, you can't expect me to be pointing a finger!"

"Why not?"

"That would be unscrupulous!"

Villon and Mallory exchanged glances. Villon asked Dickens, "You wouldn't by any chance have some scissors on the premises?"

"Oh I have some incredible scissors. One dating back to the Revolutionary War."

"It doesn't have to have a history. Just any old pair of scissors will do. I only wish to borrow a snippet of Miss Dickens's hair."

Nell glared at him. She opened a desk drawer and produced a pair of scissors and handed them to Villon. Then she snatched the wig from her head and said, "Here, help yourself." She had a close mannish bob.

"Sorry to see you snatch yourself baldheaded," said Villon.

"I'm not bald. I happen to wear my hair close cropped as a convenience for the wigs."

"You have more?"

"I have dozens. They're upstairs in my bedroom. Care to look?"

"I believe you." He snipped a strand of the wig and put it into a cellophane bag he kept in his pocket.

"Now really, Mr. Villon, you don't think I wear this thing

outside of Venice.'' She shook the wig vigorously and then fit it back over her head. "Voila!"

Hellman said to Hammett, "Fascinating morning. Why can't I have more of them?"

"Mr. Dickens." Villon's tone of voice told Bogart he meant business. Dickens stared at him while running a hand through his thick mane of hair. "Was yesterday the first time you've met the contessa?"

"Yesterday was her first time in Los Angeles, or so she told us."

"You might have met her in Europe."

Dickens smiled. "Europe is a long time ago in my life."

"So you're British."

"Yes."

"You don't look particularly British. You're so dark. Mediterranean."

"Actually I'm from Wales. There's a strain of Welsh that could easily be mistaken for Mediterranean. For instance, there's Ivor Novello. He's a famous star in England. He's Welsh. He's very dark and very swarthy."

"And incredibly handsome," said Hellman. "I've seen him on stage in London. But he happens to have Italian antecedents."

"A great many Italians emigrated to the U.K. and settled in Wales."

Sidney Heep chirruped, "And tons of them landed in Australia."

"Why?" asked Hellman, "faulty navigation?"

Villon zeroed in on Nell. "You don't look anything like your father."

Hellman said, "How can you tell?" Her remark was ignored out of kindness.

Bogart was wondering what the hell was going on. It was obvious Villon had taken an instant dislike to the inhabitants of the shop. He attributed it to the grotesquerie of Nell, though the weird Sidney Heep wasn't all that easy to take.

Nell was working on a fresh cigarette. Mallory made no effort to light this one for her. He was afraid that while bending over Villon would kick him square in the butt, and where Villon kicked, no grass grew ever. Nell exhaled a perfect smoke ring in Villon's direction by way of telling him to stuff it. "I favor my mother," she said. "She was light-skinned, light-haired, and light-headed. She lit out, so Dad brought us to the States. Fate brought us to Venice. Anything else?" The two words were more a challenge than a question. Bogart was wondering if she could beat every man in the store at Indian hand wrestling. Sidney Heep and probably Dash Hammett for sure.

"You've got the silliest damn look on your face, Bogie," commented Hammett.

"That's because I'm entertaining some damn silly thoughts," he said with a sly grin.

Villon said to the Dickenses, "Who referred the contessa to you?"

Nell Dickens crossed her legs and said smoothly with a tinge of venom, "A friend of yours, she said. Hazel Dickson. She spent some time with the contessa yesterday. Mrs. Bogart was there too. The contessa is a very dedicated woman."

"I think a very determined woman is a lot more like it," said Bogart. "For a new arrival, in under twenty-four hours she certainly has stirred a hornet's nest in this town. Herb, maybe it'd be safer to have her deported." He saw the look Nell and Edgar exchanged. "Just kidding, folks. Lily, see anything you want to buy?"

"My freedom." Hammett took her by the arm and guided her outside. They called their good-byes over their shoulders as they left.

Edgar Dickens said, "Oh dear. I had so wanted to show them my collection of literary autographs. I have George Eliot, Louis Bromfield, Booth Tarkington, Mary Roberts Rinehart."

"You seem to have a lot of hidden treasure here, Mr. Dickens," said Villon.

Dickens said with a sigh, "I keep promising myself to do an inventory. But every time I plan one I keep putting it off." He stretched his hands out expansively. "Just look at what I've got here. And look what's outside. And you've no idea what there is in the basement and the upper floor. I know, I know. I should stop stalling and get down to it. Who knows, I might find I have enough with which to retire. Are we ready for retirement, my dear Nellie?''

His dear Nellie said with a rasp, ''I haven't even had breakfast. Sidney, go upstairs and fix something.''

''What's broken?''

She shot him a look that dripped with menace and he hurried to the back of the store and the door that led to both the upper floor and the basement.

''You got any more business here?'' asked Bogart of Villon.

''Probably, but there's always tomorrow.'' He turned to Mallory. ''Who knows Jim when I might next suggest we go to the Dickenses.'' Without saying good-bye, he headed for the front door followed by Mallory who mumbled good-bye to father and daughter.

''It was nice seeing you again, Mr. Bogart. Remember me to your wife.'' Edgar Dickens stood near his daughter, looking like the grandfather in *Heidi,* smiling benevolently.

Bogart said, ''Sorry you couldn't sell us anything. Maybe next time.'' He made his exit to the chimes of ''The Land of Hope and Glory'' and wondered why he was feeling so dispirited.

As the door closed behind Bogart, Nell jumped up, tore the wig from her head and flung it on the floor. ''Temper, my dear, temper,'' cautioned Edgar Dickens.

''Oh bugger off!'' snarled Nell, hardly very Dickensian in talk or demeanor.

Outside, Hammett had spotted an outdoor café where the waiters looked fairly presentable, not always the case with Venice restaurants. They were usually unemployed actors or writers whose capabilities as waiters were usually restricted to filling glasses with water and distributing menus and then disappearing to the backyard for a smoke.

Bogart was recognized by the management and the few patrons at other tables but no special fuss was made and nobody asked for an autograph. Only tourists asked for autographs and the population of Venice was determined not to be mistaken for tourists. There was a young man in uniform, probably home on leave with a middle-aged couple who were probably his parents. The woman smiled at Bogart who nodded and then gave his attention to his four companions.

Bogart spoke first. "That little visit left me a little depressed."

"A *little* depressed," said Hellman, "one more minute in there and I'd have attacked my wrist with one of Mr. Dickens's ancient razors."

"I didn't see any razors," said Hammett. "Lily, you're always seeing things I never see."

"There was a tray of them next to a pile of what looked like opera gloves."

Villon said, "I didn't like that threesome at all. Dickens put me in mind of a defrocked priest."

"He put me in mind of another Dickens character," said Hammett. "Magwich in *Great Expectations*. You remember him, Lily."

"Why sure, we were old buddies." She was lighting a cigarette and wondering what kind of bribe it would take to get the attention of a waiter.

Hammett reminded the others, "He was the escaped convict who was young Pip's benefactor."

"I *loathe* young Pip. A parvenu upstart." Hellman was staring at four waiters deep in conversation near the entrance to the main dining room. She snapped her fingers at them. "Yes *you*. The U.S.C. Hadassah." A waiter tore himself away and came to the table. He brought with him menus and the personality of a porcupine in heat. When he recognized Bogart, he became suddenly mannerly.

Bogart took command. "Bring us pots of hot coffee and some muffins and bread and jam and butter. Can you manage that?"

"Doesn't anyone want lunch?"

"Look, son," said Bogart with the look usually reserved for the actor on screen he was about to bump off, "just bring what I ordered and if you can't cope with it send over the manager."

The waiter's face reddened. "Yes sir. Right away, sir." He hurried to the kitchen.

Villon said with a faraway look in his eye, "The escaped convict who was young Pip's benefactor. I saw the movie. Henry

Hull played Magwich. Magwich lost. What about the other two?''

"They're unreal," said Jim Mallory.

"Are you always given to understatement?" asked Hellman. "Little Nell was bizarre to say the least, and I'm being kind which doesn't happen very often."

"She looked like a drag queen," said Mallory.

Bogart disagreed. "Too off the wall for a drag queen. And I'm a drag queen maven. I used to know a lot of them in Greenwich Village when I was playing those 'Anyone for tennis?' juveniles on Broadway. The really good ones have a lot of class. They have to fight for what little respect they get so they dress expensively and act so subtly that you can't tell what gender they are. Nell's just an angry woman sticking her finger in the eye of the world and thumbing her nose for good measure. She was probably the meanest kid on her block. Caught flies, tore the wings off them, and then ate them."

"How disgusting!" exclaimed Hellman while Hammett chuckled.

Bogart resumed. "Nell's a Venice fixture. She revels in her notoriety. It's probably all the identity she's got. What else is there for her? A junk shop and the apartment upstairs. *Bleak House*. More Dickens. She's probably hugging forty and reluctantly."

"Unmarried," said Mallory, conveniently forgetting there was a moment when the lady held some allure for him.

Bogart asked, "Is unmarried a crime?"

"That wasn't meant as an insult. I meant maybe she's frustrated that the only men in her life seem to be her father and that creep Heep."

Hellman folded her arms and said, "I don't believe for one minute those are their real names. Not for one minute."

Bogart said, "You might be right. There are an awful lot of aliases out here in Southern California."

"But not nearly enough alibis," said Villon.

The waiter returned with another waiter bearing pots of coffee, baskets of bread and muffins, butter, sugar, cream, plates, napkins, and utensils. Hellman murmured, "Greeks bearing gifts.

Beware them.'' The waiters exchanged glances. Neither one of them was Greek, though each in his own mind thought he was an Adonis.

Villon said to Mallory, ''Jim. Hate to ask you to do it now but we should check the precinct.''

''No problem,'' said Mallory as a third waiter arrived with pots of jams and jellies. Mallory grabbed a muffin, split it open, slavered strawberry jam in it and set off for the parking lot.

Villon said, ''Venice is notorious for its anonymity. I had a homicide out here once and it was hell. Took months to nail the guilty party when it should have taken days. What do you think, Bogie? You're the actor. Are the Dickenses and Heep performing?''

''I think what we're seeing are masks. Those people are hiding from something. I always felt that from the first time Mayo took me there. But you see, when I first met them, I liked them. They were charming. Nell wasn't all that grotesque. She didn't wear a wig. She had her own hair. Not blonde, by the way.''

''I couldn't tell what color her hair was when she tore off the wig,'' said Villon.

''It's dyed,'' said Hellman, ''henna. Has anyone tried this blueberry jam? It's absolutely gorgeous.''

''I'm so glad you're happy,'' said Hammett.

''Who the hell said I was happy? I'm just asking if anyone's tried the blueberry jam?''

''They also brought peanut butter,'' said Bogart with undisguised distaste. ''Did we order peanut butter? I can't stand peanut butter especially when somebody else is eating it.''

''Off with their heads,'' said Hammett regally.

Bogart was removing the peanut butter to an adjacent table when Hellman cried out, ''Hey! I like peanut butter. Bring it back!''

Bogart placed the peanut butter back on the table. ''There's perverse and there's perverse.''

''Listen, smart ass,'' said Hellman, ''you know who else likes peanut butter? The Lunts.''

Bogart asked, ''What Lunts?''

"And Tallulah Bankhead. Though I dread to tell you how she eats it."

Hammett said to Villon, "None of this pointless banter is getting you anywhere, is it Herb?"

"You know, Dash, it's sometime the pointless banter that is the substance of some surprisingly solid substance. Bogie thinks we've seen masks. That threesome might be hiding from something. Banter, but very interesting banter. *Are* they hiding behind masks? Is it possible they're not what they're trying to look like? I happen to think that's a pretty damned good observation. They been in Venice a long time, Bogie?"

"Search me," said Bogart, pouring himself more coffee. "Mayo and I got hitched in August of thirty-eight, three years ago. She started her shopping sprees that Christmas. Of course I wasn't suspicious I had a demented woman on my hands because Christmas time almost everybody goes berserk with shopping for gifts. But a couple of weeks later Mayo is off and running again and running up bills and conning me into going with her when I wasn't needed at the studio which isn't too often. Jack Warner gets his money's worth out of all of us. He makes Shylock look like a shrinking violet. Anyway, Mayo had been tipped about the Curiosity Shop so there we went. It looked then like it had been around a long time. They seemed to know everybody who patronized the place. I know this: Heep is local. Told Mayo he used to teach drama. I'd hate to see his results but who knows, who can tell."

"Maybe he's having an affair with Nell," suggested Hammett.

"Why?" asked Hellman.

"Because she's there," growled Hammett, "and she's not getting any from the old man."

Hellman said, "He could be an old goat, you know."

"Well if he is," said Hammett, "he's probably happier sniffing around some other assortment of nannies."

Villon said to Bogart, "Am I right in assuming Hannah Darrow was brought here by your wife?"

"Oh yes. Hannah went along with Mayo lots of times because I urged her to in order to try and put a rein on Mayo. Sometimes I wonder if Mayo's a wife or a bad habit."

"Don't get maudlin on us, Bogart," chided Hellman, "what we need is more helpful banter for Mr. Villon."

Villon said, "I think I know why they skipped searching the basement."

"They?" asked Bogart.

"There had to be more then one. Jim Mallory hit on an idea on the drive here. He suggested Hannah Darrow was murdered because she might have recognized the ransackers."

"I like that very much," said Hammett, "very much indeed."

Bogart snapped his finger. "Hannah went with Mayo to some of the galleries. She's met some dealers. She was always giving out her special recipe for pineapple cheesecake."

"Oh yes?" asked an alert Hellman. "How does it go?"

Hammett suggested a seance. "Why don't we touch fingers and try to reach Hannah Darrow. It's a lovely day for it."

"Why don't you take a flying hop?" countered Hellman.

Jim Mallory was back. The look on his face told Villon there was trouble. "Out with it."

Mallory sat. "There was another murder last night. An interior designer named Joshua Trent."

Bogart whistled.

Villon said, "*The* Joshua Trent?"

"Could there be others?" asked Hammett innocently.

"When was it reported?" asked Villon.

"This morning. It was reported by his associate, someone named Ned Aswan."

"Oh yeah," said Bogart. "His protégé."

"You mean his lover," said Hellman.

Bogart said, "Mine not to reason why. You're so quick, Lily."

Hammett said, "Around Lily it's essential to be a moving target."

"Aswan's a very pleasant fellow," said Bogie. "Very devoted to Josh Trent."

Hellman said, "Well I hope Trent left his buddy well fixed."

"Dear Lily, always the pragmatist." Bogart winked at Hellman. "I'll have to phone Mayo and tell her. She was very fond of Joshua. Played bridge at their place quite frequently. Mayo's been after me to redo the house and so she heard about Joshua from Kay Francis and got in touch. Nice guy, Josh, real nice guy. And Herb. He was a very heavy collector. He bought and traded with others. He also did work for some of the studios when they were doing period pieces. I remember he was out at the studio a lot when they were doing *Anthony Adverse*. Poor Ned must have been wrecked by this.''

Villon asked Mallory, ''The precinct say when he was murdered?''

''Like I said, last night.''

''So how come it wasn't reported until this morning? Don't the guys live together?'' He asked the others, ''Don't they usually?''

''It's a matter of taste and preference,'' said Hellman.

Bogart said, ''They lived together and they worked together. It's a big place above Hollywood Boulevard in the hills. A section of it is their showroom and workroom, the rest is where they live, and I might tell you, quite lavishly.''

Villon asked Mallory, ''So how come Aswan waited until this morning to report the boyfriend's death?''

''He was on a job in Santa Barbara. He didn't get back until this morning when he found him.''

''You've left out something.''

''What?''

''Wasn't it ransacked?''

''Ransacked? It was practically wrecked.''

Hellman said, ''Why are some people so unthoughtful?''

NINE

VILLON DROVE WITH BOGART to the Joshua Trent house in the hills above Hollywood Boulevard. It was a treacherous drive, the roads here being narrow and winding. It's as though the area had been laid out haphazardly and at the mercy of a city planner who had taken to drink. There were many magnificent mansions to be admired and Bogart was able to identify some of them, almost all dating back to the silent screen era. "That's Falcon's Lair behind the gates on the right. Valentino built that one."

"I know it. I've been there. Wife beating. Not nice."

Villon studied Bogart's face. He wasn't all that tough looking in person. Bogart grinned. "Approve of what you see?"

"Always have. Nice of you and your friends to tag along on this case."

"Nice of you to let us. Besides, I've got a personal interest. My place was ransacked. My housekeeper murdered. I hope Warner got a studio crew over to my joint to fix it up. Not that I'm looking forward to moving back in. You sure you don't mind Hammett and Hellman?"

"Not at all. They're the comedy interest. Can always use a few laughs even when they're labored."

Bogart said, "They are not happy people."

"Aren't they a solid twosome?"

"What's a solid twosome?"

"Aren't they madly in love with each other?"

"Why Herb Villon, you sentimental *momser*. They're a convenience for each other. They're used to each other. They can just about read each other's mind. I mean take a good look at them. Lily's as homely as a can of shoe polish."

"But she's got style."

"That's for starters. She's got a great mind. She's a successful playwright. One of these days she'll get rid of her husband if she hasn't already on the quiet. She's also one hell of a cook.''

"Oh yes? She doesn't strike me as the type.''

"She's the type. She's Jewish. Southern Jewish. They're even more the type. She's perfect for Hammett. Back in the twenties he was a private eye, a Pinkerton man.''

"That's the elite.''

"I've heard he was pretty good. That was in San Francisco. That led him into short stories and he was pretty successful in magazines like *Black Mask*. That led to book offers and a move to New York without his wife and child. After a couple of pot-boilers, he hit it big with *The Maltese Falcon*. He topped that with *The Glass Key*. And *The Thin Man* dropped all the pins in the alley.''

"And since then?''

Bogart smiled. "The slow descent. The continuity for a comic strip. The script for a cheesy movie shot in New York. Some radio series. He's not a well man. Lungs or something like that. Lily takes good care of him. They're pretty straight with each other from what I can see. To tell you the truth, I'm a little surprised they're tagging along today. Hammett's always interested in police procedurals, of course. Keeps the hand in. You never can tell when he'll start up again. As for Lily, she'll do anything to keep her away from a screenplay. She likes the money but she hates the work. She'd rather be in her house on Martha's Vineyard working on a play and baking bread.'' He turned and looked out the rear window. "Our little caravan's intact in a row.''

"Ahead!'' shouted Villon.

Bogie swerved and by a hair avoided colliding with an oncoming Ford. "These damn roads! Why don't they do something about broadening them! See if they're okay behind us.''

Villon looked out the back window. "They're okay. Bogie, haven't you learned never to look out the back window when you're driving?''

"Joshua Trent. Mayo took it hard when I phoned her from the restaurant. And it's really got her frightened. I told her to stay put until I signal an all clear. 'Such stuff as dreams are made on.' Supposing we don't find this cornucopia?''

"Still have to find the murderers. I hope we're not entangled in a chain reaction. From Hannah Darrow to Joshua Trent to someone else and then further and so on.''

"L.A. will be suffering a serious shortage of art dealers and collectors. We can't have that. The town is suffering enough deficiencies as it is.''

"I'm going to suffer a lot of flack from Trent's murder. He was a heavy hitter. Very big connections.''

"He overcharged.''

Villon laughed.

"Sure! You can laugh! You've never received a bill from him. I won't even ask you to guess what he charged me for a consultation. I almost took to my bed for a week. That's it up ahead past that row of cedars of Lebanon. Lots of police cars.''

"That's just for show. For crying out loud will you look at that mansion. I mean talk about ostentation.''

In Hammett's car, Hellman said, "'Last night I dreamt I went to Manderley again.' How do you live in a place like that?''

"Luxuriously.''

"If you sat in a lap of luxury you'd slip between its legs.''

"I'm willing to risk it.''

"If you'd get back to some serious work...''

"Skip it, Lily. I guess I'll pull in behind Bogie. There's more room for a fast getaway.'' He braked to a halt and then sat saying nothing.

"Well? Are we getting out?''

"Villon intrigues me.''

"Why? He's just another everyday homegrown detective.''

"He's different.''

"I find him a bit pretentious. He name-drops a lot.''

"There are a lot of names out here to drop. I admire his nuances, his subtleties. That bit about 'banter.' It's what I did with Nick and Nora, except I didn't really carry it off all that well. They did it better in the movie. Villon's right. Let people chat away and they'll not realize how much they might be giving away.''

"Christ, you've got to be an awfully good listener for that, and I'm not a good listener. None of the Algonquin bunch were good listeners except maybe Heywood Broun. They were all too busy waiting for an opening to jump in with a wisecrack."

"You've got to be a good listener to be a good writer."

"Are you taking a swat at me?"

"No, Lily, I'm not. You didn't mean it when you said you were not a good listener. You say something like that because you want me to say "Oh Lily you're a perfectly wonderful listener. Why it's such a pleasure to watch you listening. I can see you absorbing everything with your wonderfully unique ears.' "

"How would you like a crack in the jaw?"

Jim Mallory was saying to Bogart as they walked toward the graceful, superbly designed front porch, Villon leading the way, "I thought you guys were goners back there on the road."

"I was looking out the back window."

"And Herb didn't chew you out?"

"No, he was fairly understanding. He had to be. I'm a movie star." He turned and asked Hammett and Hellman, "What do you think of the place?"

Hellman said, "I'm interested if it's priced right."

"Nothing would get you to relocate to this town."

"I'll tell you Bogie, if this town had Times Square and Fifth Avenue, the Champs Élysées and Shaftesbury Avenue, I'd give it a chance. But all it has is ratty palm trees, tatty Hollywood Boulevard, and is nothing but a couple of dozen suburbs in search of a city. We are about to be besieged by photographers and reporters. Why don't I just tell them that Hammett and I don't really belong here, that we're doing a survey for the United Jewish Appeal." They managed to make their way up the stairs of the front porch relatively unscathed. Hellman said to Bogart, "For some reason I'm feeling some sort of guilt. Is it right, our trespassing on this protégé's privacy?"

"His name's Ned Aswan."

"I mean shouldn't he be allowed the privacy of his grief?"

"Nobody grieves in Hollywood. They reminisce."

In the front hall, Villon was getting information from a detective. Aswan had found the body in the showroom that occupied

most of the first floor. The living quarters were on the next two
floors and according to the detective looked as though it had
taken a direct hit by an enemy bomber. Joshua Trent had been
stabbed in the heart and probably died instantly. The body had
not yet been removed and was still being examined by the coroner, the same man who had done Hannah Darrow's honors.
Hellman averted her eyes from the body although she could tell
the trousers and lounging jacket had that distinctive cut of London's Bond Street. Several of Trent's employees hovered about
mostly distraught upon arriving at work to find the police on the
premises and their employer murdered. Ned Aswan had spoken
to each of them offering them comfort and solace when it was
he who was sadly in need of them. The employees set about
trying to bring order to the chaos created by the ransacking while
tears ran down cheeks and there was lots of snuffling and the
expected array of expletives. Bogart spoke to some of the employees he knew and they appreciated his kindness while remembering to commiserate with him on Hannah Darrow's death. Jim
Mallory conversed with a detective who had been at Bogart's
house the previous night and said the Bogarts got off lucky. Villon was told Ned Aswan was on the next floor checking for any
missing valuables. Villon headed up the rather grand staircase
imported by Joshua Trent from a castle in Scotland. Villon gestured for Bogart, Hammett, and Hellman to follow, while Mallory
continued talking to the detective.

Hellman was impressed. She wasn't easily impressed, but now
she was impressed. The grand staircase, the imposing crystal
chandelier suspended from a ceiling two stories above. The superb and some not so superb art that hung along the walls.

"Tamara de Lempicka," Hellman told Hammett, identifying
a large oil of an aristocratic woman, with, sweetly enough, one
breast exposed. It was a beautifully formed breast and Hellman
admired it, while, Hammett was positive, envying it.

"And who is Tamara de Lempicka? Or who was Tamara de
Lempicka?"

"In the twenties, Dash, she was the darling of Parisian high
society, especially those with low morals. I'm surprised to see

her work here. In Europe, she's fallen into disfavor. Her work doesn't sell anymore.''

''Is she dead?''

''No, she's still alive. She's not old. No more than about forty or so. I met her at a cocktail party in New York a couple of years ago. I like her work. I wish I owned one. I think someday she'll be very very valuable.''

''Maybe.''

''Dash, remember how they scoffed at Modigliani? How I wish I owned a Modigliani.'' Jim Mallory was taking the stairs two at a time. Hellman snapped, ''Have you no respect for the dead?'' Mallory flashed her a look and then chose to ignore her, continuing his ascent.

The grand staircase led to an even grander reception hall that had been famous as the site of so many stupendous cocktail and dinner parties. There was more imposing artwork on the walls, all of them hanging askew, as though visited by a small army of house maids who wanted to impress the master of the house with their skillful dusting. Bogart was heartsick at the damage. He had enjoyed this room as a guest on several occasions, a warmly welcomed guest not because he was a celebrity but because Joshua Trent was a caring man who liked people and never discriminated.

From his right he heard Ned Aswan's familiar voice. ''Oh Bogie. Shambles. At last we have something in common. If Josh was alive and saw this he'd drop dead.'' They embraced. Then Bogart introduced him to Hellman and Hammett and then to Villon and Mallory.

Aswan's face lit up. ''Lillian Hellman and Dashiell Hammett. Joshua will never forgive himself for missing the chance to meet you two. He knelt at the feet of genius.''

For want of anything better to say, Hellman said, ''We're sorry we missed him, too. Bogie has told me so many wonderful things about him.''

''Just about everything about Josh was wonderful. His capacity for friendship, for loving and spreading love among his friends, his superb taste, his Toll House cookies.'' Ned Aswan was of medium height and in his late thirties with a handsome face that stopped short just this side of decadence. When he had just passed his eighteenth birthday, Joshua Trent discovered him working at a gasoline station. As the legend goes, it was something about the way he handled the gas pump that caused Trent to swoop the young innocent into his Cadillac convertible and brand him as his own. Ned Aswan never looked back because he never cared to. Here was the very reasonable facsimile of a fairy godmother who was also incredibly rich and decently attractive and offering to train him in interiors with Ned proving in time to be a very worthy apprentice.

"I don't know how I'll survive without him," said Ned.

"You'll do just fine. My money's on you, Ned."

"You're so generous, Bogie. Oh my God! Where's Mayo? Does she know?"

"I phoned her. She's at her mother's in Portland. Couldn't cope with our own disaster."

"I don't know if I can cope with this one. Does her mother have another spare bedroom?" And he suddenly exploded. "What the hell kind of madmen could do a thing like this? Murder poor Joshua! Murder him! Not just tie him up and stuff a gag in his mouth! But murder him! The monsters! May they roast in hell!"

Villon said, "Maybe he made the mistake of fighting back."

"*Joshua?* Joshua fight back? How? Oh God. When the smoke has settled I must think of a memorial service." He righted an overturned chair and sat on it. "I don't understand this! I just don't understand this! As far as I can tell so far, nothing's been taken. The wall safe hasn't been broken into. It's behind *Whistler's Uncle*. One of his lesser known paintings. There's not a scratch. There's so much in this house they could have stolen, I'm insulted they haven't made off with a thing." Mallory had provided chairs for the others and even found some ashtrays in the wreckage on the floor. Bogart and Hellman promptly lit up while Villon positioned himself next to Aswan.

Villon began, "Tell me Mr. Aswan..."

"Please call me Ned. I loathe Aswan. It's a perfectly awful name. I once thought of changing my name to Ned Hepburn because I adore Katharine Hepburn. But at the time Josh wouldn't let me because she was box-office poison. Now she isn't anymore but I haven't the strength to think of anything but getting this house back in order and oh Christ getting in touch with Josh's family...one of the secretaries can do that...and oh my God will somebody give me a cigarette?"

"You don't smoke," said Bogart.

"I do now." Bogart gave him a cigarette and lit it for him. Aswan puffed but didn't inhale. Neither Bogart nor Hammett relished hearing another fit of coughing.

Villon was speaking. "Ned, I believe you spent last night in Santa Barbara."

Ned's eyes widened. "You're questioning me! Oh my God! I can't possibly be a suspect!" He asked Bogie, "Am I?"

Bogie said, "It's just police routine."

"Oh God, I can't face questions now." The look on Villon's face told him to face questions. "Yes I spent the night in Santa Barbara at Mr. and Mrs. Samuel Potter's. I was doing an estimation for redoing their villa which is a monstrosity. I stayed for dinner and by the time we'd polished off a lot of port it was too late for me to head back to L.A. and I was in no condition to drive anyway. I left early this morning and got here around eight. Our employees don't get in until half past nine and that would give me time to shower and breakfast with Joshua which is a ritual with us so we can plan the day." His eyes were misting and Hellman was suddenly feeling maternal with an urge to take him in her arms until a cooler head prevailed. "I came in from the garage which is behind the house. It's a six-car garage except we only have five cars." He shrieked. "The kitchen! What they did to the kitchen! I was terrified by what I saw! I shouted for Josh. I ran from room to room until I was in the showroom and there he was, stabbed in the heart. So much blood, so much blood. What's that line from *Macbeth*?"

Jim Mallory provided it. "'Who would have thought the old man to have had so much blood in him?'"

"Aren't you clever. Except he wasn't all that old. He was only fifty-three and he'd kill me for telling you." He bit his lower lip. "I'm sorry. I'm not behaving well."

Hellman said sincerely, "I think you're behaving beautifully. If it was me I'd be shrieking the house down with hysterics."

Ned said, "If you care to stick around, wait until you hear me later when all this really sinks in."

"Ned, you know what a cornucopia is?" asked Villon.

"Of course I do. They're absolute kitsch. Only a grandmother would own one."

"Do you own one?"

"Oh years ago we had one. From the Henry B. Walthall estate. You might have heard of him. Joshua told me he was in *Birth of a Nation*. When he died about five years ago Joshua bought some of his effects. We didn't really want them but the family wasn't too well off and it was Joshua's way of helping. He was always doing sweet things like that."

Villon told him, "We think the killers were after the cornucopia."

"That cheesy thing?"

Bogart told him the cornucopia story. At the finish, Ned exclaimed, "You mean we had those jewels under this roof and didn't know it?" He thought for a moment. "It was quite an interesting piece, come to think of it. Samuel Goldwyn bought it from us."

"Sam Goldwyn? Maybe it was for his wife, Frances."

Hellman interjected. "Nobody gives Frances Goldwyn a cornucopia. A necklace of matched pearls or a bracelet studded with star saphires. But a cornucopia? Never."

Bogart was laughing. "I doubt if it was intended as a gift."

"It wasn't," said Ned. "It was for a movie, that awful thing Gary Cooper did a couple of years ago. *The Adventures of Marco Polo*." He paused. "This sudden quiet. You could hear a pin drop. Anyone got a pin?"

TEN

NOBODY HAD A PIN AND nobody wanted to hear a pin drop. Hellman said with irritation, "Of all the producers in this town to be involved with the cornucopia, it has to be the man I'm working for. He's probably been to my office by now, and, finding me missing, yelling his head off all over the lot."

"Screw him," said Hammett.

"You have no taste," growled Hellman. "Wipe that silly grin from your face, Bogie, it's totally incongruous."

"I grin when I'm amused. And I'm amused. I did *Dead End* for Sam four years ago. He didn't give me any headaches. I got along with him just fine. Lily, you've got to learn to curb your temperament."

"I am not in the least bit temperamental. Dash, am I temperamental?" He was lighting a cigarette so Hellman continued. "I can't stand interference. Sam's always interfering. When he hires a gifted person such as I am he should trust me. Let's go give him a hard time."

"About what?"

"About the cornucopia. He's got a fortune under the studio roof, the very thought of it might bring on a stroke."

"If it's the one we're looking for."

Villon asked Bogie, "You game to take on Goldwyn?"

"What the hell," replied Bogie. "He's got a great liquor supply. I could use a drink."

Ned Aswan nimbly leaped to his feet. "Let me see what I can find."

"Oh no. Don't you bother yourself," said Bogie. "You're in mourning."

"Oh no," said Ned softly. "I'm not mourning Josh. I'm celebrating him. I know this will sound maudlin, but he gave me my life. My opportunity to become somebody." He smiled.

"Now it's my turn. Now I pick up the torch and run with it. I shall help someone make something of themselves the way Josh helped me." He happened to look at Mallory and smile. Mallory's face went ashen. Ned looked at Bogie. "I know there's champagne in the refrigerator."

Bogart said, "Forget it, Ned. Herb here's got a heavy schedule and he's kind enough to let us participate. You might have heard I'm about to start a new movie from a book by our friend Hammett here. A detective named Sam Spade. I'm getting a lot of pointers from Herb."

Villon smiled. He was feeling good. Bogart getting pointers from him. He heard Hellman say, "Another silly grin! It's epidemic!"

"Bogie," said Villon, "you've made my day."

Hammett was at a window that overlooked the front porch. "They're taking the body away."

Ned howled. "Oh no! Not until I've said good-bye!"

Villon stopped him from running downstairs. "Ned. He's being taken for an autopsy. They'll let you know when to claim his body. Probably some time tomorrow."

"Autopsy," echoed Ned. "What an awful word."

Villon said to Bogart, "I repeat, you game for Goldwyn?"

"Don't you have to stick around here?"

"To do what? My men are all over the place and I trust every single one of them. My forensics team is one of the best in the country. Let's get going." He put a hand on Ned Aswan's shoulder. "I know you'll be all right."

"I'll be just dandy." His voice was flat and morose. He looked around the once lavishly appointed room now in a pitiful state. "I never realized how big this place is. When you're happy, size doesn't matter."

Hellman spoke the thought that had just come to her. "Ned, why don't you come back to the Garden of Allah with Dash and me. It's crazy for you to stay here by yourself until some sort of order is restored."

"I'm not afraid. I know Josh is looking after me." Hellman felt her skin crawl but said nothing. She foresaw an awful lot of conversations between Ned Aswan and the shade of Joshua Trent. Well why not. He would find it comforting.

Bogart said to Hellman, "You and Dash jumping ship?"

"I relish no confrontation with Mr. Goldwyn at the moment. Okay with you, Dash? We grab some lunch someplace and go sit by the pool and splash everyone?"

"'Whither thou goest,' my love," said Hammett as he bid Ned a warm good-bye and led Hellman to the grand staircase. Over his shoulder he called to Bogart and Villon, "You know where to find us if you get lonely."

Mallory wished Ned well and Villon and Bogart took more time with him. Villon handed him a card. "If you think of something or if you need me, here's my card."

"I'm so grateful. You're so kind." He pocketed the card. "It's hard to believe the gossip about police corruption." Villon winced while Bogart took Ned's arm and squeezed it reassuringly.

"Now I don't want you in this place getting depressed all by yourself."

"You mean I should invite a few friends over to get depressed with me?" asked Ned airily. "Actually, 'Butch' Romero and some friends are coming by later to take me to dinner. It'll be more like a wake." He paused and smiled. "It's like I said. We'll celebrate Josh's memory."

"Drink one for me," said Bogart as he released Ned's arm. He hurried down the stairs with Villon and Mallory in pursuit. Mallory caught the eye of a pretty secretary who at some other time might have signaled encouragement. He made a mental reminder to return with some trumped up excuse to see Ned Aswan and another go at the handsome woman. Villon said to Mallory, "Call the precinct and let them know we're off to the Goldwyn studios and not for screen tests. I'll stay with Bogie and make sure he keeps his eye on the road."

Mallory trotted to the unmarked police car leaving Villon to field questions from the reporters who were still milling about. The photographers concentrated on Bogart while reporters wanted to know what was his connection to the investigation. Bogart reminded them he'd been victimized the previous evening and continued the myth of studying Villon for his new picture. He figured the least he owed Jack Warner was some gratuitous plugs. Villon said, "Should we maybe phone ahead and let Goldwyn know we're on our way?"

"Don't worry. He'll be there. Sam's one landlord who can always be found on the premises and that often includes Sundays." At Hollywood studios before unionization, it was a six-day working week. Very often it was a seven-day working week with no overtime, something about which Bogart did a lot of grousing.

In the car, Bogart said, "I better refill the tank." Villon suggested a station at Hollywood Boulevard and Fairfax Avenue which was conveniently en route to the Goldwyn studios on Santa Monica Boulevard. They passed Mallory who was talking into the car radio and Bogart maneuvered carefully down the drive past badly parked police and press vehicles, unaware the departure was being watched by Ned Aswan from an upstairs window. Ned's face was tear stained. He hadn't lost a friend and a lover, he'd lost a father. He covered his face with his hands and whispered, "Help me. Please help me."

In Bogart's car, Villon said, "It's better to have Hellman as a friend, isn't it."

"So you noticed. I don't think she realizes she's so mean and ornery. It's second nature to her. Dash says it's her protective armor."

"Protective from what?"

"Everything and anything. She and my wife are sisters under the skin. Everybody's against them. Everybody's out to get them. Be on the offensive before they get a chance to attack you. This business is loaded with their carbon copies. Crawford. Connie Bennett. Boy there's a bitch on wheels if ever there was one. Like I said before, Cagney and Davis. On the other hand, there're the sweethearts. Barbara Stanwyck for instance. A broad from Brooklyn and doesn't forget it. Irene Dunne. A real lady with a great sense of humor. Joan Blondell. She's my angel. If both of us were free I'd ask her to marry me, but she's stuck with that putz Dick Powell. Glad Lily and Dash pulled out?"

Villon shrugged. "People don't bother me. If they're here,

they're here, if they're not, they're not. I've taught myself to tune out. That's mostly thanks to my beloved Hazel who by now is finished at the beauty parlor and has her antennae out trying to track me down.''

"You ever going to marry her? I don't notice her wearing an engagement ring. If you *are* engaged, let me tell you something I once overheard my mother telling one of my sisters. 'Long engagements are hard on short tempers.' One of the few times she ever gave them any advice that I knew of. She didn't like them. Hey! There's the gas station!" He pulled in, rolled down his window, said to the attendant "Fill it up!"

The goggle-eyed attendant asked, "Are you really him?"

"Yeah," said Bogart, "I'm Stan Laurel."

"Ah g'wan," said the attendant, while Bogart groped for his wallet.

Villon said, "Be nice to him. He might be the next Ned Aswan."

After they left the filling station, Bogart asked Villon, "What do you think, Herb? Although I suppose it's too early to tell. There being only two ransackings so far. Do you suppose it's the start of a pattern?"

"Like I said, it could very well be. Your mother-in-law and you were ransacked because Captain Methot was the start of the Yellow Brick Road. That's the countess and her bunch. I'm convinced they did the job in Portland and did it badly. Your wife pointed out what a cinch it was for them to make it here from Portland with plenty of time for tea. As for doing your place and murdering Hannah Darrow, their only alibi is each other. But somehow, I can't buy them as killers.''

"Why not? Marcelo Amati strikes me as being hot-blooded."

"That's because he's your stereotype hot-blooded Italian and as an actor you're always dealing with stereotypes. But let me tell you, Bogie, in my experience with so-called hotbloods and hot tempers it usually turns out they've mostly got piss in their veins. As to Joshua Trent, whoever did your housekeeper did Trent. Same modus operandi. Same kind of violence. Same kind of anger. This person is very familiar with the world of L.A. dealers and collectors. With Joshua Trent they were starting at the top. Big bucks and big contacts. They'd be in a position to get their hands on hidden treasures. Most of these people are duplicitous. Most of them are always suffering a slow cash flow. They live high off the hog because they're expected to. But it's a rough go. The trick is, did Joshua Trent know the origin of the cornucopia story or was he as much in the dark as Ned Aswan appeared to be?"

"I think if Josh suspected he had a hidden treasure, he'd have unsealed it and looked."

"Maybe he did," said Villon.

Bogart was lighting a cigarette. "Ned would have known."

"You're right. So if they had the treasure, they didn't know it and sold it to Goldwyn for of all crazy coincidences, *The Adventures of Marco Polo*."

They were nearing the studio. Bogart bore down on his horn as a teenager on a bicycle cut across him and sped into a side street. Bogart was furious. "And I suppose if I had hit him, you'd have booked me for manslaughter!" He turned into a dirt road that led to the studio entrance. He pulled into the gate. The guard recognized him and smiled.

"Hiya Bogie! Long time no see! Gonna be doin' a pitcher with us?"

Bogart remembered his name. "No Isaac, I don't do quickies."

"Ho ho! Let the boss hear you say that. I don't have you on my visitor's list." Villon flashed his badge. "Say! Who you after?"

"Goldwyn," said Villon.

"No! What's the beef?"

"Just after some information."

Isaac looked from left to right and back again, as though there might be some danger of being overheard. He asked conspiratorially, "Morals?"

"I don't know," said Villon, "I suppose he has some."

Isaac guffawed. He said to Bogart, "He's still in the same building."

"Thanks Isaac." Slowly, Bogart drove ahead and carefully. There was unusually heavy pedestrian traffic. "Sam must have rented a lot of space this month. A lot of independent producers use Sam's lot. He offers top facilities and a good dining room. On the other hand, a lot of producers steer clear because Sam is always sticking his two cents in. Ever cross paths with him?''

"Oh yeah. Back in twenty-nine. A series of killings involving Diamond Films. Remember Alexander Diamond?''

"Sure. "If It's A Good Film, It's a Diamond.' ''

"Goldwyn was a friend of Diamond's." He chuckled. "Diamond was having trouble with an actress who was forever forgetting her lines. Goldwyn is supposed to have suggested she might be suffering from magnesia.''

"It makes for a good joke," said Bogie, "but all those Goldwynisms were and still are dreamed up by a smart press agent. You don't get to the top of the heap where Goldwyn is by being a Mrs. Malaprop. There's a parking space. God is on my side. I've never seen the lot this crowded.''

Sam Goldwyn had been presiding over his kingdom for almost two decades, when he broke away from Metro-Goldwyn-Mayer to go it as an independent. He let them keep his name and they let him keep his integrity. He had only a few stars under contract, but they were top drawer. His major asset was Ronald Colman who he nursed successfully from silents into talkies. He developed Gary Cooper into a major star. His only serious misjudgement was the Russian actress Anna Sten who was very beautiful and a very good actress but not in English. She cost him a lot of money, a blow he was a long time recovering from. Goldwyn's near-implacable taste in film properties was now legendary. Most importantly, he invested his own money. He earned millions and poured it back into his own productions. He happened to be standing at a window that overlooked the entrance to his building, hands folded behind his back, deep in thought, when he saw Bogart and Villon approaching. He was pleased. The man with Bogart seemed familiar but he couldn't place him. Goldwyn went to his desk and signaled his secretary on the intercom. "I'm available now." He was positive Bogart and his friend were coming to see him. Who else would a star like Bogart come see at his studio? The secretary announced Bogart and Villon.

Goldwyn was standing, arms outstretched as the door opened

and Bogart came in with Villon. Magnanimously, Goldwyn cried, "Hungry Bogart! What a nice surprise!"

Bogart winced. "Sam, you old gonif." They shook hands. "This is Herb Villon. He's a detective with the downtown precinct. You might remember him from those Alexander Diamond murders."

"Of course! How could I forget such a clever detective!" He hadn't the vaguest remembrance of ever having had met Herb Villon. "Sit down, boys, sit down. Terrible thing that happened to you, Bogie." He said to Villon, "I assume you're heading the case and tracking the murderer. That's why you come to me? Maybe I'm the murderer?" He laughed. "They write stories about how I murder the English language. Believe me. I'm not all that exclusive. I also murder French and Spanish." He winked at Bogie. "Something tells me you could use a little schnapps. How about you, Herb Vilson?"

"Villon."

"So what did I say."

"You said "Vilson'," said Bogart, knowing Goldwyn had mispronounced his name deliberately.

Goldwyn said, "Maybe I was thinking of Woodrow Villon." He was at his well-stocked bar.

Villon said, "I never drink while on duty."

"So make believe you're not on duty. You're in Sam Goldwyn's office, so have something. Some bourbon? Some rye?"

Villon said, "Have you got some seltzer water?"

Goldwyn snorted. "You heard of a Jewish producer who doesn't stock seltzer? By us it's better then a blood transfusion. Bogie?"

"Scotch'll be fine."

"I've got a great brand here. Smuggled to me exclusively from Mexico. You can imagine what the war is doing to the scotch industry. War." He shook his head from side to side. "Everything's rationed. What I go through getting film stock!"

Bogart smiled. "But you get it."

"Of course I get it. We all get it. We need entertainment and the movies are the number one entertainment in the world next to sex, and it's less energetic. Talk about sex, how's your wife Mamie."

"Mayo."

"Mayo?" He was pouring the scotch. "When did she change it?"

"Come on, Sam, we're here on serious business." He brought Bogart his drink and then found a seltzer bottle and squirted a glass full for Villon.

"So get serious. I'm stopping you?"

"There's been another murder. Maybe you haven't heard about it. Joshua Trent."

"My God. I wonder if my Frances heard. Joshua Trent? But how? Why?" Bogart told him the how and the why.

"And I bought this cornucopia for *Marco Polo?* Maybe I did and maybe I didn't."

"You did. Ned Aswan says you did."

"If he says I did, then I did." He buzzed his secretary. She entered immediately, a handsome middle-aged woman named Sarah with a pleasant smile and a no-nonsense look that bespoke efficiency.

"Sarah. You know what's a cornucopia?"

"Yes, I do."

"Do we have one?"

"We had one."

"What happened to it?"

She sounded as though he should remember what happened to it. "It was sold at the auction!"

"Aha! The auction. So the auctioneer would have a record as to who bought it." He told Bogart and Villon, "Last year I set up an auction to get rid of a lot of junk that accumulates. Made a nice profit. That's because at a Sam Goldwyn auction people bid more than at an ordinary auction. You remember the auctioneer?"

"How could I forget. It was my cousin Herman Zabin."

Goldwyn said to Bogart and Villon, "See. We keep everything in the family. If it isn't her family, it's my family. Sarah, phone your cousin and tell him to look up the cornucopia and to who did he sell it.'' She nodded and left. ''While we're waiting, let's discuss a movie, Bogie.''

''You got a movie you want me to do, you discuss it with Jack Warner. He's very particular when it comes to lending actors.''

''From Jack Warner I wouldn't borrow a cup of sugar.''

''He probably wouldn't lend it. It's rationed.''

Sam Goldwyn was back on the track with murder. ''Joshua Trent murdered. What won't they think of next?'' He asked Villon, ''You got any clues?''

''I haven't got much besides my suspicions.''

''I can tell from looking at you that your suspicions are good suspicions. Just like my Frances. She's very good with suspicions.'' He rambled on about his wife and his son and Bogart and Villon refused refills. Sarah returned at last with a paper in her hand.

''Sorry it took so long. Herman had to dig in his files. Here. I've written down the buyer's name, address, and phone number.''

Villon took the paper and read aloud, ''Mrs. Angelica Harper.''

''Oh boy,'' said Goldwyn.

''That sounds like you know her,'' said Bogart.

''By the way,'' said Sarah, ''there's a Mr. Mallory waiting for you.''

Villon asked, ''Why didn't you show him in?''

''Well actually,'' said Sarah, ''I was going to announce him but he said he'd just as soon wait.''

Villon went to the door and opened it and said to Jim Mallory, ''You suddenly shy or something?''

''Well through the door I heard Mr. Goldwyn going on about his wife and son and I didn't want to interrupt.''

''Okay, we're about to leave.''

Bogart asked Goldwyn, ''Who's Mrs. Angelica Harper?''

''You never heard of her? Well, she's an artist. Not just an artist, but a highly eccentric one. In fact, she's crazy. It would be just like her to bid for a cornucopia. Maybe she doesn't have it anymore. You better call her. Here, use the phone.''

Villon dialed and by the fifth ring Mrs. Harper answered. Villon introduced himself and explained about the cornucopia she'd bought at auction.

"The cornucopia! Of course! You're a detective? Wonderful! You can help me. Do you have my address? Come right over!" She slammed her phone down.

Villon said to Goldwyn, "She sounds a little off center."

"Not just a little, believe me. My Frances bought one of her paintings. She wanted to come stay with us for a few days until the painting adjusted to its new home."

"I see," said Villon. "One of those. Well Bogie," he looked at the address on the paper, "she's not too far from here. Down the road a piece on Fairfax Avenue. Thanks for your help, Mr. Goldwyn, good to see you again."

"Anytime. Now that you know the way, don't be a stranger. Tell me Bogie, maybe you can break your contract with Jack Warner?"

ELEVEN

THE HOLLYWOOD GRAPEVINE crackled with the electricity of hot news. Joshua Trent's murder was definitely hot news. Even as Sam Goldwyn entertained Bogart and Villon, Trent's murder was a special flash on local radio stations. The former screen queen Marion Davies heard it at her palatial beach house in Santa Monica while sharing martinis with Mary Astor. Both women had known Joshua Trent. It seemed that every woman connected with films was acquainted with Joshua Trent. They were sitting on a veranda that overlooked the beach, though the house itself was surrounded by a ten-foot high protective wall atop which were layers of barbed wire that could cause instant electrocution if touched. Armed guards patrolled the premises with trained police dogs. It seemed to Mary Astor there was a small army of these guards. She was tempted to ask Davies how she lived this way, wasn't it uncomfortable, wasn't it scary and then she looked at Davies leaning over in her chair to catch every word coming from the console radio. The woman's face was a blank, a heavily made-up blank.

"A knife in his heart," said Davies, "just like Bogie's housekeeper. Mary, I think there are maniacs on the loose."

"What's so special about that in this town?" Astor sipped her martini reminding herself to restrict her intake to two glasses as the martinis served in the Davies household were notoriously potent and there was a dinner engagement in Holmby Hills that night awaiting her attendance.

Davies said, "I think I'll ask Bill to hire more guards. Double what we've got."

"Seems to me you've got a good-size private army as it is."

"Them? Them on the beach? They're on the lookout for Jap invaders in case there are any on the way. Bill says there's going to be trouble with Japan."

"Why?"

"Why not?"

Bill was the powerful newspaper tycoon, William Randolph Hearst. Marion Davies had been his mistress for close to twenty-five years, he having plucked her from the chorus of a Ziegfeld Follies, determined to possess her physically and to make her a major star of motion pictures. Both of his ambitions where she was concerned cost Hearst millions of dollars. Surprisingly enough, Davies turned out to have a delicious sense of humor which worked well for her in several films, and for over two decades. She even succeeded in talkies despite a pronounced stutter which she learned to control and finally retired in 1938 after a succession of flops. On her retirement, she had millions of dollars, owned real estate on both coasts, including an office building on the southeast corner of Park Avenue and East 57th Street. Her jewelry collection, of course, was impressive and blinding.

The newscaster signed off and Davies turned off the radio. "Mary?"

"Yes, Marion?"

"You're a pretty smart kid, right?"

Mary Astor smiled. "Sometimes too smart."

"There's no such thing as too smart," said Davies, stirring the pitcher of martinis on the table next to her and then refilling her glass. "You know a lot about everything. What's a cornucopia?"

Astor told her.

"A horn of plenty? What the hell's a horn of plenty?"

Astor gestured with her hand. "All this. You live in the midst of a horn of plenty. Of course all your wealth is a metaphor."

"What's a metaphor?"

"An example. A horn of plenty and great wealth are often synonymous."

"What's synonymous?"

"Let's go back to cornucopia."

"This horn of plenty." Davies was getting warmed up to the subject. "Is it anything like a ram's horn?"

"I don't think I've seen a ram's horn."

"Oh sure you have. It's what the Jews blow on Yom Kippur eve. That's their highest holy day. I had a Jewish lover who taught me all this stuff. The Jews call the ram's horn a shofar. You know when my lover said he had to go to shul that night...shul, you know is a synagogue...because they were going to blow the shofar. I misheard what he said and thought they were going to blow the chauffeur which near convulsed me..."

"Marion?"

"What."

"That's an old one."

"Yeah, but it's still good. I pulled it on Bill before you got here and he went *heh heh heh*. For Bill, that's a belly laugh. He called me from the castle. He's up there for a couple of days. He says we had a cornucopia someplace. If it's up at the castle, they'll never find it. So much damn junk up there. Y'know, there's crates of stuff Bill's brought from abroad that have never been opened?"

"I know. You showed me the last time I was there."

"Oh I did?"

"You did." She could tell the martinis were having an effect. Lunch had been promised but there was not a sign of it.

"Well if it's not up at the castle, it must be here someplace. And say!..." She sat up and looked like an obscenely evil child, "if it's the same one that has them ransacking and murdering, I've got a hidden fortune." She contemplated what she had just said. "And I need a hidden fortune like I need a third tit. And I don't relish the thought of being ransacked or murdered."

"You've got nothing to worry about what with your guards and their dogs."

"Honeybunch, believe me, there are ways of getting in and out of this place without being caught. I know. I've done it. Often."

"What about the high wall and barbed wire?"

"Mary, do you know how often this dump's been broken into? Bill keeps it out of the papers when it happens to discourage any copycats. But they keep on coming. This joint's a real challenge. A good crook, and by good I mean a crackerjack, a whiz, a topnotch professional can get into and out of any place if he sets his mind to it. When I was in the Follies I met a lot of shady characters and from them I learned plenty.''

"I can pick a lock,'' continued Davies.

"You can't.''

"Sure can. With a bobby pin. Bill gave up locking me in my room because I was as good an escape artist as Harry Houdini.'' She suddenly went all dreamy. "God Harry was a great lay.'' A butler materialized. "What do you want?''

"Luncheon is served.''

She said to Mary, "It's always luncheon. It's never lunch. And it's never ever 'Soup's on' anymore.'' She said to the butler, "Okay, okay, Jeeves. We're coming.'' She struggled off the chaise longue on which she'd been reclining.

"His name isn't really Jeeves, is it?''

"How the hell should I know? Never saw him before this morning. Boy, war sure is hell. Can't hold on to the help anymore. They're going off to factories and shipyards where they get paid a fortune.'' She took Mary Astor's arm. "Let me help you, dear, you're a little unsteady.''

"Which way do we go?'' asked Astor.

"Straight ahead and turn left at the Rembrandt. Christ, I hope it isn't chicken à la king again.'' She brightened. "Maybe it's a big fruit salad. All laid out in a cornucopia. Hmm. I wonder if we have that effing thing. So you're signed to Warner now. Son of a bitch ruined my career. That last stinker, *Ever Since Eve*.'' She shook her head. "I hear they're still fumigating the theaters.''

"Do you miss making movies?''

"Nah! I only made them because Bill wanted me to. There's only one thing I miss about making movies.''

"What's that?''

"Screwing my leading men. Ha ha ha ha ha!''

FAIRFAX AVENUE was one of the cosier streets in West Hollywood. It was predominantly Jewish and also famous for Hollywood High School which produced a good share of movie personalities. Bogart and Mayo in their happier days came here at least once a week on a Friday, a few hours before the start of the Jewish Sabbath to shop for such goodies as smoked salmon, smoked whitefish or carp or sturgeon, challah bread, onion rolls, pickled herring in sour cream or au naturel, chicken noodle soup, matzo balls (Mayo, on her first time here with Bogart asking in all innocence, "What kind of balls are matzo balls?"), stuffed derma, gefilte fish, brisket of beef. Bogart's mouth was watering.

"Say Herb, how's it if I pull into Canter's parking lot?"

"I'm all for it, but first let's attend to Angelica Harper. She sounded a little frantic on the phone." Bogart had driven a block past Fairfax Avenue's commercial area. Villon was looking ahead through the windshield. "There's a very strange-looking house ahead on the left on a very large lot."

"Where?"

"You blind? The gray thing with the turrets. Looks like an imitation castle."

Bogart laughed. "Oh sure. I've passed it dozens of times. Do you suppose that's Mrs. Harper's?"

"Pull over. There's a mailbox with an address printed on it."

Bogart pulled over. The address on the mailbox confirmed this was the residence of Angelica Harper. There was a short road behind a locked gate that led to what seemed to be a moat over which there lay a drawbridge. "There's a speaker in the gate," said Bogart. "I'm going to park here. It looks safe."

They left the car and went to the speaker. There was a button that Villon pressed. No response. He pressed again. Bogart was staring up at a turret and said, "'Rapunzel, Rapunzel, let your hair down.'"

They heard what they supposed was Mrs. Harper's voice. "Yes?"

"Mrs. Harper. I'm detective Villon!"

"But mais oui! Le gendarme! Au secours!" They heard a buzzing noise and the gate clicked open. "Entrez! Entrez! Bienvenue or whatever the hell you're supposed to say."

Bogart and Villon looked at each other. Bogart said, "This is not real."

"This is Hollywood," said Villon. "For Hollywood, this is real." They passed through the gate and walked to the drawbridge. Bogart looked in the moat. "Real water." He grimaced. "And lots of dead things."

Villon said, "The drawbridge is a fake." At the end of the drawbridge was a wooden door. Villon tried the knob and pushed it open. They walked into what was probably a reception room, though it held very little furniture. There was a long wooden table that Villon tested by shaking it. It was quite sturdy. Around the table were about a dozen wooden chairs that Bogart thought were probably fifteenth century in design. There were tapestries on the walls depicting medieval knights jousting and hunters stalking deer and wild boar and to Bogart's delight, the fairy tale heroine Rapunzel with her mile of blonde hair floating down from a window at the top of a turret where she was imprisoned.

"I know," said Villon. "It's a movie set." There was a circular wooden staircase that led up a long flight to a balcony that seemed to lead to a hall and other rooms. On the opposite wall just past the balcony was a double door. From behind the double door came the unlikely sounds of a harp being plucked. Bogart recognized the melody, "I Dreamt I Dwelt in Marble Halls."

"Most inappropriate," said Bogart, "there's not a slab of marble in sight."

"I think we're supposed to go through the double doors," said Villon.

"I hope we're not interrupting a recital," said Bogart.

Villon pushed open the double doors. They entered a studio that was two stories high and aglow in sunshine pouring through the glass roof overhead. There was indeed a harp and playing it was a very thin little lady of an indeterminate age with a beatific expression on her face. Several feet beyond her was a platform with an easel and canvas and daubing at the canvas wearing a smock and a beret with a devil-may-care attitude was undoubtedly their hostess, Angelica Harper, holding a palette in her left hand and a brush in her right. She was probably sixtyish, but, as Bogart noticed, she had very shapely legs. Bogart was known to be a sucker for a shapely leg. Her smile was beguiling, enticing. "Mes amis! Vous avez arrivez! Which means, My friends, you have arrived at last!" She laughed. "I'm terribly pretentious! In time you'll get used to it." She said to the harpist, "That was just fine, Letitia. Absolutely splendid." She said to the men, "Letitia is practicing to be an angel." Having divested herself of her painting appurtenances, Mrs. Harper slowly walked down the six steps that led from the platform, while Letitia curtsied and then scampered out a door that in a flash Bogart saw led to a kitchen.

Villon introduced himself and Bogart.

"Of course I recognize Mr. Bogart," said Mrs. Harper. He took the hand she extended and shook it. She seemed disappointed. Hand kissing was an art that had eluded Bogart. Likewise Villon who shook hers lightly. She indicated a sofa and some easy chairs in another corner of the room where apparently she occasionally held court. "I can offer you port or chablis." Both men refused. "It's just as well. The glasses are a bit dirty." She looked at four glasses on a nearby table that held the bottles of port and chablis. "In fact, they're filthy. I must have a word with Letitia. In fact, I shall have several words with Letitia. She keeps house for me in addition to providing mood music that I require when I'm working. I'd say she was a treasure but she isn't. She's been with me for years, ever since my husband died." She was seated in an easy chair that resembled a throne. "My husband built my castle. He designed it."

"He was an architect?"

"He was an idiot," she said with a charming smile. "But he was rich rich rich!" Her arms were outflung and there was a lascivious look of ecstasy on her face. "Archibald Harper was a rogue, but never a peasant slave. He based this castle on the one Douglas Fairbanks had designed for his *Robin Hood*. Doug was a good friend, he visited often. These are all my creations." One of her hands was making lavish circles in the air drawing their attention to the walls which were crowded with framed canvases of varying sizes and dimensions. Angelica Harper's works covered a broad canvas of their own. There were still lives and portraits of celebrities from the historical past. There was one of a nurse who Bogart assumed was probably Florence Nightingale though he found the leer on her face somewhat confusing. There was a pretty good one of Rasputin, the mad monk with a soulful expression that seemed somewhat out of place.

Villon seemed mesmerized by a huge canvas of nymphs and

satyrs cavorting in a forest glen with the god Pan tootling his pipes and it was all refreshingly pornographic. All the while they studied her work the artist rewarded them with a monologue about herself and her art.

"On the far right you have Marie Antoinette in the kitchen at Versailles icing the cakes for the poor. Just below her is George Washington crossing the Delaware and he is violently seasick. To the right of George is Alexander Graham Bell phoning information for a number and below him is Betsy Ross tearing the flag apart because she's displeased with the color arrangement." She stopped speaking. They stared at her. She shut her eyes and after a few beats, reopened them slowly. "Gentlemen. I am psychic. There is a sword of Damocles dangling over both of your heads. There are ectoplasms of death surrounding your bodies." Bogart considered screaming but didn't want to alarm Herb Villon. "I know the tainted history of the cornucopia you're looking for. It may be mine. It's sealed. I've never tried to open it. I like things to be left intact. It's depicted in a painting I sold to the Goldwyns. I know about your house being ransacked and your housekeeper murdered, Mr. Bogart. Quelle tragedie. And Mr. Villon, I know about the ransacking at Joshua Trent's and his tragic death. Un autre tragedie." She smiled. "I've taken up studying French. You'll forgive my occasional Gallic interjections. Mr. Bogart, do you perhaps speak any French?"

Bogart said, "Un peu."

"Oh you do, you do! How clever you are." She had crossed to a wall behind them and stood in front of the portrait of a handsome man who seemed rather effete, or that was how Mrs. Harper had caught her subject. "This is Joshua Trent." The portrait nowhere resembled the grotesque corpse they had seen earlier in the day. "The mouth is not as good as I wanted it to be because he never shut it. Talk talk talk a mile a minute. Gossip gossip gossip. But a kind man and a generous one. Of course you know he was murdered."

"I'm assigned to the case. Remember the cornucopia."

"Indeed. As there are those who remember the Maine." She walked slowly back to them. "Then you've met Ned Aswan. I assume he inherits everything." She smiled. "Being men of the world, we accept that they were a homosexual relationship." She paused for a moment. "Thank God I never married a homosexual. They're so fussy about their kitchens. In the kitchen I'm a slob. My husband Archibald wouldn't let me near it. His was the magic touch with aspics and kasha varnishkas. After his death, Letitia inherited the responsibility. She wields one hell of a can opener. But I have not digressed too far from the cornucopia to lead you back." She was back in the chair. "Such a lovely design."

"May we see it?" asked Villon.

"Mais c'est impossible."

"You don't have it?"

"I loaned it to a friend who admired it so and wanted it for the centerpiece of her Thanksgiving table. For weeks I've been trying to reach her by telephone but she doesn't seem to be answering the phone. She's a bit on the private side, a little reclusive I'd say though given to the occasional Thanksgiving gathering. She's a bit of a mystic like me and given to long days of meditation. You know what the French always say, Cherchez la femme!"

Bogart groaned inwardly. He was hungry. He wanted to be seated at a table at Cantor's and munching on a half sour pickle while making a selection from the vast menu that promised monumental indigestion. "I'll phone my friend again." She went to a sideboard where there was a telephone hidden under a doll wearing a voluminous eighteenth-century ball gown. First she opened a drawer for her address book. She found the number and then raised the doll revealing the telephone. Villon looked at Bogart and shrugged, and Mrs. Harper dialed. She hummed "La Marseillaise" while she waited and then spoke, "Kito? It's Mrs. Harper again. I *must* speak to Mrs. Brabin." Her sigh was one of vast exasperation. "I am tired of indulging your mistress. I'm sending two gentleman to collect my cornucopia. One is Mr. Villon who is a detective with the Los Angeles police department and with him is a very famous movie star, Humphrey Bogart." They heard a screech coming from the phone. Mrs. Harper said, "Kito, control yourself. It's only a movie star. It's not the second coming of Christ. They'll be there shortly." She slammed the phone down. "Kito's a fan of yours, Mr. Bogart."

"I heard. I'm only a movie star."

"I'd love to paint you, Mr. Bogart. You have a most revealing face."

"Oh yes. What does it reveal?"

She said mysteriously, "Much more then you do. It was so nice having you." She told them Mrs. Brabin's address.

Villon said not without a trace of irony, "It was so nice being had by you. We'll find our way out."

Her voice sang in their ears as they left. "Remember! Those swords dangling over your heads! 'Forewarned is forearmed.'"

Letitia had made her way back to the harp and plucked away at the strings. Villon recognized "I'll Be Glad When You're Dead, You Rascal You."

They hurried outside and into the car. Bogart lit a cigarette. He exhaled some smoke, turned on the ignition, let the engine warm for a few seconds and then said to Villon, "Eh, mon vieux, peut-être Cantor's?"

Villon exploded. "For crying out loud stop the frog crap and let's go to Canter's!"

TWELVE

THE LOOK ON BOGART'S FACE was sheer bliss, as he and Villon waited to be seated. The hostess was a tall, vastly overweight bleached redhead with a fixed smile and incredibly long, ominous looking fingernails. Villon thought in her spare time she might be a professional wrestler. As she advanced on them standing behind a velvet rope, the fixed grin broadened into a smile that revealed a slash of purple gums. There were also teeth but the gums predominated. Bogart recognized her from earlier visits.

"It's been so long since we've seen you, Mr. Bogart. Remember me? I'm Pearl. I'm sure you don't remember my name, nobody does." She smiled at Villon. "And you are?" head cocked slightly like a nearsighted pouter pigeon.

"Hungry," said Villon taking no pains to mask his impatience with oversized and overaged coquettes.

Bogart intervened. "This is Detective Villon, he always gets his man."

Pearl asked with a sly smile, "Does he always get his woman?"

Villon stared at her. "Does he maybe get seated and a shot at the menu?"

"Would you prefer a booth or a table?"

"A booth. How about that one straight ahead next to the one holding some people we know." Bogart nudged Villon with an elbow. Bogart's eyes directed Villon to the booth in question. He saw Sidney Heep with a woman he didn't recognize.

"Who's the broad?" asked Villon as Pearl unclipped the velvet cord and indicated they follow her.

"Her name's Lucy Darrow."

"Any relation to your housekeeper?"

"Her daughter."

"Well now isn't this a how-dee-do," said Villon.

"How-dee-do," repeated Pearl, "I recognize that. It's Gilbert and Solomon."

Sidney Heep saw them coming and under the table nudged Lucy Darrow with his knee. This annoyed her and she looked at him questioningly. His eyes led her to Bogart and Villon. Bogart now saw both were nursing draught beers. The dish of sour pickles, sour tomatoes, red peppers, and sauerkraut seemed untouched. Bogart hungered to attack it.

"Well Lucy, what an unexpected pleasure seeing you twice in one day. Meet Mr. Villon. He's a detective. He's trying to find your mother's killer."

Pearl said, "I've left menus on your table. Enjoy your lunch." Bogart thanked her and she favored him with gums again as she walked away.

"Mr. Heep," began Villon, "you're a long way from home."

Heep squinted up at him from behind his glasses. "I'm making my rounds. Today I see dealers and collectors. See what they've got to sell. Find out what they might be interested in buying."

"Come across any cornucopias?" asked Villon.

"No," snapped Heep. "I'm having a bad day. A very bad day. It began with you people this morning and then Joshua Trent is killed and we were old friends. The only nice thing to happen to me today was running into Lucy and she's in mourning for her mother."

"Say Heep," asked Bogart, "you know an artist named Angelica Harper?"

"She's nuts."

"So you know her. You deal with her?"

"Her stuff's too expensive. She thinks she's Mary Cassatt reincarnated."

"Some of her stuff is pretty good, I think," said Bogart. "She's got an interesting portrait of Joshua Trent. He was a pretty good-looking guy."

"Pretentious."

"The portrait or the subject?"

Heep said, "I knew Joshua Trent when he was a snotty hustler trying to work some of our richest boobs."

"I guess he succeeded," said Bogart.

"He certainly did."

"I thought you said you were old friends."

"We most certainly were. Joshua bought a lot of tchotchkes from us. So? I don't mince words. He began as a snotty hustler and became terribly pretentious. Terribly grand and terribly rich. I'm not telling you anything I didn't tell him." He said to Villon. "Are you assigned to Joshua's murder, too?"

"It all comes under the umbrella called cornucopia," said Villon. "Got any theories?"

"About what?" asked Heep.

"About who's the crazy behind these ransackings and the killings?"

"I'm not one given to theories. If I was, I'd be in detective work."

"How about Dickens and Nell? They discuss it with you after we left this morning?"

"You were very rude to Nell. You shouldn't be rude to Nell. Just because she's so garish and otherworldly. Nell's an original. She's very clever. A very smart businesswoman."

Bogart asked Lucy, "You find a dress for your mother, Lucy?"

"I've seen some potentials." She indicated a notebook on the table. "I've jotted them down. I suppose I'll be at it all day. Maybe tomorrow, too. Mr. Villon, when can I find out when my mother's body will be released? I've made a reservation for her at Utter McKinley's funeral parlor. It wasn't easy. They're very heavily booked. They've given me a selection of times for the chapel. I've got a priest standing by. Everything's set. All I need is my mother." Heep patted her hand. She gave him what Bogart supposed was a grateful look. "It was Mother who introduced me to the Curiosity Shop. I found it very curious. Mr. Heep has been very kind. I'm so glad we ran into each other today."

Bogart said, "We'll let you get on with your lunch."

"It's taking an awful long time," said Lucy. "The restaurant's very crowded."

Bogart nudged Villon. "Let's order." They said their good-byes and went to their booth. Bogart attacked the dish of relishes and selected a half sour pickle. He munched contentedly as he opened the menu. Villon was preoccupied. "What's bothering you, Herb?"

"Lots of things are bothering me."

"Such as?"

"Those two in the next booth, for instance."

"Careful, they might hear you."

"With all this din going on around us? They're lucky if they can hear each other."

"What about them?"

"They didn't happen to run into each other."

"You're positive?"

"No, I'm not positive. But I trust my instincts."

"What are you going to eat?" asked Bogart.

"Whatever it is, I'll regret it." Villon studied the menu. Bogart saw Lucy and Heep leaving.

"They're leaving."

Villon peered around the edge of the booth. "I don't think they ate any lunch."

Bogart said, "I don't think they ordered any."

"Then why come to Cantor's?"

"Because it's one of those places where they don't expect to run into anyone they know." Bogart smiled. "What's the matter, Herb. Didn't you ever make dates with women you didn't want to be caught seeing?"

"All the time," said Villon with the air of a practiced man about town. "I never thought of meeting a date in this place."

"Why? You an anti-Semite?"

"Oh shut your face. Me an anti-Semite. I like that a lot. Hazel Dickson is not Hazel's real name."

"No kidding. What's her real name?"

"I can't pronounce it. Neither can Hazel. That's why she took Dickson." A waiter stared down at them. He had a large Adam's apple and his ears stuck out. He reminded Bogart of the comic strip character Happy Hooligan. He stood with pad and pencil poised for their orders.

"Are you ready to order?" asked the waiter in a thick, middle-European accent that made Bogart curious.

"Where you from?" asked Bogart.

"Don't ask," said the waiter with a sigh.

"You're a refugee, aren't you?"

"Everybody on earth is a refugee. We are all looking for a safe harbor. Some of us will find our safe harbor and the less fortunate won't. That is Kossow's law."

"Who's Kossow?" asked Bogart.

"Me."

Bogart laughed and order a triple-decker special. Villon decided on a sardine and mayonnaise on white bread and heard the waiter say under his breath, "Goy."

Bogart asked the waiter, "You an actor, Mr. Kossow?"

He hit the right nerve. "An actor? Am I an actor? You want to know who I am? You have heard of Stanislav Kossow?" He held up a hand. "Don't speak! Of course you have not heard of Stanislav Kossow. You have not had the glorious opportunity to see him! My Hamlet! My Macbeth! My Romeo! My etceteras! In Czechoslovakia I am their Laurence Olivier. You asked where I come from and I said 'Don't ask,' well now you know why I warned you. Mine is another of the hundreds of thousands of tragic stories that cross the thresholds of this free world. Yes Mr. Bogart. I recognize you. Don't look so modest. You're a star. Make the most of it." He leaned forward with his eyes popping. "Because it won't last forever?"

"He's giving me the creeps," said Villon in an aside.

Kossow looked over his shoulder to ascertain if Pearl was within hearing distance and scold him. "Mr. Bogart, I will do anything. Bits, extras, walk-ons." He smiled. "Perhaps you can arrange a screen test?"

Bogart said, "Call me at the studio tomorrow. I'll leave your name at the switchboard. Stanislav Kossow."

"You remember my name?"

"Why not? I only heard it a minute ago."

Villon pleaded, "Kossow, will you please place our orders?"

"Immediately! At once! Mr. Bogart, I kiss your hand!" He hurried off.

"Who knows?" said Bogart, "he might be the next 'Cuddles' Sackall."

Villon asked Bogart, "You think Heep and Lucy Darrow are what the columnists might call 'a thing'?"

"Maybe. What if they are. What's it got to do with the case?"

"How do I know? I'm open to all suggestions. I've got a clueless case to deal with."

"What about that strand of hair from my place?"

"Unreal. Useless. That's why I thought it might match that wig of Nell's. But I don't think she wears that thing anyplace but in the store. She'd stand out like the red light over the entrance of a whorehouse. I also think there's more to the Curiosity Shop than meets the eye."

"Such as?"

"Edgar Dickens. That trace of an accent. I've got a good ear for accents. I come up against them all the time and I know how to identify them."

"Always on the nose?"

"Give or take. Dickens's accent is not Welsh. Because the Welsh, they have a lovely lilt to their voices. A cousin to the Scotch brogue."

"The brogue is too thick for me."

"Okay, then an Irish accent. I mean a real homegrown Irish accent, not an exaggeration like Barry Fitzgerald's." He speared some sauerkraut. "I'm telling you Dickens is from somewhere in the Mediterranean Sea. Italy's my guess."

"I didn't notice any statues of Christ or nuns or crucifixes in the shop."

"They're there," he stated positively. "Upstairs someplace or in the basement."

"What's all this got to do with the cornucopia?"

"I don't know. I'm shadowboxing. I'm catching flies. That's how it always is with me at the beginning of a case. It's like

running into an alley and finding there's no way out at the end
You got to turn around and go back and follow something else
Very frustrating. Very aggravating. Very stimulating. By God
here's Kossow with our order. How'd you get it so fast, Stanis
lav?''

"I promised they would cater my big party!" he told them
eagerly as he placed their sandwiches on the table.

"When you having this big party?" asked Bogart.

"When I sign my contract with Warner Brothers! And you are
both positively invited!"

Bogart didn't know whether to laugh or cry.

"NOW THIS is a very impressive piece of real estate," said Villon
to Bogart as they pulled up in front of the Brabin estate in Brent
wood.

"Why does a dame who lives in a palace like this have to
borrow a cornucopia for a Thanksgiving dinner centerpiece?"

"That's why she lives in such splendor and elegance. She'
thrifty."

"Or has a rich husband."

"Who is also thrifty." Villon suggested Bogart drive up the
circular roadway and park next to one of several impressive pil
lars at the front of the house. Bogart drove in and parked under
a shade tree.

"Mrs. Charles Brabin," said Villon. "That name strike
bell?"

"I don't have any bells for it to strike. There's somebod
peeking out at us from an upstairs window. Feel like playing
Living Statues?"

"Let's not horse around. I've got to be taken seriously." They
were now standing at the most impressive front door with it
sculpted panels and an immense door knocker that might hav
been silver. "I don't think I can lift this knocker," said Villon

"You don't have to. There's a bell button." Bogart's inde
finger connected with the bell button that was in a side panel to
the right of the door. More chimes. Villon thought just abou
everyone in Hollywood must have a set of chimes attached to

their door. These chimes played "In the Hall of the Mountain King," and from behind the door, though slightly muffled, sounded ominous and foreboding. The sky was clouding over and Bogart feared they were about to lose their bright, sunny day. They heard the pitter-patter of what might be tiny feet hurrying to the door. The door was pulled open by a diminutive Japanese man who was smiling from ear to ear and, thought Bogart, beyond the ears.

"Welcome, Humphrey Bogart, welcome." He bowed several times. "It is an honor to welcome you to my house!"

"You're Mrs. Charles Brabin?"

"Oh no. She is meditating but will soon be finished. I am Kito, a most important member of the household without whom the Brabins could not survive."

Modest little devil, thought Bogart. Kito ushered them into the downstairs hall, shut the door and then scurried in front of them, leading the way to a huge, rococo furnished and decorated living room. The clock had been turned back, and this was at least two decades ago. Everything was brocades and velvet and a grand piano with a Spanish shawl draped across it. An original Tiffany chandelier hung from the ceiling and across an oversize divan was thrown a leopard skin. There was a polar bear skin on the floor, the bear's head oversize and its mouth open, revealing ferocious teeth. There were several end tables that held lamps with bases that were the heads of saints or Egyptian houris with legs extended and quaintly enough, Bo Peep with her crook looking not for her sheep but as though she was dying to get laid, or so thought Villon. He was given to flights of erotic fancy on the rare occasion he found himself in such exotic surroundings. This was a touch of old Hollywood, the Hollywood that was once so gloriously outrageous. The Hollywood of the woeful scandals that brought down such celebrities as "Fatty" Arbuckle, William Desmond Taylor, Wallace Reid, Mabel Normand, and countless others.

A strange, sickeningly sweet odor attacked their nostrils. Bogart looked around and saw Kito lighting a stick of incense protruding from the belly button of a statue of Buddha in the corner of the room. Bogart noticed an exquisitely wrought marble stair-case leading up to a pair of blood-red drapes that hid, probably, a hallway. At the foot of the staircase was a good-size gong.

Bogart realized he hadn't identified Villon and corrected the oversight. Kito bowed to Villon who was wondering if the little man's name was on a secret roster of Japanese names compiled by the FBI for immediate round-up and detention in the event of a war with Japan. Bogart, among others, was perplexed as to why in some quarters Japan was seen as a possible threat to the nation's security. He studied Kito. This little man a threat? He realized Kito was holding a pen and an autograph album under his nose.

"Please Mr. Bogart, would you sign my album?"

"Sure," said Bogart, and scribbled his name.

"Oh sir, please. Above your name please write 'To my good friend Kito.'"

Bogart smiled. "No problem."

"Oh sir, you are truly my most favorite actor in all the world. I see your pictures many times. I have seen *High Sierra* eight times."

"No kidding? By now you should have built up an immunity to it."

Villon glanced at his wristwatch. He was anxious to get on with it. "How much longer will Mrs. Brabin be at her medita-tion?"

From upstairs, they heard a bell tinkle.

"Aha!" said Kito. "The meditation is completed. Madam will be preparing to descend." He hurried to a cabinet, opened its doors and exposed a Victrola. He wound it up hastily and then placed the arm holding the needle into the starting groove. They heard the haunting strains of "Pale Hands I Love Beside the Shalimar." Kito hurried to the gong and struck it three times very slowly. It reverberated through the room. Kito hit a light switch at the foot of the stairs that were now enveloped in a clear, pink light. At the head of the stairs, a woman's hands parted the bloodred drapes. They saw a middle-aged woman wearing a black dress that reached her ankles and covered her

ms. Her rich raven-colored hair was pulled tightly back from
er head ending in a lavish chignon. Her face was alabaster
hite. Her lips were richly ruby red as were her fingernails.
lowly she descended the stairs staring down at Bogart and Vil-
n. They heard Kito declare, "Gentlemen, Mrs. Charles Bra-
n."

Of course, thought Bogart, of course. Charles Brabin had been
film director but it was his wife who had garnered the celebrity.
rs. Charles Brabin. I'll be damned. He wondered if Villon rec-
gnized the greatest vamp of the silent cinema, Theda Bara.

THIRTEEN

"HOW NICE TO WELCOME YOU to my home, Mr. Bogart." He
voice was a mellifluous contralto. She was smiling at Villon
"And Mister...?"

"Detective Villon."

"Oh my. Is there some fine I've forgotten to pay?" The me
shook hands with her and Bogart marveled at how youthful sh
looked until he realized she couldn't be much older than hin
She'd made her last film fifteen years earlier and at the time wa
not quite thirty years old.

Villon said, "Angelica Harper sent us. She phoned to let yo
know we were coming."

"She spoke to your servant, Kito," said Bogart.

She was draped across the sofa on the leopard skin. Boga
and Villon sat in chairs opposite her. Bara snapped her finge
at Kito and told him to shut off the Victrola and to kill the blu
light on the staircase. Without asking if either man cared fo
some, she told Kito to bring tea. Kito bowed and backed his wa
out of the room still grinning at Bogart who didn't quite kno
how to respond or if he was expected to.

Mrs. Brabin said to Bogart, "Don't be discomforted by th
perpetual smile. We never know if he's happy or if he's dyspe
tic. At times we wait, after Kito has left the room, if the smi
remains behind like Alice's Cheshire cat. Kito can also be terrib
forgetful. He did not give me the message. I don't scold Kit
because then he sulks and the atmosphere becomes unbearable.
She smiled at Villon. "Are you selling tickets to the policeman
ball? My husband and I don't socialize very much but we'
happy to give donations for widows and orphans."

"I'm not selling," said Villon, "I'm investigating."

"I see," her voice was subdued but her face showed curiosit

"And for some reason your investigation has brought you to me."

"You borrowed a cornucopia from Miss Harper," Villon reminded her.

"Yes. This past Thanksgiving, an interesting object. I wanted it that one time for a table decoration. I knew I'd never use it again and there was no point in buying one of my own. So I borrowed hers. All terribly simple. Oh dear. I suppose she's still irked I didn't invite her to the dinner. I couldn't. There were ten guests and my husband and myself. That's twelve. Had I invited Angelica, that would have made thirteen at the table. As you know, superstitious people consider thirteen a very unlucky number. Kito is terribly superstitious. He won't serve a table holding thirteen people. Kito is priceless." Her smile was a tacit request for understanding. "Angelica isn't."

"There's always somebody who's expendable," said Bogart. "Especially in Hollywood."

"Yes, in time it happens to many of us." There was a warm twinkle in her eye. "I think you recognize me, Mr. Bogart."

"You haven't changed a bit. You look the same. Maybe my friend here doesn't recognize you. Herb, the lady was very famous once. Theda Bara."

Villon brightened. "That's who you are! I knew I'd seen you somewhere before."

Mrs. Brabin leaned forward. "Tell me, is there a connection with the murder in your home, Mr. Bogart, and that of my dear friend Joshua Trent to Angelica's cornucopia?"

"Do you know the legend of the cornucopia?" She didn't and Bogart told her. Kito brought the tea and served it along with some excellent petit fours.

"And you think when you find the cornucopia you will have found your murderer?" She was nibbling a biscuit and knew she shouldn't be. She had gained weight and had been advised by her doctor to lose it. She loathed advice.

Villon said, "I don't know that at all. If you have the cornucopia, I don't think you murdered for it."

"Why not? I was famous for my interpretations of monstrous

vampires. Sometimes life imitates art." She laughed. "Quite honestly, I wouldn't know how to commit a murder. I'm a nice Jewish girl from Detroit who had fame thrust upon her by a ruthless producer named William Fox. But unlike the fame, the name Theda Bara lives on. I'm always in crossword puzzles! 'Vamp Bara! Twenty-one Across.'" A troubling thought assailed her. "Mr. Villon, if I were in possession of the cornucopia, I'd be in danger of being ransacked and murdered."

"It's a possibility," said Villon.

"Well what a relief. I don't have the cornucopia."

"Where is it?" asked Villon.

"As far as I know, it's back with Angelica."

"But it isn't," said Villon, "that's why she sent us here."

Mrs. Brabin was on her feet and pacing. "Now that's very odd. I know I gave it to someone to bring to Angelica. Well, Angelica is so flighty, she might have forgotten it was returned to her. Oh wait a minute! I remember! I entrusted it to Karen Barrett! She lives near Angelica and said it would be no problem to drop it by the next day. Do you suppose she didn't?"

"Looks like it," said Villon.

"Now that's not very nice of her. Do you at all remember Karen Barrett? For a while there she was very successful as a serial queen. You know, like Pearl White and Ruth Roland. Her big success was *The Terrors of Thomasina*. It was fifteen chapters of absolute nonsense in which she disguised herself as an alley cat and went around rescuing people from predicaments they had no right getting themselves into. This is terribly naughty of her." She crossed to the gong and gave it a thumping whack. "Poor Karen's been having a hard time of it. She's been on welfare. I have her for dinner as often as possible though she makes my husband nervous. Poverty tends to give him the hives. Other people's poverty, that is."

Kito entered and of course remembered to bring the smile with him. "Kito, please phone Karen Barrett. I don't remember her number."

"I remember the number, Mrs. Brabin. I remember all your

numbers, Mrs. Brabin.'' He went to the table at the far end of the couch and dialed.

Mrs. Brabin was back sitting on the couch. "Like too many of the silent era, Karen didn't invest wisely. Nor did she marry wisely all four times. Charles and I, as you can see, are among the fortunates. When I was a Fox star I got stock from the old Fox and it has multiplied and now it's Twentieth Century-Fox.''

"Not bad,'' said Bogart.

She shrugged. "The tip of the iceberg.''

Bogart said to Villon, "What's that crazy look on your face?''

"Where's Jim Mallory? Where'd we lose him?''

"Maybe he decided to go back to the station. We passed him in the car checking the precinct on our way to Angelica Harper.''

"He was probably called back,'' said Villon. "And no way of telling us. I'll check in as soon as Kito is off the phone.''

Kito had been off the phone for a while waiting for a chance to speak. He finally caught Mrs. Brabin's attention.

"Yes, Kito? What about Miss Barrett?''

"I'm sorry to tell you, the phone has been disconnected.''

"Oh dear, that doesn't bode well, does it. Perhaps it's just a matter of her being delinquent with her bill. Kito, give the gentlemen Miss Barrett's address.'' She said to Villon, "I assume you want to check into this.''

"Very definitely. Mrs. Brabin, may I use the phone? I'd like to call my precinct. I seem to have misplaced my associate.''

"Please do.'' As Villon availed himself of the phone, Mrs. Brabin said to Bogart, "Is detective work your hobby, Mr. Bogart?''

"No, not at all. I'm with Villon because of the murder and the ransacking in my house. Some other friends of mine were along with us but they dropped out.''

"Isn't it rather unusual for detectives to let outsiders tag along with them?''

"Herb Villon isn't your everyday run-of-the-mill detective. He's a maverick. He hears a different drummer. If I was in the way, he'd get rid of me. But Herb likes someone along with him and Jim...Jim Mallory. His associate. Nice young man with a tendency to occasionally wander off as like right now. When last seen he was reporting to the precinct on his car radio. Maybe he was called back.''

''Maybe he was kidnapped,'' suggested Mrs. Brabin, as though kidnapping was a common occurrence.

''No, he's quite safe,'' said Villon, returning from the phone. ''He's at Cedars of Lebanon Hospital.'' Bogart was startled. ''Ned Aswan tried to commit suicide.'' Bogart was on his feet.

''Joshua's Ned Aswan?'' asked Mrs. Brabin. When Villon said ''Yes,'' she said, ''Oh how terrible! Kito! You must take him some chicken soup.'' Kito was handing Villon a slip of paper on which he had written Karen Barrett's address. Villon slipped it into a pocket.

''Is it bad?'' Bogart asked Villon.

''When is it ever good. He drank poison. Something they use on furniture. He's in a coma but they think he'll come out of it.''

''You going over to the hospital?'' asked Bogart.

''No need to. Nothing I can do. Jim's got it covered. The place is swarming with reporters and photographers and the big question from them is, did Ned Aswan commit the murder.''

''Oh for crying out loud,'' said Bogart.

''Right,'' agreed Villon. ''He was in Santa Barbara when the murder was committed. Jim checked the people Ned was with. He's got a solid alibi.''

Mrs. Brabin said softly, ''I had no idea love could be so powerful.''

Bogart said, ''Maybe it was fear.''

Mrs. Brabin said, ''Oh. Do you suppose he thought the murderer might come back for him?''

Bogart said, ''He wasn't afraid of dying. The suicide attempt is your proof. He was afraid of living. That's my theory and I'm not all that much of a philosopher. Thanks for the hospitality, Mrs. Brabin.''

''My dear Mr. Bogart, it was hardly any trouble and very much worth it. I haven't had such a wonderful time in ages. Cornucopias, murders, ransackings, a suicide attempt. I can't wait for Charles to get back. He'll never believe a word of it.''

Kito chimed in. ''Oh Kito will back you up.''

''He'll believe it even less. Good-bye, gentlemen. I do so hope we'll meet again but under happier circumstances.'' She followed them out and stood in the doorway of the house, waving as they got into the car. Bogart beeped the horn by way of farewell and Mrs. Brabin's face beamed a splendid smile.

NELL DICKENS was pacing back and forth in the rear of the shop, puffing a cigarette and sounding very agitated. ''You had to meet her at Cantor's. Half of Hollywood eats in Cantor's!''

''Did I know Bogart and the cop would show up?'' Sidney Heep was not happy.

''What's the fuss?'' asked Edgar Dickens. ''You and Lucy are acquaintances. You ran into each other. Cantor's was convenient. Why behave as though a crime was committed?'' Nell started to speak but Edgar Dickens cut her short. ''You're both making too much of this. So Villon thinks I'm Italian. Well, he's a pretty smart dick but I'm not easy to trace. It's years since I left Italy. I served my sentence. I paid my debt to society or whatever corny phrase you care to substitute. I'm sure Mr. Villon has never heard of Nino Brocco. Why should he? He was a small boy when Nino Brocco was arrested for forging fake art treasures. Nino Brocco has been Edgar Dickens for a very long time now. Edgar Dickens is an American citizen.''

''You fraud,'' snorted Nell.

''The dead man was an American citizen. When I took his name from a stone in the cemetery, I checked on him and he was indeed a born and bred American. Forging the appropriate documents reincarnating myself as Edgar Dickens was child's play.''

Dickens was seated at his desk and Nell stared down at him. ''Villon is a very smart cop. If he thinks he's on to something with you and your possible Mediterranean origins, if he needs to he'll try to make something of it. He's got two murders to solve.''

"I didn't kill anybody," said Dickens. "You know I didn't kill anybody."

Heep piped up. "You're forgetting something."

"What?" snapped Nell.

"La Contessa di Marcopolo. For an old lady, she has a very sharp memory."

"Why not. Decades ago I deflowered her. A woman never forgets the man who took her virginity." He smiled. "She was so easily seduced."

"She could make trouble," said Nell. "She as much as threatened it yesterday. She worries me."

"She won't make trouble," said Dickens confidently.

"She will if she doesn't retrieve the cornucopia," said Heep.

"She never had the cornucopia so she has nothing to retrieve," said Dickens.

"She's determined. I think she's dangerous."

Dickens said, "It's as though this murderer had access to my records. I'm very meticulous about who we do business with. Who sold to us. Who bought from us. Who traded what with us. The Bogart tragedy, of course, is related to the ransacking of his mother-in-law's apartment. That of course had to be Marcelo Amati and Violetta Cenci. But they didn't have murder on their minds. They tricked the woman out of the apartment. But the Bogart ransacking is something else. It wasn't them. They wouldn't have killed the housekeeper. Someone else has taken over. I'm sure Herbert Villon is smart enough to be thinking along the same lines. You know something, Nell?"

"What?"

"At this moment, I don't think it's such a good idea for anyone in this town to admit to owning a cornucopia. Especially a sealed one. Sidney, give me that green ledger on the table there. I want to see who we've sold and traded the blasted things."

Nell said, "We'd have known if we had the right one. It must be damned heavy."

"True. Lots of sealed cornucopias are darned heavy, filled with all kinds of objets d'art. Who knows? Maybe we had it after all."

Nell said unpleasantly, "You trying to give me a stroke?"

"You're not the stroke type, my dear." He took the ledger from Sidney Heep and riffled the pages. The pages were stiff from age. There were water stain and food stains and little chicken scratches that Dickens didn't bother to decipher because he knew he couldn't. He lingered over a few transactions because they evoked pleasant memories of bargaining and friendly haggling. That's what buying and selling and trading had been about. How shrewdly could you beat the other guy down.

Hannah Darrow. Joshua Trent. There would be more killings. And if he knew it, Herbert Villon knew it. Dickens wondered who beside himself had a register of cornucopia owners. Perhaps it wasn't necessary. Perhaps there was but one authentic one. The one the Baron di Marcopolo entrusted to Jack Methot. Where had Jack Methot stashed it? Had he in turn entrusted it to anyone. His daughter Mayo?

"Such a sigh, Edgar," said Nell, "such a long, long sigh."

"Such an awful predicament. And such fruitless murders, I think." He slammed the ledger shut. "The hell with it. Let Villon do his own solving."

JOSHUA TRENT'S secretary, Zelda Sweet, the one who Jim Mallory had given the eye earlier that day, was glad he was back so soon, but sad that he was asking questions about Ned Aswan's attempted suicide. She liked Ned Aswan as well as she had liked Joshua Trent. They were decent employers and not given to innuendo. They were interested in women only as clients. With them you didn't have to worry about sexual harassment or veiled threats if you refused to unveil.

"I think you should attribute his attempted suicide to a sudden case of despondency," suggested Zelda to Jim.

"There's no such thing as a sudden case of despondency," said Jim who had taken some training in psychology when he decided to go into police work. "Despondency has to accumulate and develop until it becomes dangerous."

"You mean like a kid brother? I've got a rotten kid brother."

Jim Mallory wasn't interested in her rotten kid brother. "He always given to moods?"

"Ned? Well, he had a quick temper. And he was abnormally precise about everything. Look Mr. Mallory, Josh was the sun around which Ned orbited. Josh was his life. He was his father, mother, uncle, sister, and brother. Josh's world was all the world he knew. It was all the world he wanted to know. Ned was just plain afraid to continue on his own. This business was Joshua Trent, and underline the name. Ned doesn't know peanuts about business. He knows how to make estimates but it's Josh who knows how to rob...figure the costs. You taking all this down?" Jim nodded. "Am I any help?"

"You're lots of help. How long have you worked as Mr. Trent's secretary?"

"Little over five years."

"You happy here?"

"Until this morning. I don't think there's going to be any more business conducted here once the smoke clears. I know the contents of Josh's will. He dictated it to me. Ned gets almost everything except for some small bequests to a few friends and employees and a marble torso of a prizefighter he's bequested to Mae West."

"Nice lady. Was involved in a case with her once."

"Ned has no family. But with the kind of money he's inheriting, he can buy himself one."

"When are you free for dinner?"

"You name it."

"I'd like to do it tonight, but I'm not sure if I can. I have to find my partner and see what more needs to be done."

"You have to find a murderer."

"We'll nail him."

"Maybe it's a her."

"Maybe it's a him and a her. Who knows? That's what's so fascinating about murder. You never know who you're going to find waiting at the end of the trail. So, when do you quit work?"

"Tonight, who can tell. The place is such a mess. Ned had invited company for tonight and I'm still trying to track down some of them to call them off.'' She wrote something on a slip of paper and handed it to him. It was the office number and her home number. ''You'll find me at either place. Unless I'm on a bus in between.'' She smiled. ''You'll find me.''

FOURTEEN

ONCE AGAIN BACK ON Fairfax Avenue, Herb Villon asked Bogart to pull over to an outdoor phone. He called the precinct to give them Karen Barrett's address to be passed on to Jim Mallory when he checked in which Villon knew he did frequently. The phone was outside one of West Hollywood's tonier and more expensive beauty salons, Mr. Gwen. Hazel Dickson was at the counter settling her rather exorbitant bill. Hair dyes that obliterated the former color of roots, a facial, a manicure, a full-body massage, a pedicure, and lots of gossip always took their toll. Through the plate glass window Hazel saw, to her joy, her beloved Herb Villon talking on the phone accompanied by meaningless gestures, unless you heard what he was saying. Hazel thrust some bills into the cashier's hand with instructions to distribute them as tips and then hurried out to the street to surprise Villon.

He was hanging up the receiver when he heard the familiar Dickson voice greeting him. He was genuinely pleased to see her and proved it by kissing her cheek. "What are you doing here?" he asked.

She pointed to the beauty salon. "My home away from home. I told you I'd be spending hours here." She looked into the car. "Hi Bogie!"

Bogie lowered a window. "Hello gorgeous, you look good enough to eat."

"Don't talk dirty. There are women with toddlers in carriages who they have a bare memory of conceiving. What have you accomplished, Herb?" It didn't take Villon long to cover the territory he and Bogart had covered. "Theda Bara, for crying out loud. I wish I'd been there."

Herb was glad she hadn't, but didn't say so. "We're on our way to Karen Barrett's, want to tag along?"

"Karen Barrett, for Pete's sake. Isn't there anyone on your list who's made a talkie? Mmmm," she mmmm'd, "Karen Barrett on welfare. Louella will love that one. Back in the good old bad old days she, Karen, and Marion Davies used to pal around a lot. I'll see if I can get Louella to put the touch on Davies for Barrett. Davies is always good for a touch. She has a list of dependants longer then her arm. Where does Barrett live?"

"Down the block past Angelica Harper's dump and a left turn. Where's your car?"

"In the lot behind the salon. Give me a minute and I'll tail you."

Five minutes later, Hazel had rescued her car from the parking lot and two minutes later was tagging Bogart to Karen Barrett's place. Ned Aswan's attempted suicide didn't sit well with Hazel. She liked him and his nutty sense of humor, like the time he came to Cesar "Butch" Romero's Hallowe'en party in drag and passed himself off as his own twin sister, a gag that collapsed when Marlene Dietrich took him aside and advised him to use a depilatory.

In Bogart's car, Villon wondered if it would be appropriate to put his hand over his heart as they passed the Harper castle. Bogart said, "I wonder if I should be hurt she didn't ask me to sit for my portrait. Some of her stuff's pretty good. John Decker once asked me to sit for him in that filthy house of his on Mulholland Drive. I figured what the hell why not and arrived at the appointed hour of ten in the morning. Well let me tell you, never before have I stepped so gingerly into a drunken nightmare. His easel was set up under a gigantic skylight covered with bird droppings and rotting greenery probably blown there years earlier by a Santa Ana. On a podium was a throne chair in which I was supposed to sit, except it was already occupied by W. C. Fields who it was obvious was a bit incontinent. Sprawled on a couch was Errol Flynn and sprawled on Flynn was a nubile sweetie who, I might tell you, now has a stock player's contract at Warner's. They were but a small part of the population in that room.

There was at least another dozen alcoholics in various stages of inebriation. Even the houseboy who admitted me had trouble standing erect. It was a scene of such complete perversion that would have appealed to Hogarth's shade had it been haunting the place.''

"Where was Decker?" asked Villon.

"He was presumably upstairs asleep. Obviously there'd been an all-night orgy and as Errol's doxy was obviously underage, I made tracks fast and drove to the nearest church. It being Sunday I did not go in but for my own peace of mind I recited a couple of Hail Marys and a Stations of the Cross and then drove home to Mayo, spoiling for a really hot knock-down-drag-out and, bless her heart, Mayo didn't disappoint me. Have I passed Barrett's place?"

Villon was staring past Bogart out the window. "I think this is it here." Bogart pulled over to the curb and parked. Hazel parked in front of him, sparing him a dented fender by a very narrow margin. The three stood on the sidewalk staring at a two-level apartment complex that at one time in its existence must have been a favorable address. Bogart later described it to Mayo as what appeared to be rows of rabbit warrens that were semi-detached and undoubtedly semi-inhabitable. Attached to an outside wall was a directory on which Karen Barrett was indeed listed. Hazel said in her usual optimistic way, "I hope Barrett's not our second suicide of the day."

"Bite your tongue," said Villon. "I need her." They climbed the cement stairs to the second level. Villon was in the van. Now they were standing in front of the door to Karen Barrett's apartment. Her name was in a slot over a bell. Villon pressed the bell. They waited. He pressed it again. The door opened a few inches. There was a protective chain.

"I'm a friend of Mrs. Brabin's. She sent me and my... er...associates to see you."

"Why?"

"To ask some questions."

"What kind of questions?"

"If you'll let us in, I'll give you some samples."

"Don't try to kid me. You're here to dispossess me." The fear and the pathos in her voice affected the three.

Villon's tone of voice was gentler. "Miss Barrett, I'm Detective Herbert Villon. It's to do with the cornucopia Mrs. Brabin gave you to deliver to Angelica Harper the day after Thanksgiving."

"Oh God." She shut the door. They heard the chain removed and then the door opened. Karen Barrett wore what was once a Japanese kimono, held in place by a strip of what might have been curtain material tied around her waist. A worn, tired snood held her hair in place and her feet were encased in scuffs that were frayed at the edges. It was a one-room apartment with two windows on the wall opposite the front door that looked out on a courtyard. There was a sofa that Hazel assumed opened out into a bed, a table, and four kitchen chairs, a half-sized refrigerator, a stove, a sink, and a door that opened onto a small bathroom. On a shelf above the sink Bogart spotted a box of dry cereal, a can of condensed milk, a box of soda biscuits, a few canned goods, and a near-empty gin bottle. Déjà vu, thought Bogart. A replica of the roach-infested studio he lived in when he first came to seek his fortune in New York. There were some bits of clothing strewn on the floor and the couch.

Karen Barrett wore no makeup, and was still a handsome woman despite the evidence of vicissitude. On the table was an ashtray and a pack of cigarettes and a book of matches. "Forgive the mess," she said in a voice tortured by too much cigarette smoke and too much gin and too much talking to herself, "it's the maid's day off." She gestured at Bogart. "You're Bogart, right?"

"Right," said Bogart, managing what he hoped was a friendly and sympathetic smile.

Barrett looked at Villon. "So you must be Herbert Villon. Very fancy monicker, I must say, so I've said it." She looked at Hazel Dickson. "I know, don't tell me. You're the Spirit of Christmas Past, back in the days when there used to be Christmas." Her words were soaked in gin. "Have a seat. Anywhere you like. They're equally uncomfortable." Bogart saw the phone on a small end table at the end of the sofa. He sat on the sofa next to the phone. The sofa was lumpy. "You can't use the phone because it doesn't work. It's been disconnected. How do they expect you to pay your bills if you can't get work and haven't got a dime to call your own?" Mayo's spending sprees were flashing through Bogart's mind. He made a mental note to give her some swift kicks in the behind when next he saw her. Better yet, he might go home and pack all her clothes and send them to Karen Barrett except they weren't the same size, Mayo was petite, Barrett was tall and with an athletic body. Serial screen queens had to be athletic in the silents. They didn't have doubles. They did their own stunts and survived to give interviews about their athletic prowess.

There was a knock at the door.

"Oh shit!" exclaimed Miss Barrett. "That's him. From the sheriff's office with my dispossess. Where the hell do they expect me to go? Griffith Park?"

There was another knock at the door.

Karen Barrett squared her shoulders and shuffled to the door, a brave action more conducive to a brief appearance before a firing squad. She opened the door and Jim Mallory said, "Is Detective Villon here?"

Karen Barrett's smile was like a klieg light at a Hollywood Boulevard premiere. "Who gives a damn if he is or isn't. You're absolutely adorable. Come right in. And you're blushing. I haven't seen a man blush like that since I seduced a teenager who wasn't worth the trouble." Barrett shut the door. "Well, there must be some hope coming out from under the rocks. Mr. Villon, introduce me to this improvement." Villon introduced them. "Mallory. Jim Mallory. Any relation to Boots Mallory? Cute kid who did some features at Fox in the early thirties. I don't know what's become of her."

"I do," said Bogart, "she's Jimmy Cagney's sister-in-law, married to his brother Bill."

"Well what do you know about that," said Barrett. Jim Mallory told her Boots was no relation. "I'm sorry I've got no refreshments to offer you," she said, obviously determined to hold on to what few belts of gin remained in the bottle, "but I'm fresh out. Sit down, Jim. The kitchen chairs are serviceable." He chose to remain standing by the door as though a hasty exit might soon be called for.

"About the cornucopia, Miss Barrett," began Villon.

"I was afraid you'd get back to that." She pointed to a small radio on a shelf above the refrigerator. "I know all about the murders. I was one of the first to give Joshua Trent a break." She paused. "He stopped returning my phone calls. Funny, but just telling you that, it still hurts." The others in the room were veterans of unreturned phone calls, although Hazel tended to get violent about it and send threatening letters to constant offenders.

The silence in the room was broken by Jim Mallory. "Herb, should I check the precinct?"

Hazel said, "You'll have to use drums. The phone's disconnected."

Barrett said with a small laugh, "What's worse, I'm fresh out of drums." She stood in front of Villon and saluted him smartly. "Sir, I'm a disgrace to the regiment and I throw myself on your mercy. I know that somewhere under your skin there beats an understanding heart. But in dire need of food and to pay my electric bill, I hocked the God-damned thing."

"Jesus," said Villon.

"He also existed on handouts," Barrett said. She sat at the kitchen table and lit a cigarette. She asked no one in particular, "I still got some looks. Do you think I could make it on the streets? Maybe I should try Chinatown. There they don't give a damn who they sleep with as long as the price is right."

"Now don't you talk that way," said Hazel softly. "Remember, in every cloud there's a silver lining." Bogart strained to hear a sad violin but no sounds were forthcoming. "You used to be a good pal of Marion Davies's, why haven't you asked her for help."

"I'm too ashamed."

"But you mustn't be!"

"But I am. In those days, I used to pick up the tabs. For Marion it was a fresh experience and Louella was always a freeloader." She fiddled with the snood for a moment. "Funny how many people drop out of your life when you're no longer picking up the checks." She now wore a tender smile. "I used to love to take people out. Well, them days are gone forever." She shuffled to a table where she kept her handbag. It was the table with the phone next to where Bogart was sitting. "Here's the pawn ticket." She fumbled with the purse. "Leo Bulgari's on Sunset near La Brea. There's three brass balls hanging over the entrance, one more than Bulgari has. Though he's usually pretty fair." She was staring into the purse.

"There's nothing wrong, is there?" Bogart asked with a smile.

She said nothing. Her eyes were misting up. She sat next to Bogart and rummaged in the purse. She was careful not to expose the twenty dollar bills Bogart had surreptitiously slipped into the bag. She didn't want to embarrass either herself or Bogart. She found the pawn ticket, shut the handbag and leaned across Bogart to replace it on the table. She arose and took the ticket to Villon. He studied it.

Villon said, "Bulgari's not all that generous."

She stared him in the eyes. "I had some good meals and saw a couple of good pictures, and if I'm under arrest, you'll have to wait while I get into something glamorous."

Bogart spoke swiftly. "You're not under arrest. Certainly not for hocking some crappy thingamabob." His words were directed at Villon.

"Of course you're not under arrest. Mrs. Brabin would have to file a complaint, and I doubt she'd do that. She sounded as though she's very fond of you."

"Yes, I guess she is even though I outlasted her in pictures. We got our start around the same time, but after five or six years of them, the public grew tired of vamps. They grew tired of my serials too but I was able to move into adventure pictures and Westerns. As a matter of fact, I did some talkies. Cheapies on Poverty Row. I made three for a couple of rats who were lowercase impressarios. The evil of two lessers." She smiled at Villon. "Mrs. Brabin wouldn't file charges because the thing didn't belong to her. It belongs to Angelica Harper."

"She won't file charges," said Bogart, "or I'll file charges against her for having a musician on the premises without a license."

"I had no idea you were so civic minded," said Villon.

"Neither did I," said Bogart. "I think we've taken up enough of Miss Barrett's time."

Jim Mallory held out a pad and pen to Karen Barrett. "Miss Barrett, may I have your autograph?"

"Oh shit, you've got to be kidding!"

"It's for my mother. She's a big movie fan. I know she'll be tickled pink to have it."

"Well, okay." She took the pad and pen. "What's your mother's name?"

"Mary Bessie."

Hazel crossed her eyes. Karen Barrett wrote a message and signed it with a flourish. She returned the pad and pen to Mallory and then on impulse patted his cheek. "You're too handsome to be a cop. Maybe Mr. Bogart can arrange a screen test."

"No way," said Mallory, "I'm very happy where I am."

Villon said, "Come on, let's be on our way." He was holding the door open. "Thanks a lot, Miss Barrett. You've been very helpful. If you ever need me, I'm at the downtown precinct." Hazel and Mallory filed out.

"Mr. Bogart?" asked Barrett. "Could I see you alone for a minute?"

Bogart said to Villon, "I'll be right down." Villon shut the door.

Miss Barrett retrieved her handbag and extracted five twenty dollar bills. "This is a new experience for me. Usually men took money from my handbag, not put money in it. Mr. Bogart, this is very generous of you and I shall cry myself to sleep tonight and a lot more nights after. It's too much. I can't take all this."

Bogart made a fist. "You want a rap in the kisser?"

"You sound like one of my husbands."

"Get your phone back on again. It can't be all that much."

"It isn't."

"Treat yourself to a new dress. Then phone me at the studio.

I'll leave your name at the switchboard. They're always hiring stock players. Lots of old-timers. We've got Monte Blue and Wheeler Oakman and Larry Steers and probably when my time comes maybe somebody will do me a good turn with a stock contract. Only one thing, and forgive me for saying it because I'm sure you know my reputation for downing a few belts, but don't spend too much on gin.''

"Oh honest to God, I won't. Now I can go back to bourbon!''

Bogart laughed and hugged her. "Christ but how you gals are made of sterner stuff.'' He had the door open. "Get the phone back on and be sure to phone me, I want to see you on the set of my next picture.''

He shut the door. She stood staring at it. She stared at the twenty dollar bills she was clutching. She replaced them in her purse. She went to the bathroom where she had left the glass in which were dissolved twenty-three sleeping pills. She poured the contents of the glass into the toilet bowl and flushed it. She rinsed the glass thoroughly and placed it on the rim of the sink. She stared at herself in the mirror in the door of the medicine chest above the sink. She removed the snood and stared at her mess of gray hair. "Girl, you're getting yourself a rinse and a dye job and a very fancy set and you're going to phone Humphrey Bogart as soon as the juice is back on and get your tail over to Warners and take whatever they offer you. He's not handing you a line either, honey, and he didn't suggest beddy-bye. He's the real article.''

She stripped, ran the shower, stepped under it, and for the first time in too long a time, remembered what it was to be happy.

On the street, the others watched as Bogart rejoined them. He said to Mallory, "That was damned nice of you to ask for her autograph. That was really damned nice.''

"But I meant it. My mother's movie crazy. I try to get her all the autographs I can. So help me, it's true!''

Hazel asked Bogart, "How much did you slip her?''

"What are you talking about?''

"I saw you slipping those bills into her handbag. Nice job of sleight of hand if I must say so myself.''

"And you have," said Villon.

"Hazel, if I see anything about this in somebody's column, and I read everybody's column religiously, like every other egomaniac in this town, I'll slap you bowlegged."

"She's already bowlegged," said Villon.

"You shut up!" scolded Hazel. To Bogart she said, "I have every intention of telling Louella about Karen's bad luck because I know Louella will help. She's not completely a mean old bitch. And Louella will pass it on to Marion who's a good Joe and will probably invite Karen over to share a fifth of gin."

"Karen prefers bourbon." Bogart looked at his wristwatch. "The day's growing shorter, Herb. What's the name of that pawnbroker?"

"Leo Bulgari."

"Oh yeah. Him with the three brass balls. Let's get going."

Villon was reading Mallory's mind. "You can phone the precinct from Bulgari's. Oh Christ, I almost forgot, there's so much going on with this case—how's Ned Aswan?"

"They expect him to pull through. I had a long talk with Josh Trent's secretary, Zelda Sweet, back at the house. It seems that he's always needed Joshua Trent to stabilize his emotional insecurity."

Bogart asked, "I'm sure Trent left him very well fixed."

"According to Zelda Sweet, more then very well fixed."

Villon asked him, "When you having dinner with her?"

Mallory blushed. "What do you mean?"

"You're blushing so you know what I mean." Villon said to Bogart, "Jim's a sucker for a pretty face. But nothing comes of it. He's still single. He never gets engaged."

"Hell," said Mallory, "engaged means a ring and who can afford a ring on my salary."

Hazel said to Villon, "You earn more then he does."

Bogart asked, "You following us, Hazel?"

"I don't like that smirk, Mr. Bogart."

"I never smirk, Hazel. My upper lip's too stiff. Funny, with my stiff upper lip I don't understand why I'm never offered no British parts. What do you think, Hazel?''

She said as she got behind the wheel of her car, "Scrub it, sweetheart. They've already done *Little Lord Fauntleroy*.''

FIFTEEN

"LEO BULGARI." VILLON spoke the name with a hint of contempt.

"Your paths have crossed before, I take it."

"Many times. He's so crooked he gives corruption a good name. He's a Turk. We know he's a fence but we've never caught him at it. He calls himself the pawnbroker to the stars. You'd be amazed at the number of names who have utilized his services. He's so greedy, he does house calls. He preys on has-beens like Karen Barrett. Too many silent screen actors had absolutely no business sense whatsoever. The exceptions were Mary Pickford and Charlie Chaplin and some shrewd mothers. Pickford's mother. The mothers of the Talmadge sisters and the Gish sisters. Very clever with a buck and demons at the bargaining table. But ladies like Karen Barrett, they didn't have mothers. They had husbands. Bloodsuckers who bled them dry. You slip her much?"

"A hundred."

"Very nice. It's tax deductible. Charitable contribution."

"Forget it." Bogart added, "And I don't want Mayo to hear about it. Spread the word. Especially to Hazel."

"Tell her yourself. Up ahead, I see three brass balls."

"That's Bulgari's place." He looked out the rear window. Mallory was right behind them, and behind him was Hazel who was more concerned with examining the recent repairs to her face in the rear mirror than she was with the oncoming traffic in the adjacent lane.

Bogart saw a space and parked. Mallory did a U-turn into a small lot that was adjacent to a hot dog stand. Hazel joined him. Traffic was surprisingly light for the late afternoon and Mallory and Hazel were able to make it across the street to join Bogart and Villon in safety. The pawn shop had two display windows offering unredeemed objects for sale. There were items of jewelry, a variety of watches and musical instruments, fur coats and jackets, cameras, radios, dishes, silverware, and linens.

"Look," said Bogart, "the cornucopia."

The cornucopia was set in the center of a display. Bulgari had placed a card alongside it on which he had printed, IS THIS THE HORN OF PLENTY?

"Brazen bastard," said Villon.

Hazel said, "So that's what a cornucopia looks like. I wouldn't give it as a wedding gift to a couple I disliked."

"It's sealed," said Bogart. He and Villon looked at each other. "You know, Herb, at the end of *The Maltese Falcon* when they find what they really think is the bird they're looking for, it turns out to be a fake."

"You trying to tell me something?"

"I'm trying to tell you not to be too disappointed if this thing is filled with crackerjacks."

"Bogie, to me the cornucopia is an afterthought. I'm trying to catch a killer. He's going to kill again. He's undoubtedly gotten his hands on a list of cornucopia owners. This could spread into an epidemic."

They heard a bell tinkle as the pawnshop door was pulled open. "But of course! It is my old friend detective Villon! I thought I recognized you! And my heavens! Do I see before me Humfairy Bogart?" Leo Bulgari was possibly five foot seven inches tall. He seemed taller because he wore a fez on his head with a gold tassel that dangled to just below his left ear. He was fat and his stomach bulged over his trousers belt. He was brave enough to wear an earring at a time when only certain kinds of men favored earrings. Bulgari's earring was a crescent moon worn on his right lobe.

Bogart mumbled, "This, I suppose, is Bulgari?"

"Yeah. The fez is familiar," said Villon.

"I don't go for that Humfairy business. He trying to be funny?"

"Ask him."

Bulgari said to Hazel, "That is a delightful brooch you are wearing."

"And shall continue to wear," said Hazel.

For a man of his girth he bowed gracefully, one hand extended by way of inviting them into his store. Hazel was the first to enter followed by Mallory and Villon. Bogart managed to disguise his distaste as his eyes met Bulgari's. "I am a great admirer, Mr. Bogart. You have given me very many pleasant hours." Bogart managed a smile that Bulgari could interpret any way he saw fit. Bulgari shut the door and offered them chairs and Turkish coffee. Hazel sat. Nobody wanted coffee. "And how may I help, Detective Villon?"

"You know what I'm after. A certain cornucopia."

Bulgari clasped his hands together and his eyes beseeched the ceiling. "What is it all of a sudden with cornucopias?"

Villon said, "Bulgari."

"Yes?"

"You're overplaying." Bulgari unclasped his hands. "That one in the window."

"It is worthless. Unless you care to buy it."

Villon handed him Karen Barrett's pawn ticket. "Is this the ticket for the thing in the window?"

Bulgari examined the ticket. "Ah yes. Miss Barrett. An unfortunate victim of circumstances. Are you interested in redeeming the object? Twenty-eight dollars."

"What! You gave her fifteen dollars."

"In a rash moment of generosity. It has been here a long time and each day the interest on the loan increases."

"That wasn't Miss Barrett's to hock. It belongs to someone else."

Bulgari shrugged. "That is not my concern."

"Take it out of the window. I want to examine it."

"Take my word. It contains nothing of value. It is sealed because I sealed it myself. These things are dust catchers."

Villon said to Mallory, "Jim, get it out of the window, pronto."

Jim reached into the display and removed the cornucopia.

Bulgari hovered behind Mallory. "Careful, careful. Don't throw anything over."

Mallory carried it to a desk. Villon said to Bulgari, "Unseal it." Bulgari shrugged. He took a pen knife from his pocket and with elaborate care unsealed the tin foil that obscured the cornucopia's interior. "Surely your friend could tell by its light weight that it contains nothing as heavy as gems."

Villon pulled back the tin foil. He knew he'd find nothing of value. He was enjoying harassing Bulgari who he seemed to have forgotten was unharassable. Bulgari said, "You see. There is only wads of cotton. So, do you wish to redeem the item?"

"I'll think it over."

"As you wish. It might interest you to know I have had another inquiry. A gentleman inquired on behalf of a royal personage."

"La Contessa di Marcopolo."

"Aha! You know about her. Her emissary tells me this cock and bull about her father and I humored him."

"Were you successful?" asked Villon.

Bulgari shrugged. "He was a most disagreeable person. Very good looking. But very impatient and quick-tempered. Italian. They are usually very quick-tempered, and now that they are allied with the Nazis, I trust them even less."

"Spoken like a true patriot," said Bogart, enough iron in his voice to construct a battleship.

Villon asked, "You've got other cornucopias?"

"Only this misbegotten one. You doubt me? Look around. You will see no other cornucopias."

"You've got a basement."

"There is nothing of value down there. I assure you. No cornucopias."

"I might come back with a search warrant," threatened Villon.

Bulgari clasped his hands together. "How often have you threatened me with search warrants!" Bulgari said to the others, "It is a little game we play, but he never returns with a search warrant."

"You do business with Edgar Dickens?"

Villon's question seemed to catch Bulgari by surprise. "Dickens?"

"You know who I'm talking about. The Old Curiosity Shop in Venice. You guys are always buying and selling and swapping with each other."

"Ah! Of course! Today my brain is like a sieve. Whatever is there tends to slip through. Yes of course I have dealt with Mr. Dickens. And I may as well tell you I've also dealt with Joshua Trent. But this you have probably already surmised. We are a closely knit community here in Los Angeles. We know each other well. We buy, we sell, we trade, we haggle, we threaten, we fight, and then come to an agreement." He added soberly, "But, my friend Villon, we do not commit murder."

Villon's hands were on his hips. His voice rasped. "Bulgari, are you a citizen of this country?"

"Soon. Soon. Very soon. I shall throw a banquet in my honor."

Bogart said to Hazel and Mallory, "The bastard'll probably charge admission." He didn't give a damn if Bulgari heard him or not. He disliked the man and was not about to make any bones about it. "Herb, we have to hang around here any longer? I need fresh air."

"Let's go," said Villon.

"Villon!" The Bulgari charm had evaporated. "Do not threaten me. I will not tolerate being threatened. I conduct my business with decorum. I have no police record. I have never been charged. So do not threaten me."

Villon left without saying a word. Hazel and Mallory followed. Bogart stopped in the doorway, turned, and said to Bulgari, "I don't like the way you pronounced my name, fatso. Get it right. It's Hum*free*. Right?"

Bulgari shrugged. Bogart left. The four huddled on the sidewalk. Bulgari watched them through a window. He wished he could read lips.

Bogart was saying, "That was a very unpleasant experience. I should have decked him. I need a drink. I need a couple of drinks. I'm going back to the Allah and check for any messages.

Mayo may be looking for me. And the studio. Anyone care to join me?''

Villon said, ''Thanks, Bogie. But Jim and I should get back to the precinct. We've got a lot to do. You going home, Hazel?''

''If that's a hint, I'm not taking it. I'm tailing after you two bums so I can use the john and the telephone and then Herbert Villon, you're taking me to dinner.''

''You're taking me. It's your turn.''

''Gee,'' said Mallory, ''then I can invite Zelda Sweet to dinner.''

''Zelda what?'' asked Hazel.

''Come on, come on,'' said Villon, ''let's get going. Bogie, if anything turns up, I'll call you at the hotel.''

''Thanks, Herb,'' said Bogart. He got into his car and was soon heading to the Garden of Allah, which was only a five-minute drive from the pawn shop.

In the bar of the Garden of Allah, Dashiell Hammett and Lillian Hellman were going through the motions of holding court. With the strong-willed characters inhabiting the bar at cocktail time, a favorite sport was jockeying for position. Hellman had been holding somewhat spellbound an audience consisting of Dorothy Parker, her husband Alan Campbell, Robert Benchley, and the portly Sidney Greenstreet. She was telling them about the encounters at the Curiosity Shop and the tragedy at Joshua Trent's estate. She repeated the incidents well and with enough dramatic intensity that there were no inane interruptions with the usual fatuous wisecracks. At one point Mrs. Parker insisted the butler did it but Hellman insisted there was no butler, in Trent's case, only a lover and an assortment of employees. Then surprisingly enough, especially for Hellman rarely given to compliments or kind words, she waxed generously enthusiastic about Herb Villon.

''He sounds absolutely spiffy,'' said Mrs. Parker. She indicated her husband. ''When Alan gets killed in action, I'll look up your Detective Villon.'' Campbell didn't look kindly on her statement but kept his peace. He had no intention of seeing action. He had wangled himself into Special Services where he would write scripts for army films.

"Seems to me," said Benchley with a chuckle, "what this case needs is your thin man, Dash."

"He wouldn't be of any use," demurred Hammett.

"Your modesty is appreciated but most unbecoming," said Benchley, "Nick Charles would have this case solved in about the time it takes him to drink four martinis."

Hammett said to Hellman, "Here we go again." He said to Benchley, "Thanks to the film series, you're under a bit of a misapprehension. Nick Charles is not the thin man."

"Applesauce," said Mrs. Parker.

"He's not applesauce either," said Hellman.

Hammett retrieved the spotlight. "I repeat, Nick Charles is not the thin man. In my book as in the first movie of the series, the thin man is the elongated shadow on the wall of the murder victim. The building janitor tells Nick he saw a thin man, meaning that shadow on the wall. There. You have it from the horse's mouth which is as dry as hay and in desperate need of sustenance. The liquid variety."

Hellman shouted for a waiter and then waved at Bogart who was headed for the bar. He signaled he'd join them as soon as he got himself a drink.

Mrs. Parker asked Hellman, "Any news about the wife?"

"She's no wife, she's a bad habit. As far as I know she's still up north with Mama. For Bogie's sake and sanity let's hope she decides to stay there."

Alan Campbell said, "She won't let go of him. Not now. Not while his career is swinging into high gear."

"Why beloved," said Mrs. Parker, "is that why you won't let go of me?"

"Just say the word," said Campbell, "and you're a free woman."

"Balls."

"That's not the word."

Bogart joined them and sat next to Hellman. "Well, you character assassins, been having a field day?"

"As a matter of fact," said Hellman, "we've been discussing another assassin, the one who did in Josh Trent and your house-keeper. Well don't sit there as though you're waiting to audition for something. What have you guys been doing? What did you find out? Was useless Goldwyn of any use?"

Bogart lead them to Sam Goldwyn and from Sam Goldwyn to Angelica Harper and her castle that had Benchley fascinated and wondered if she'd be a fit subject for the two-reelers he wrote and starred in at M-G-M. Bogart said probably and then went on to Mrs. Charles Brabin, relishing the looks on their faces when he identified the lady as the old silent screen vamp Theda Bara.

Hammett said dreamily, "She used to give me an erection."

"Did she charge much?" asked Hellman.

"This Kito," asked Greenstreet, gratified to finally put an oar in, "was there anything suspicious about him?"

"He grinned. Very big grin. Very big teeth. Why suspicious, Sidney? You think he might be a spy?"

Mrs. Parker contributed, "Possibly a rear admiral on a secret mission."

"He didn't have much of a rear," said Bogart. "And stop interrupting." He moved onward to Karen Barrett and her sad state of affairs, sidestepping his contribution to her of a hundred dollars.

"There's an awful lot of that going on in this town. Even Louis B. Mayer has some of them under stock contract. May McAvoy, Barbara Bedford, Aileen Pringle." Benchley shook his head and sipped his drink.

"In her day Pringle made him millions," said Greenstreet.

"Her day's passed," said Bogart, "so why don't I get on with it?"

"There's more?" asked Mrs. Parker, who was showing signs of fatigue.

"There's a Turkish delight," Bogart told her. He launched into the incident with Leo Bulgari with relish and a side order of venom, describing his girth, the earring, the fez, and the worthless cornucopia.

"It wouldn't be worthless if it had contained the jewels," said Hellman.

"Your Bulgari sounds like someone Eric Ambler might have created. He was very big with Turkish scoundrels," said Greenstreet.

Hellman was on a trail all her own. "Maybe it did contain the jewels and he's got them stashed away some place."

"I do wish somebody wants another drink," said Mrs. Parker, "it's too early to think about breakfast."

"You haven't had dinner," said her husband.

"Oh. I hadn't noticed."

Hellman said to Bogart, "If you haven't got any dinner plans, join us. We're thinking about Musso and Frank's."

"Sure. But listen. Are you in a rush about dinner?"

"Hell, no," said Hellman, "I'd rather hang in here for a few more drinks and wait for Dotty to drop something quotable." Mrs. Parker behaved as though she hadn't heard her. She hadn't dropped anything suitably quotable in a long time. In time it would be discovered that bitchery was more her forte then wit.

Bogart said, "Why don't I meet you back here in a couple of hours. I want to go over to the house to see if the Warner crew's got it anywhere near back in shape."

Somebody might have heard him but he doubted it. They were heavy into a discussion of Theda Bara and her Japanese servant and, wondered Mrs. Parker, do you suppose they might be having an affair right under Mr. Brabin's nose?

In the lobby, Bogart stopped at the desk to see if he had any messages. There was one from the studio to remind him of the rehearsal the next morning and Bogart told the clerk he'd be back in a few hours. He hurried out of the lobby and into the parking lot and was soon on his way to Brentwood.

There was a lot crowding his mind as he drove into Laurel Canyon Road. There were victims and an attempted suicide and an unknown assassin and the Goddamned cornucopia and Villon and Mallory and Hazel Dickson and a silent screen vamp and her Japanese houseman and a ditsy artist and a lady very far down on her luck. He stopped for gas at his usual station near his home and soon he was driving into his street and wishing he hadn't left the Garden of Allah.

There was a blue coupe parked in front of his house and inside the house he saw a light in the foyer. He wondered if the coupe and light connected to one of the Warner crew. He left his car and went up the walk to the front door. He put his key in the lock. It was unlocked. He entered and crossed from the foyer into the living room.

There wasn't a sign of the crime. The Warner's crew had done a superb job. No one ever would have suspected that a murder had taken place. All the place lacked was the little woman to welcome him home with his pipe and slippers in place. He went into the kitchen and then traveled to the den. He went upstairs. His and Mayo's room was immaculate. Also the guest room. At the end of the hall was an unused room, presumably for a live-in servant but Hannah Darrow had used it as a work room for herself and where she kept a few things such as a smock, an extra dress, and extra shoes. It hadn't even been examined to see if it had been ransacked. Bogart saw a light coming from under the door. That was very curious.

Bogart slowly walked down the hall to the door. When he reached it, he listened for a sound from within. He heard nothing. Abruptly, he pushed the door open. "What are you doing here?" he asked.

Lucy Darrow looked startled.

SIXTEEN

SHE WAS SITTING AT WHAT looked like a small desk, but when opened it was a sewing machine. On the desk was a shopping bag into which Lucy was folding garments. "Oh! You frightened me. I phoned you here and at the hotel to tell you I'd like to collect my mother's things, but I couldn't find you." She indicated the shopping bag. "Her smock, her aprons, her slippers..." her voice faded away.

"How did you get in?"

"The men from Warner Brothers were just leaving. They let me in. Actually, my mother kept a spare key in the apartment that I was going to return to you, I intended to use it." She folded and packed as she talked.

Bogart leaned against the door with his arms folded. "You find the dress for your mother?"

"Finally. It's in the car. I'm taking it to the funeral parlor. They're delivering Mother tomorrow morning."

"Why did you and Heep leave Canter's without having your lunch?"

"Oh, that. I wasn't hungry. Sidney wanted to get back to Venice. I wanted to get back to finding mother's dress. Is that man a really good detective?"

"Herb Villon? He's aces. You finished here? I've got a dinner date."

"Yes, this is it."

"You could have borrowed a suitcase."

"This shopping bag's fine. Thanks just the same." He held the door open for her. She walked past him and he switched off the light. He followed her to the foyer downstairs. She talked as they walked. "I haven't chosen the time for the services. Probably the day after tomorrow at noon. I need time to notify her friends.''

''Why don't you run a notice in the *Times?*''

''That's an idea. Except it's too late to place it today. Mother didn't have that many friends and as to relatives, there's only my aunt and she has no family. I'm an only child. I never knew my father. He died before I was born.''

''Sorry about that.''

''Oh,'' she said airily, ''you don't miss what you never knew.'' In the foyer, she rummaged in her handbag for her car keys. ''And oh, here's the house key.'' He pocketed it. ''Is Mr. Villon close to finding the killer?''

''He needs the lucky break.''

''The lucky break? What's that?''

''What every detective prays for. A phone call with some information that leads to the killer. Or the killer to make a slip and do something suspicious or say something suspicious. Detectives never know where it's going to come from. But sooner or later, it comes.''

''And the cornucopia?''

Bogart said, ''I wish I'd never heard of the damn thing.''

She said dreamily, ''I wish I had a cornucopia. I wish I could find it.''

''Why not? Everybody has a right to their dreams. I'm curious, Lucy. Do you mind if I get a little nosy?''

''Not at all.''

''Are you and Sidney Heep what they call an item?''

''Mother only introduced us a short while ago. I like him, but I really don't know him all that well. Did we look that intimate at the restaurant?''

Bogart shrugged. ''There's intimate and there's intimate. Now I hate to hurry you on your way...''

''Of course. Your dinner date. I'll let you know about the service.'' She grasped the shopping bag and hurried out of the house. Bogart stood in the doorway watching her. Something bothered him. He couldn't put his finger on it, but something bothered him. As he shut the door, the phone rang. He went to the living room, sat in the chair next to the phone and picked up the receiver. "Hello?" It was Mayo. "The house is in tip-top shape. How'd you guess I was here?"

"The clerk at the hotel told me. Are you staying in the house tonight?"

"If I'm in shape to get back."

"Meaning?"

"I'm having dinner with Lily and Dash at Musso's. I'm picking them up at the Allah."

"Why aren't you meeting them at Musso's?"

He looked at the ceiling in exasperation. "Because it's easier to round them up at the Allah. When I left them, they were drinking with a gang of professional drinkers and you know what that can lead to. I spent the day playing detective with Herb Villon. Lily and Dash joined us for a while but then left us when we had to go see Sam Goldwyn."

"What the hell does he have to do with the case?"

"I'll start at the beginning." He recapped the day's activity ending with the unpleasantness at Leo Bulgari's.

"Well," said Mayo, "all that and Theda Bara, too. Listen, my mother wants to tell you something. That's really why I'm calling."

"Aw. I thought it was because you missed me."

"Only when I take aim," she retorted.

He snapped his fingers. "I knew there was something wrong in this room."

"What do you mean?"

"I'm sitting here talking on the phone and nothing's gone whistling past my head."

"You big sap. Here's Mother."

Bogart heard some fumbling noises as the phone was passed from daughter to mother and then winced as her sharp voice sliced into his ear. "Hello Humphrey."

"Hello Evelyn. How are you?"

"Much better now that Mayo is here with me." Hypocrite, thought Bogart. I can still picture your sigh of relief complete with sound effects as you saw your daughter off to New York that landmark day so many years ago. "Humphrey..." The way she pronounced his name it was like having an ice pick plunged into him. "Mayo and I have been talking about the ransackings, of course. Frankly it's all we can think about. My apartment is still a bit of a mess though Mayo's been a dear helping me straighten out."

He heard Mayo say with irritation, "Oh for crying out loud, Mother, get on with it."

"Don't be so impatient, Mayo!" bristled Evelyn.

Bogart thought, throw something, Mayo. Hit her with a pillow.

"Now Humphrey," said Evelyn. "In all this horror and confusion I forgot something that might be helpful to the police."

"The Portland police or the L.A. police?"

"If it was the Portland police we wouldn't be phoning you, would we?"

"You've got a point there," he said, and thought, and hold on to it especially if it's very sharp.

"That large carton of my husband's in your basement."

"I know where it is. You don't have to worry about it. It wasn't broken into."

"Yes, Mayo told me. Humphrey, I think that's the carton with the false bottom."

He sat up. "You kidding me?"

"You know I never kid. I suppose it's safe to tell you now, he's been dead long enough."

Bogart refrained from telling her that some people are never dead long enough as he was afraid she'd take it personally.

"How shall I put it without making it sound too illegal? Oh well, in for a penny, in for a pound." Haven't heard that one in a long while, thought Bogart. "Jack kept an apartment in Shanghai. For his long stayovers." The devil, thought Bogart, grinning. "He would pack his belongings into that carton and of course have it delivered to his apartment."

Bogart asked, "And what did he pack into the false bottom?"

She said briskly, "He smuggled, to and fro. Don't ask me what kind of contraband he dealt in because what I have expressed is a suspicion, it's not a statement of fact." She paused for a moment. "He did bring me the occasional vial of perfume, frivolities like that."

"I think that was very thoughtful of him."

"Yes, I suppose it was. Anyway, Humphrey. It's worth a go. I don't know how it opens but if it's the right carton, then I suspect the cornucopia might be there."

Mayo pulled the phone from her mother's grip. "Bogie, you get right out of that house!"

"Why? I own it."

"The ransackers aren't stupid. It might occur to them the carton might have a false bottom."

"But they never touched it in the first place."

"Please, Bogie," she pleaded. He was touched by her concern.

"You might be right. There've been a lot of people in and out of here the past twenty-four hours. After the police left a crew came in from Warner's and set the place to rights. And oh yeah, when I got home tonight, I found Lucy Darrow in that spare room Hannah used to work in."

"What was she doing there?" asked Mayo with a soupcon of suspicion.

Bogart recognized the suspicion. It was a constant with Mayo. "She tried to rape me." Mayo shrieked. "Calm down, kiddo, calm down. I'm only kidding."

"I wouldn't put it past her, what with her record."

"What record?"

"I never told you before?"

"What the hell are you talking about?"

"She's been hospitalized." She paused. "Mental problems."

"You mean she's nuts?"

"Relax. She's been out a few years now."

"Now you listen to me, when they're nuts they're nuts and they stay nuts. Come to think of it, this morning she gave me Hannah's keys to the house."

Suspicion again. "When this morning? Where?"

"Come on, kid. You know she was coming to the Garden of Allah to pick up her mother's handbag. That's when I got back Hannah's keys. When I found her here she said the crew let her in on their way out. But she could have used Hannah's spare key."

"What spare key?"

"The one Hannah kept in their apartment in case of an emergency."

"What emergency?"

"I don't know. Make one up. Listen, I've got to track down Herb Villon. I'm hanging up."

"Wait!"

"What?"

"I love you." She slammed the phone down. He smiled. He searched in his pocket address book, found Villon's number and dialed it. Jim Mallory answered the phone.

Mallory said, "Detective Villon."

"Come off it, Jim, I know it's you."

"Bogie! I've been ringing you. Your line's been busy. And we're just on our way out."

"Hold your horses, I've got to talk to Herb. It's important. It's a lead."

Villon snapped his fingers and Mallory handed him the phone. "Bogie. We've got an emergency. You can meet us at Bulgari's."

"Why there, for Chrissakes!"

"Because, old buddy, he's been found in his apartment in back of the store with a stab wound in his chest."

"Is he dead?"

"Very."

"Well that's a relief. I'll be right over."

"Don't rush. Drive carefully. He's not going anywhere."

A few seconds later, Bogart was going through the house bolting windows and doors. In the kitchen, he locked the door leading to the basement and pocketed the key. He hurried to the front door, pulled it shut after him and double-locked it. In the street, twilight now descending, he looked for the blue coupe. There was no sign of it. He got into his car, and was soon on his way to the pawn shop at Santa Monica and La Brea.

Humfairy Bogart.

Bulgari, it serves you right.

Dash and Lily. Dinner. Damn. He saw a drugstore with phone booths and pulled over. He got through to the bar but there was a delay getting Hammett or Hellman. Bogart nervously jingled coins in his pocket. He could hear laughter and the sound of the cash register and then finally Lillian Hellman asked, "Hello?"

"It's Bogie, Lily. Listen, something important's come up. I can't make dinner."

"I didn't know you could cook." The slur in her voice was overpowering.

"My apologies to you and Dash."

"Why? Because you can't cook?"

"Lily," he shouted, "I won't be at Musso's."

"I don't blame you. The food's lousy."

"Good-bye, Lily!" He slammed the phone down and raced back to his car.

Lillian Hellman managed to make her way back to her group.

"Who was that?" asked Hammett.

"Some son of a bitch who can't make dinner because he can't cook. Well personally, I think he's having a nervous breakdown. Where's my drink?"

"In your hand," said Hammett.

"Oh."

Bogart was feeling a tingle. What Bogart had told Lucy Darrow earlier, a detective waits for a break, and now Bogart felt the break was at hand. His palms were sweating and his upper lip felt stiffer and of all times to be hungry. Ahead he saw the three brass balls. He also saw police cars and photographers and groups of people clustered on both sides of the streets. He decided it would be wiser to distance himself. He parked half a block away, locked his car, and walked to the scene of the crime. Villon or Mallory had apparently ordered the area in front of the store to be cleared as Bogart saw policemen ordering onlookers and reporters and photographers to back away. Meanwhile, an ambulance pulled up and two orderlies descended into the street. They went to the rear of the vehicle, opened the door and pulled out a bound stretcher. They carried this into the pawn shop little realizing a movie star was following in their wake. Hazel Dickson was using the shop's phone telling somebody somewhere that the pawnbroker to the stars had been redeemed at last. Bogart pinched her cheek as he passed her and entered the rear of the shop. He found himself in a pleasant, one-room apartment complete with kitchen and bathroom and barred windows that overlooked an alley. Leo Bulgari lay face up, eyes half open in appraisal of nothing. The forensics men were busy as always. Villon motioned to Bogart when he saw him enter and pointed his face at a shelf laden with cornucopias. Bogart whistled while Jim Mallory was cursing the fate that brought about the circumstances keeping him from the desired company of Zelda Sweet.

"The only good thing about being here," said Villon, "besides the beached whale on the floor is that I didn't need a search warrant. There's more in the basement."

"So he's been collecting them," said Bogart.

"I would assume they've been amassed over the years. There was a time when these things, filled with fruits, candies, cakes, or flowers were a popular decoration."

"What's the basement like?" asked Bogart.

"You wouldn't want to live there."

"I'm not apartment hunting. Any leads? I'm only asking you that because I've spoken that line so many times in so many pictures."

"Well I figure this is the scenario. He closes shop—you might have noticed the sign in the door window apologizing for being closed, please call again. He comes back here to do the day's figures. You'll notice on the desk over there there's a ledger open and a pile of receipts and a pen. I suspect he was waiting for someone."

"Wouldn't the closed sign discourage them?"

"You forget, Bogie, all residences in tinsel town come with back roadways for garbage collection." He indicated a door in the back wall. "There's the back door. You notice it is equipped for a bolt but the bolt is resting against the wall and not in place where all good bolts should be because the killer left by the door he entered with and of course could not bolt the door behind him.''

The coroner, who Bogart recognized as the same one who had examined Hannah Darrow and Joshua Trent grunted as he got to his feet, being slightly arthritic. Bogart asked Villon, ''He your favorite coroner?''

''He my only coroner. I'm thinking of adopting him.'' He looked at Mallory. ''Jim, a hangdog expression doesn't become you.''

Bogart asked, ''Who found the body?''

''Some extra walking his dog saw the door ajar and knowing there's a pawn shop here suspected the possibility of foul play, and since his dog was a savage French poodle he felt it safe to investigate. He saw fatso and the blood and called us and here we are. And there's little else we can do here.''

The orderlies needed some policemen to help them lift Bulgari onto the stretcher and strap him in. Bogart clucked his tongue. ''There goes an awful lot of halvah. He got a family?''

Villon pointed to some framed pictures on the desk. One was a chubby woman and the other was three chubby children, two boys and a girl. ''We're tracking them down,'' Villon said. He bent down and picked Bulgari's fez from the floor. He offered it to Bogart. ''Souvenir?''

''I'll pass,'' said Bogart.

''Now what's this about a lead?'' asked Villon.

''Hell yes. I went back to my place to see if the Warner crew had cleaned it up, which they did. I found Lucy Darrow there.''

''Alone?''

''Quiet as a mouse.'' Bogart recapped the incident and then continued with the phone call from Mayo and her mother. Mallory had joined them and was enjoying the small smile on Villon's face. It was always a small smile when he thought he was on to something promising. Never a broad grin or a whoop of joy, just the small smile in case he was in for a disappointment. Villon was always careful to cover himself.

''A secret compartment,'' echoed Villon. ''Gee, I used to love them in spy movies. I always wanted to come up against a secret compartment, and my dream is about to be fulfilled." He thought for a moment and then asked Bogart, "You think there's anything significant in the fact that she's served time in looney bins?"

"I reserve opinion. Outside of the fact that he was undoubtedly a rat, who do you suppose had it in for Bulgari?"

"I can't give you names but I can give you types. But my guess is, he's tied in with the cornucopia. Bogie, I've been playing with this idea since we parted company earlier. I think Bulgari was part of a group pledged to find the bloody thing and if there was a treasure, they divide it. I figure with all his cornucopias they suspected he found the right one but hid the gems until the time was safe to convert them into cash. Now I'm not accusing anybody, but there was the strong possibility that the members of this cabal could have been in addition to Bulgari, Edgar Dickens and his little Nell, Sidney Heep, Joshua Trent, and Ned Aswan..."

Bogart's eyes widened. "That could explain the suicide attempt!"

"That's right," said Villon. "Not that he lost his beloved, but that had he been at home and not in Santa Barbara, he could have bought his passage to forever."

"What about the other ladies? Bara, Mrs. Harper, Karen Barrett."

"Red herrings. Bara's a rich lady with a rich husband. Angelica Harper knew of only one cornucopia and that's the one Bara borrowed and Barrett hocked. But there is a lady who I think might have been involved."

"Who?"

"Your housekeeper. Hannah Darrow."

SEVENTEEN

BOGART WAS SCRATCHING his chin. "Hannah Darrow. Talk about your least likely suspect even though she was a victim. Well, let's take it from the top." He walked to a kitchen table and took a seat. Villon and Mallory joined him. Hazel Dickson walked in and asked if they were holding a seance and why. Villon told her to sit down and not move her mouth unless there was gum in it. Hazel started to bristle but a wink from Bogart which was both friendly and wise caused her to settle down and listen. "I think it begins with my wife." Villon nodded agreement. "She and Hannah spend a lot of time together. Mayo's not working and lonely. So she gets chummy with Hannah who's a nice lady and also a smart one. They do a lot of jawing and learn a lot about each other. Hazel, when she finally feels comfortable about it, tells Mayo about her daughter, Lucy. Mayo tells her about her mother and what a famous news hen she is in Portland. Then she gets going on her father and he's a hell of a lot more colorful. Sea captain on the Orient run and that's pretty exotic. And about the most exotic thing that Hannah heard about in Hollywood is Grauman's Chinese. Mayo is a great one for icing on the cake so she tells Hannah about the cornucopia. Hannah loves it and tells her daughter Lucy who's the dreamy type with a faulty mechanism between her ears and she looks into cornucopias. She probably begins by looking it up in the dictionary."

"And then comes the Old Curiosity Shop," interjected Villon.

"Most likely. Mayo has brought Hannah there and that leads to Lucy's introduction to the place. And whether this is conjecture or not, Lucy and Sidney Heep hear harp music when they look at each other."

"I may weep," said Hazel.

"You may just shut up and listen," said Villon.

"Edgar Dickens has cornucopias but they're not the one they want. Dickens is chummy with Joshua Trent and Ned Aswan. They do a lot of buying, selling, and trading in addition to interior decorating. Trent and Aswan get all steamed up. They agree to join the hunt."

"Not knowing where to begin?"

"They begin with Mayo. Hannah knows she's got her father's carton there among other things. She offhandedly wonders if Mayo has the cornucopia and Mayo just as offhandedly tells her no she doesn't because Mayo doesn't know anything about it except what her mother told her. And Mayo doesn't give diddly piss for it because all Mayo wants is a job in a movie or a fistfight with her husband to prove she's as much of a man as he is."

Villon said, "All this is recent."

"It has to be. What sets it into motion is the arrival of la Contessa di Marcopolo. She and her gang..."

"There're only three of them," Jim Mallory reminded him.

"And not your usual crowd," said Bogart. "They ransack my mother-in-law's place and then hightail it here. Mayo's mother calls her and Hannah Darrow overhears. She tells the others. And one of them gets very greedy, and knowing that with la Contessa in the picture time is growing short, ransacks my place not knowing Hannah is still there, probably up in the workroom she used. Hannah hears the noises and investigates and catches a knife blade, probably from my own kitchen." He said to Hazel. "We have some very fine cutlery."

Hazel said while looking coldly at Villon, "I might borrow one."

"Then killing Hannah inspires the killer to fresh heights. Gets rid of what the killer thinks is excess baggage, such as Joshua and Ned. Joshua's available but Ned isn't, but so it shouldn't be a total loss when the opportunity presents itself, Joshua is wiped out. Ned can be taken care of later."

"But why ransack the place?" asked Villon.

"Look," said Bogart. "Joshua Trent once sold a cornucopia to Sam Goldwyn. Stands to reason he has been in possession of others. He might still have them."

Hazel said, "Then the people out at the Old Curiosity Shop and the countess and her playmates are marked people."

"But not easily disposed of," said Bogart. "Countess and friends are in a hotel suite and for the most part travel together."

Villon said, "On the other hand the killer knows they don't have the cornucopia. Why bother to kill them? At least not now. Wait until they get their hands on it if they'll ever get their hands on it. As to Edgar Dickens and his crowd of two, he doesn't have the treasure either. There's only one person left to kill."

"Who?" asked Hazel.

"Me," said Bogart.

"She could have done you when you found her in the house," said Villon. Hazel and Mallory were bemused. Found who in what house?

"It wouldn't work. The house has already been searched. Go through the motions again? Stupid."

"So where do we find the murder weapon?" Mallory asked.

"In my kitchen. All washed and dried and magnetized hilt in place on the wall above the work counter. That's really why she went back to the house. After she murdered Leo Bulgari who she knew was a nuisance and couldn't be trusted."

Hazel exploded. "Who the hell are you talking about?"

"Oh didn't you know?" asked Bogart. "Lucy Darrow, my housekeeper's daughter. A lady with a dream." He paused. "Poor bitch, she's better at creating nightmares." He said to Villon, "I locked up my place tighter then a drum, but I'd still like to get back there and examine that carton."

"What carton?" asked Hazel.

"One with a secret compartment," said Villon.

Very annoyed and perplexed, Hazel said, "You guys had better watch out. I'm going to scream."

Villon patiently told her about Mrs. Methot's phone call to Bogie and about the benighted Lucy Darrow.

"Well why in God's name don't you arrest her?" asked Hazel.

"On what charges?" asked Villon. "All we've got to work with is a supposition. And it's nice thinking, Bogie, really good."

To Hazel he said, "But I haven't a shred of evidence against her. And another thing, she didn't work alone."

"I had an idea you had an idea," said Bogart.

"Those ransackings. No one person could have pulled them off."

"You think it was Sidney Heep?"

"The most likely, isn't he?"

"Because we saw them together once?"

Bogart smiled. "You're a cautious little devil, aren't you?"

Villon smiled in return. "I could get into a lot of trouble for false arrest. And to make accusations without a solid body of proof could lead to cases of libel and slander."

Hazel gasped.

Villon asked her, "Indigestion?"

Hazel said, "It suddenly dawned on me what you're saying! You're saying Lucy Darrow murdered her own mother? It's unthinkable!"

Bogart said with equanimity, "Many's the time I thought of slaughtering mine. She wasn't a very nice person and one of the meanest bitches crawling around on all fours. She was hell on my sisters and me, hadn't the vaguest idea what love and affection meant. My sister Pat ended up in an institution."

Villon asked, "I wonder if she ever ran into Lucy?"

Bogart laughed. "Opposite ends of the country."

Villon was on his feet. "Let's get going to your place, Bogie. I've been having one of my tingles and I don't want to give it a chance to decelerate. Cheer up, Jim, it's still early. You might still have time to catch up with Zelda Sweet."

"By the time I catch up with her she may not want to be caught up with," replied Mallory dispiritedly.

Hazel patted Mallory's cheek. "Now Jim, my mother has two favorite expressions where getting involved with someone else is concerned. Her favorite is, 'There's a cover for every pot.' Her other one is, 'If you miss the bus, there'll be another one along in fifteen minutes.'"

Villon asked, "Hazel, have you ever thought of murdering your mother?"

Villon and Bogart walked to Bogart's car. Mallory's unmarked police car was parked outside the pawn shop and Hazel's was across the street in the hot dog stand's lot. All would rendezvous at Bogart's house. Hazel bought a hot dog and a soft drink to eat on the drive to Brentwood. Mallory, after a moment's thought, dashed back into the pawn shop and phoned Zelda Sweet at her home, fingers crossed that she'd be there. The gods were smiling at Mallory and Zelda was at home and promised she'd wait for Mallory to call back, probably within an hour. Zelda's mother scolded her daughter for making herself so available to a man, especially one she had just met today. It was at a time like this that Zelda entertained the notion of murdering her mother.

At Cedars of Lebanon hospital, Ned Aswan's private room resembled an arboretum. When he came out of his coma, he squealed with delight at the sight of the wreaths, vases filled with flowers, and lovely floral arrangements that filled the private room. The nurse told him he'd probably be able to go home within a day or two and the news did not please him. He knew why Joshua was murdered and that it could very well soon be his turn. Which one of those greedy bastards did it, he wondered. After the nurse left, a young police officer came into the room, took off his hat and hung it on a door hook, and sat on a chair facing Ned Aswan with a pleasant look on his face.

Ned asked, "If I'm under arrest, what for?"

"You're not under arrest. I've been assigned to protect you."

"From who? Or is it "From whom'?"

"I can't help you there. But I can help you here. I don't know who's after you because I don't think Herb Villon knows who's after you but I'm here for safety's sake. My name's Amos Colbert like in Claudette but no relation not even distant. Lots of pretty flowers. Smells like a funeral parlor. Oh. Sorry."

"You're right. It does smell like a funeral parlor. It's all those goddamn gardenias. Do you know how long I've been out of it?"

"Not long at all. Not as long as most botched suicides. Oh. Sorry."

"No need. I did botch it. I need Josh to count the correct amount of pills. You can't swallow too many and you can't swallow too few. How long have you been with the police?"

"A little over a year. I guess I'll be going into the army soon, however."

"And when you get out, back to the police?"

"If I survive, I suppose so."

"Have you ever thought of being an interior decorator?" He hoped he didn't sound coy or effeminate or on the make, which he did and he was. But Amos Colbert was something rare and unique to Hollywood. He was an innocent.

"You know, I'm glad you asked. I know who you are and I was too shy to ask, you just out of a coma and all that." As though one was given to going into and coming out of comas with alarming frequency. "Well, in school I was pretty fair in my art classes. My teachers told me I had a nice sense of style and color. Do you think I ought to set my sights on something more fulfilling then being a cop?"

"Amos," said Ned with what he hoped was a provocative smile framing his mouthful of capped teeth, "I think we were destined to meet."

In Bogart's car, Villon was telling him, "You've seen Lucy a couple of times."

"Three," corrected Bogart.

"She strike you as someone freshly derailed?"

"I can't make a judgment, Herb. I mean, I know a lot of nut cases in addition to my sister." He reeled off, "Jack Warner, Peter Lorre, my wife..."

"Hazel's aghast at the thought of Lucy having murdered her mother."

"Well Hazel's another one of the walking wounded who believes in the sanctity of motherhood. This morning I liked Lucy at the Garden of Allah. Although presumably in mourning, she was doing a good job, I thought, of facing up to it and getting on with the burial. She asked me to speak at the funeral."

"Well, you're proven box-office."

Bogart smiled. "At Canter's I began to wonder what she was

doing with a creep like Sidney Heep. But I have to remind myself there's a hell of a lot of my fellow players sharing their beds with creeps and worse, so there's a lot of truth in that saying there's no accounting for tastes. Then when I found her in my house packing her mother's stuff, there was something very creepy about her. I'm wondering now if she's the murderer and if I had found her in the kitchen cleaning the knife, would I be here discussing her?''

"Well you wouldn't for a couple of good reasons. The first being you caught her with the knife and the second being she has no option but to kill you as you've caught her with the goods.''

"Well I'm awfully glad I didn't catch her in the kitchen.'' He thought for a moment. "I wonder which knife it was if it was one of our cutlery. If it's the carving knife, there'll be no beef carved at our table ever again. How'd Jim Mallory beat us here?''

"He passed us a little while ago. You're not exactly a demon at the wheel.'' Bogart pulled up behind the unmarked car and a few seconds later, Hazel parked behind them and joined them on the sidewalk.

"Where's your handkerchief?'' Villon asked her.

"What do you need with my handkerchief?''

"There's mustard on your chin.''

"Thanks,'' she rasped, extracting a handkerchief from her handbag and wiping her chin.

"A little more to the left,'' said Villon.

Bogart was unlocking the front door. He entered and turned on the foyer lights. Villon's voice prevented him from going any further.

"Hold it, Bogie. Let Jim and me proceed.'' Villon indicated for Mallory to do the upper floor. Hazel stood with Bogart as Villon went quickly from room to room. "Okay down here!'' Villon shouted.

"Likewise up here,'' shouted Mallory. He descended rapidly and the three followed Bogart into the kitchen. He unlocked the basement door, switched on the light and led the way to the storage room. He opened the door and there was the carton as it had been left when they last saw it, bound with a strong cord.

"Well, gentleman, with any luck, do you suppose this is the end of the rainbow with the pot of gold?" asked Hazel.

Bogart said, "Hazel, I feel more like Pandora about to unleash the Furies. Anybody know how to open a secret compartment? I've never had to deal with one before."

Villon said, "Jim, you're the mechanical one. Have a go at it."

Hands on hips, Jim slowly circled the carton, examining the bottom with great care. He cut the rope binding the carton with his penknife.

"If we have to, we can slash the thing open," said Villon, always the pragmatist.

"Patience, Herb, patience. I see a smudge. The kind of smudge made by dirty fingers." He knelt and pressed the smudge. They heard the sound of a release of springs and a section at the bottom of the carton popped out slightly. Mallory helped it by prying with his fingers. There was an object wrapped in oilskin held together with masking tape. Mallory tightened his grip on the penknife.

Villon said, "It looks about right for a cornucopia. Cut it open, Jim."

Bogart said, "'Such stuff as dreams are made on.'" And then added, "And also nightmares."

EIGHTEEN

FOR BOGART, THERE WAS something incomplete about this moment in the basement. It lacked the sweep and the majesty of a Max Steiner score, very exotic, very oriental, with a clash of cymbals to underline the moment of discovery.

"It looks like nothing special to me," rasped Hazel, shattering Bogart's fantasy. Jim Mallory picked up the package and carried it to the bar.

"Is it heavy?" asked Villon.

"It's heavy," Mallory told him.

Bogart and Villon exchanged looks. Hazel went around the bar for a better position for the unveiling. Mallory unwrapped the oil cloth and pushed it to one side. Under the oilcloth was brown wrapping paper. "It's an awful lot of wrapping," said Mallory.

"Captain Methot was a bit of a fussbudget," Bogart told him. "That's where Mayo gets it from."

With care, Mallory removed the wrapping paper. There was indeed a cornucopia. It had a very beautiful, very elaborate design that twisted from its tail to its broad mouth.

"It's a dragon," said Villon.

"In China, they're very big with dragons," said Bogart. "Is the mouth sealed with cement?"

Mallory tested it with a finger. "It's putty. Just plain old putty."

From the strange look on Hazel's face, Bogart could tell the basement had been invaded. He said to Villon, "I think we've got company. Hazel, we got company?"

"Why yes," said Hazel, "and he's absolutely gorgeous."

Marcelo Amati was pointing a revolver at them from the bottom of the stairs. "Will the detectives put their weapons on the bar, please. Very slowly. Very gently. No sudden movements. I'm a crack shot and totally without mercy." Violetta came down the stairs behind Marcelo, and behind her, very regal, with the look of a panther about to pounce on its prey, came the Contessa di Marcopolo.

"How nice to see you again so soon," trilled Hazel as she clutched her handbag tightly. "I love your dress, Contessa."

La Contessa reacted without removing her greedy eyes from the cornucopia. "It's a Chanel."

"Very tasteful," said Hazel winsomely. Bogart was wondering if he was in the middle of a dangerous situation or at the closing night of a drawing room comedy that had been slaughtered by the critics.

"That is indeed my cornucopia," whispered the Contessa. "The dragon tells me. It is the true cornucopia, not the bargain basement garbage we saw in Venice." She looked at Bogart. "We were positive it was in your wife's possession. You are Mr. Bogart, aren't you?"

"I'd better be. Why didn't you find it last night?" asked Bogart.

"We weren't here last night," said Marcelo, sounding a bit offended. "Had we been here last night, the housekeeper would still be alive. We are adventurers, not murderers."

"Oh my precious cornucopia! You are mine at last!" cried la Contessa.

Villon was moving slowly and subtly to Hazel's side.

Violetta spoke up. "Let's take it and leave."

"What's the rush?" asked Bogart. "You won't get very far with it."

"Do not threaten us, Mr. Bogart. We are not secondary players in your grade B movies."

"Aw now don't be so insulting and condescending; some of them pictures were pretty damn good. It's not nice to be insulted when you're a guest in my house, especially an uninvited one. I suppose you used a skeleton key."

"Mr. Bogart, forgive me if I sound like an ungrateful guest, but the security in this country lacks a certain savoir faire, a je ne sais quoi. In my country, a child could pick your locks without so much as a by-your-leave.''

"Okay, big mouth, drop the gun.'' The voice came from the staircase. "My gun's bigger then your gun and my trigger finger is itchier.'' She spoke over her shoulder, "Come on down, baby doll. I've got the drop on them.'' Nell Dickens was a vision in black leather from head to toe. Behind her, Lucy Darrow came slowly down the stairs, Rebecca in search of her Sunnybrook Farm.

"Anybody else?'' asked Bogart.

"Just us chickens,'' said Nell. Lucy had walked slowly toward the cornucopia seemingly hypnotized.

"Where's Heep? Where's Daddy?''

Nell smiled. "Daddy? You mean Edgar? He's not my daddy. He's my husband. I married him when he was Nino Brocco years ago in Italy.''

"Aha! I knew it!'' cried la Contessa. "I thought he was familiar. Nino Brocco! Master thief! Criminal! Forger of works of art and masterpieces! And you,'' she pointed a finger at Nell, "you shall not rob me of my heritage. It is my cornucopia! My father's!'' She pointed a shaky finger at Bogart. "His father-in-law stole it!''

"Now not so fast, Contessa,'' Bogart said swiftly, "I never held any brief for Jack Methot but in this country you're innocent until you're proven guilty.''

"In my country you would get the firing squad!'' countered the countess.

"I find that a little impetuous.'' From a corner of his eye, he could see Hazel Dickens very carefully opening her handbag. Villon was now at her side and Bogart repositioned himself so that they could not quite be seen by the others. "Are Heep and Daddy waiting in Lucy's blue coupe or do they have wheels of their own?''

"When last seen they were suffering smoke inhalation. The shop caught fire.''

"What a shame,'' said Bogart, and he really meant it, "there goes another of Hollywood's priceless landmarks." He looked at Lucy. "Lucy, I'm disappointed in you."

She was wide-eyed with amazement. That Bogart would be disappointed in her was unthinkable. She liked him. She respected him. And she told him as much. The innocence she managed to project was almost touching in its sincerity.

"But Lucy. Matricide!" exclaimed Bogart.

"What?" she asked, face screwed up with questioning.

"*Matricide.* A fancy word for murdering your mother."

"I didn't murder my mother. Why would I murder my mother? Nell murdered my mother. With your bread knife."

"Oh well that's a relief," said Bogart, with a quick look at Villon and Hazel. Villon had Hazel's gun but was in no rush to make his move. Here was the lucky break every detective prayed for. Mallory was closest to Lucy and he was prepared to use her as a shield should there be much cross fire. "Nell, that wasn't nice murdering Hannah."

"She did a damn fool thing. She was the one who grabbed the knife in the kitchen. She came at me. She didn't see Lucy. She didn't know Lucy was with me. That's right, isn't it, baby doll?"

"Yes. That's right. You tripped her. Then you jumped on her and got the knife from her and we took it with us to use on Joshua Trent and that smelly pawn broker and..."

"It was very nice of you to bring it back and clean it and place it where it belonged," said Bogart.

Lucy said with pride, "My mother taught me to clean up after using anything and put it back where it belongs."

"You're not mad at Nell for killing her?"

"I could never be mad at Nell. She was so good to me in the hospital. She helped me to survive. Nell loves me."

"That's for sure, baby doll. Now pick up that thing and let's get going. And don't come chasing after us, coppers, because you can't. We've slashed your tires."

"Mine, too?" asked an incredulous Bogart. "They're brand-new, damn it! I just bought them!"

"Mr. Bogart, this is neither the place nor the time for a temper tantrum. We'll just collect our spoils and be on our way."

"Miss Dickens," said Villon, "I think mine is a bit bigger then yours. And I don't give a damn who I kill."

Nell wheeled on him but Villon was too fast for her. He pulled his trigger and caught her in the shoulder. Mallory was fast and picked up Nell's weapon and Marcelo's. Marcelo made a move toward Mallory but Villon shouted a warning. Mallory spun on his heel and his right fist connected with Marcelo's fragile jaw. Villon sent Hazel to the phone to call the precinct while he reclaimed his and Mallory's revolver.

"I want my property!" bellowed la Contessa. "It is mine, it is rightfully mine!" Violetta went to her side to comfort her. Bogart helped Marcelo to his feet. La Contessa was at the bar stroking the cornucopia, tears in her eyes. "This is the only link left to my father. It is all I have. It's mine."

Lucy knelt beside Nell, cradling her in her arms.

"Oh my God! It's true! The Curiosity Shop's in flames!" cried Hazel.

Bogart said to Nell, "My God but you're an evil bitch. Are Dickens and Heep dead? Did you murder them?"

Nell said matter-of-factly, "We just tied them up. Edgar is indestructible. I'm sure he's been rescued." She yelled at Hazel. "Do you mind getting me an ambulance."

"Not at all," said Hazel, "and I'll tell them to bring along a box of straitjackets." She did as she promised.

Villon and Mallory herded the others together at the far side of the bar. Violetta held Marcelo's hand while la Contessa made unpleasant whimpering noises. Lucy helped Nell to her feet and then provided her with a chair. Bogart viewed the miscreants with a mixture of contempt and amusement. Then he turned to Villon. "Hey Herb, I'm rehearsing a scene similar to this tomorrow except the company I'll be with is a hell of a lot more appealing."

Hazel was finished with the phone for the moment. She'd soon be peddling her story to the highest bidder. She reclaimed her gun and plopped it into her handbag. "Good old Harriet, at last you served a purpose." Thanks to Villon she had a permit. She had no need of the gun until now. She couldn't hit an elephant if it was standing next to her.

Bogart picked up Mallory's penknife. He stared at the cornucopia. He said, "Herb, I claim the rights to do the honors. It's been taking up space in my basement all these years."

"It's mine! It's mine! It belongs to me!" blubbered la Contessa.

"Oh be quiet!" scolded Marcelo, anxious to see what the object contained.

"I'm cutting your allowance!" snarled la Contessa.

All eyes were on the cornucopia. Bogart dug into the putty slowly. He cut away small pieces. Behind him he heard heavy breathing. The air was so thick with tenseness it could have been cut with a machete. Tiny beads of perspiration were forming on Bogart's upper lip and forehead. In the distance they were alerted to the sound of approaching police sirens. Villon's and Mallory's eyes were on their captives. Villon honestly didn't give a damn what the cornucopia contained. He had his murderer, assuming Nell Dickens would confess to all, aided and abetted by Lucy Darrow.

Hazel Dickson watched Bogart pull a hand full of jewels from the cornucopia's gut as though he were eviscerating a chicken!

"Mine! They're mine!" screamed la Contessa.

Hazel dug around in her handbag and found a jeweler's loupe. She screwed it into her eye and picked up a jewel for a very close Dicksonian examination. She was her mother's daughter. She examined a second and then a third. She smiled at Bogart and then at Villon and then turned to la Contessa. "It's all junk, sweetie."

"No! No! It can't be!" La Contessa seemed on the verge of swooning, and if she did, Villon wondered who among them would be brave enough to risk a hernia by catching her.

"Paste," said Hazel. "You can buy better at the five-and-ten." They heard the police cars arriving followed by an ambulance. La Contessa sagged against the bar. Then by way of reassurance, picked up one of the fake jewels and held it up to the light. It looked like an emerald, it almost felt like an emerald, but as

Hazel later told her mother, it belonged on a stripper's brassiere. Villon shouted up to the reinforcements who came tramping down into the basement. Hazel lost no time and phoned her scoop to the *L.A. Times.* Mallory was ready to commit a homicide by strangling Hazel for grabbing the phone before he could reach Zelda Sweet. Villon said to an officer, "This is Nell Dickens. Book her on suspicion of multiple murder, suspected arson, and endangering my life."

"Arson my eye!" shouted Nell. "Lucy set the fire, I didn't."

Lucy's eyes were aglow. She endearingly misquoted Edna St. Vincent Millay. "'My candle burns at both ends...oh what a lovely glow.'"

Bogart said to Villon. "I suppose she'll plead insanity."

"Why not?" replied Villon, "she's cornered the market." Villon turned Marcelo, Violetta, and the contessa to the charge of two other officers. "Menacing with weapons, obstructing justice," and fixing the countess with a steely eye, "and a pain in the ass."

She said something to him in Italian, which though he did not speak the language, he got her message.

Hazel got off the phone and Mallory captured it. Bogart looked around the basement and said to Villon, "Looks like Warner's going to have to send me a fresh crew tomorrow to clean up this mess. You need the cornucopia as evidence."

Villon laughed. "'Such stuff as dreams are made on!' The Boulevard of Broken Dreams! Look at Jim. He looks like a teenager who just got himself a prom date."

"Give him a break, Herb. Send him on his way." Bogart raised his voice. "Last one out turn off the lights! I'm going to get very very drunk." He spat an expletive. "But first I've got to phone Mayo and her mother." In the living room, he sat down next to the phone. He looked at the ceiling and said, "God give me strength and may *The Maltese Falcon* be the hit I have a feeling it's going to be. And then I suppose we might follow it with *The Chinese Cornucopia.*" He dialed as he said, "God forbid."

THREE DAYS LATER, the day before the start of the actual shooting of *The Maltese Falcon,* Mayo returned from Portland with her mother in tow. The driver of the cab that brought them from Union Station brought in the bags. Then he brought in a small carton which Mayo asked him to put on the kitchen table. Evelyn Methot looked at the living room as she removed her gloves. "The place looks awfully good. You'd never know a brutal, bloody murder took place here." The cab driver returned from the kitchen, accepted his tip from Mayo with a bewildered expression on his face and wondered if this place had any connection to the murders that had made headlines recently, the ones involving Humphrey Bogart. As he left, Bogart drove up and parked. The cab driver recognized him at once and was delighted.

"Say, Mr. Bogart, is this your place?"

"Yeah."

"Where the murders took place?"

"Singular, son, just one murder here. I don't want to make a pig of myself."

"I guess I just brought home your missus and her mother."

"I'll never forgive you."

Bogart entered the house. He could hear Mayo and Evelyn upstairs in the guest room. He shouted, "Hey you two! Cut the chatter and let's get to the martinis." He threw his hat and his script on the couch as Mayo came hurrying down the stairs and into his arms. They kissed as Evelyn followed Mayo down the stairs. "Well Humphrey, you're looking well despite your recent ordeal."

"Hello Evelyn. Welcome," he lied and kissed her on the cheek. "Sorry about the cornucopia. You can have it back from the precinct anytime you want it. They don't need it."

She took his hand. "Come with me, Mr. Bogart." She led him to the kitchen. Evelyn followed them. She patted the carton box on the table. "We've got a little surprise for you."

Bogart stared at the box with suspicion. Mayo demagnetized a knife from the wall.

"That's a bread knife," said Bogart.

"As Gertrude Stein would say, Bogie, 'A knife is a knife is a knife.'" She cut the rope with which the carton was bound.

Evelyn said, "After you called us the other night, I suddenly remembered. When I was ransacked, I had some items out being cleaned and repaired. Well, dear boy, *this* was one of them."

Mayo had the carton open. She lifted out a beautiful cornucopia sealed at the mouth with putty. It too had an elaborate dragon design.

"It's sealed," Bogart said lamely.

"That's right. Jack refused to unseal it. He'd been warned against it."

"What do you mean 'warned against it?'"

"The dealer who sold it to him said it had a curse," Evelyn said with an icy smile. "He who dares to open it shall meet a horrible death."

Mayo held the bread knife out to Bogart, the other hand on her hip. "Go ahead, honey, I dare you."

SOMEWHERE SOUTH OF MELROSE
by Maxine O'Callaghan

MY WORK as a private detective tends to send me off in all directions from my home base down in Orange County, but it had been a while since anything had brought me to Tinsel Town. Now I was here because of where I'd grown up and the people I'd known back then, cruising slowly down Hollywood Boulevard past Vine and wondering when the place had started to look like a foreign country.

I had a sudden vivid memory of being jammed into an old convertible, of a giddiness compounded of youth and beer bought with phony ID, of crowding into theaters that were still the place to be for first-run shows and sightings of movie stars, as well as some lusty teenage groping. Today the Chinese was one of the few still open and doing business. The Hollywood Theater was now a Guinness Museum, and the Vogue had become a center for paranormal research.

Never mind the nice new buildings scattered among the old, compliments of the riots a few years back. Even in a wash of glorious noon-high sunlight there was still a seedier, sadder air. Maybe it was the preponderance of fast food joints, tattoo parlors and body-piercing shops, or the fact that the tourists gawking at the inlaid stars on the sidewalks were outnumbered by hookers and drifters.

Or maybe I'd just edited the memories, letting years of movies and TV shows add a golden, glamorous skrim. In any case I was already regretting the nostalgic impulse that had sent me blocks north of my destination. I turned on a cross street and headed south.

Past Melrose things got worse. No seedy glitter here. Just plenty of graffiti, dirt and hopelessness as I located the address and found a place to squeeze the van in along the curb.

I counted a good dozen homeless people who sat in the lip of shadow cast by the old three-story building, where most of the downstairs windows had boards instead of glass. One lone bag lady shuffled along the street, pushing a shopping cart. A cluster of homeboys eyed me from their station by a bus stop bench.

A holster, clipped to the back waistband of my slacks, holds my mini-automatic. I took my .38 from the glove box and let it keep the Beretta company. The artillery made me feel only slightly better, but since chances were good that I'd come back to find a window in the van smashed and the interior looted, at least I could take some comfort in knowing that the revolver wouldn't be stolen and used in a drive-by.

I climbed out of the van, already having second thoughts. This might be Crystal Landry's last known address, but she'd lived here more than twenty years ago. I'd bet that even in its heyday the apartment-hotel was a place for transients where no questions were asked or forwarding addresses given. So what were the chances Crystal was around, or that anybody here remembered her?

Nil to zero.

Still, since the guilds had no record of Crystal, and I'd struck out at the library for the Academy of Motion Picture Arts and Sciences, this was all I had left.

As I locked the van, the homeboys began to drift my way. They wore no common colors, so I guessed they were just your average, nonaffiliated gangbangers. Somehow this did not make me feel more secure. Sunlight glinted off an earring, a nose stud, a length of shiny bicycle chain pulled through one fellow's belt loops.

Oh, yeah, I was in a foreign land, all right, and the natives were restless.

IF ANYBODY ASKED I'd tell them I grew up in L.A., which to most people means Hollywood, and I did. Well, I lived a few freeway miles east in Altadena, close enough. That's where I had gone to high school with Crystal Landry—and with Alan Weems, who was now my client.

Alan had tracked me down, using, of all things, one of those chatty letters from one of our ex-classmates, trying to tempt us into coming for a reunion. You know the kind of letter, lots of rah-rah and hyped-up success stories about the alumni designed to make the rest of us want to come and bask in reflected glory. This one included me on the roster of interesting grads. While I missed most successful and most prolific childbearer, I did get a mention for most unusual occupation, including a description of my work that somehow made me sound like a cross between Miss Marple and one of the sleazier sex kittens from a James Bond movie.

When the letter was followed by a phone call from a member of the reunion committee, grown desperate enough to beat the bushes, I begged off, saying I was packing my knitted shawl and stiletto-heeled boots and flying off that weekend to South America to seduce the head of the Colombia drug cartel. Sitting across my desk from me in my Santa Ana office after the reunion was long past, Alan confessed that he had attended, the first time he'd ever been to one of the shindigs, and then only in the hope of seeing Crystal.

"She didn't come," Alan said. "I found out she wasn't even on the mailing list."

Men change a lot after their teens, I had discovered, a lot more than women, and he looked only vaguely like the boy I'd gone to school with. The long-limbed grace was hidden behind some extra pounds and an improperly tailored suit, the track-star confidence chipped away by continuing doses of reality that life keeps handing out. His thick, sun-streaked hair had thinned and darkened. His clear blue eyes had crow's-feet at the corners and watched the world with caution.

"I couldn't believe how disappointed I was," he went on. "How I'd built it up in my mind. And afterward, well, I just couldn't stop thinking about her. God, Delilah, we were so crazy about each other."

"Oh, yeah," I said.

I'd never been included in their inner circle, but I certainly remembered the supercharged glow that seemed to radiate when the two came together.

They were the perfect couple, above all the teenage angst, destined for happy-ever-after. A little envy there, I admit it. I'd spent my high school days walking a fine line between adolescent rebellion and keeping my nose clean. Or at least clean enough so nothing got back to my tough-minded dad who had spent enough years on the L.A.P.D. to have little patience with minor acts of anarchy.

Trying not to sound too wistful, I said, "I figured you and Crystal for a sure thing."

"Yeah," Alan said. "Me, too."

But when he left for Berkeley that fall, Crystal went off to look for the real Hollywood in Burbank and Culver City. And it was scary how quickly she vanished, Alan said. Her phone was disconnected just before Thanksgiving. By Christmas there was nobody at her last address who remembered her. And the aunt who had raised Crystal after her parents died had moved away, leaving no forwarding address.

Crystal might have been a star in all those high school productions of *West Side Story* and *A Midsummer Night's Dream*, but I'd bet her luminous beauty dimmed considerably next to the megawatt competition, and none of those big fantasy-factory doors ever opened. At any rate, I'd never spotted her on the screen, big or small. Alan said he hadn't, either.

"For a long time I kept looking," he said, "but I guess it didn't happen for her."

Meanwhile, Alan's heart mended, after a fashion. He met somebody else, fell in love and got married. The childless marriage ended in divorce a few months before the reunion. Which explained why Alan became obsessed with thoughts of what might have been.

Psychologists testify to the power of that first deep love, how the remarkable pull of it continues to alter our lives. I know about this firsthand because I'm the person who gets to look at the old pictures and listen to the longings that never seem to go away.

So these folks come to me, and more often than not I find their lost love. What's amazing is how in a lot of cases passion does rebloom. Sometimes, once in a while, there are even happy endings.

Not always, however.

Too bad I didn't remember that before I went to look for Crystal.

"PICK YOUR BATTLES," my dad had told me the day I graduated from the police academy. "Don't die stupid."

I always try to heed my father's advice, even though it means I have to overcome my natural tendency to dig in my heels and stand my ground. Besides, I wasn't getting paid for this kind of duty. So I had already backtracked a couple of steps toward the van when a lowrider Cutlass came barreling up and spared me the embarrassment of a full retreat.

The homeboys piled in, off to more important targets, saying goodbye with catcalls and obscene gestures that crossed all language barriers.

I picked my way through the litter outside the hotel and tried not to breathe too deeply. A little harder to ignore the eyes that watched me. Impossible to shrug off the sense of hopelessness that was as palpable as the smells.

If the building had ever had air-conditioning, it no longer worked. Inside, the floor was sticky under my feet, the air thick with trapped heat and the odors of cigarette smoke, greasy food and despair. I took some comfort from the fact that some twenty-plus years had passed since Crystal had lived here. Surely it couldn't have been this bad a place back then.

The first door on the right had a grimy plaque that read Manager. A knock brought a prolonged fumbling with several dead bolts, accompanied by a litany of curses, and finally a woman squinting through a crack in the door. I got an impression of frizzy red hair, overbaked skin and rampant paranoia, honestly earned, in my opinion, by living here.

Neither my state ID nor my declarations of trustworthiness cut any ice with her. But when in doubt, keep talking. I did, and suddenly said the magic word.

"*Crystal?*" she said. "Good God, Crystal *Landry?*"

"You knew her?"

"*Knew* her? We were roommates," she said, opening the door. What can I say? Sometimes you get lucky.

INSIDE the one-room studio apartment a floor fan ground away, but did little to cool the stifling air. The weak breeze didn't even ruffle the pages of tabloids and soap opera digests heaped on a coffee table in untidy stacks. Pillows in shades of fuchsia and pink and a few brightly colored Mexican throws failed to hide the murky browns of threadbare carpet and a sagging couch. About the only thing that would have helped this place was a major earthquake with an epicenter at Sunset and Vine.

Shafts of early-afternoon sunshine beamed through boards that covered the window, reflecting off a gallery of framed pictures on the walls. A few were in color, but mostly they were black and white, the kind of publicity photos that arrive on a casting director's desk by the truckload. All of them were of the same young woman, marginally beautiful with a cloud of auburn hair. It took a moment to realize the woman in the photographs was my hostess.

She said her name was Heather Blake. "Well, my *stage* name," she amended, closing the door behind us and engaging all the bolts. "Who did you say you were again?"

"Delilah West."

She shook her mass of overpermed hair, unable to place me, so obviously my fame had not spread north of the Orange County line.

"Kathleen Turner played a private eye," she said. "Some Polish name. Never heard of her, either."

Beyond slender, Heather was bone thin, a gauntness that made me think of eating disorders or the possibility that the long sleeves of her electric blue caftan might hide needle tracks. Right now cheap rum was her drug of choice, mixed with Slim Price cola. There were bottles on a counter in a small kitchenette, and she had a few ounces left in a chunky amber glass.

"Want one?" she offered.

"No, thanks," I said. "Can we sit down and talk about Crystal?"

"Sure. Why not?"

She took one end of the couch. I took the other. It was as uncomfortable as it looked, and the pillows didn't help. Sweat oiled my face, and I was thinking that claustrophobia was a real possibility if I had to live in this cramped, closed-in place.

"You said you were roommates," I prompted.

"Yeah, we were. Right here. Well, upstairs. At first we had singles, but once we got to know each other, it made sense to share. Of course, that ended pretty soon after Carl arrived."

"Carl?"

"Carl—what was it?" She sipped her drink and tried to remember. "Dal—something. Dalpert, I think. God, I still can't believe it. I mean, Crystal could've *gone* somewhere, you know? I mean, look at me. I've been in over a hundred movies and *gobs* of TV shows. I got my AFTRA card. I've worked with Sly and Sharon and Tom, *every*body. I'm reading for a part on 'Baywatch' next week."

"Back up," I said. "You're saying that Crystal gave up on acting?"

"Worse than that," Heather declared, adding with equal amounts of scorn and disbelief, "she went off with Carl to *Fresno*. And she *stayed*. I think she must've *married* the guy."

IT TOOK ANOTHER rum and coke and a pint or two of sweat but I got a fairly good summary of Crystal's brief stopover in Hollywood. She and Heather had plastered the town with head shots, got a couple of gigs together as extras, and had gone to some parties. Between the lines I read of Crystal's plunge into the sleazy swarm of wanna-bes and hangers-on attracted to the sweet promise of fame and fortune like flies to honey.

It was hard to believe she had forgotten Alan so quickly and fallen for somebody new, but maybe she bought the romantic movie myths and saw Carl as a white knight come to her rescue. This was not Heather's opinion, however.

"Guy was so *off*," Heather said. "I kept going, *Crys,* what are you *thinking?* But she wouldn't listen to me."

"What do you mean, off?" I asked.

"You know, a little weird, like he knew something he wasn't telling."

Turns out Carl hadn't revealed much of anything, at least not to Heather. She thought he was a few years older than Crystal. Although he didn't have any visible means of support, he had a red Mustang and enough money to party.

"Was he trying to get into the film business?" I asked.

"Carl? No way," she said. "I don't know *what* that guy was into. I got up one morning, and they were gone. Here I thought Crys and me were friends, and she didn't even say goodbye."

"She was going steady with somebody from high school," I said. "She never even sent a Dear, John letter. He came here looking for her at Christmas, but nobody told him any of this."

"Her old boyfriend Alan? Well, you know, people were always coming and going, so by Christmas there might have been a whole new bunch living here. I was out of here by then. Never thought I'd be back, but I heard about this job last year and—" She gave an elaborate shrug. "Hey, it's *temporary.* Just until something happens. You can't give up, you know? You just can't give up and go to friggin' *Fresno,* or Oakville, or wherever the damn place was."

But her words had lost the ring of conviction. She went to find some certainty in the rum bottle, and I let myself out, wondering if my luck would hold and I'd find Crystal up in the Fresno area.

Well, mine did, but I soon found out that Crystal's luck had quickly run out.

I AVOIDED ANY MORE nostalgic side trips, found a brand-new Burger King, and used my cell phone to call my assistant, Danny Thu, while I sat in the drive-through and waited for my late lunch. These days I have Danny make computer searches before I undertake any major treks to look for people, especially when the hunt would involve a trip to Fresno in July.

Danny called up an Internet directory that gave two Dalperts in Fresno and one in Oakville, which looked from my three A's map to be a small town about fifteen miles away. None of them had Carl for a first name. After I finished my Whopper, I tried the listing in Oakville first. A man answered and said yes, he was Paul Dalpert.

"I'm looking for *Carl* Dalpert," I said, "and I was wondering if you were related."

There was a moment of heavy silence, then he said, "How did you get this number? Who is this?"

"I found you in the phone directory," I said. "I'm a private investigator and—"

He cut in, demanding, "Is this some kind of sick joke?"

"No, sir," I said. "I would just like to find Carl. Do you know where he is?"

"Yeah, I know," he said harshly. "My son's buried over in St. Michael's Cemetery. Her, too. It's been more than twenty years, lady. I don't appreciate having that mess dug up. So leave us alone, and don't call here again."

HER, TOO.

I sat for several moments with the disconnect tone humming in my ear, thinking about the last time I'd seen Crystal. It was shortly after graduation, just a brief meeting at the Galleria. She was with a gaggle of friends. I was alone and rushing through some necessary shopping, no mall rat, even then. I'm not sure we said more than hello. But I do remember how she was always in motion, her long blond hair catching the light and the big green eyes alive with excitement.

One of the current favorites in the lexicon of psychobabble is *closure*. I hate the term and think that those who bandy it about so freely understand nothing of the true nature of grief. So I didn't think what I would find up in Oakville would provide any neat ending to Alan Weems' quest. Still, I was getting paid to fill in all the painful blanks, to tidy up all the loose ends. And in this case I had enough personal emotion invested to want to finish the job and do it right.

So even though I could probably have found out by telephone

whether Crystal was dead and buried in St. Michael's Cemetery, I left L.A. and drove north through cotton fields, orchards and the simmering heat of the San Joaquin Valley.

There was about an hour of sunlight left when I got to the graveyard just outside Oakville. Even though there was no administration office in the small cemetery, it was easy enough to find Carl. His family had been here long enough to stake out a whole section of plots. But the bright twilight was fading to purple dusk before I found the other marker over in a corner I'd bet was Potter's Field. Just a small rectangular block of concrete set into the earth so a mower could do an unimpeded sweep of the weedy grass. It contained only Crystal's name and nothing else to mark her passing.

WITH LOTS OF PEOPLE traveling, I had to settle for an Econo Lodge on Route 99. I was tired, and once in my air-conditioned room, I had no desire to go out in the heat, so I ordered a pizza. While I waited for the delivery, I tried Mr. Dalpert again. All I got was the answering machine, then and later on my second try. I left polite requests to speak with him about his son and Crystal, not surprised when he didn't call back.

After a restless night listening to the semis highballing it past the motel, I got up early and went to find breakfast and then in search of the details of Crystal's death.

Paul Dalpert was the logical place to start. I located his house about a quarter of a mile up a gravel road just off the highway. It was a square frame, no-nonsense dwelling that must have once been way out in the country and now was right at the city limits. An old Chevy Suburban sat in the driveway. Keeping a wary eye out for dogs, I went to knock on the door. Nobody answered.

Not willing at this point to stake out the place, I wrote a note on one of my cards, telling where I could be reached, stuck it in the screened door and went back into town.

At 9:00 a.m. it was already oppressively hot. The catalpa trees in the small central square were dusty and droopy. Yellowing grass crunched under my feet as I crossed over to city hall, an old two-story stucco building that took up one side of the square.

A clerk told me I'd find death records at the county building over in Fresno. No, sorry, she'd lived in Oakville for only five years, so she knew nothing about anything that had happened before that time.

Well, I knew there was a good-sized newspaper in Fresno where I could also do some research. Before resigning myself to hours of squinting at microfiche, I noted that the local police shared the building, and I thought it couldn't hurt to stop in and ask a few questions.

The police department was housed in an area not much bigger than my two-room office suite back in Santa Ana. A big reception desk took up most of the front room. Behind it, a little tank of a woman was sorting mail. Mid-fifties, I guessed, with short salt-and-pepper hair and rings on almost every finger of her sturdy hands. A plastic sign said she was Delores Krantz.

Two small desks were crammed into the space behind her. One was empty. A young male officer sat at the other, dunking a tea bag in a foam cup and staring glumly at the contents of a thick file folder. Just beyond him a frosted door read Chief of Police.

Ms. Krantz gave me the once-over, and I was sure that regardless of who sat behind that closed door, it was she who really ran the place. I told her what I was looking for, and from the sudden, measuring look in her eyes, I had no doubt she could've told me what I wanted to know.

Instead, she said politely, "I'm sorry, but you'll have to speak to Captain McEndree about that."

But I would not be speaking to him that morning since he was in a meeting with the mayor. There was nothing for it but to go on over to Fresno. And for all the information I found there in the official records and old newspaper accounts, I couldn't shake the feeling that only somebody who knew the people involved would be able to tell me what had really happened.

POOR CRYSTAL. She never had a chance to engage in the make-believe violence of films. Instead, she'd found herself involved in the real thing with Carl Dalpert. Their Bonnie-and-Clyde saga had enjoyed front page coverage in Fresno for only a day, however, before being upstaged by a double homicide involving a city councilman.

From the newspaper accounts and the facts I already knew, I pieced together the story. The trip from L.A. to Oakville had taken approximately five weeks, a route that began with a jaunt up the coast. There, somewhere around Santa Barbara, Crystal and Carl had added a third person to their party, a young woman named Jolene Walker, and it was Jolene who provided most of the sordid details of what followed.

According to her, she'd been hitching rides, trying to get to San Francisco, when Carl picked her up. Within a day she became a virtual prisoner, fed booze and pills and handcuffed to the bed in various motels and tourist cabins, except when she was taken along on the half dozen armed robberies her captors pulled off as they hopscotched from the coast to the central valley. Lots of lurid sexual innuendo but nothing specific.

For their last hit, Carl targeted a gas station on Highway 41 on the outskirts of Fresno. Big mistake. The owner's son was a California Highway Patrol officer, off duty, helping out his dad.

Again only sketchy details, but a shoot-out took place, during which the patrolman was wounded. Carl and Crystal, dragging Jolene along, ran out and jumped in the car. The officer managed to stagger outside in time to fire at them as they started to speed away, killing Carl. Driverless, the car skidded into a gas pump. Jolene was thrown from the car just before the pump exploded. Somehow the patrolman got Crystal out of the burning vehicle, but she was DOA at the hospital. Jolene suffered a concussion, and it was two days before she regained consciousness.

When she did, the officer corroborated her story of being a victim, remembering the way she had screamed for help as Carl dragged her from the station after the robbery attempt. No charges were filed against her.

The CHP officer's name was Patrick McEndree.

COMPARED TO THE PICTURE that had run in that old newspaper account, the sandy hair was a little grayer, and there was a hint of jowls on the handsome face. Still, I thought the years had been kind to Chief of Police Patrick McEndree. He looked like a man who'd made himself a comfortable life and had settled in to enjoy it.

One wall of his office was papered with civic awards, along with several photos of himself as coach of Little League teams, and one of two young look-alikes in uniforms who had to be his sons. There was another picture on his desk, but it was angled so the light reflected off the glass. I got a vague impression of the boys again, this time posed with a woman that I took to be their mother.

"I have to warn you," he said. "My kids and their team are playing Clovis this weekend. I have to get out of here in about fifteen minutes and go practice with them."

He sounded affable enough, but the candid blue eyes were wary and growing a little wintry as I told him of my connection with Crystal and that I was looking for details to fill in what I'd learned.

He said, "If you read the story in the papers, I don't see what else I can tell you."

"Did you try to contact Crystal's family? I know she had an aunt."

"*I* wasn't in charge of the investigation, the county sheriff was. But I'm sure an attempt was made. All we had was her name and that she came from L.A. Maybe you ought to talk to the sheriff."

"I'd like to talk to *you*," I said, "because you were there. Look, the case is closed. It's not like I'm asking for confidential information. I'd just like to understand a little more about what went on during that spree. The whole thing is so out of character for Crystal."

"Yeah, well, Carl's family thought the same thing," he said dryly. "In their opinion, your friend led their boy astray. But one way or other, Ms. West, you've been in the cop game long enough to know people are totally unpredictable."

He'd checked me out while I was reading old newspaper files. So he was competent if not cooperative.

"Still," I said, "maybe if I could talk to Jolene Walker—do you know what happened to her?"

"Yes, but I'm not going to tell you," he said. "One thing I will say, I know for a fact she can't help you." He put both hands on the desk and pushed himself to his feet.

"You said fifteen minutes."

"I've decided I need to get an early start," he said evenly, coming around the desk and moving over to open the door for me. "Go home, Ms. West. It's an old story, over and done with."

I hated to admit it, but I thought he was right. I stood up, ready to head back to L.A.—and got a good look at the picture on his desk.

"Nice family," I said, trying to cover my hesitation and the sudden leap of knowledge as I stared at the woman in the photo, remembering there had been no pictures of Jolene or Crystal in the old newspaper articles.

Saying, "Thanks for your time," I beat it out of there so I could get to my van before he could leave the station.

EITHER I DID A GOOD JOB of tailing McEndree or he wasn't as competent as I thought. At any rate, he drove to a house on the edge of town without appearing to make me. Home, I presumed, a nice little ranch house that was old enough so you could tell a room had been added and for some walnut trees to have grown into a shady canopy over the yard. He went inside and reappeared a few minutes later, dressed in jeans and a T-shirt.

Two exuberant young boys bounded out with him. From where I sat in the van half a block away, I could hear their voices, high but still distinctly male, yelling, "Bye, Mom," to the woman who came out to wave them off.

She stood for a few moments, watching them go, long enough for me to get a good look at her face through the zoom lens of my camera. Time might have dimmed the glow, but even without makeup and with the blond hair scraped back in a ponytail, she was still a beautiful woman.

I sighed, put down the camera without taking the picture, and watched her go back in the house. Sat there for a while and weighed my obligation to my client against the bewilderment and pain that my report could bring to those two little boys, a devoted husband and a woman who had made her choices years ago.

Obligations be damned.

I drove away and left Crystal and her family alone.

COUNTY RECORDS IN FRESNO confirmed a marriage between Patrick McEndree and Jolene Walker six months after the shoot-out at the gas station. So my hunch was right: McEndree didn't know his wife's real identity. If he had, if he'd been protecting her secret, I'm sure I'd never have gotten a look at that picture on his desk.

Two things seemed obvious to me. One was that it had been Crystal who was victimized by Carl and Jolene on that nightmare trip. The second was that there had been some mix-up about her identity after the aborted robbery when Crystal lay unconscious in the hospital, and that she had gone along with the mistake when she woke up. What I wanted to do was go back, knock on Crystal's door and ask her why. Instead, I headed south to Orange County, trying to decide what to tell Alan.

In the end I endured my twinges of conscience and simply said that Crystal had died in an automobile accident. Alan didn't press for details, saying only that he had to know, and now that he did, he could let her go.

Despite my guilt at lying to a client, I knew I'd done the right thing. Crystal had her own reasons for abandoning her old life. While I'd never know what they were for sure, I could make a few guesses.

Growing up as the prettiest girl in school would have come with the freight of expectations—her own and everybody else's. I'd bet she really believed she was going to take Hollywood by storm. Maybe her rude awakening had also included a flash of the future, a premonition of what her friend Heather had become. Or maybe she just couldn't face admitting failure to her aunt, to Alan, to everybody.

If I gave it some thought, I could come up with some darker scenarios. God knows the Hollywood scene abounded with them.

In any case she'd been desperate enough to go off with Carl Dalpert, a stupid mistake that might have proven fatal. Instead, fate had stepped in to offer her a new life. Well, she'd made her choice just as I'd made mine, and finally I thought I understood why. Because the Crystal Landry whom Alan and I had known really died, along with her Hollywood dreams, not in Fresno but in that old hotel somewhere south of Melrose.

DEATH
OF A DUSTBUNNY
CHRISTINE T. JORGENSEN

A STELLA THE STARGAZER MYSTERY

When Elena Ruiz disappears,
five-year-old Steven Holman is convinced
that a vampire has taken his nanny.
Stella the Stargazer, astrological adviser
to the lovelorn, is certain there are no
vampires, and she also knows that
Elena wouldn't walk away from her
charge. Only Steven has the clues to
her disappearance. So Stella has taken
over Elena's job temporarily to find
her friend.

Between comforting the boy and
trying to put her own haphazard life
in order, Stella discovers a trail that
leads to monsters of a very human sort....

Available May 1999 at your favorite retail outlet.

Look us up on-line at: http://www.worldwidemystery.com

If you enjoyed this short story, act now to receive other

Maxine O'Callaghan

mysteries

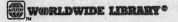